IN SAFETY KEEP

"Do you think he would physically harm his son?" Grant asked.

"Yes," Vanessa whispered. "I'm terrified that he'll not only have us followed, but that he'll come and get us himself. Roddy's afraid of that as well."

Grant sat motionless in the darkened car. "You must get away from here as soon as possible. I can help you, but you'll have to believe that I'm on your side."

Vanessa hesitated.

"Do you trust me? Or do you think I'm one of your husband's hired investigators?"

She looked directly into his face, disturbed by the strong pull of attraction she'd been trying to resist ever since they'd first met.

Grant leaned forward, his entire body emanating an intensity, like a magnet she couldn't resist. "Let me take you and Roddy back to California with me. I won't allow any harm to come to you or to your son."

Vanessa desperately wanted to trust him. . . .

**"EXCITING . . . PASSIONATE . . .
REALISTIC . . . TENDER.
SUSAN BOWDEN WRITES MOVING
AND INSIGHTFUL NOVELS OF LOVE,
LOSS, AND CHANGE."
—*Romantic Times***

Say Goodbye to Daddy

Susan Bowden

A SIGNET BOOK

SIGNET
Published by the Penguin Group
Penguin Putnam Inc., 375 Hudson Street,
New York, New York 10014, U.S.A.
Penguin Books Ltd, 27 Wrights Lane,
London W8 5TZ, England
Penguin Books Australia Ltd, Ringwood,
Victoria, Australia
Penguin Books Canada Ltd, 10 Alcorn Avenue,
Toronto, Ontario, Canada M4V 3B2
Penguin Books (N.Z.) Ltd, 182–190 Wairau Road,
Auckland 10, New Zealand

Penguin Books Ltd, Registered Offices:
Harmondsworth, Middlesex, England

First published by Signet, an imprint of Dutton NAL,
a member of Penguin Putnam Inc.

First Printing, August, 1998
10 9 8 7 6 5 4 3 2 1

 REGISTERED TRADEMARK—MARCA REGISTRADA

Printed in the United States of America

PUBLISHER'S NOTE
This is a work of fiction. Names, characters, places, and incidents either are
the product of the author's imagination or are used fictitiously, and any resemblance to actual persons, living or dead, events, or locales is entirely
coincidental.

For my darling daughter Katherine,
who is also my beloved friend.
Thank you for the insight and
joy you have brought to my life.

Say Goodbye
to Daddy

Chapter 1

Standing outside Strathferness Castle, in that shadowy time between dusk and nightfall, Vanessa felt an intense pang of sadness as she gazed up at the floodlit granite walls and the medieval peel tower. They held bittersweet memories for her. Memories of her meeting with Colin and their wedding here only a few months after that meeting.

The wind had whipped up since the morning. It was now gusting from the north, a harbinger of snow. When Roddy had woken this morning he'd been disappointed that it wasn't a white Christmas, but now it looked as if he might wake up to snow tomorrow instead.

Vanessa pulled her down-filled coat more tightly about her as she walked down the gravel path, through the archway, and into the garden. In summer it was a riot of color, coaxed to life each year by Fiona's devotion, but now it lay dormant, the ground flint-hard and unworkable, the only sound the dry rustle of the giant thistles as the wind swept through them.

Vanessa shivered. The rustling made her think of arid old age . . . yet she was still young, only thirty-two, with many years ahead of her.

She wandered down the path to the little lake, now covered with a thin layer of ice, but not yet thick enough for skating. She was reminded of the skating pond in Assiniboine Park at home in Canada and skating there with her best friend, Jill. "I wish you were here now," she whispered.

The sound of the heavy front door thudding shut in the distance brought her to her senses.

"Vanessa!" her father-in-law's voice shouted, sounding remarkably loud in the winter stillness.

Perversely, she ignored him, rubbing her gloved hands up and down her arms to try to warm herself.

"Vanessa!" This time Sir Robert's voice had an edge of annoyance to it. "Where are you?"

"Down by the pond," she shouted back as she climbed up the slippery bank. "I'm coming." She walked to the castle, guided by the floodlights, to find Sir Robert in the doorway.

"We thought you were upstairs. Then Fiona came down and told us you'd gone out quite a while ago." He pushed open the door and ushered her peremptorily into the hall. "What the devil were you doing out there?"

Vanessa was tempted to say, *Sorry I didn't ask for permission,* but sarcasm usually passed right over Sir Robert's head. "Just walking. Thinking. Clearing my head after that huge meal." Still shivering, she drew her gloves off and rubbed her hands together.

He tried to assist her out of her coat, but she stepped back from him and shrugged herself out of it, only then allowing him to take it from her. In those infrequent moments when they were alone together, his antagonism was particularly tangible. Colin's father had never been able to accept that his son had married an actress, and a Canadian actress, at that.

"Avoiding our company?" he asked, giving her a malicious smirk over his shoulder as he hung her coat in the large hall closet. He was far shorter than his son. Colin had inherited his mother's height and aristocratic bearing. Sir Robert was a small, wiry Scot, and he and Vanessa stood eye to eye; two people with no earthly reason to like each other and nothing in common, apart from the bonds of family.

"Not at all," Vanessa said in reply to his question. "Where is everyone? In the library?" She walked

ahead of him, not wanting to be alone with him more
than was necessary.

As she crossed the stone-flagged hall she could hear
voices from the library. Opening the library door, she
was greeted by the welcome warmth from the log fire
in the stone fireplace and an equally warm welcome
from Roddy, who sprang up from the puzzle he was
doing on a large tray by the hearth.

"Nanna found one of her old wooden puzzles," he
said. "Come and see. It's a picture of Strathferness."
He pronounced the word in the Scottish way, with an
emphasis on the *R*'s. Vanessa had to smile. Roddy's
accent always became more Scottish when he visited
the ancestral home. He obviously caught it from
Morag Lindsay, the housekeeper, who had the soft,
lilting accents of the Highland Scot.

"For God's sake, Roddy, speak properly," Colin
said. Roddy's attempts at a regional Scottish accent
were strongly discouraged by both his father and
grandfather. "Where the hell were you?" Colin
asked Vanessa.

She could tell that he was still under the influence
of all the booze he'd drunk before and during the
Christmas dinner. He was slumped on the deep-
cushioned sofa, his long legs stretched out before him.
Beneath them slept Hamish, one of the two family
collies.

"I went out for a walk." Vanessa sat down on the
hearthrug beside Roddy. "I needed some exercise
after that dinner."

"I told them that's where you were," Fiona said,
looking up from her tapestry frame. "But they were
worried."

Not them, thought Vanessa. Not the stalwart
Craigmore men. They didn't worry about their wom-
enfolk, unless it affected themselves in some uncom-
fortable way. She turned to smile at Fiona, who was
perched anxiously on the edge of her high-backed
chair, her thin legs crossed at the ankles. "I'm fine."

"You might have taken the dogs out with you if

you were going for a walk," was all that Colin said, proving Vanessa's point that her husband hadn't been at all worried about her. There had been a time when he would have walked with her, strolling hand in hand around the grounds of the castle, but that time was long gone.

"It's probably too cold for the dogs," she said. "Feels like snow, I'm afraid."

"Oh no." Fiona's hands fluttered in her lap. "I do hope we won't be snowed in. Robert dear, should we perhaps get the chains put on—"

"For God's sake stop flapping, woman." Her husband sat down in his leather chair. "It is not going to snow." Having made this pronouncement, he lit his pipe and leaned forward. "That piece goes there," he told Roddy, puffing smoke into his face, to Vanessa's intense annoyance. Grabbing the puzzle piece from Roddy's hands, he set it in place. "There you are."

"I knew it went there, Grandfather," Roddy told him severely. "I wanted to keep it in my hand so I could match other pieces with it."

Sir Robert grunted. Puffing a final cloud of smoke in Roddy's face, he retired behind the Christmas edition of the *Sunday Times*.

Good for Roddy, Vanessa thought. At seven, her son was nicely developing his own brand of confidence, even to the point of standing up to his formidable grandfather. If she had her way, that was how it would always be.

Roddy's father was another matter entirely, of course. It remained to be seen what Roddy's relationship with Colin would become. At present, Vanessa acted as a buffer between her son and his father's increasingly uncertain temper, but for how long could that continue?

As she helped Roddy with the puzzle, following his instructions about what pile of pieces went where, and which section he would permit her to work on, Vanessa sensed that Colin was watching them. A little shiver ran across her shoulders. She turned to confirm her suspicions. Yes. Colin had set down his copy of *Racing Guide* and was observing them with narrowed eyes.

Roddy looked up and saw his parents silently regarding each other. "You want to help with the puzzle, Daddy?"

"No, thanks. I had my fill of your grandmother's puzzles when I was growing up."

Vanessa saw Fiona's face turn a delicate pink beneath the halo of fine gray hair. She wished to God that her mother-in-law wasn't quite so sensitive. Surely after all these years of living with Craigmore men she should have developed a thicker hide. Sometimes Vanessa wanted to take the narrow shoulders in her grasp and shake some ginger into her, but it was probably too late to change her now. "I thought you liked doing jigsaw puzzles," she said to Colin, trying to lighten the situation.

"Not much," Colin said. "And Amanda loathed them."

"What did I loathe?" asked his sister from the doorway, entering in the middle of the conversation.

"Ma's puzzles," Colin said, and again retired behind his paper.

Amanda came and flung herself down on the sofa beside her brother. "Can't you leave your wretched horses alone for one day in the year?" She smacked the paper from his hands. "Come on, Col, it's Christmas Day. A day for the family."

Colin rolled his eyes. "God help us. Okay, okay. What shall we do, play charades?"

Roddy clapped his hands. "Cool, charades!"

"Oliver hates charades," Amanda said.

"Who cares about Oliver? Vanessa loves charades." Colin smiled indulgently at her. "Don't you, darling?" Despite the rift between them, he was still immensely proud of her work, although she'd only done a supporting role in a Sir Walter Scott television serial this year.

"But Vanessa's a professional," Sir Robert said.

"She should be good at the game, even if she is somewhat of a lapsed actress, as you might say."

Vanessa gave her father-in-law a sweet smile, at the same time wishing him in hell. She'd had plenty of offers for theater and movie work, but all of them would have involved being out every night or having to live away from home for long periods of time, and she was no longer willing to leave Roddy alone with his father. "I don't think you need to be a professional actor to play charades, do you?"

Sir Robert's eyes glowered at her over his horn-rimmed reading glasses. Then he cleared his throat loudly and returned to his newspaper.

This whole scene was a charade, a pretense, thought Vanessa. It would make a perfect setting for one of those Victorian dramas. The library of an ancient castle with a massive pine tree in the corner, beautifully decorated. The perfect happy family Christmas.

Except that no one was truly happy at this particular moment . . . other than Roddy, perhaps. And the dogs, stretched out before the roaring fire.

"Where is the delightful Oliver, by the way?" Colin suddenly asked his sister.

"Still sleeping it off, the drunken swine. He must have had a whole bottle of champagne to himself." Amanda took her brother's hands and dragged him up from the sofa. "Come on, you lazy lump. Stir yourself."

Colin put his arm around Amanda in a rare display of affection. How different they were, thought Vanessa. Amanda short and dark like her father—but petite rather than stocky—with that mass of dark curling hair a frame for her heart-shaped face, and Colin tall, with the Nordic gold hair and classic features that had first attracted Vanessa to him nine years ago.

Colin's hair was starting to fade to silver, but Roddy's gleamed as bright as a gold sovereign in the dancing firelight. Vanessa couldn't resist leaning forward to rumple it.

"Don't," Roddy said, pushing her hand away. Despite his momentary enthusiasm for charades, he was still concentrating on his puzzle.

"Okay, Roddy," Colin said. "Put the puzzle away and let's get going on charades."

"Not yet, Dad."

"I said, put it away, Roderick."

The familiar edge to Colin's voice made Vanessa's heart pound.

"Not yet," Roddy insisted. "I want to finish this corner first. See, it's the peel tower. It won't take long."

Colin's face flushed crimson. "No, it bloody won't." Before anyone had time to stop him, he kicked the tray over, scattering the wooden puzzle pieces across the floor, his foot coming dangerously close to Roddy's face.

Roddy sprang up. "You bastard!" he yelled. "You spoiled my puzzle."

Colin's eyes narrowed. "What did you call me?" He grabbed Roddy's arm.

Vanessa held her breath for a moment. She scrambled to her feet. "Leave him alone, Colin," she said in a low voice.

Colin turned on her. "Who bloody well asked you?"

"For God's sake, Colin, what did you have to do that for?" demanded Amanda.

"I won't have him defying me like that. He has to learn."

"One month at boarding school," Sir Robert said, "will soon smarten him up."

Over my dead body, thought Vanessa.

Roddy stood very still in his father's grip, screwing up his face in a desperate attempt not to cry.

Vanessa knelt down. "Come and help me pick up these pieces, Roddy," she said, trying to keep her voice low and calm. Heart racing, she held out her hand to him.

Roddy looked up at his father, but Colin didn't release his grip on him. "It's time you and I had a talk," he told his son, and began leading him to the door. Roddy cast a pleading look backward.

"Come on, Roddy," Amanda said, before Vanessa had time to say anything. "Let's pick these up and see what we can salvage." She knelt down on the hearthrug and turned the tray over.

Vanessa flicked her a look of gratitude and mouthed the word *Thanks*.

"Get away from that, you stupid dog." Amanda shoved at Hamish, who was nosing a puzzle piece beneath the footstool. "Come on, Roddy," she said impatiently. "Let's get these picked up before Hamish eats some of them. There's nothing more useless than a puzzle with missing pieces. If we all look for them we should manage to find them. Come on, Father. You, too."

Sir Robert glanced from Colin to Amanda and then, grumbling beneath his breath, pushed back his chair and knocked some pieces toward them with his walking stick.

Vanessa saw Roddy glance up at his father. Colin's grip relaxed a little, allowing Roddy to slide away. The boy flopped onto his knees beside Amanda, as if he realized that she was his refuge.

Someone in the room released a long, relieved breath. Probably Fiona.

"Oh, look at that, Roddy," Amanda said. "The peel tower section is still intact. Isn't that good?"

Vanessa marveled as everyone set to in the search for the scattered pieces. To her amazement, after a few moments of hesitation near the door, even Colin came back to join in. Another Craigmore family disaster diffused. This time, thanks to Amanda.

As she helped sort out the puzzle, Vanessa felt sick at the thought of what might have happened had Amanda not intervened. And all at once, she knew that this could not, must not, happen again.

No more second chances, no more giving in to Colin's promises that this would be the last time he would lose his temper . . . or drink too much . . . or go off on gambling sprees. It was imperative that she make a decisive move, for Roddy's sake as well as her own, before something unspeakable happened.

Chapter 2

By the time they'd finished playing charades, it was nearly midnight. Despite Colin's assertion that she loved charades, Vanessa actually loathed them. She'd never been able to understand this strange desire of the British to make fools of themselves in childish games at family gatherings. She also felt exhausted from trying to maintain the facade of having a good time, when her mind was in such a turmoil.

Roddy had fallen asleep on the sofa a couple of hours ago, his earlier upset seemingly forgotten.

"Time that boy went to bed," Sir Robert said. "Come along, Roderick," he shouted. "Long past your bedtime."

Roddy started up, jolted from his sleep.

"For heaven's sake, Father," Amanda said. "You'll scare the boy to death. Why don't you carry him upstairs?" she suggested to Colin.

"He's getting far too heavy to be carried."

"Oh, don't be such a misery. Here, I'll carry him if you won't."

"What a nag," Colin grumbled, but he went to his son and picked him up. Eyes closed in sleep again, Roddy sighed, his arm flopping down to hang loose like a rag doll's.

"I'll come with you," Vanessa said, tucking Roddy's arm back across his chest. She wanted to make sure that Colin didn't stumble on the stairs.

Roddy awoke as his father lowered him onto the large tester bed with the cozy velvet curtains that he loved to pretend was a tent somewhere in Africa. "Night, Daddy."

"Night, son." Colin hesitated and then said, "Sorry about the puzzle."

As she watched Roddy's arms reach up to Colin's neck, Vanessa was torn by sadness. Roddy loved his father, but he never knew what to expect from him, an apology or an attack.

Colin was at his worst when he came to Strathferness. Not only did he drink too much, but he was also more volatile and aggressive. It was as if he wanted to prove himself the tough father in front of his own father. Somewhere, deep down, Colin loved his son, but he had been so programmed by his own father that he rarely showed his affection for him. Most particularly not when Sir Robert was around.

Sensing that it was now safe to leave them alone together, Vanessa tiptoed from the room. As she came downstairs, she found Fiona waiting for her in the hall at the foot of the stairs, a mohair shawl about her shoulders.

"Are you all right, dear?" she asked.

Vanessa nodded.

"What about Roddy?" Fiona's hands twisted and untwisted in a constant motion of anxiety.

"He's fine." Vanessa hesitated, and then said, "I wish Colin could learn to control his temper. Roddy just doesn't know where he stands. One minute Colin's laughing and playing with him, the next he blows up at the smallest thing."

Fiona glanced about her and then said in a lowered voice, "His father is the same, I'm afraid." Her face looked gaunt in the dim light of the hall, the shadows emphasizing the angular face. "One never knows when he . . ." Her voice trailed away, leaving her sentence incomplete, but her meaning was obvious.

"It's not good for a child," Vanessa said, her mind focused on Roddy. "Children need to have consistency."

The library door opened, issuing light and warmth

from the interior of the room. "What are you two women doing whispering out here in the hall?" demanded Sir Robert. "Come on in or you'll freeze."

He was right. It was bitterly cold out in the stone-flagged hall, the wind whistling in beneath the front door and swirling about their feet, despite the stuffed patchwork snake that lay across the foot of the door.

Fiona had clutched at Vanessa's arm when her husband came out, her thin fingers digging into her flesh. Vanessa was furious that this frail, gentle woman was moved to such fear by her bully of a husband. She drew Fiona's arm through hers and marched her past Sir Robert into the library. "Come on, Mother. Let's both have a good dose of that delicious cognac Colin brought. Warm ourselves up before we go to bed." She went to the drinks trolley and lifted the heavy crystal decanter.

"I'll get it," Sir Robert said, taking it from her. "You need only ask, my dear," he added in a tone of resentment, as if she'd criticized his hospitality. "Are you sure you want brandy?" he asked his wife. "You know how it gives you a headache."

"I . . . well . . . yes, I suppose that's true," Fiona fluttered. "I'd better not," she said, giving Vanessa an apologetic smile.

Vanessa took the glass of cognac from Sir Robert and went to warm herself by the fire. Amanda looked up from where she lay on her stomach in front of the fireplace, apparently not caring that she was getting wood ash on her sequined gold-silk tunic. She had started the puzzle again, expanding the peel tower section. Vanessa wasn't sure that Roddy would appreciate someone doing his puzzle when he wasn't there to supervise.

"Don't worry," Amanda said, reading her mind. "I'll break it up before I go to bed. Puzzles sooth the nerves."

Vanessa glanced across at Amanda's current lover, Oliver Hapgood, a man several years younger than Amanda. He was playing some solitary card game at the large table by the window. Vanessa could feel the tension between them. They'd obviously been fighting. What a family!

She glanced at her watch. It was almost twelve-thirty. As soon as she'd downed her drink, she should be able to escape to bed. It had been a long, stressful day and she felt exhausted.

"How's Roddy?" Amanda asked, her gaze still on the puzzle.

"He's fine. Colin's still with him." Vanessa hesitated. "Thanks for—"

"Of course he's fine," Sir Robert said, breaking into the conversation. "Trouble with women is that they fuss around their children far too much. That's why it's important to get boys off to boarding school, away from too much feminine influence."

Vanessa clamped her lips together, determined not to rise to his bait.

He sat down in his favorite chair—its cover of brown hide was so old it was worn almost through to the interior padding—tapping his pipe against the granite fireplace. "Women make boys soft. It's a tough world out there."

This time Vanessa couldn't resist responding. "What about girls? They have to deal with this tough world, too."

"Well, you know what I think about that. Oh, it's fine for a young woman to have a career to keep her out of mischief until she gets married, but after that she should be at home with her children, not letting someone else raise them."

"Like nannies . . . or a boarding school, for instance?"

Sir Robert gave her a dark look, his mouth tightening beneath the small military mustache. Although it had been far too good an opening to miss, Vanessa immediately regretted her impulsive words.

"I can't believe you said that," she heard Amanda mutter beneath her breath.

Amanda was right. There was little point in raising

the dangerous subject of boarding schools again. They'd had one huge argument about it yesterday, just before they'd left for the midnight Christmas service.

Vanessa sprang to her feet. "I'm going to bed," she said, before Sir Robert had time to reply. "I can't keep my eyes open."

"I think that's a good idea," Fiona said, looking immensely relieved. "I believe I shall do the same." She turned to her husband. "If you don't mind, dear?"

"Do as you please," he said, obviously disgruntled. "I was hoping you would stay to carry on the debate," he told Vanessa, "instead of making a cowardly retreat to your bed. I always enjoy a good discussion."

"But you don't really discuss, do you? You give your opinions and then browbeat everyone else into agreeing. And if they don't, watch out for fireworks."

His sea-green eyes narrowed. "I am sorry to have earned such a bad reputation with you," he said softly, "merely because of a difference of opinion over schools for Roddy. But then how could I expect you, a foreigner, to understand a tradition that has been part of our lives for decades, even centuries?"

Vanessa bristled at being called a foreigner. "A tradition that has kept the class system going in this country," she said hotly. "Besides, it isn't even a typically Scottish tradition. It's English, adopted by those Scots who wanted to be more English than the English themselves."

Sir Robert's face was beet red, but his reply was interrupted by Amanda noisily tipping all the jigsaw pieces into the box and rattling them about as she broke up the puzzle.

Vanessa seized the opportunity, hurriedly saying good night to everyone, kissing Fiona on the cheek, and escaped into the dimly lit hall, still clutching her glass of cognac.

"I switched on your electric blanket," Fiona's voice wafted up from behind Vanessa as she ran up the stairs.

"Thanks very much," she called back . . . and almost

collided with Colin, who was standing at the head of
the stairs.

"Going to bed?" he asked.

"Yes." She walked past him and went down the
shadowy corridor, which was lit only by forty-watt
bulbs in the two wall fixtures. To her dismay, Colin
followed her.

She wished they could have had separate rooms.
After all, they no longer slept together at home nowadays. Vanessa had moved into the spare room to avoid
any more fights about him coming home so late or his
drinking or the latest unpaid bill—but, most of all, to
avoid his lovemaking.

Last night he'd fallen asleep on the sofa in the library and hadn't come upstairs until dawn. Tonight,
it seemed, she wasn't going to be quite so lucky.

"Is Roddy asleep?" she asked, pushing open the
door to the Blue Bedroom and switching on the light.

"He is. I read him some *James and the Giant
Peach.*"

She gave a faint smile. "He loves that book." She
put her glass on her bedside table. He came to the
foot of the bed. "Colin, I—"

"You look tired. Want me to rub your back for
you?"

She stepped around him, grabbing her green velvet
robe from the padded bench and holding it like a
shield in front of her. "No, thanks. What I want is to
get a good night's sleep. I'm really tired."

He came to her then, taking her limp hands in his.
"I can give you a sleeping draft," he whispered, his
arms sliding around her.

Her hands were firm, pushing him away, her heart
beating painfully fast. "No, Colin."

"What do you mean, 'No, Colin'? You're my wife."

"Not for much longer."

"Oh, don't start all that crap about separating
again."

Straightening her shoulders, she faced him without
flinching. "This time I mean it."

"I've told you before, this is all a load of rubbish. We can work things out, you know that."

"No, I don't know it. I've given you so many chances and every time you've screwed up. I'm tired of your excuses. I'm tired of you begging my forgiveness after another affair or another big loss on the horses or another threat to hurt me. This has to stop, Colin."

He put his arms around her again, pulling her against him. "You're just tired, that's all."

He tried to kiss her, but she turned her head away, so that his mouth grazed her ear. She stood quite still now, not even trying to fight him. It was amazing how the old magic had completely disappeared.

At first it had been like a constant fireworks display, all brilliance and excitement. She'd fallen madly in love with the clever young stockbroker, dazzled by his charm, his position, and his success. Since then, with the upheavals in the financial world compounded by his own blunders, his success had waned, but she'd tried to reassure him, telling him she hadn't married him for money. Her love for him had blinded her for a long time after their marriage, so that even after a fight he'd been able to woo her over. But now there was nothing, not even the slightest spark to fan into a flame.

It was that thought, more than anything else, that brought tears to her eyes, sliding down her cheeks.

He released her and stepped back. "For God's sake turn off the waterworks. You know how I hate it when you cry."

"Not half as much as I hate it." Vanessa went to the box of tissues on the dressing table, ripped a few out, and blew her nose. "I'm going to ask your mother if I can sleep in another room."

"Don't be so bloody ridiculous."

She looked directly at him. "I'm also going to tell your family that our marriage is over."

"Over my dead body you will."

The tone of menace sent shivers through her, but

when she spoke, her voice was calm and firm. "I was on the brink of telling them this evening, but I didn't want to say anything in front of Roddy."

"You mean you were going to tell them on Christmas Day? Bloody nice of you, I must say!"

"Well, I didn't. Apart from anything else, everyone was so upset by your behavior I thought there'd be a huge row."

"What do you mean, my behavior?"

"Kicking Roddy's puzzle over. It was just another instance of your recent irrational behavior with him."

"That's crap! You've spoiled him, that's what's wrong. Raising him like an American brat, instead of a future British baronet. You don't exert any discipline. My father agrees with me that you've spoiled the boy."

"If shielding him from your violent rages is spoiling him, then that's what I do. And if you're going to quote your father to me, I'm getting out of here right now. I've had just about all I can take of the great Sir Robert."

Suddenly all the stuffing seemed to seep out of Vanessa, and she was left feeling hollow. She sank onto the couch by the fireplace with its unlit electric fire, her head in her hands. "I'm fed up with fighting you over everything, Colin. I'm sick of veering between hopes that you'll change and fears of what you'll do next."

Colin fell on his knees in front of her, burying his head in her lap. "Stay with me tonight," he murmured. "For old time's sake."

The wheedling tone reminded Vanessa of Roddy. *Just another little story, Mum. Just one more.* The difference was that Colin wasn't a child, he was a grown man. A man who frequently behaved like a child. In the early years of their marriage, she'd been patient with him, knowing what a hellish upbringing he'd had.

In times of weakness or intimacy he'd told her about his life at the strict boarding school in a remote part of the Highlands, where he'd been sent at the age of eight. Of how every year he'd pleaded with his father not to send him back there, but Sir Robert had ignored him.

Yet Colin had put Roddy's name down for that very same school, assuring her that everything had changed for the better. "They have a separate prep school for the younger boys now," he'd told her, "so Roddy can go there next September, after his eighth birthday. And they even take girls in the sixth form."

Big deal. A handful of girls in grade twelve. Talk about tokenism!

"Please don't leave me, Van." Colin's arms gripped her around her knees.

"For heaven's sake get up, Colin." She pushed him away and stood up, turning from him, not wanting to see his face. "You only want me because there isn't anyone else around. I told you weeks ago that I wasn't sleeping with you again, and I haven't. Frankly, even if I wanted to, do you really think I'd risk it, when I don't even know who you've been with? You must think I'm downright stupid."

His face was chalk-white. "So this time you really mean it?"

"Got it at last. I'm going to tell your family tomorrow morning." Then she would leave immediately with Roddy and drive back to Edinburgh, but she wasn't going to tell Colin that. She could hardly remain at Strathferness once she'd told the family she was going to divorce Colin.

He lowered his head to glare at her like a belligerent bull. "If you leave me, don't expect to keep Roddy. I'll fight you in court for him."

"Save your money. You haven't a chance in hell of getting custody." Her tone was scathing. "What sort of parent have you been? Half the time you're in London—"

"You're a bloody liar! I spend nearly all my spare time with Roddy nowadays."

"A few hours a week. The rest of the time you're

either at the racetrack or with a woman. Or both. You haven't a hope of getting Roddy."

"Don't expect a Scottish court to give you custody," Colin shouted. "Not when Roddy will be the heir to a Scottish title and estate one day."

"You don't really think they'll take that into account, do you? Not with your record as an absentee father." Vanessa crossed the room to take her night-dress from beneath her pillow, trying to hide the fact that her hands were shaking. Even discussing the possibility of a custody battle made her feel physically ill.

"Have you been to a lawyer?" Colin demanded.

"Yes, I have. I wanted to know what the procedure was for a separation. But now I intend to file for a divorce. I think I have sufficient grounds."

He stared at her, as if only now beginning to understand what was happening to him. "Do you, indeed?" he said in a thin tight voice that reminded her forcibly of his father. "I warn you, a divorce won't come easy. I'll fight you over everything."

"I thought you might." She picked up her cosmetics bag and robe, and faced him. "I'm going to find somewhere else to sleep."

"No need. I wouldn't sleep with you now if you begged me on your knees." Colin strode from the room, slamming the door behind him.

It was a tremendous relief to have him on the other side of the door. Just to be sure, Vanessa turned the heavy key in the wrought-iron lock. Then she sat on the edge of the bed, staring at the hunting tapestry that hung on the wall, until the faded colors blurred before her eyes.

Outside, in the hall, Colin heard the rasp of the key in the lock. The sound filled him with a mixture of rage and despair. It seemed symbolic somehow of his life, another door closing, locking him out. And this time it could mean the loss of the only thing he now had left. The one thing in his wretched, pointless life worth having. His son.

Chapter 3

Vanessa awoke to the sound of knocking on her door and Roddy's voice shouting, "There's been lots of snow, Mum. I want to go out and play in it."

Vanessa leaped out of bed. "Coming," she shouted. She hid the suitcase she'd packed last night, pushing it into the back of the wardrobe, and then unlocked the bedroom door.

Roddy was already dressed in parka, boots, and a tartan woolly tuque. Behind him came Morag Lindsay, the Craigmores' housekeeper, who'd been with the family since before Colin was born. She carried in the morning tea tray, her round face red from the exertion of climbing the stairs.

"Oh, Morag, I do wish you wouldn't do this. You make me feel so guilty." Vanessa took the tray from her and set it down on the little oval table by the fireplace.

Morag looked shocked. "Not bring your morning tea? The day I don't bring everyone their tea is the day I'm carried out of this place in my box."

Vanessa had to smile. "You're a dear. Thank you."

Hands on her ample hips, Morag stood there in her floral pinafore—which she wore only in the early morning, replacing it later with a severe navy wool dress with a white collar. "Young Roddy here insisted on dressing so he could play outside in the snow. I hope that's all right."

"Of course it is. Thanks, Morag."

"Get dressed and come outside with me," Roddy begged his mother. "Please."

"Just one cup of tea to wake me up and—"

"But the snow'll all be melted," Roddy protested.

"No, it won't," Vanessa said firmly. "I'm not wasting this lovely tea Morag's made for me."

"Yucky tea! Hurry up, then."

Vanessa smiled at Morag. "The impatience of youth."

"Shall I switch on the gas fire?" Morag asked. "It'll be toasty warm in a minute."

Vanessa pulled her robe around her shoulders. "Sounds lovely, but a fire would make me too comfortable and then I wouldn't want to go outside. I don't think Roddy would be too happy about that."

"I definitely wouldn't," said Roddy.

"Oh, you! You're a pest." As she hugged him, Vanessa smiled at Morag over her son's head. "He loves the snow."

"Well, the lad is half Canadian, isn't he?" Morag said, tweaking the bobble of his hat.

Morag's acknowledgment warmed Vanessa. None of the family seemed willing to accept this simple fact. "Yes, he is."

The sounds of dogs barking came from outside the window. "See," Roddy said, his face crumpling in dismay. "The dogs are out already." He raced to the window and climbed up on the window seat.

Morag unloaded the tray and set out the morning tea on the table. It consisted of the usual complement of silver teapot—although Morag frequently grumbled that "wally pots" made far better tea—rose-strewn china, and a plate laden with thick, golden shortbread and chocolate digestive biscuits.

Roddy clambered down from the window seat. "I'm boiling hot," he complained, tugging at his jacket.

"I'm not surprised, with all those clothes on," Vanessa said. "You go on down and play with the dogs. I'll have my tea and then throw on some clothes. I'll be there in about fifteen minutes, okay?"

He was already out the door, speeding down the hall.

Morag shook her head. "I wish I had that bairn's energy." She eyed the empty space in the bed beside Vanessa. "I brought Mr. Colin's tea, but I'll take it away again. Have you any notion which room he'd be in?"

Vanessa felt her face grow warm. "No, I'm sorry I haven't."

"I'm the one that's sorry." As she poured out a cup of tea for Colin, Morag sighed and shook her head. She heaped one of the small plates with some of the biscuits. "I'll be taking this to him, wherever he is." Morag carried the tray to the door.

"Thank you, Morag," Vanessa said. "Thank you for everything."

"You're most welcome, pet." Morag hesitated, then said, "You've done your best. No one can do more than that."

Vanessa got up to open the door for her.

"If there's anything I can do to help, you need but ask," Morag said.

Vanessa thought of the plan she'd made last night. "Well . . . there is one thing. I need to talk to the family this morning without Roddy there. Do you think you could manage to take him somewhere for a while?"

Morag frowned. "That bad, eh? I am sorry." She heaved a wavering sigh. "Aye, I'll take him to the lodge. The McIntyres have some new puppies he's been wanting to see."

"Perfect." Vanessa went out into the hall with Morag. "Would you mind keeping him at the lodge until I come and get him? It might be a while."

"Fine. You'll speak to Roddy later, though, won't you? I think he guesses there's something strange going on."

"Does he? Did he say so?"

"Well, not in a manner of speaking, but in a round-about way. He told me you and Mr. Colin sleep in separate rooms at home."

"Ah, yes." Vanessa felt her face growing warm beneath Morag's steady gaze. "Don't worry, Morag, I'll tell him later on today." When she'd left Strathferness, Vanessa added to herself.

"I must be going before this tea's stone cold." Morag started off down the hall.

Vanessa drank a cup of tea, but she didn't feel the least bit hungry. She tried to eat one piece of shortbread. Even that was too much. It stuck in her throat, its sugary sweetness setting her teeth on edge.

Within minutes she was dressed in ski pants, a thick fair-isle sweater, and a parka. This would probably be her last day at Strathferness. She wanted Roddy's memories of this day with his mother to be happy ones, not sad.

When she went outside, the crisp coldness made her catch her breath. She smiled, a feeling of nostalgia for her home and family in Winnipeg sweeping over her. When she'd called her parents yesterday they'd told her there had been a new fall of snow on Christmas Eve and she'd envied them. Now, as she gazed at the white world and breathed in the pungent fragrance of pine trees, it was like being home again.

She awoke to reality when a snowball hit her full in the face. "Gotcha!" Roddy shouted.

"No fair," she spluttered, wiping snow from her eyes and mouth. "I wasn't ready."

After a brisk snowball fight, they had races across the paddock and threw sticks for the dogs, forming trails and footprints in the once pristine snow. Then Amanda joined them, and she and Roddy proceeded to roll down the bank by the putting green, with the collies rushing at them, barking excitedly.

When Amanda grew tired and told Roddy she had to take a rest, Vanessa seized her chance. "I want to speak to the family this morning," she told her sister-in-law, as they sat down on a bench together.

"About you and Colin?" Amanda asked. Vanessa nodded. Amanda took a long draw on her cigarette. "I found him asleep on the library sofa again this morning."

Vanessa's lips tightened. Damn him! Did he have to make such an advertisement of it? "I'm leaving him. I want to tell the family what's happening before they hear it from someone else."

"Oh God, must you?" Amanda rolled her eyes.

"Yes, I must. I know Colin won't, so I have to do it."

"What a time to choose! Christmas. Oliver here. . . . Couldn't you have waited for a better time?" Amanda flashed a sardonic grin at her. "When I'm back in London, for instance?"

"Sorry, but it can't wait any longer."

Amanda heaved an exaggerated sigh. "Okay. I'll see if I can persuade Oliver to go for a walk with me. He loathes the cold, but I'll do what I can."

"I'd rather you were there when I tell them."

"Oh shit! Why do you need me?"

"I just do."

"Okay, I'll be there. One word of warning, though. Don't expect me to give you open support against my family."

"I wouldn't expect you to do that." But Vanessa knew Amanda's ability to intervene in explosive situations without seeming to take sides. "You don't seem surprised."

"That you're going to divorce Colin? Why should I be? My beloved brother's a prat. I've often wondered why you didn't leave him a long time ago."

Vanessa sighed. "Because I used to love him very much. Because I took my marriage vows seriously."

"More than he did, I bet."

"But mainly because of Roddy. I may be old-fashioned, but I think a child is better with two parents, if that's possible."

Amanda took off her ski gloves to blow on her hands. "What changed your mind?"

"Oh, just everything seems to have escalated recently. You know how Colin is." Vanessa preferred not to go into the gory details with Colin's sister. "But mainly for Roddy's sake."

"Well, just remember I sympathize with you, even if I don't speak up for you against the family." Amanda brushed snow off her sleeves. "I hope you realize what you're taking on. The Craigmores of Strathferness can be a formidable bunch when they close ranks. Look what happened to Alastair."

Vanessa didn't know what exactly had happened to Colin's younger brother. All she knew was that he'd run off to Australia many years ago. "I know hardly anything about it. Colin won't talk about him. All he said was that his brother was a layabout and was probably rotting away in some jail in the Australian outback. When I asked your mother, she told me Sir Robert won't allow anyone to mention his name. She was so upset that I didn't dare bring up the subject again."

Amanda looked away, as if she regretted having mentioned her younger brother. "Let's just say that Father and Alastair never saw eye to eye. God, it's bloody freezing out here. I'm going in. Coming?"

"Not yet. I want to spend a little more time with Roddy. I love this weather."

Amanda gave her a quizzical look. "You do? Oh, of course you would, having been born near the Arctic Circle. Come on, you lazy hound," she yelled to her father's old black Labrador. They were off in a flurry of snow before Vanessa could respond to her taunt.

They went inside twice to get warm and to get dry gloves, but Roddy kept insisting on going out again. "The snow could melt, you know, Mum," he kept reminding her. But when his lips started turning blue and his third pair of mittens were soaking wet, she told him they had to go in.

"Not yet," he protested. "I'm fine. Honest I am."

"I believe Morag said something about hot chocolate with marshmallows."

That was incentive enough. He called to the collies and raced back across the paddock with them, their barking and his shouts echoing in the still, crisp air.

Vanessa stood there, wishing she could capture this moment, protect it with shatterproof glass, and keep it forever.

The ancient castle stood gray and indomitable against the pale blue sky. Racing toward it, feet kicking up arcs of snow, was her son, who would one day inherit the castle, together with all the land that surrounded it, and the distillery two miles away that gave much-needed jobs to the local people. Only then, when Roddy was the Laird of Strathferness, Vanessa thought, would she be able to return to this place she had come to love. Perhaps by that time the bad memories would have dissipated.

"Come on, Mum," Roddy shouted, and she ran across the field to join him. They went into the castle together, pausing first in the tack room, where they dried the dogs with pieces of rough toweling before allowing them inside.

Vanessa deposited Roddy in the kitchen with Morag, as planned. Then she dashed upstairs before anyone else could see her. She fetched the suitcase from her room and then went into Roddy's room, where she hurriedly gathered up his clothes and portable toys, squashing them all into a big nylon hold-all.

Thank God for the old back servants' staircase, she thought as she made her way back down the narrow stone steps again, this time very carefully, carrying both her own suitcase and the heavy bag containing Roddy's things. From the kitchen she could hear Roddy's laughter blending with Morag's gusty chuckles.

She went out by the scullery door, cutting across the yard to get to the stables. The dark green BMW stood outside, as there was not enough room, with everyone home, to garage all the cars. They had driven here separately. Colin had wanted to go to Strathferness a few days before Christmas and Vanessa had had to wait to wrap up a commercial she'd been taping for the Scottish Tourist Board.

Heart pounding, she put the bags in the trunk. Then she locked it again, checking the petrol gauge, and made her way back to the house. Before she went inside, she checked to make sure there was no one around, praying that she hadn't been seen.

She left her parka and boots by the back door, hoping no one would move them, and then went down the passageway and into the gold morning room, the brightest room in the house. Facing south, the room reflected the sun—which unfortunately rarely shone in the winter—with its flocked gold-and-ivory wallpaper and gilded picture frames.

Vanessa waited there until she heard the kitchen door open, followed by Roddy's excited voice saying to Morag, "Five puppies? Wow! Maybe I can have one." Then the back door slammed. Shortly thereafter came the hum of the Land Rover's engine. Treading lightly, Vanessa crossed the hall to peer out the stained-glass window, and saw the rear of the Land Rover disappear around the bend of the driveway.

She released her breath in a huge sigh of relief. Thank God for Morag, she thought. That was one major hurdle jumped.

Chapter 4

They all looked up when she came in. Fiona in her high-backed chair, working on her tapestry, glasses perched on the edge of her nose. Colin stretched out on the couch, eating an apple and reading the newspaper. Amanda still working determinedly on the puzzle, which she had moved from the hearth to the small inlaid-mahogany side table. Sir Robert reading a copy of *Scottish Field*, his stumpy corduroy-clad legs stretched out on a leather footstool, hogging most of the heat from the blazing log fire.

As usual, Fiona was the first to greet her. "Good morning, Vanessa dear."

Vanessa came to kiss her soft cheek. She smelled of lavender, as if she were an old lady instead of a woman in her mid-sixties. "Morning, Fiona." She used the name deliberately, to distance herself from the one member of this family she still genuinely cared for.

"You must be cold after being outside for such a long time."

"Not really. Roddy and I kept moving all the time."

"Colin dear, let Vanessa sit there so that she can get warm."

Colin lowered his newspaper, his eyes meeting Vanessa's. Slowly, he took his feet, one by one, from the couch.

"No, don't worry," Vanessa said. "I'm not going to sit down."

Sir Robert put down his magazine. "We missed you at breakfast."

"Roddy couldn't wait to get out in the snow."

Vanessa avoided looking at him. She moved to the center of the room and stood behind the couch, very much aware of the back of Colin's head, resolutely turned away from her.

"Something on your mind?" Sir Robert asked.

"Very much so." Vanessa took a few steps backward, to find herself hemmed in by the bookshelves. She drew in a deep breath, redolent with that musty leather smell of old books. "I have something to tell you all."

Colin cursed beneath his breath.

"It isn't pleasant, but I wanted you to know before you hear it from some other source." Vanessa cleared her throat and swallowed hard. "I am very sorry to have to tell you that Colin and I are getting a divorce."

Now Colin's head turned. "Oh no, we bloody aren't. You're the one who's doing the divorcing, not me."

Vanessa stiffened. "I'm sorry. Colin's right. I am leaving Colin. I am applying for a divorce. But whoever's doing it, the effect is the same. We won't be living together anymore."

Sir Robert was on his feet. "This family doesn't believe in divorce." Hands clasped behind him, he stood with his back to the fire to make his pronouncement. "We have never had a divorce in the Strathferness branch of the Craigmore family."

"Well, there's always a first time for everything." Vanessa saw Fiona flinch. She hadn't meant to be flippant, but Sir Robert's attitude infuriated her. *Calm. Keep calm,* she told herself.

Fiona turned her face to Vanessa. It was filled with pain and apprehension. "Have you tried marriage counseling, Vanessa dear? Might it not be of some help to you and Colin?"

"Actually, I have. But as Colin refused to go with me, it was a total waste of time."

"Shrinks are a bloody waste of time," Colin muttered.

"I agree with Colin." Sir Robert moved his feet a

little wider apart, settling himself in for a long harangue. "Too much washing dirty linen in public nowadays. Look at Charles and Diana before their
divorce. All those wretched television interviews. People should be able to sort out their problems in private, by themselves."

"They should," Vanessa agreed, "but only if there
is some sort of dialogue between them. However, I'm
not here to discuss our marital problems with you—"

"Why not?" Sir Robert demanded. "Isn't that what
families are for?"

"You just said that people should work out their
problems in private."

"I meant within the family, of course."

"Not this family. I'm not prepared to—"

"You haven't even had the courage to tell us why
you're leaving Colin."

"You haven't given me the chance. Besides, that's
between Colin and me."

Colin moved to sit on the arm of the couch. "Be
my guest," he said, waving his hand. "I wouldn't mind
hearing your reasons myself."

"You know them already."

Colin smiled at the room in general. "She doesn't
like my interest in horse racing—"

"Gambling on horses," Vanessa interjected.

"Good God, woman," Sir Robert spluttered. "Everyone in Britain has a flutter on the ponies now
and again."

"Colin's gambling is hardly just a flutter. And, by
the way, please don't call me 'woman' in that way. I
find it offensive." Vanessa was standing near enough
to Amanda to hear her heartfelt, "Amen to that,"
although she doubted anyone else could have heard it.

Sir Robert's face was beet-red. "It is a Scottish expression, totally innocuous when used with the
family."

"At the very least it's outdated and today's women
find it demeaning, family or not." Vanessa saw Sir
Robert's eyes narrow and his lips purse and knew

that—even if he hadn't been before—he was now her enemy, for having rebuked him before his wife and children.

She also saw the pink flush in Fiona's face before she ducked her head to hide it, and immediately regretted having caused her embarrassment. But when Fiona looked up again, Vanessa caught a gleam in her eyes that she didn't remember ever having seen before, and she wondered.

"This must be very difficult for Vanessa," Fiona said in her soft, tentative voice. "Shall we hear her out?"

"There really isn't any more to say. Other things have alienated me and Colin, but they are private matters. I merely wanted you to know that I intend to file for a divorce, before you heard it from someone else."

"What about Roddy?" Sir Robert asked.

"What about him?" Vanessa rapped back.

"You realize that if you separate from Colin we will make sure you never see the boy again."

Rage suffused Vanessa. For a moment she felt like springing on him like a panther, ripping his eyes out.

"Hold on, Father," Amanda said. "This isn't the Middle Ages, you know. You can't do that."

Her father glared at her across the room. "Keep out of this, Amanda."

Colin spoke. "If this nonsense of a divorce ever happens—which, by the way, I doubt it will; it's just Vanessa being her melodramatic self, as usual—but if it does, naturally we'll make arrangements for her to see Roddy occasionally."

Vanessa boiled over. "You're blind," she said. "So wrapped up in your selfish selves that you can't see reality. Colin would never in a million years get custody of Roddy. That's one of the main reasons I'm divorcing him. He's not a fit father. For one thing, he's hardly ever home. For another, Roddy's afraid of him, and—"

"You're talking utter rubbish," Colin shouted.

"Am I?" Vanessa turned on him, breathing fast. "Well, we'll see about that when the time comes. For now, I need some time to think. After the New Year, I'm going to Canada to visit my parents for a couple of weeks. When I come home we'll work things out with our respective lawyers."

"Where's Roddy?" Colin suddenly asked.

Vanessa was prepared. "Morag's taken him to visit her sister." She hated lying, but she knew that she must. Their violent reaction to her announcement made her realize that she would have to use her backup plan after all, much as she didn't want to.

"Her sister?" Sir Robert repeated. "But Morag's sister lives near Beauly, doesn't she? That's miles away. They won't be back for lunch. Really, she should have asked us first."

"I told her it was okay," Vanessa said. Now came the worst part. "When I go to Canada, I shall be taking Roddy with me. I promised him that, one day, I'd take him to Canada in the winter. I think this would be a good time."

"Roddy's not leaving the country with you," Colin said flatly. "He's staying here at Strathferness with me."

Vanessa's heart beat painfully fast. "I didn't intend to go until after the New Year." Which had been true, originally.

"You won't take him with you to Canada, or anywhere, at any time. As far as Roddy is concerned, you either stay with me as my wife or you say good-bye to him."

"You can't stop me from taking him for a holiday to see his other grandparents," she said through dry lips.

"Oh yes, he can, lady," said Sir Robert. "Yes, he can. I'm going to ring my lawyer right now. I intend to ask him to make an immediate application to the Sheriff's Court for an interim custody order."

"But you can't ring Ewen today, Robert dear." Fiona's hands gripped the top of her tapestry frame. "Surely he'll be at home for the holidays."

"I don't give a damn where he is. When I speak to him, he'll recognize the urgency of the situation. I shall instruct him to engage the best advocate in Scotland to take up the case." He glowered at Vanessa. "You've chosen the wrong family to play games with, madam."

Amanda scraped back her chair and stood up. "Excuse me," she said, "but I think I've had enough." She walked past Vanessa without looking at her and left the room, slamming the door hard behind her.

Vanessa suddenly felt very alone. "Is this what you want?" she asked Colin.

"Sounds good to me." His eyes avoided hers. "Unless you want to change your mind."

"No, I'm sorry I can't. I've given you so many chances . . ." she told him, beneath her breath. Gripping the back of the sofa, she drew herself up and faced Sir Robert. "Interim custody order or not, the court will never give Colin sole custody of Roddy. Not after they've heard what I have to say."

"My dear girl." Sir Robert was smiling now. "You're living in a dream world. The Sheriff Principal is a good friend of mine. In fact, I know the entire panel."

"Even you can't buy off a group of judges," Vanessa told him.

"There's no need to buy anyone off. Do you really think that a Scottish court would allow you to take Roddy away to Canada with you? A child who will one day be the heir to an ancient Scottish title and estate?"

For a moment Vanessa said nothing. Then she looked at Colin, his head averted, and Fiona, her eyes downcast, and back at Sir Robert, smiling his triumphant smile at her. "You're right," she said. "I certainly did choose the wrong family."

Head erect, she walked from the room with stiff legs and closed the library door quietly behind her.

Her heart jumped when the door opened again and Colin followed her into the hall. "Where are you going now?" he asked.

"Back to Edinburgh," she told him. "I can't stay in this house one moment longer."

He moved toward her. "For God's sake, Van. Give it up. Let's try again to make a go of it."

"No, Colin. It isn't just the two of us anymore. It's Roddy on one side and you and your father on the other." She gave him a sad smile. "As I said, I chose the wrong family."

She walked away from him.

"Go to hell, then," he shouted after her. He stormed into the kitchen and she heard the clink of a bottle against glass.

No doubt Sir Robert was dialing his lawyer's number at this very moment. Hands shaking, Vanessa quickly dragged on her parka and boots and then went out the back door. She couldn't risk waiting even one more hour. Her emergency plan would have to go into action immediately.

Chapter 5

Morag Lindsay sat in the cozy front room of the gamekeeper's lodge, only part of her mind listening to what Annie McIntyre was saying. But then, that was nothing new. Annie always blethered away about nothing, her conversation filled with unimportant details.

". . . so I says to Angus, 'There'll be no dead birds coming into my house, and he says to me . . .'"

Morag's mind drifted away again, her gaze resting on Roddy's shining head as he played with the four golden retriever puppies before the fire. She loved this boy as if he were her own. Despite his strong resemblance to his father, his personality reminded her more of the other boy. The one that had gone from Strathferness forever.

Morag blinked rapidly and, pretending she had to scratch her arm, drew back her cardigan sleeve to glance at her watch. They'd been here almost an hour. She wished she were a fly on the wall so that she could hear what was happening at the castle. Whatever it was, it was going to be hard for the lad's mother.

Roddy's laughter rang out, bringing her back to reality. "He's biting the other one's tail. Don't do that! It could hurt." He dragged the two puppies apart and held one of them on his lap. "Doesn't it hurt when they bite each other?" he asked Annie, the puppy wriggling in his hands.

"They just nip at each other, that's all. Their mum'll soon tell them off if they go too far."

"She's asleep. She can't see what they're doing."

"Don't you believe it." Annie leaned down from her old rocking chair to pat the retriever stretched out across the hearth. "She's got her eye on them all the time. You'd best put the puppy down now, Roddy, or she might get upset."

Roddy set the squirming puppy back in the basket. "Please may I have a piece of cake, Mrs. McIntyre?" He looked at Morag as he asked the question.

"Of course you can," Annie said.

She cut a large wedge of raspberry sponge and was about to hand it to him when Morag intervened. "Wash your hands first," she told Roddy. "You've been playing with the dogs, remember?"

Roddy jumped up and dashed off into the hall.

"He's a fine lad, that one," Annie said. "When does he go off to boarding school?"

Morag's heart lurched. "This year, at the end of August."

"Poor bairn. He's so young. He'll miss his mother, and she him."

"He'll be fine," Morag said curtly. "His father survived and so will he." She heard Roddy's feet out in the hall. "No more talk of school, mind," she said with a warning frown at Annie, as the door opened.

Roddy had almost finished his second slice of cake when Morag heard the sound she'd been listening for, a car engine. She got up from her chair so suddenly that the retriever lifted her head and growled at her.

"That could be your mother, Roddy," Morag said, going to the bow window and lifting the net curtain to peer out.

Ice patterns frosted the window, making it difficult to see. She was able to discern a car, but not which one.

A car door slammed and then the doorbell rang. "Shall I go?" Roddy said, already running into the hall.

Annie started to lift her bulk from her chair, but Morag stayed her with a hand on her shoulder. "I'll go. It'll be Mrs. Craigmore come for Roddy." She went out into the dark hallway.

The bell rang continuously now. Roddy opened the door. "Hi, Mum."

"Hi, darling." His mother stood there, her face almost hidden by the fur-lined hood of her coat. Morag switched on the light. "Hello, Morag." Vanessa's dark eyes looked enormous in her pale face. "We have to go right away," she told Roddy. "Where are your coat and boots?"

"My boots are right here."

"Put them on. Quickly." As Vanessa stripped off her gloves, Morag could see that her hands were shaking. "Would you help him, Morag, please?" she said. "Where's his parka?"

"I'll get it." Morag opened the door of the hall cupboard and took out Roddy's coat.

"Why do I have to go so soon?" Roddy protested, as she held it out for him. "I want to stay with the puppies."

"We have to go now," Vanessa said, bending to do up his boots.

Roddy dragged his foot away from her. "I'm not a baby," he said scornfully. "I can do my own boots."

"Then do them. Quickly."

Morag's heartbeat quickened. She met Vanessa's eyes over Roddy's head. The pupils were wide and she could actually hear the younger woman's hurried breathing.

Annie came out into the hall. "Mrs. Craigmore, it's grand to see you. Won't you come in and have a cup of tea?"

Vanessa continued doing up the zipper on Roddy's coat. "Thank you, but I don't have time today, Mrs. McIntyre. Perhaps another time."

"Are you taking the laddie away already? He's barely had time—"

"I'm sorry, but there's a . . . bit of an emergency. We must go now. Come along, Roddy." She turned to the door.

Roddy hung back. "I don't want to go."

Morag stood between them, Roddy on one side, his mother on the other. If she grabbed Roddy now, maybe she could race upstairs with him, run into a bedroom, lock Vanessa out. But were there locks on the bedroom doors? Would Roddy come with her? How could she explain to him that he shouldn't go with his mother, that maybe she was about to do a bad thing?

She was torn, not sure whose side she was on. Again, she met Vanessa's gaze. This time the look of mute appeal was unmistakable. Then Vanessa turned to open the front door, letting in a rush of frigid air.

"Kiss Morag good-bye," Vanessa told Roddy.

Roddy looked at her, wide-eyed. "But I'll see her—"

Morag stepped forward and enveloped the boy in her arms. "Good-bye, my pet," she whispered, and then kissed him on the forehead.

"What about me, don't I get a kiss?" Annie said.

Roddy hesitated. He wasn't really into kissing people nowadays. Then he ran to give Annie a perfunctory hug, and dashed back to his mother again, catching her sense of urgency.

Morag stood at the top of the steps, shivering from more than the cold. The car's engine was still running. For a quick getaway, she said to herself.

"Get in the car," Vanessa told Roddy. She went down the three steps and then turned to look back at Morag. "If you really care about Roddy," she said in a low voice, "please don't go back home yet. They think you've taken him to Beauly to visit your sister."

"Why would they think that?"

"Because that's what I told them. If you stay here for a while longer, I'll be able to get a good start."

"You're not going back to the castle, then."

"No, I'm not."

"What's to stop me phoning or driving back there as soon as you've gone?" Morag demanded, annoyed that Vanessa would expect her to be disloyal to the family.

"Nothing. Nothing except your concern for Roddy's welfare."

"Where are you—"

"The less I tell you, the better it is for you. That way you can tell them you know nothing about my plans, and it'll be true."

Roddy opened the car door again and leaned out. "I thought you were in a hurry," he yelled.

"I am. Coming right away." Vanessa turned back to Morag. "Do it for Roddy, not for me," she said, and then ran to the car.

The car sped off, the wheels kicking up gravel. Morag watched it until it turned into the road and was out of sight.

"That was strange," Annie said from behind her. "What's the emergency? She never said, did she? She must have been going to fetch the doctor. Someone must be sick up at the castle. Probably Lady Craigmore. She's not at all strong, poor woman." She took Morag's arm. "Come on inside before you perish from the cold. We dinna want you sick as well."

As Annie led the way back into the snug front room, Morag passed the telephone on a cluttered table in a corner of the hall. She hesitated for a moment.

"Do you want to phone up to the castle to see what's the matter there?" Annie asked.

Morag was tempted. Then, recalling the panic in Roddy's mother's eyes, she shook her head. "I'm sure there's nothing much wrong or Mrs. Craigmore would have said so. Let's have another cup of tea and a look at those photos of Tommy's new baby, shall we?"

I've made my choice, she thought as she settled into the chair again. She hoped to God she wouldn't come to regret it.

Chapter 6

More than an hour had passed since Vanessa had left with Roddy. Morag was falling asleep from the combined effect of the heat from the fire and Annie's constant blethering. She stretched her aching arms and shoulders. "Time I was going."

Annie glanced at the clock on the mantelshelf. "Where does the time go to, I wonder? Angus'll be in for his tea soon. I should start getting it ready. Just cold chicken left over from yesterday's bird." She sighed. "Now that Tom and Sally are in Australia I don't bother with a turkey. It's not worth it for just the two of us."

Morag gathered up her knitting, carefully rolling it up. She was glad she'd brought it with her. It had helped to keep her calm all this while. "At the rate Roddy's growing I'm hoping this pullover won't be too small for him." She stuffed it into her knitting bag.

"Aye, he's growing fast."

Morag stood up abruptly. "Thanks for this, Annie. It's been a good wee rest for me. Now I must get back before they wonder where I've got to."

"They know where you are, don't they?"

"Of course." At my sister's house in Beauly, Morag thought with a wry smile. Her stomach churned at the realization that they would soon know otherwise.

A damp mist had closed in, obscuring the trees and the hills beyond them. She was glad she hadn't far to drive in this miserable weather. She shivered, thinking of Vanessa and Roddy, wondering how far they were going today. And where.

As she drove slowly up the winding driveway to the castle, she felt sick with dread at the thought of having to face the family. Whatever Vanessa was planning, they would say she'd been her accessory, wouldn't they? She could imagine Sir Robert's rage when he discovered that his grandson was not with her at all, but with Vanessa.

She didn't have to wait long. As soon as she drove into the stable yard at the rear of the castle, Sir Robert came out in his thick tweed jacket, followed by Colin. They must have been standing at the back door, waiting for her.

"He's not with her." A gust of wind carried Sir Robert's words to her as she got out of the car.

And she heard Colin's response. "Oh shit."

Sir Robert strode forward to grasp her arm. "Where's Roddy?" He was so close she could smell the whiskey fumes on his breath.

"With his mother. Why?"

The grip on her arm tightened. "His mother? I thought you were at your sister's in Beauly."

Morag forced a smile. "Whatever gave you that idea, Sir Robert?"

Colin came forward, his eyes narrowing. Morag felt menaced by the two of them crowding in on her. It had all been a terrible mistake. She should never have let herself get involved.

"Never mind," Colin said. "Where have you been?" Their breath plumed like white smoke into the whirling snowflakes.

"At the lodge."

"At the lodge?" Sir Robert repeated incredulously. "All this time you've just been at the lodge?"

"Of course. I took Roddy to see the new puppies at the McIntyres. I promised him I'd take him ever since—"

"Never mind that. Where is Roddy now?"

"Could we go inside, please? I'm frozen stiff out here in the cold." Morag pulled her arm free of his painful grip and marched ahead of them to the back door, her heart beating sickeningly fast.

She reached the door, with them following close behind, and turned the doorknob. To her great relief it turned—and opened. She felt safer inside the house.

Someone was standing there in the darkness. For a moment she thought it was Vanessa, but then she saw that it was Amanda. Thank God for small mercies, she thought. Amanda would make sure they didn't do her any harm.

"What's going on?" Amanda asked.

Before Morag had time to answer, the men crowded into the narrow passage by the kitchen, bombarding her with questions.

"Was Roddy with you at the lodge?"

"He was."

"Was Vanessa there with you, too?"

"Aye, she was."

"When did she and Roddy leave?"

"Would you mind if I took my coat off before I answer any more questions?"

"Forget your bloody coat," Colin said. "Tell us where Vanessa has gone with Roddy."

Ignoring him, Morag broke away from them to hang her car jacket up in the closet. This time it was Colin who grabbed her, swinging her around to face him. He lowered his head to glare at her. "You'd better tell me the truth or—"

Amanda stepped in. "Get your hands off her, Colin." She pushed herself between them. "Go into the library and get warm," she told Morag.

Morag was only too happy to set some space between her and the Craigmore men, but she knew that it would only postpone the inevitable for a moment or so. In all her years at Strathferness Sir Robert had never actually abused her physically, but when it involved his grandson she suspected he was capable of doing anything.

When she went into the library she found Lady Craigmore standing near the door, obviously listening to what was going on. She grabbed Morag's hands as she came in. "Are they all right?" she whispered. "Nothing bad has happened to them, has it?"

Morag had time only to shake her head and say a hurried, "No, no. They're fine," before the others came in behind her.

"Sit down," Sir Robert barked at her.

Morag perched on the edge of the couch, hands clasped tightly in her lap.

"Would you like a sherry to warm you up?" Amanda asked her.

Morag nodded.

"A Bristol Cream?"

"Yes, thank you."

Colin started in on her again before she had time to take a sip from the crystal glass filled with sweet sherry. "Why did you pretend to go to Beauly with Roddy?"

"I didn't pretend anything," Morag said, indignation sharpening her voice. "I told Roddy's mother I was taking him to see the puppies at the lodge."

"So she lied to us, damn her," Sir Robert said to Colin.

"Why would Vanessa lie?" Lady Craigmore asked. "Actually, I'm not quite clear what has happened. Is Roddy with Vanessa?"

"Why don't you go and rest for a while?" Sir Robert said, his voice laced with annoyance.

"I've only just come down from my rest, remember?"

"Right. Well, let me ask the questions, my dear. We want to find out as quickly as possible what has happened to Roddy."

"But if he's with his mother nothing has happened to him, has it?"

Colin turned on her. "For God's sake, Mother, shut up!"

Lady Craigmore's thin frame seemed to shrink into her chair, her pale blue eyes downcast, hooded by translucent lids.

"I'm sorry, but you really must let Father and me deal with this." Colin turned back to Morag. "What time did Vanessa take Roddy from the lodge?"

Morag frowned, as if she were trying to recall the exact time. "I'm not quite sure. Annie and I had been talking a fair while. And Roddy was playing with the puppies. It must have—"

"How long since she left the lodge with Roddy?" Sir Robert demanded.

This time Morag had to tell the truth. After all, they only had to ask Annie to confirm it. "More than an hour."

"An hour!" Colin shouted. "What the hell have you been doing there all this time?"

"I have been visiting with Mrs. McIntyre." She drew herself up and looked him straight in the eye. "I would remind you, Master Colin, that the day after Christmas has always been a holiday for me. I need my rest after all the work on Christmas Day."

"That's not what I meant, and you know it. Why didn't you call to tell us that my wife had taken Roddy?"

"Why on earth would I do that?" Morag asked. "She's his own mother, isn't she?"

"That's not important," Sir Robert said impatiently. "What matters is where they've gone. Did Vanessa say where they were going?" he asked Morag.

She glanced away from his reddened face . . . to catch sight of Lady Craigmore's expression. She was surprised by the intensity of her gaze. It was as if she were trying to infiltrate her mind. "Why, Edinburgh, of course," Morag replied, with only a moment of hesitation. "Where else would they go but back to their own home?"

"Did she actually say that was where she was going?" Colin asked.

Morag frowned, trying to recall what had been said between her and Vanessa, but her memory had been blurred by anxiety. "I really canna remember. I'm sorry."

"Even if she intends to go away somewhere," Colin said to his father, "she'd have to go back to Edinburgh to get some more clothes, wouldn't she?"

Sir Robert frowned. "Unless she'd packed for herself and Roddy beforehand. How many suitcases did she bring with her, does anyone know?"

"Just the one," Morag said. "I helped her unpack. And one bag for Roddy, of course."

"But she could have had more bags in the boot of her car, couldn't she?" Sir Robert said.

Colin's eyes widened. "If she did, it could mean she intended take Roddy out of the country. I'm going to phone the police."

"No, Colin. Not the police." Lady Craigmore's voice sounded so forceful that Morag barely recognized it. "We cannot have the police involved in a private family matter like this."

"For God's sake, Mother. She could be kidnapping Roddy." Colin's hand hovered over the telephone.

"You can't kidnap your own child," Amanda said.

"You can if it's against the father's wishes."

"No, you can't."

"Whose side are you on?" Colin demanded.

"No one's." Amanda shrugged. "I'm neutral, as always. But whether you like it or not, it's not an offense for Vanessa to take Roddy anywhere she pleases, unless you've got sole custody. And you haven't yet, have you?"

"Damn. If it weren't vacation time we could have that interim order right away," Sir Robert said. "Especially now that she's taken Roddy." He turned to Colin. "Regrettably, I have to agree with your mother. I don't think the police could or would take action on this. Until you get custody nothing can be done officially."

Colin strode to the door. "I'm not going to wait around doing nothing."

"Where are you going?" his father asked.

"To Edinburgh. I've got the Jag. Vanessa doesn't like driving fast. If I drive like hell I can catch up with her, perhaps even be there at the house when she arrives."

"What if she doesn't go to the house?"

Colin met his father's gaze. "Then I'll take the motorway to Glasgow. There are only a couple of flights to Canada every day. It should be fairly easy to find her at Glasgow Airport tomorrow morning."

"She may not go to Canada. Hasn't she got some actor friends in America?"

"If she's leaving Britain at all, she'll go to Canada, I'm sure of it."

"Just out of interest," drawled Amanda, "exactly what are you planning to do if you find her, in Edinburgh or Glasgow? Drag her back to Strathferness by the hair?"

Colin turned on her. "You're such a bitch!" For one horrible moment, Morag thought he was going to hit his sister.

Amanda stood her ground without flinching. "Just asking."

"I'll tell her she can go to hell for all I care, but that Roddy is coming home with me."

"And will you tear him apart between you? That would make an interesting spectacle at Glasgow Airport."

Colin gave his sister a faint, unpleasant smile. "I know Vanessa. She'd do anything to avoid upsetting Roddy."

"Ah." Amanda leaned back in her chair and blew out a puff of cigarette smoke. "A little bit of wholesome paternal blackmail. What a shit you can be, brother mine. No wonder Vanessa's left you."

"At least I have a child to care about. With the fruits you hang around with, you can't even get pregnant. But maybe that's the idea. Where is the delightful Happy Hapgood, by the way?"

"I sent him off to the pub to get him out of the way of my so charming family. He's going back to London tomorrow. I had intended to go with him."

"Before the New Year?" her mother said, shocked. "You always see the New Year in at Strathferness."

"Well, please don't stay on my account." Colin glared across the room at Amanda. "You're no help, just a bloody hindrance."

Sir Robert intervened. "That's enough from both of you. You're upsetting your mother."

He was right. Lady Craigmore was sitting glassy-eyed in her high-backed chair, her face deathly pale, as if all the blood had drained from it.

Morag went to her. "This is all too much of an upset for you. You should be lying down. I'll take her upstairs," she told the family.

Sir Robert came to his wife's side and took her limp hand in his. "Morag's right, my dear. You mustn't let this worry you. I'll soon have it all settled, so that Roddy will be back here with us before you know it."

His wife looked up into his face and then took his arm to lever herself out of her chair. "Will you take me upstairs, Robert?"

"Morag or Amanda will take you. I have several telephone calls to make."

Lady Craigmore subsided into her chair. Colin came to her. He bent to give her a hurried kiss on the cheek. "And I have to dash off. Father's right. We'll have Roddy back here by tomorrow at the latest. We'll all be bringing in the New Year together, I promise you."

His mother gave him a wan smile.

"I'll phone Ewen again, tell him what's happened," Sir Robert said.

"I'd rather deal with the legal side myself," Colin told him.

"Better that I do it," his father said impatiently. "Leave all of that to me. Your job is to get after her."

It was always the same, Morag thought. Colin trying to take control, his father refusing to relinquish it. As usual, Colin gave in to him, the way everyone did in this house.

"Okay. But you can tell Ewen I'll speak to him when I get back with Roddy." Colin turned back to the door. "I'm going to grab a sandwich. I don't want to have to stop to eat."

"I can get that for you," Morag said.

But Colin totally ignored her offer, as if she hadn't even spoken. "I'll ring you as soon as I get to Edinburgh," he told his father. "The roads should be fairly quiet today. Once I'm on the A9 I'll be able to hammer down to the motorway. You never know, I may even catch up with Vanessa by the time she reaches Pitlochry."

"Want me to come with you, for company?" Amanda asked.

Colin looked surprised. "No, but thanks for asking. I'm better off on my own."

"Please drive carefully, Colin dear." His mother looked as if she wanted to say something else, but the words never came.

"I always do." Grim-faced, he lifted his hand to them all and left the room.

Chapter 7

Darkness comes early in the Scottish Highlands in the winter. Fortunately it had been light for the early part of the drive. But when Vanessa took the narrow road that wound around the loch, the mist had suddenly descended, obscuring the view of the snow-capped mountains and of the road ahead of her. It was as if a fluid white shroud had been thrown over them, blotting out sight and sound. Although she knew the road well, she had been forced to slow down.

All the time she was driving, she kept glancing in her mirror, expecting to see Colin's Jaguar suddenly appearing behind her. For all she knew, he could have left Strathferness just a few minutes after she did. If that were the case, he could catch up to her any time now. Colin always drove fast. Nothing would slow him down, not even this damned mist.

When they reached the A9, the main road south, they were able to speed up, but the mist still ebbed and flowed, sometimes closing in on them completely so that Vanessa could only inch forward, other times suddenly lifting to show the road stretching before them, the hills towering on both sides.

There were only a few other vehicles on the road, most of them going south, and the silence was eerie.

Roddy peered out the wide window. "It's sort of creepy, isn't it?" he said uneasily.

"Yes, it is. But we know the road well, don't we? It's not as if everything isn't there. We just can't see it, that's all."

"Can we put some music on now?"

"Good idea," Vanessa said. "Let's have *Nutcracker*. That's nice and Christmasy."

Roddy selected the CD from the case and put it on.

The sounds of Tchaikovsky's lush score did nothing to allay Vanessa's fears. She would have preferred to drive without music, but knew that the silence and the claustrophobic mist were getting to Roddy.

She drove on, tightly gripping the steering wheel, concentrating hard on the road before her. "Tell you what," she said eventually, allowing herself to relax for a moment. "Why don't we guess where we are and see if we're right every time the mist lifts?"

They played this game all the way to the Pass of Killiecrankie, which, fortunately, was one of the less misty parts of the road. As they drew nearer to Pitlochry, Vanessa was starting to think that she might just pull this off, that Colin wouldn't catch up with her, when Roddy said he needed to go to the loo.

"Can't you wait a little longer?" Vanessa asked.

"No. I have to go now. And I'm hungry, too."

"There's some chocolate bars in that bag." She nodded to the bag at his feet.

"I want a hamburger."

Oh God! She should have known this would be too good to last. "Okay. We'll stop at the Little Chef, but it has to be a very quick stop."

If Colin was closing in on them he'd be bound to check in the roadside restaurant. There were hardly any other places to stop unless you went right into Pitlochry.

As she climbed out of the car, her legs almost crumpled beneath her. She grabbed onto the door to balance herself. Her entire body was stiff from the tension of driving through that mist, never knowing when Colin would appear out of it. She also realized that she, too, was dying to go to the loo.

"If you're finished first, get in line, if there is one," she shouted after Roddy, who had sprinted to the door as soon as the car stopped.

She had parked in the darkest corner of the parking

lot. A useless precaution, she knew. If Colin was looking for the BMW he would find it, wherever she
parked. She walked to the restaurant entrance, realizing that she was starting to feel—and think—like a
fugitive.

As she was washing her hands in the washroom, she
looked at her reflection in the mirror. Her thick dark
hair—which she wore just above shoulder length so
that she could easily tuck it under wigs for the cos-
tume shows—was escaping from the confines of the
woolen hat she had pulled on. Her face was almost
devoid of makeup and she had bitten her bottom lip
so much as she drove that it had been bleeding.

"What a mess!" she said aloud.

A woman came in as she spoke. She was clad in
one of those huge all-in-one nylon suits that rustled
loudly as she walked. She looked like an ad for Mi-
chelin tires.

"Bloody cold, in'it?" she said in a south London
accent.

Vanessa nodded and smiled. She didn't want to become engaged in a conversation. Although she had
lost her Canadian accent, she had a rather unusual,
low-timbred voice, which tended to identify her far
more than did her attractive, but definitely not beautiful, face. She quickly applied some lipstick and went
out before the woman could say anything more to her.

There was a small queue of people waiting for tables. Roddy was standing in line, as she'd asked him
to do, but he was also talking to the young woman
who stood in front of him. And he'd taken off his
tuque.

Vanessa's heart plummeted. If Colin came asking
questions, he'd soon discover that a golden-haired boy
of about seven had been seen there.

She joined Roddy in the line.

"Hi, Mum."

"Hi, darling." She glanced at her watch. "Remember now, we can't stay long."

The restaurant was surprisingly busy. After being

surrounded by so much silence and white darkness, the buzz of voices and clatter of crockery were reassuring.

"Are we running away?" Roddy suddenly asked.

The woman he'd been speaking to turned around to look at them, frowning.

"No, no, of course not," Vanessa said. "Don't be silly."

"Then why do we have to hurry?" His young voice seemed to ring through the restaurant.

She put her finger on her lips. "Ssh! Not so loud. We want to get . . . where we're going before it's your bedtime."

"I can sleep in the car."

"Sure you can." Vanessa smiled. "I just don't like driving in the dark for too long."

"Especially in this weather," the young woman chimed in. "That's a friendly wee lad you have there," she said in a Glasgow accent. "He's been telling me all about his Christmas."

Vanessa's smile froze on her face. "Has he? He's quite a talker."

"I asked him his name, but he said he couldna give it to strangers."

Thank God for that, at least.

"Very polite about it he was," the woman assured her.

To Vanessa's relief the woman and her silent partner were led away to a table. Then it was their turn. She ordered a hamburger and apple pie and ice cream for Roddy and some chicken soup and a cheese sandwich, with a pot of coffee, for herself. Although she wasn't at all hungry, it might be a long time before they were able to eat again.

"Can I talk now?" Roddy asked, when he'd taken a few bites from his hamburger.

"Of course you can."

"I know you didn't want me to talk before." He lowered his voice. "Are we running away from Daddy?"

Vanessa froze. She returned the suspended soup spoon to her bowl of soup. "Not really." She swallowed hard, searching for the right words. "I'll tell you all about it when we get back into the car."

"Then you'll find some other excuse."

"No, I won't. That's a promise. I just don't want to talk about private things here, okay?"

"Okay." Roddy went back to his hamburger. "But we are running away, aren't we? That's why we have to hurry."

She didn't want to scare him, to have him watching over his shoulder all the time, as she was. He was nervous enough nowadays, often suffering nightmares and biting his nails. "We're hurrying because we have to catch a plane. Now no more questions," she said firmly, "until we're back in the car."

"A plane," he said in an elated whisper, his eyes alight with excitement. He subsided when he saw her warning frown, but, as he ate his pie and ice cream, he kept jiggling in his seat and giving her little conspiratorial grimaces.

It wasn't going to be easy to explain. She wished she could do it without adding more stress to his young life. After all, that was one of her main reasons for leaving Colin.

When they went out into the cold parking lot, he let off steam by running to the car with his arms outstretched, imitating plane noises.

The stop had held them up for forty minutes. Vanessa took out the AA book of road maps and turned on the interior light.

"Where are we going to on the plane, Mum? Where?"

"Hush a minute. I want to study the map."

What would Colin expect her to do? More and more, she was trying to get into his mind, to anticipate how it would work. She could keep on the main road to Perth and then take the motorway directly to Edinburgh—which was what Colin would be expecting. Or she could strike out on one of the other roads. But if she turned off and took another route she would be slowed down considerably, and could also very well get lost in this weather. Indeed, some of the roads could be impassable after the snowfall.

She closed the map book. It would have to be the predictable motorway. She wished she had planned this more meticulously last night, but she'd hoped then that it wouldn't be necessary. Her original plan had been to take Roddy back to Edinburgh and leave for Canada a few days later. She should have known better.

Besides, she wasn't one for planning ahead. In the past, she had made decisions on the basis of intuition, impulse, rather than careful planning. Unfortunately, that had often landed her in hot water. But now it was imperative that she concentrate and make the right choices. If she didn't, the consequences could affect Roddy's entire life.

She turned off the light and started backing out.

"You said you'd tell me—" Roddy began to protest.

"I will. But it's getting late. We have to keep driving." She glanced down at Roddy. "Got your seat belt on?"

"Of course. Tell me now, Mum," he insisted. "Are we running away?"

"Sort of."

"I knew it."

She drove out from the parking lot, pulled the car onto the inside lane of the highway, and changed immediately to the faster lane. Despite her concern about lost time, she had to admit she felt better for the break.

"Daddy and I have decided to get a separation," she said, once she had settled into a steady speed.

"I thought you might," Roddy said, his matter-of-fact tone surprising Vanessa. "You keep fighting. Just like Alan McKinnon's parents. They're getting a divorce. Are you and Daddy getting a divorce?"

Vanessa hesitated. "I'm afraid so. We both still love

you very much, but we don't feel that way about each other anymore."

"I don't think Daddy loves me."

"Of course he does. He loves you very much."

Roddy picked up Rex, his favorite green dinosaur, burying his face in its worn velvety cover. "He's scary when he's cross with me," he mumbled into the stuffed dinosaur.

"Oh, everyone's scary when they're cross. I'm scary when I'm cross."

"Not the same way. He makes my tummy feel like it's full of snakes."

A chill ran down Vanessa's spine. She glanced in the mirror, saw that there was nothing behind her, and quickly pulled across both lanes, to draw up on the verge of the road.

She reached over to take Roddy in her arms. His eyelashes were damp against her cheek. "No one's going to hurt you, darling. Not when I'm here."

"Alan's going to live with his dad. That's because he's a boy, he says." He lifted his face to look into hers. "Will I have to live with Daddy?"

"No, sweetheart. You won't. I'll make sure of that."

"Won't I ever see him again?"

"Of course you will. You'll see him for holidays and maybe Christmas and—"

"But you'll be there, too, won't you?" His eyes looked enormous in the semidarkness.

"Yes, Roddy. Whenever you're with Daddy I'll always be there, too."

She could feel the release of his breath against her neck. "That's okay, then." He drew away from her. "I don't want to lose Daddy forever, you know."

"I know." She started up the car and moved to the outside lane once again.

"Where are we going on the plane?"

"To see Gran and Grampa Marston."

"To Canada?" Roddy yelled. "We're going to Canada?"

"We are." Vanessa smiled at his enthusiasm.

"Does Daddy know we're going to Canada?"

"Not really. He doesn't want us to go. He wanted us to stay with him at Strathferness."

"So he's going to be cross with us, right?" His voice wavered a little.

"A bit."

"That's why we've got to hurry, so he won't catch us."

"Oh, I don't think he's going to bother to try to catch us." Vanessa tried to make her voice as light and casual as possible. "Daddy wants to stay with the family at Strathferness. He's just a bit annoyed that we aren't with him, that's all."

Roddy sat for a while, thinking. "Are we flying to Canada tonight?"

"No. All the planes to Canada have left already. We're going to catch the first one to leave, but we have to take a short flight somewhere else to get it."

"Where?" demanded Roddy.

"That's a secret. Wait and see. It'll be a big surprise."

She hoped it would be a big surprise for Colin, as well. So much of a surprise that he wouldn't be able to anticipate what she was doing.

Chapter 8

Colin hesitated when he reached the Little Chef near Pitlochry. He was trying to get into Vanessa's mind, anticipate what she might have done. Less than a year ago, he'd have said he knew her well enough to be able to read her easily, but she was different now. Tougher, more complex, more aggressive. Look at how she'd stood up to his father during the last couple of days!

He didn't want to think about that.

The heavy mist in the hills and the snow drifting across the road in exposed areas had delayed him. He'd made shitty time, but Vanessa would have done far worse.

In fact, he wouldn't be at all surprised to find her inside the restaurant with Roddy. It was the obvious place to stop, and he knew that Vanessa would put Roddy's needs before her own desire to keep going.

He parked and went inside. The restaurant was full, the bright lights and chatter a shock after the quiet hum of his engine and the muffled soughing of the wind. He took a look around, but there was no sign of Vanessa or Roddy.

"Table for one?" asked the hostess, picking up a bright laminated menu.

Colin thought for a moment. "No, thanks. Just a coffee to take with me." He drew out his wallet. "I was wondering if you might have seen this woman and child in here today." He showed her a recent picture of Vanessa and Roddy.

"I only came on my shift a few minutes ago." She looked at him with suspicion. "Are you the police?"

"No." He flashed a smile at her. "My wife and son left ahead of me with the other car. We'd arranged to meet here. I'm rather concerned that they're not here. The weather's pretty bad out there," he added in explanation. "I'm just hoping they haven't broken down somewhere."

"Och, you poor man. What a worry! I'll speak to Peggy. She's been here a good wee while." She called one of the waitresses over. "This poor man's looking for his wife and wee boy. Have they been in, do you know?"

Colin held out the photograph to the waitress, who pushed back the fall of sandy hair from her eyes. "Aye, they were here. I served them myself. Such a lovely lad and so polite, too. He even—"

"Can you tell me when that was?" Colin burst in impatiently. "When did they leave?"

"I can tell you exactly. It'll be on their bill." She turned to the hostess. "Have you got it there?"

The hostess went through the pile of bills and drew one out. "Is this it?"

Peggy glanced at it. "Aye, that's it. Hamburger, soup, and cheese sandwich. They paid at five-fifty."

Colin's heart leaped. That was a little less than an hour ago. As he'd hoped, despite Vanessa's earlier start, he'd made better time than she had on this part of the journey. "Thank you." He took a five-pound note from his wallet and handed it to the waitress. "Thanks very much," he said as he strode to the door.

"What about your coffee?" the hostess called after him.

"Forget it," he called back. He pushed the door open and went out into the night.

Driving south to Perth, he felt his elation at being so close on their tail slowly seeping away as he tried to work out what was the best thing to do now.

He could speed down to Edinburgh as fast as he could and go straight to the house. Vanessa had said

she was going home, but could he believe her? What
if she was making for Glasgow Airport to catch a flight
to Canada?

Vanessa had spoken of going to Canada after the
New Year. Perhaps she'd try to change her tickets to
an earlier departure. If so, he should be making for
Glasgow, not Edinburgh.

But there wouldn't be any more international flights
from Glasgow Airport until tomorrow, would there?
Where would she go to sleep overnight?

His mind whirled. Damn Vanessa! Damn her to
hell! His hands tightened on the steering wheel. If he
had her here now, he'd take that slim throat of hers
between his hands and squeeze tightly, just like he did
that time a few months ago when she accused him of
having it off with Sonya, a friend of hers. He'd known
a heady sense of power when he saw the look of sheer
terror in her eyes before he released her.

From that time on he'd found that the one way
he could control her was by threatening to hurt her
physically. Although he never did much to her, the
threats alone had been enough to stop her bloody nag-
ging about his gambling or his drinking or his women.

He'd never expected that she'd actually carry out
her threat to leave him. She'd put Roddy's welfare
before her own for so long now that she seemed to
have accepted living with him, letting him do his own
thing, for Roddy's sake. After all, wasn't that what
most sophisticated couples did? Live and let live. His
own father had had plenty of bits on the side, but his
mother had remained untouched by it all. Of course,
knowing his mother, she'd have been totally unaware
that anything was going on.

The trouble was that Vanessa wasn't from their
world. His father had warned him before their marriage, but Colin had been too much in love with her
at the time to listen to reason. Besides, marrying
someone against his father's wishes had made him feel
powerful and independent. And it was the fact that
Vanessa was different from the women of his world

that had first attracted him to her. Her impulsive, down-to-earth manner and lack of guile had been like a breath of fresh air in his narrow, boring life.

But then it all went wrong. After a while, he began to find Vanessa just as boring as all the other women had been, and he looked for other, more exciting stimuli.

Perhaps Vanessa would have continued to go along with things as they were if it hadn't been for his sudden renewed interest in his son. He'd never been close to Roddy as an infant, but now that he was turning into a person in his own right, Colin had suddenly discovered the joy of having someone in his life who loved him unconditionally.

He started taking Roddy out to pantomimes or museums, playing cricket in the garden with him, turning up at his school sports' days to cheer him on as he ran the egg-and-spoon race. Being a father had turned out to be a surprisingly pleasurable and rewarding experience.

But with this new closeness came a more relaxed attitude from his son. When Roddy started answering him back and defying him, Colin decided it was time he got involved in his son's upbringing. His mother had spoiled him. It was time he was disciplined. He needed to be prepared for the ruthless world he was about to enter.

And for the bullies he'd meet up with in school.

The thought of his golden-haired, sensitive son trying to face up to some of the louts he might encounter at boarding school literally sickened Colin. It was up to him, the boy's father, to prepare Roddy for that ordeal, to wean him away from his adoring mother and toughen him up.

Vanessa's stubborn resistance to sending Roddy to his old alma mater, the school to which the Craigmore males had gone for more than a century, was the main reason for everything escalating to this crazy end. The virtual kidnapping of his son.

Colin put his foot down harder on the accelerator.

"Bitch!" he yelled into the cavern of the car, his own voice reverberating in his ears. "You'll be sorry." He turned on the radio. It was playing some raucous heavy metal music that suited his mood perfectly, the bass pounding out in time with the violent beat of his heart.

As he hurtled through the darkness, Colin swore that he would find his son and that Vanessa would pay dearly for having kidnapped him.

Chapter 9

When he reached Edinburgh, Colin hit a bad traffic snarl. Seething with frustration, he revved the engine at every red traffic light and holdup.

Once he had cleared the worst of it, he put his foot down. When he turned with a screech of tires into his street on a hillside in a solidly upper-class area of the city, he saw, with a huge sense of relief, that the lights were on in the porch of their granite-built Victorian house. He drew up outside, unable to see over the stone garden wall topped by a high privet hedge. Slamming on the hand brake, he jumped out to open the gates to the gravel driveway.

Vanessa's car was not there. Nor, when he opened the garage door, was it parked in the garage.

"You bloody idiot," he told himself. "You should have known she wouldn't come back here." Cursing, he opened the front door and stepped inside.

He was wrong. Vanessa and Roddy had been . . . and gone. There were signs of hasty packing everywhere. Drawers half open, clothes spilling from their hangers, the hall closet door swinging on its hinges. Plastic *Jurassic Park* dinosaurs lay scattered across the floor, as if Roddy had begged his mother to let him take them, and Vanessa had said, "No," and knocked the box from his hand.

That made Colin even more furious. Using his full force, he kicked the closet door closed, splintering the wood panel. Despite the unearthly silence, he ran upstairs, yelling for Roddy. There he found more open drawers and doors, their contents spewing out, silent

witnesses to the frantic haste of those who had been
there.

His first impulse was to smash everything in sight.
He picked up one of Vanessa's favorite crystal scent
bottles from the collection on her dressing table and
dashed it against the full-length cheval antique mirror
he'd bought her in Italy for their fifth anniversary. The
oval panel of glass shivered for a moment and then
dissolved in a jagged crack.

He indulged himself in the wish that it had been
Vanessa's face he'd shattered. "Bitch!" he yelled, scattering all the bottles on the dressing table with one
sweep of his arm. The smell of expensive perfume
filled the air.

Then reason set in. He began talking himself down,
knowing that the next thing he did must be the right
move, or else. But clearing his head was easier said
than done. He'd had a few fast beers on the way
down. That—and the bitter disappointment of thinking that he'd arrived in time and finding he'd missed
them—made his mind feel thick and slow.

He went downstairs again, turning into the dining
room to get himself a whiskey. But his hand stilled
above the decanter. "No. No more booze," he told
himself. He had to keep his mind sharp.

He stood in the middle of the elegant room that
Vanessa had redecorated only last year with her usual
good taste, damn her! Although he'd agreed that it
needed brightening up, she'd spent a lot more on the
redecorating than he'd expected and he'd told her so.
"I'm not bloody made of money," he'd yelled at her,
as she stood, erect and white-faced, by the lovely
Georgian sideboard, her excitement at showing him
the newly finished room draining away.

"We decided on this together," she'd reminded him.
"You said you wanted to do it."

"Not at this cost, I didn't," he'd roared back at her.
He hadn't told her, of course, that he'd had a big loss
on the horses just the day before, when he'd taken
some Japanese clients to the Ascot races.

God, he was thirsty. His hand hovered over the whiskey decanter again, but he turned away and went into the kitchen to get himself a drink of water. A collection of fridge magnets cluttered the refrigerator. Vanessa was a great collector of all kinds of rubbish. Everywhere he looked reminded him of her.

Under a maple leaf magnet was Roddy's latest drawing, a spaceship he'd done after he'd seen *Star Wars*. As he looked at it, tears stung Colin's eyes. "Roddy," he whispered. His son's name seemed to act as a kind of catalyst. His mind miraculously cleared and he was filled with anger again, only this time he was determined to use the anger constructively to fuel his thought processes.

"Think, you bloody shithead!" he shouted at himself, striking his forehead with a balled-up fist. "Or you'll lose your son forever."

She'd said she was going to Canada to visit her parents. That mean Glasgow Airport. There wouldn't be any more flights leaving for Canada today. That meant she'd have to stay in a hotel tonight. Where would she stay? Probably not at the upmarket hotels where he'd expect her to stay. But there were plenty of other, smaller hotels in Glasgow. Even if he rang every hotel in the city, would she have used her own name? Surely not. And certainly not her married name.

So he was back to square one. Every fiber of his being was telling him to call his father, ask his advice. But he rebelled against the voices inside his head. He could just imagine it. "What should I do, Father?" How often had he turned to him and had to endure scathing criticism before he got the advice he needed?

No, this time he'd do it by himself. He wouldn't return to Strathferness until he could go there triumphantly, with Roddy at his side, proving to his father that he could manage very well without him.

The telephone rang suddenly, startling him as it pealed out in the numbing stillness of the house. He hesitated, but then, realizing it could be Vanessa, he picked up the receiver.

"Colin?" said his father's voice.

For one suspended moment Colin was tempted to put the receiver down again. He could hear his father's voice repeating his name, growing more exasperated. He put the receiver to his ear. "Yes, I'm here."

"I know that. Are they there?" his father barked.

"They were. But they'd gone by the time I got here."

"Damn! How do you know they were there?"

"She packed in a rush. Doors and drawers open."

"Damn," his father said again. "I thought you might have got there in time."

"I drove as fast as I could," Colin said, his voice sharp with annoyance. "The roads were a mess. You can blame Morag for not telling us in time."

"I do. I have. I've told her to pack her things and leave by tomorrow morning."

That was how his father worked. Fast and lethal. Like a well-honed axe. No thought of where Morag would go after living at Strathferness for almost forty years.

"Good," Colin said. "If Morag hadn't covered for Vanessa I'd have Roddy now."

"Well, no point in wasting time crying over spilled milk. We must decide what to do next."

"I have. I'm going to Glasgow right away. She can't get a flight out to Canada tonight. It's too late. She'll have to stay in a hotel. Don't worry, I'll track her down." Colin's voice held a confidence he didn't really feel.

"How the hell will you do that?" his father demanded. "There are dozens of hotels in Glasgow."

"How many women with small boys will have checked in without a reservation, though? Precious few, I should think."

"A hotel's not likely to give out that information."

"I can think up a plausible story. You'd be surprised."

"Damn right, I would."

Colin felt like swearing down the phone at his father, but knew there was no point. He'd done that many times before, and had to come crawling back with an apology.

"No," his father continued, "your best bet is to be at the airport early tomorrow morning. Hang around the check-in counters for the flights to Canada until they turn up."

"That was my backup plan."

"You'll never find her in a hotel. The airport is the place to go. How can we be sure she'll go to Canada?"

"Where else can she go?"

"She's a fool if she does. If she turns up at her parents' home in Winnipeg, we can easily get Roddy back."

"I'll contact the police right away."

"Don't bother. There's no point. Until we have a court order she can take Roddy anywhere she likes. No, just go to Glasgow Airport tomorrow and then come back here directly, whether you get Roddy or not."

Somewhere during the conversation Colin realized that, once again, he had lost control of the situation. Now, sitting far away in his battered leather chair, his father was giving him orders, pulling the strings.

"We have to make sure we get this thing done legally," his father continued, "so that we can tie that wife of yours up in knots. I tell you, once Roddy is back with us, I'm going to make sure she never gets her hands on him again, whatever it takes."

"I'll keep in touch," was all Colin said, and he replaced the receiver before his father could say any more.

He felt as he always did after a conversation with his father. Diminished, without value, demoralized. Whatever he did now, however successful he might be at getting Roddy back, his father would imply that Colin could never have done it without his help.

"You stupid shit!" he yelled into the void. "You

had to pick it up, didn't you?" He pounded the telephone with his fist, making the bell ping, but it was himself he was really pounding.

He looked around the kitchen in a daze, seeing and yet not seeing the copper pans on the wall and the marble countertops. One thing was certain. He couldn't stick around here, just waiting until morning. If he did that he'd drink himself into a stupor and be wasted in no time. No, he'd do what he'd said he was going to do. Go around all the Glasgow hotels with the picture of Roddy he had in his wallet. And, by God, he'd tell them the truth. That his wife had kidnapped his son and he wanted to find them before they left the country. That would surely get people on his side.

And just think how it would feel to bring Roddy back to Strathferness tomorrow morning, proving to his father that he could do it without any help from him.

Spurred on by this thought, Colin ran from the house, sprang into his car, and tore off down the street, making for the fast motorway to Glasgow.

Chapter 10

The taxi wound through narrow, cobbled streets, and then drew up before a tall, gabled building. Beyond it, the light from the street lamp glistened on the dark water.

"Can you guess where we are?" Vanessa asked Roddy when they got out of the taxi.

Roddy peered up at the tall, thin buildings and then down the street to the water. "Looks like Holland," he said.

"Right first time. It is Holland."

"You are in Amsterdam," the taxi driver told Roddy in perfect English, as he swung their luggage out onto the cobblestoned road. He jerked his head toward the water. "That is the largest canal, the Singelgracht." He picked up the bags and carried them to the hotel entrance. "Are they expecting you here?" he asked Vanessa.

"They should be. I called them from the airport. They said someone would be here to let us in."

As she spoke, the door opened and a man in a white shirt and black waistcoat came out to help them in with their luggage. Vanessa paid the taxi driver with some of the Dutch guilders she'd bought at Edinburgh Airport, and followed the man inside.

"Why are we in Amsterdam?" Roddy asked, peering around the narrow foyer of the small hotel.

"I'll tell you when we get to our room," she whispered. She went to the desk as the hotel porter or receptionist, or whatever he was, went behind it to register them. He was friendly and quietly efficient.

"I'm sorry we're so late," Vanessa said, as she signed the register *Vanessa Marston*.

"This is not late for Amsterdam, Mrs. Marston. Many of our guests do not return until three or four o'clock in the morning. Amsterdam rarely sleeps."

"Well, we're certainly going to sleep. We'll see Amsterdam in the morning. Can you have someone wake us at seven?"

"Certainly."

"Can we get breakfast that early?"

"Of course." He leaned over the counter to point the way. "Down the hall and into the room on the right."

"Thank you."

She had deliberately chosen a small hotel away from the center of the city. Although she'd picked it at random, she seemed to have chosen well. There were vases of delicately colored freesia on the counter and the small, highly polished tables in the foyer. From the cheerful-looking bar across from the front desk came the sound of soft music and the hum of conversation.

"Will you need a taxi in the morning?" the man asked.

Vanessa frowned, trying to gather her thoughts. Ever since she'd left Strathferness everything had been done on impulse, so that planning ahead seemed more than usually difficult. "We have to be at the airport around twelve."

"Schipol?"

She hesitated, not quite recognizing the name the way he pronounced it.

"The international airport," he said.

"Yes, that's right."

"I will order it for you. For eleven o'clock tomorrow morning."

"Will that be enough time to get us there?"

"More than enough. You will also have time to visit the Rijksmuseum in the morning before you leave."

Looking at art galleries was the last thing Vanessa

felt like doing, but she would have to fill the time somehow. She certainly didn't want to wait around at the airport, expecting Colin to appear at any moment. "Would I need a taxi to get to the museum?"

He gave her a patient smile. "It is only a few minutes' walk from here. You will have plenty of time."

How matter-of-fact and quietly self-confident the Dutch were. This mixture of patience and assurance was just what she needed.

He ducked beneath the counter and brought out a map, opening it up. "Here we are and here is the museum." He refolded it and handed it to her.

Vanessa took the map without looking at it. "Thank you. You've been very helpful."

He rang the bell and asked the young man who appeared from the bar to take them up to their room. It was small and neat, with plain utilitarian furniture. Two narrow beds with white bedspreads, a simple dressing table, and a small wall closet.

Vanessa shivered as she looked around. She was feeling desperately tired and the room both looked and felt cold.

"There is a heater here." The young man turned it on and a gush of warm air came into the room. "Would you like anything else?"

"Would it be possible to have some tea?"

"It would be faster if you come down to the bar. I will provide it for you."

"Thank you." Great, she thought. That would give her a chance to telephone her parents in Canada as well. Since she'd arrived at Edinburgh Airport she hadn't been able to get time away from Roddy to call them. She handed the man a green ten-guilder note, hoping she'd given him enough, and closed—and locked—the door behind him.

"What's this thing?" Roddy was in the bathroom, investigating.

"What?" Vanessa peered into the bathroom. "Oh, that's a bidet."

"What's it for?"

"It's to wash your feet—or your bottom."

"My bottom!" Roddy shrieked with laughter, strad-dling the bidet and bouncing his behind on it. "I'm washing my bottom. I'm washing my bottom," he sang out.

"Ssh! You'll wake everyone up. I'm going down-stairs to get some tea. Would you like anything? Some milk?"

"Coke," Roddy shouted. He was extremely overtired and becoming obnoxious.

"No Coke. Milk. And maybe some cookies if you're good. I'll see what I can find." She unlocked the bag she'd helped him pack. The house in Edinburgh seemed like another world now, but, in fact, it was only a few hours since they'd left it.

"Can I watch the telly?"

"Television," she corrected automatically. "Okay. After you get your 'jamas on."

"Will they speak double Dutch on the television?" Roddy rolled on the bed, yelping with glee at his joke.

Vanessa rolled her eyes. "Groan," she said. "I'm sure you'll be able to find something in English."

She was at the door when she suddenly remembered where they were. Amsterdam. Sin City. "On second thoughts," she said quickly, "don't turn the television on until I get back. Get washed and ready for bed first."

"Oh, Mum!" he moaned, but subsided when she gave him one of her special "looks."

The bar was so cozy, with a crimson deep-piled car-pet and dark wood, that she was tempted to stay there for a while, but knew that she couldn't leave Roddy. She ordered tea for herself and some milk for Roddy, plus a couple of large slices of a delectable-looking apple spice cake, crusted with brown sugar on the top.

"I'm just going to make a telephone call," she told the bartender. "I'll be back in a few minutes." She went to the public phone booth in the foyer, which fortunately had a door to ensure privacy.

Her mother answered the phone. When she heard

the familiar voice, Vanessa found it impossible to speak for a moment, so that her mother had to say, "Hello," again.

"Hi, Mum. It's me, Vanessa."

"Hi, darling. This is a surprise. I didn't think we'd hear from you again until New Year's. Is everything okay?"

"Fine." Vanessa paused, not sure how to explain without worrying her mother. "I've got a surprise for you. Roddy and I are flying over to spend New Year with you and Dad."

"You're kidding!"

"No, I'm not. We're taking a KLM flight from Amsterdam to Minneapolis tomorrow."

"Amsterdam! Is that where you are now?"

Vanessa hesitated. Damn! She shouldn't have told her mother where she was. "Yes."

"Why Amsterdam?"

"I'll explain tomorrow when I see you."

"Okay. That is a lovely surprise, sweetheart. Did Roddy have a good Christmas?"

"He can tell you himself when he gets there. Is Dad there?"

"He's out shoveling snow. Would you believe we had more snow this morning and—"

The bartender appeared in the hall, bearing a tray.

"Hang on, Mom. I have to do something. Don't go away."

Vanessa quickly signed the bill and then went back to her mother. "I can't stay long. I'm in a public call box."

"What the heck are you doing in Amsterdam?" her mother demanded. "Why couldn't you fly from Scotland?"

"I'll explain when I get home."

"You sound a bit odd. Is something wrong?"

"I'm fine, Mom. Don't go on. I'm in a hotel and I have to get back to Roddy right away. Have you got a pen and paper?"

"Yes."

"I'll give you both flight numbers and the time the Northwest flight from Minneapolis arrives in Winnipeg." Vanessa read them out.

Her mother repeated them to her. "We'll be at the airport to meet you. Give our love to Roddy."

"I will. He's very excited about seeing you."

"We are, too. I wish I knew—"

"Don't worry, Mom. I'm fine. I'm a big girl now, remember? Able to take care of myself."

"I know that." A small pause, and then her mother said, "See you tomorrow, sweetheart. Your Dad will be thrilled."

"He's not the only one. Give him my love." Vanessa hesitated and then said, "If anyone calls, please don't tell them where I am."

"Who'd be calling?" her mother asked. Then she gave a stifled little gasp. "You mean Colin. He doesn't know where you are?"

"Colin—or anyone else," Vanessa said, ignoring the question. "Don't tell anyone that you've heard from me, okay?"

"You're scaring me, Vanessa."

"There's no reason to be scared. Just don't tell anyone other than Dad that I've called."

"If someone does call to ask about you, I'll tell whoever it is that I haven't heard from you since Christmas Eve," her mother said in a firm voice. "Is that right?"

"Perfect. I'll explain when I see you. Love you. 'Bye." Vanessa replaced the receiver before her mother could ask any more questions.

She slept badly, waking frequently from unsettling dreams. But when the telephone rang she was in such a sound sleep that Roddy answered it before she could get to it.

"Hello, this is Roddy Craigmore," he said, as she'd taught him. "Is that Daddy?"

For one horrible moment Vanessa froze, but then

Roddy handed her the receiver and said, "It's a man telling me the time."

"Thanks, darling." Heart racing, she took the receiver from him and thanked the operator.

"From now on let me answer the phone, wherever we are," she told Roddy as she got out of bed.

"Why?"

"Because it could be someone speaking another language." It was a lame reason, but the only one she could think of on the spur of the moment.

"What about in Canada?"

"There, too."

"But don't they speak English in Canada?"

"Most people do," she had to admit, "but some speak French."

"Only in Quebec. You told me that."

"Some people in Manitoba speak only French."

"But why would they be—"

"No more questions. You can ask me anything you want about Canada when we get on the plane. But now we have to hurry up and get dressed and have breakfast. We want to see a little bit of Amsterdam before we go to the airport."

As she stood in the shower, deliberately keeping the water cool to wake herself up, her mind darted from one thought to another. She was like Roddy, brimming with unanswered questions.

Last night, Colin would no doubt have discovered that they weren't at home in Edinburgh. What would his next move have been? Would he have called her parents? Would he have gone to Glasgow Airport, as she hoped he would, thinking she'd fly direct to Canada from there?

Breakfast was served in a bright room with small tables covered with crisp white tablecloths. She and Roddy were the only guests there.

"I hope we're not too early," Vanessa said to the rosy-cheeked girl who greeted them at the door. She looked as if she should be wearing clogs and a white, winged cap, but she was dressed, disappointingly, in a white blouse and short black skirt that hugged her ample bottom.

"No, no. You are not first." She led them to a small round table by the electric fire set into the blue-tiled fireplace.

Roddy eyed the large basket that sat on the table. It was filled with delicious-looking rolls and slices of various kinds of bread: brown, white, some studded with plump raisins or caraway seeds. Beside it was a dish of sliced meats and sausage.

While Roddy pigged out on several slices of bread spread with apricot jam and then made himself a sandwich with slices of succulent pink ham, Vanessa ate a pear and banana from the fruit tray she was offered and drank strong coffee laced with cream.

The Rijksmuseum turned out to be quite a success for both of them. Roddy was particularly taken by Rembrandt's *Night Watch*. "Wow! That's awesome. I've never seen such a gigantic picture. It's the size of the whole wall. He must've used a ladder to paint it."

"I imagine he did."

Vanessa enjoyed the lovely Vermeer painting of a kitchen maid pouring milk, with its realistic depiction of loaves of crusty brown bread, "Just like we had for breakfast this morning," she said, but Roddy found that far less interesting.

Their brief tour ended with a visit to a nearby pancake restaurant. They sat on a wooden bench at a long table and both ordered puffy, crisp apple pancakes liberally dusted with powdered sugar, each the size of the large dinner plate they were served on.

"Wow!" was all Roddy could say before he tucked into the pancake, quickly deflating it with his fork and covering his mouth with the white sugar.

Vanessa was glad that the diversion to Amsterdam had proved to be such a success. The last thing she'd wanted was to transfer her own fears to Roddy and have him constantly looking over his shoulder, as she was. In a way, she wished they could hide out in Amsterdam for a few more days, but she knew that Colin would already be using every resource possible to find them. The quicker they got to Canada, the better. In Canada she had family and friends she could trust implicitly.

Here, she was too close to Scotland. And she was growing more certain every minute that Scotland now spelled danger to her son.

Chapter 11

The following evening, Colin turned into the long curving driveway to Strathferness Castle. The probing light from his headlights picked out the frosted trees and the fields beyond them covered with ice-coated snow.

Despite the heat in his car, Colin shivered. He was returning home a failure, as always. Last night, with the icy rain spilling down, he'd driven and walked the streets of Glasgow, searching for Vanessa and Roddy in all the larger hotels—and most of the small ones, as well—with absolutely no success. Eventually he'd booked into the last seedy hotel he'd visited, slept on a lumpy mattress for a few restless hours, and then took off for the airport before seven in the morning.

He'd stayed at the airport—grabbing a piece of sausage in a bap for his lunch, afraid even to go to the lavatory in case he'd miss them—until the last flight to Canada had taken off.

Although no one would give out names on their passenger lists, he was quite sure that if his wife and son were flying to Canada from Glasgow he would have seen them. Vanessa had tricked him. As he drove around to the garages by the stables, Colin felt yet another surge of fury at the thought of her. Because of bloody Vanessa, he had to return to his father, tail between his legs, and confess that he'd screwed up.

When he went into the castle, he could hear voices from behind the closed door of the library. His father's and another male voice. Stretching his neck and shoulders to relieve the tension, Colin opened the door and went in.

"Ah, and here he is at long last," his father said, as if Colin had just run downstairs from his bedroom. "You know Ewen McKay, of course."

Colin turned to his father's solicitor and shook his hand. "Hello, Ewen. Thanks for coming."

"Tough drive, I should imagine," Ewen said succinctly.

"Very."

Three years ago, the head of the law practice the Craigmore family had used for almost a century had died. Ewen McKay, his junior partner, had succeeded him. Like a new broom, he'd swept the old firm into the twentieth century. Despite his personal misgivings about Ewen, Sir Robert had kept his lucrative business with the firm, recognizing Ewen's undoubted ability.

Before his father could offer him anything, Colin helped himself to a whiskey and cut a wedge of Cheddar from the cheese board on the coffee table. "Excuse me, but I haven't eaten since I left Glasgow," he said, sitting down by the fire across from his father. "What's been happening here?"

Ewen leaned forward, folding his thin hands together like a praying mantis. "Before we start in on that, your father tells me that you had no success in finding your wife and son in Glasgow."

"None at all."

"Would you tell me exactly what has happened since your wife left Mrs. McIntyre's house?"

"Has Mrs. Lindsay—"

"I have interviewed Mrs. Lindsay. I want to know now what you have done since then."

Colin told Ewen about his journey to Edinburgh, the empty house with its signs of hurried flight, the search in Glasgow last night, and his long wait at the airport this morning.

"So it is likely that your wife has either remained in Britain or flown to Canada from another airport. Perhaps from London. Wherever it was, it is now too late to intercept her. She will be en route to Canada at this moment. That is, if she is going to Canada."

"I'm sure she is," Colin said.

"Does she have many friends here in Britain?"

"Yes, of course. In her business—"

"Friends who would be prepared to hide her and her child from her husband?"

"I think so," Colin said slowly, reluctant to admit that many of Vanessa's friends in her world of theater and television sympathized with her.

Ewen made a note on his lined pad of paper. "I shall need a list of all your wife's friends here in Britain."

"Wouldn't it be better to make sure she's not in Canada first?" Colin didn't see the point of broadcasting the fact that Vanessa had left him unless it was absolutely necessary.

"Naturally."

"Ewen's not a fool," Sir Robert said, his tone suggesting that Colin was. "He wants you to telephone your wife's parents and—"

"Not yet. Not until we actually have the court order." Ewen turned to Colin. "I have arranged for a hearing regarding the interim custody order for ten tomorrow morning."

"That was fast. What are my chances of getting custody?"

"Interim custody? Almost certain. Taking a child out of the country—if that is what your wife has done—without the other parent's knowledge or consent is definitely frowned upon."

"Appalling," Sir Robert said. "And even more appalling to involve our housekeeper in it, as well."

As if on cue, the door opened and Colin's mother came in, followed, to his surprise, by Morag Lindsay herself, bearing a tray.

"Not now, Fiona," Sir Robert said impatiently.

As if she hadn't heard her husband, Fiona smiled at Colin and came to kiss him. "Hello, dear." Her cheek felt as soft as rose petals. "Morag and I have

made some roast beef sandwiches. I saw you drive in
and thought you might be hungry."

"I am. Starving, actually." He gave her a grateful
smile and then tackled the plate of sandwiches, studiously avoiding either thanking or even looking at
Morag.

"Help yourself, Ewen," Fiona said, and then went
to sit in her usual chair a little distance from the fire.
She smiled at Morag. "Thank you, Morag."

Sir Robert's face was scarlet. "What the devil is that
woman still doing here?" he demanded, the instant
Morag had left the room.

"I'm sorry, dear, but she can't leave in this dreadful
weather until I have found her somewhere to go."
Fiona blinked her pale blue eyes, gazing at him like
a startled doe. "I'm sure that it was never your intention to have her leave until I had found her another
situation, was it?"

Aware of Ewen, Sir Robert cleared his throat and
said, "No, no, of course not. But I want her gone as
soon as possible."

"Of course, dear. In the circumstances I am sure
that is what Morag wants as well."

Colin couldn't contain himself. "Who the hell cares
what she wants? Honestly, Mother, you are sometimes
so dense it makes me—" He stopped short, aware of
his father's scowl. "I'm sorry," he said with a heavy
sigh, "but Morag Lindsay is the main reason Roddy
isn't here."

"She has been dealt with. Let's leave it at that." Sir
Robert turned to Ewen. "Perhaps we should adjourn
to my study to discuss this further."

Fiona's thin hands twitched in her lap. "Roddy is
my only grandchild. I should like to be here when you
are talking about getting him back to us. Would that
be all right, Ewen?"

Ewen inclined his head in an old-fashioned little
bow. "But of course, Lady Craigmore."

Colin exchanged glances with his father, for once in
full agreement with him. Much though he loved his

unworldly mother, she was bound to be a hindrance in the discussion.

"Should we call Amanda in as well?" Fiona asked.

Ewen glanced at Sir Robert's face, which looked as if it might explode any minute, and hastily said, "No, no, that won't be necessary, Lady Craigmore."

"We get this order for custody tomorrow," Sir Robert burst in as Ewen was speaking. "What then?"

"*If* we get the order," said Ewen, "we must then find Colin's wife and son and request that they return to Scotland. Then arrangements can be made between Colin and his wife for his son's future."

"Surely she cannot have any say in Roddy's future when she has kidnapped him—"

Ewen held up his hand. "I know how upset you are about this, but it is not a kidnapping."

"What if she refuses to come back to Scotland?" Colin demanded.

"Good question," his father said.

Fiona smiled at Colin. "I am sure Vanessa will return once she knows that you want to discuss all this amicably."

"God's sake, Mother." Colin heaved an impatient sigh. "Vanessa and I have gone way beyond amicable discussions."

Ewen tapped his pen on his pad of paper. "Let us keep to the discussion of practical questions, shall we? If, as Colin suggests, his wife refuses to return to Scotland with Roddy, we must then instigate a search."

"Get the police on to it," Sir Robert said.

"That's what I think we should do," Colin agreed.

Ewen rubbed his chin with his bony fingers, a sure sign that he was getting impatient. "The police cannot be involved yet."

"I don't think they should be involved at all," Fiona said.

Sir Robert turned on her. "If you're going to keep interrupting us, we'll take ourselves off to another room."

Again, it was as if she were deaf to what he had

said. "If you go to the police the press are sure to hear about it. Only think what a dreadful scandal it would be."

"Why on earth would the press be interested?"

"Oh, my dear Robert." Fiona gave a little laugh. "Vanessa is a television actress. Colin is the heir to the title and to Strathferness. It would be a great story for the media. Can't you see the headlines? '*Actress Kidnaps Baronet's Grandson.*' "

"You are quite right, Lady Craigmore," Ewen said. "There is no need to go to the police with this. If Colin's wife has gone into hiding and refuses to return, we can use private investigators to track her down. There are ways of hounding her until she will be happy to submit. For now, we shall secure the interim custody order and then inform her that she must return Roddy to Scotland."

"If we can find her," Colin said gloomily.

"We will begin by telephoning her parents tomorrow," Ewen said. "Even if she is not with them, they will probably know where she is. If you like, I will speak to them."

"No, I'll do it," Colin said hastily, feeling that everything was being taken out of his hands. "I think I know them well enough to be able to tell if they were lying or not."

Ewen raised his thin shoulders in a slight shrug. "Very well. But may I suggest that you deal with them with the utmost diplomacy for now."

Colin didn't trust himself to answer that one. He disliked the solicitor even more than his father did. The feeling, he was sure, was mutual.

"Getting the order is only the start of a number of moves you will have to make," Ewen told Colin.

"Such as?"

"That will be up to your own lawyer to decide. You have not engaged me." Ewen gave Colin a prim little smile.

"Well, as my father's footing this bill, give me some free advice."

"You may not like it."

Colin felt like strangling him. "Give it to me, anyway." He glanced at his mother. "Unless you think my mother shouldn't hear it."

"On the contrary. I believe that my advice encompasses the entire family."

"Right, let's bloody well hear it then." Ewen's pedantic statements were driving Colin crazy.

"Should we ask Amanda to come in?" Fiona asked. "Ewen did say that his advice was for the entire family," she said apologetically to her husband.

Ewen cleared his throat. "I meant the family in residence at Strathferness, Lady Craigmore, but by all means call in your daughter if you wish."

Fiona glanced from her husband to her son. "I can explain everything to her myself later," she said, subsiding into her chair.

Ewen turned to Colin. "If, as I understand from Sir Robert, your goal is to secure full custody of Roddy, you will have to prove that you are fit to be his sole parent."

"Therein lies the rub," Colin heard his father mutter.

"Fit not only financially but also emotionally. You must be prepared to have social workers prying into your life, asking personal, intrusive questions that will infuriate you, all the time knowing that a wrong answer could jeopardize your chances of gaining full custody."

"I realize that," Colin said. God, what a pompous prat Ewen could be!

"You must also show that Roddy would have a full, structured home life with you. Were you living at all times with your wife?"

"Yes."

"That isn't so," Sir Robert told Colin. "You were living with her on and off. Half the time I'd telephone the house and you wouldn't be there."

Colin glared at his father. "Thanks, Father."

"I can't help you if you're not honest with me,"

Ewen said in a frosty voice. "And another thing. You should be able to convince the court that there is full family solidarity." The solicitor looked at them, one by one, over his glasses. "To be honest, Colin, the ideal solution would be for you to move in with your parents."

Sir Robert gave a bark of laughter.

Colin's expression, too, must have startled Ewen, for he hastily added, "At least until you are given permanent sole custody. That way you can be seen to be providing Roddy with a satisfactory home, two loving grandparents, and a solid family life."

"He'll be going to prep school in September," Colin said. "As a boarder. What's the point of having to make such a drastic change in all our lives?"

"As I told you," his father said to Ewen, "that was the main reason Vanessa's taken him. She doesn't want the boy to go to Colin's old school. She's Canadian, of course. Boarding schools aren't their tradition."

"I understand that. But I should advise you to play down the part about boarding school." The solicitor's lips formed a dour smile. "Not everyone shares your enthusiasm for sending an eight-year-old boy away from home for his schooling."

Including Ewen himself, it seemed. Understandable, thought Colin, considering Ewen's father had been a butcher in Inverness.

"I would like to take issue with you on that subject."

Seeing that his father was about to start an argument about schools, Colin jumped in. "Considering you have been in this from the start, Ewen, I'd like you to look after the case."

"Are you sure about that?" Ewen adjusted his glasses and gave him one of his shrewd looks. "I call a spade a spade, you know. Don't expect me to gloss things over just to please you."

Hot anger surged through Colin, but he held it in

check. "I won't. The goal is to get my son back. That is all that matters."

"Good." Ewen got to his feet, unfolding his spindly frame. Although Colin was tall, Ewen was taller by a couple of inches. He gave Fiona a little nod of the head. "Good night, Lady Craigmore."

She held out her hand. "Good night, Ewen. Please give your dear mother my best wishes for the New Year when it comes. She keeps well, I hope."

"She does. Still very active with the Social Advice Bureau. I will pass on your good wishes to her."

Sir Robert got up, his black Labrador springing up beside him. "I'll see you out."

"No need." Colin was already ushering Ewen out.

"You'll allow me to see my solicitor from my home." His father stalked across the room, pushing between them to lead the way out.

Behind him, Colin met Ewen's glance and saw a fleeting glimmer of sympathy in his eyes, before the lawyer turned away and followed Sir Robert out into the hall.

Damn Ewen! Colin didn't want to be pitied by a jumped-up butcher's son. Damn them all. Colin watched the tall lawyer and his father's stocky frame as they crossed the hall, his father talking, pointedly emphasizing his words, as always, like a boxer jabbing with his fists. All at once, despite the vastness of the echoing hall, Colin felt utterly trapped.

Chapter 12

Although it was dark, Vanessa was able to make out the endless stretch of flat prairie fields and then the two winding rivers, the Red and the Assiniboine, all covered in snow. The city below looked like a fairyland, lit up by twinkling lights. She hugged Roddy, blinking back tears. "Almost home," she whispered, as the plane flew over the downtown office blocks of Winnipeg and then banked in preparation for its landing. Safe at last, she added silently. Rather melodramatic, but that was exactly how she felt.

"Wow! What a lot of snow!" Roddy said, as the plane came nearer to the ground.

"You can say that again," said the burly man sitting next to Vanessa. "Unfortunately it lasts all year."

"That's a slight exaggeration," Vanessa protested.

"How would you know?" the man asked.

"Because I was born and brought up in Manitoba, that's how."

"You'd never have guessed it from your accent," the man muttered.

"My mother's an actor," Roddy said proudly.

"Is she?" The man peered at Vanessa. "Movies or TV?"

Vanessa frowned at Roddy. "What did I tell you?" she warned him beneath her breath.

Roddy subsided. "Sorry," he whispered.

"My son likes to make up stories," Vanessa told the man. She turned her back on him and pulled a black tuque over her hair, which she'd dragged back from her face. With her hair tied back and without makeup, she could look quite plain and ordinary, thank heavens.

As soon as she came through to the baggage carousel, she caught sight of her parents. They were standing by the window, their faces almost pressed to it in their eagerness to see them.

"There's Gran and Grampa," she told Roddy. But he had already seen them and was dashing over to the window to wave back at them.

It took only a few minutes to get through customs and then they pushed their luggage cart through the automatic doors, to be enveloped in welcoming arms.

"Hi, Mom," Vanessa whispered against her mother's fur collar, smelling the familiar smells of Ombre Rose mixed with peppermint.

Her mother held her for a moment and then touched her face. "It's all right, sweetheart. You're home now."

Vanessa nodded, unable to say more.

When they went outside, the intense cold knifed into her. "My God," she gasped, "I'd forgotten how cold it is here in the winter."

"We're having the worst winter in years," her mother said. "The windchill's making it about minus fifty today." She bent to make sure that Roddy's hat was well down over his ears, then hurried him over the pedestrian crossing to the parking lot.

The bitter wind made Vanessa's eyes water. By the time they reached the car she could barely see.

"Get in," her father told her, as he put their bags in the trunk. "I plugged in the interior heater, so that should have kept the car fairly warm."

Not much, thought Vanessa as she sat shivering in the back of the car with Roddy huddled against her. But once they got going the car soon heated up.

For the first few minutes, Roddy chatted away, asking about the boy who lived nearby and did they still have Sooty, their black cat, mercifully covering the anxiety they all felt, staving off the inevitable questions.

When Roddy fell silent, slumped into a half sleep against her side, Vanessa asked, "Did anyone call for me?" She had to know.

"Only Jill," her father said.

"Is she back in Vancouver?" Vanessa asked eagerly.

"Not yet. She was calling from New York. She said she'd had one of those weird feelings you two girls used to have. She felt it on Christmas Day. She thought you were in some sort of trouble."

"Oh God," Vanessa whispered. She remembered wishing Jill was with her when she'd walked by the frozen lake at Strathferness on Christmas Day.

"She said she'd be back in Vancouver tomorrow evening. We didn't tell her you were coming," her mother quickly added, turning to look back at her, as they crossed the bridge to River Heights. "You did say not to tell anyone."

"I didn't mean Jill, but that's okay. I'll call her tomorrow."

"I'm keeping the answering machine on all the time," her father said in a low voice.

Vanessa leaned forward. "Thanks, Dad. I'll explain everything later."

"That's fine."

He was a man of few words. Solid, dependable. At times, when she was a teenager, she'd wondered how this rather mundane, boring accountant could ever have been her father. Now she was grateful for his quiet strength.

Her mother would be harder to deal with. They were more alike, she and Lynne Marston. Artistic, emotional, impulsive. All these traits Vanessa had inherited from her mother. It was her mother who'd encouraged her to audition for the National Theatre School and then, later, to go to England. Her father thought acting was too unstable a career. Vanessa was his only child. He'd wanted her to be an accountant or a lawyer, something safe and lucrative.

Her mother had won out, as usual. Vanessa had come to realize that her parents' marriage was one of opposites. Ying and yang. They worked well together, but it hadn't been easy for Vanessa, growing up with two such diametrically opposed personalities. Her mother's volatility and her father's rigidity. Miraculously, both had mellowed over the years, each taking on some of the other's characteristics. Her mother had grown a little calmer and her father more flexible.

"Almost home," he said, turning into their street. The large leafless elms on both sides of the narrow street formed an archway of wintry branches against the dark sky. Christmas lights festooned most of the houses and many of the trees in the front yards.

Vanessa sighed. "How lovely it looks. It hasn't changed a bit."

Her father chuckled. "I shouldn't think it would have, considering you were here eighteen months ago."

She had to laugh with him. "Sorry. I'm just so glad to be home."

Roddy was asleep within an hour of their arrival. He was exhausted from the long journey plus all the accumulated excitement of Christmas and the stressful two days since they'd left Strathferness.

Stressful for her, at least, Vanessa thought. As she looked down at her son, curled up in bed in the room next to hers, covered by the bright patchwork quilt her mother had made for her twelfth birthday, she felt a rush of mixed emotions. Relief at being home again. Safe. But for how long? In these days of modern technology it wasn't easy to hide, however far—or fast—you ran.

She couldn't stay here for more than a few days. Once Colin knew she'd left the country, this was the first place he would try. Besides, she didn't want to embroil her parents in her problems.

She told them so when she went downstairs to join them in the family room. "We can't stay long," she said, after telling them everything that had happened.

"Colin will know I'm here. Actually, I'm surprised he hasn't called."

Her father frowned at her over the top of his glasses. "Afraid he'll turn up?" he asked.

"Yes, I am. I don't want a big scene in front of Roddy."

Her mother sniffed. "Don't you worry about that. I'll be happy to deal with Colin myself."

Vanessa gave her a faint smile. "I know you would, Mom, but fighting Colin doesn't achieve anything."

Her father leaned forward to throw another birch log on the fire. It flamed into life, burning brightly in the brick fireplace. "Exactly what does your coming here achieve?" he asked, as he sat back in his adjustable armchair. His tone was patently disapproving.

Vanessa felt as if she'd been attacked. "You think I should have stayed in Scotland? Risked losing Roddy completely?"

"Don't be so ridiculous, Hugh," her mother said. "You heard Vanessa. It's not safe for her and Roddy to be around Colin anymore."

Hugh Marston rubbed the tips of his fingers together in that annoying little habit of his. "I know Vanessa. Like her mother, she has a tendency to exaggerate things."

Anger surged through Vanessa, but she forced her voice to remain steady. "Not this time, Dad. I wish I was exaggerating, really. For Roddy's sake."

"And this thing about boarding school. You knew when you married Colin what his family traditions were. How different they would be to ours. I warned you about that when you got engaged, remember?"

"For heaven's sake," Lynne intervened, before Vanessa could reply. "Our daughter's come home to find refuge from an abusive husband and this is the way you treat her. Shame on you, Hugh."

He sighed. "I'm sorry. I don't mean to be critical of you, Van. I'm just trying to get to the facts, that's all. I really don't know what running away from the situation achieves."

Much as she loved her mother, Vanessa would have found it easier to deal with her father had she not been there. She knew that she needed to remain calm while she tried to explain the exact situation to him. Somehow her mother's emotional reaction to her problem made her wonder if she, too, had overreacted.

Then she thought of Colin's increasingly violent outbursts over the past few months and Sir Robert's expression when he'd told her that if she left Colin she would never see Roddy again, and she knew that she had acted in a rational way. That taking Roddy out of their reach was the right thing to do.

"They told me that they intended to apply for custody and that I would never be given access to Roddy."

"That's nonsense," her father said. "Just wishful thinking on their part. As his mother, you have a right to have access, to have joint custody, in fact."

"But they will send him to boarding school. There's no doubt about that. You know how I feel. It could ruin his life. Famous people have talked and written about the horrors of their childhood spent in boarding school."

"It's barbaric, sending an eight-year-old child away from his home." Her mother drew a tissue from her sleeve. "Surely you can't think it's a good thing, Hugh?"

"It's not something I would agree with, no," her husband said. "But I'm sure that things have changed in British schools since the bad old days. Why didn't you try to get Colin away from his family, sit down with your lawyers, the pair of you, instead of running away? Surely Colin would have agreed to a reasonable compromise."

Vanessa shook her head. "I've tried talking to him, Dad, but Colin's not a reasonable man anymore. I'm afraid he's changed a lot even since you last saw him. He's absolutely irrational on the subject. Besides, he's so rarely at home lately that I haven't been able to talk to him about anything. And he refused even to discuss a separation. That's why I had to spring it on his family like that."

"If he's that unreasonable, I should think you will probably get custody."

"Not if I want to take Roddy away from Scotland."

"Why on earth not?"

"Because he's the eventual heir to Strathferness, that's why." She was trying to be patient with her father, but his devil's advocate stance was really annoying her. "Unless I get some unusually progressive judge, they're going to say that Roddy must be raised by his father and his father's family, and go to a Scottish school, to prepare him for his position as head of the family estate and the family firm."

"Exactly," said her mother. "Everyone will be against Vanessa because she's Canadian, not British."

Vanessa sighed. "No, Mom, my nationality has nothing to do with it. You don't understand—"

"Of course I understand."

Vanessa blinked. "This isn't getting us anywhere," she said wearily. "I thought you'd see why I came here, Dad. But perhaps no one can understand unless they've been around the Craigmore family for a while."

"I warned you—"

"Yes, I know you did." She was trying hard not to lose her temper. "But I was in love with Colin. I wasn't interested in hearing about different attitudes and all that garbage. To be perfectly honest, I thought you were being ridiculously narrow and old-fashioned."

"I probably was," he admitted.

"Not really. Now I'm starting to think you were right. Our backgrounds really were too different. I was happy to go along with Colin's way of life when there were just the two of us, but once Roddy was born everything changed. He wasn't just our child, he was the family heir and, as such, became the property of the family. I found that hard to take. His father's interference in Roddy's upbringing caused a lot of the fights between Colin and me." She paused for a moment. "Now that I think about it, that's really how the rift between us began."

"So his father was really the cause of your breakup," her mother said.

Vanessa grimaced. "Colin's drinking and gambling was the main cause." She hadn't told them about Colin's women. Her parents didn't need to know about that.

"I've only met Colin's father a few times," said her mother, "but I didn't like him from the first time I saw him."

"Well, we all agree on that." Hugh turned to Vanessa. "Have you worked out what your next move will be?"

She hadn't, of course. Beyond getting to Canada, the future was a blank. "I think that depends on what Colin does. I thought I'd stay here for a few days, see whether he gets in touch with me, and then act accordingly."

"You stay here as long as you like," her mother said. She stood up. "I'm going to put the kettle on for more tea. Are you sure you don't want me to cook you something?"

"No, thanks, Mom. It's too late for me to eat anything more than a sandwich, and I've had two already."

"We'll have some Christmas cake. I know how you love my cake."

When her mother left the room Vanessa exchanged looks with her father. "You'd better eat a bit of it, or else!" he said, grinning.

Vanessa's responding smile faded. "Do you really think I should have stayed in Scotland? I actually toned down the stuff about Colin, for Mom's sake. I am genuinely scared for Roddy."

"Has he hurt him physically?"

"Not yet, but I think he might. It's mostly emotional stuff now, so that I can't really prove anything against him."

"You should get a psychologist to assess Roddy."

"Good idea." This was more like it. This was what she needed, practical suggestions.

"I think your plan to wait and see what Colin's next move will be is a good one. Don't do anything rash."

Their eyes met. "I was scared, Daddy. Not for myself, but for Roddy. That's why I ran. I don't want him to get his hooks into Roddy."

"Colin?"

"Both of them. Colin and Sir Robert."

"You make Colin's father sound like some sort of monster. He can't be that bad."

She bit her lip. How could she explain someone like Sir Robert to her father? Straightforward and warmhearted himself, he couldn't begin to comprehend the complexities of such a man. "I'm not the first in the family to run away," she said eventually, fixing on a practical illustration.

"Oh?"

"Colin had a brother who ran away from home at the age of seventeen."

"I didn't know that."

"No. Nobody's allowed to mention his name. But Amanda told me about him."

"Is she in touch with him?"

"No. As far as the family's concerned he doesn't exist. So, you see, I'm not the only one."

"I must say the family does seem to be rather dysfunctional."

Vanessa had to laugh. "That's putting it mildly."

"What's so funny?" her mother asked, carrying in the tray bearing her special Christmas teapot and a plate heaped high with slices of her fruitcake and an assortment of Christmas cookies.

"We're talking about dysfunctional families."

"Ours isn't that bad, is it?" Her mother sat down on the sofa beside Vanessa.

"Not ours, Mom." Vanessa leaned over to hug her. "Ours is a little nutty at times, but great." She looked at them both. "Thanks for giving us such a warm welcome when we landed in on you without much warning."

"No need to thank us. That's what parents do, darling."

"Some."

"Anyway, I think your father could have been a little more welcoming."

"Dad was fine. He was being Dad, keeping my feet on the ground, as always. I need that, especially now. You're both great."

"Help yourself to cake. And I made some of those almond butter cookies that you love."

"Just now?" Vanessa teased her.

"No, of course not."

"I can't believe you still bake all this stuff. Who eats it?"

"We give it to friends, neighbors. Can't visit people empty-handed, can you?"

"I suppose not." Vanessa took a small piece of fruit-cake and a cookie.

"Trouble is, we get landed with other people's cookies in exchange. I've put them all in the freezer." Lynne poured them all more tea. Then she sat back, looking from Vanessa to Hugh. "What have you decided to do?"

"Stay here for now," Vanessa told her mother.

"What if Colin follows you here?"

"I hope I can get away before he does, but Dad thinks I might be able to deal with him better if his father isn't around," Vanessa added doubtfully. "He said Colin and I should try to work it out with our lawyers."

"I'm not so sure," her father said unexpectedly. "Normally, that would be the case. But from what you've told us, I suspect that Colin's father might be helping him financially. Am I right?"

"Yes, I'm afraid so," Vanessa had to admit. "There are gambling debts and . . ." Her voice trailed away. She found it embarrassing to tell them about Colin's failings as a man as well as a husband and father.

Her father's expression was grim. "That will make it more difficult for Colin to act independently of him." He let his breath out in a long sigh. "I still think that you may have been a bit too impulsive rushing off with Roddy like this. But now that you're here, it's probably best to wait and see what Colin does next."

Chapter 13

They didn't have to wait long. A few minutes after seven o'clock the next morning, the telephone rang. Vanessa had been up since five-thirty and was in the den watching an old Doris Day movie with the sound turned low. She ran to get the phone before it woke up her parents.

Then, just as she was about to lift the receiver, she remembered. Her heartbeat skittered as she realized how close she'd come to answering it.

She heard the bathroom door open. "I've got it," her father said in a loud whisper from the upstairs landing. He answered with the portable phone just as the machine was about to click in.

Very carefully, Vanessa picked up the receiver in the kitchen and held it to her ear, at the same time sliding her hand across the mouthpiece so that no one would hear her breathing.

"Mr. Marston? This is Colin Craigmore."

It was Colin at his most formal, his voice sounding particularly British upper-class. Vanessa's heart started pounding. *Say something, Dad,* she wanted to yell, when the silence stretched on.

"Hello, Colin," said her father at last. "Sorry, I'm still half asleep. You woke me up. It's only just after seven in the morning here, you know."

Good old Dad. Attack is the best defense.

"Oh, sorry." Colin sounded rather taken aback. "I thought you'd be going in to work today."

"No, we have the entire Christmas week off. What can I do for you?"

"Is Vanessa there?"

"Vanessa? Sorry, this is a very bad line. I can't hear you properly."

Colin rallied. "Oh, I get it. She's told you to say she's not there, right? Well, Mr. Marston, even if that's true, no doubt you'll know where she is. And, even more important, where my son is. I want you to give Vanessa a message."

"A message? Right. I will if I can."

"Perhaps you should get a piece of paper and a pen."

"I am perfectly capable of taking a message, Colin."

Despite her tension, Vanessa couldn't help smiling at the dry rebuke.

"I'd rather you wrote it down," Colin insisted. "I want you to get it exactly right."

How dare he speak to her father as if he were a senile old man! Vanessa was tempted to take over, but common sense kept her hand gripped tightly over the mouthpiece.

"Very well. I have a pen and paper. Give me your message."

"Kindly tell Vanessa that we had a hearing in Edinburgh this morning and that I was granted interim custody of Roddy."

"Interim custody? What does that mean?"

"It means that she bloody well has to get Roddy back here right away, or else."

"Or else?"

"Or else we'll apply to the Manitoba court to have the order carried out. If Vanessa ignores it, she'll be in breach of the order and in contempt of both courts. Tell her that. I'm sure you don't want that sort of publicity, do you, Mr. Marston? Winnipeg's not that big a town that it could be hushed up, is it?"

"Thank you for sharing this information," Vanessa's father said.

She admired his restraint. Her heart was beating so fast now that it felt as if it would leap out of her chest.

Her father's lack of emotion got to Colin at last.

"Damn you!" he yelled down the phone. "Tell her she'd better get Roddy back here double quick or she'll pay dearly for it. Tell her I'll be on her tail, one step behind—"

The quiet click told Vanessa that her father had cut Colin off midsentence.

The bedroom door opened. "What did he say?" her mother asked. She was the only one not to have heard both sides of the conversation. There was a murmur of voices and then the bathroom door opened and closed.

"You're a pain in the butt, Hugh Marston," Lynne shouted, "you know that?"

"Come on down, Mom," Vanessa quietly called up to her. She didn't want to wake Roddy, who was still sleeping. "I'll make some fresh coffee."

Her mother was down in a flash, hastily tying the cord of her pink velvet dressing gown, her ash-blond hair in a tangle of curls. "Did *you* hear what Colin said?" she asked Vanessa, as she opened the freezer door and began searching inside it. "Your father wouldn't tell me."

"I'll tell you in a minute. What are you looking for?"

"Cranberry muffins. Ah, here they are. We'll heat a few in the microwave."

Vanessa shook her head. "You certainly did enough Christmas baking. I think you must have known we were coming."

"You know me, always prepared. Besides, I like to think you *might* be coming. Christmas isn't the same without your children, you know, however old they are." She gazed with open affection at her daughter.

"Oh, Mom." Vanessa hugged her tight. "I'm glad we're here, but I'm so sorry it had to be this way." She drew away and got down plates and mugs from the china cupboard. "I really wanted to come home for Christmas this year, but it was such a hassle with Colin's family. The whole week of Christmas and New Year is like a royal command performance."

"What do you mean?"

"Everyone has to be there, at Strathferness, or there's trouble. Amanda hates it so much she usually just comes for the one day and then finds some excuse to escape, but then she has to come back for the New Year."

"What a very strange family. Poor darling, it must be terrible for you having to be with them."

Vanessa didn't want to think about Strathferness. "Mmm, these smell terrific," she said, as she took the steaming muffins from the microwave. "How on earth did you find the time to do all this? I should have thought Christmas would be the busiest time for you at the store."

"It was a madhouse. For the last two weeks until Christmas Eve, I stayed open until nine every evening. This was a much better year than last year for sales."

"Great." Her mother had been a women's fashion buyer at Eaton's Department Store for many years, but lost her job when the head office in Toronto took over. Buying the little gift store on Academy Road had been her father's bright idea and it had worked wonders for her mother. "I even managed to sell some of my own little herb pillows."

"You're an absolute wonder, Mom. I don't know where you get the energy from."

"You know me, I have to keep busy or I go crazy."

Vanessa smiled to herself. Her mother was a little crazy whatever she did, but she loved her just the same. "Where's Dad?"

"He's shaving. He wouldn't tell me what Colin had said, but he seemed pretty upset."

"I can tell you. I listened in."

The coffee finished dripping with a loud gurgle. Her mother poured it into the mugs and they sat down at the dining room table. "Was it bad news?"

Vanessa picked out a cranberry from her muffin and ate it. "Let's say that they certainly haven't wasted any time. The Scottish court's granted Colin what he calls interim custody."

"Oh my God!" Her mother's hand went to her throat. "What does that mean?"

"I'm not quite sure. We'll have to find out. But I think it means that Colin is to have sole custody of Roddy until we have a proper legal battle over him."

"Oh no, Vanessa. That's absolutely terrible."

Vanessa's jaw tightened. "I'm not giving him up. I won't allow Colin to have him."

Her father appeared in the doorway, dressed in a green tweed sweater and jeans. His face was grim. "Did someone bring the newspaper in?"

"I did. It's in the den." Vanessa pushed back her chair. "I'll get it."

Lynne poured him some coffee. He sat down heavily, pushing aside the white poinsettia plant in the center of the table.

"There you are." Vanessa handed him the folded paper. "One *Winnipeg Free Press*. More snow expected."

He grunted in response.

"I'm sorry about the call, Dad. I should have spoken to Colin myself."

"I didn't mind speaking to him." He folded the paper and put it under his chair. "But this is far more serious than I thought, Vanessa. A court order. You can't ignore court orders. Colin means business. You will have to go back to Scotland."

Vanessa's eyes widened. "You don't mean that."

"I certainly do. You must go back, hire a good lawyer, and—"

"And take my chances on losing Roddy completely," she interrupted. "Is that what you mean?"

"Now you're being melodramatic. There's very little chance of you losing Roddy."

"But what if she does?" Lynne asked, her voice rising. "If she takes him back to Scotland and then loses him, she can't get him back again. What then?"

He turned on her angrily. "Stop encouraging her. Both of you are overreacting. This is real life, for God's sake, not some soap opera."

Despite the constant warm air blowing from the

heating ducts, Vanessa felt cold shivers running through her. "I'm well aware of how real it is." She drew in a deep breath. "I am not overreacting. I happen to be closer to this than you are, Dad. I know what the situation really is. Colin is dangerous. Colin's family is poison. At least his father is. I will not allow them to take my son away from me, even temporarily."

"Colin is the boy's father and—"

"Why is Grampa mad at Mummy?"

They all froze at the sound of Roddy's voice. Blond hair rumpled, he stood in the hallway in his Dalmatian pajamas, blinking in the light.

Vanessa went to him. "He's not mad at me, darling," she said brightly.

"He's mad at Daddy, then. I heard him say something about Daddy. Was Daddy on the phone?"

"He was. He just wanted to make sure we'd arrived safely, that was all."

"Oh, okay." Roddy yawned and hoisted up his pajama trousers. "Didn't he want to speak to me?"

"We thought you were still asleep," Vanessa explained. "Are you hungry? Gran's made some super cranberry muffins."

"Yummy." He kneeled on a chair and helped himself to a muffin.

Vanessa gave him a plate. "No crumbs, please." She gave her father a faint smile and then turned away. "I'm going to have a shower," she murmured, and went upstairs.

As she stood in the shower, the warm water pouring down her face and body, she wished it could wash away her disappointment.

No one understood. She'd hoped that her parents would, but they were reacting the wrong way. Her father was seeing things from both sides and thought she was exaggerating everything. Her mother was on her side, but she was being a melodrama queen, which only upset Vanessa more.

She rubbed conditioner into her hair. She was on her own. That's what it came down to. She would have to think clearly, be sure she was making the right move each time, because there was no one to get her out of it if she took a wrong step.

One thing she knew. Now that Colin had the court order, she couldn't stay here. She'd have to move on. The only other person she could trust to help her was Jill. She'd call her tonight.

"Please God, don't let Colin come here before I can get away," she whispered into the steam.

Once she'd made her decision she felt more able to face her parents. She dressed in warm wool tights, black corduroy stretch leggings, and a thick-knit, cherry-red sweater that reached almost to her knees, and went downstairs.

"Sorry I got mad," she told her father. "This is all very difficult for me."

"What have you decided to do?" he asked rather guardedly.

"I think you should go see our lawyer," her mother said, before Vanessa could reply, "tell him what's happened and ask his advice."

"Scottish law is different, Mom. It's not even the same as English law." She glanced at Roddy, who was listening intently while humming and eating at the same time. "Why don't we all just have a good time today? What's the weather like?"

"It's going to be warmer," her father said.

"How about a horse-drawn sleigh ride? Do they still do those? We used to have them for birthday treats, remember?" In her own ears her voice sounded artificially hearty, forced, but at least she was trying, for Roddy's sake.

"I'll check in the yellow pages," her mother said.

"Isn't it rather cold for a sleigh ride?" her father asked.

"Not if we wrap up warm. Roddy and I can go. You and Mom can wait in the car."

Her mother at last got into the act. "I think they do sleigh rides on the river at the Forks," she said with enthusiasm.

"What's the Forks?" Roddy asked.

"It's where the two main rivers, the Red and the Assiniboine, meet," his grandmother told him. "It's also where the native tribes used to meet. And now everyone gets together there and has fun. It's a big meeting place."

"What do you do there?"

"You can eat all kinds of different food and ice cream and hot donuts. You can buy vegetables and fruit at the big indoor market. And skate on the outdoor skating rink."

"Skate!"

"That's right. Did you bring your skates with you?"

Roddy looked crestfallen. "I don't have any."

"A Canadian boy without skates? We can't have that, can we?" She exchanged smiles with Roddy's grandfather.

"Maybe we can rent some," he said. He winked at Roddy's grandmother. "Why don't we go down to the rink and see?"

"Good idea," Lynne said. "We could skate and then go inside and have some hot chocolate."

"Sounds great." Roddy grinned up at his mother. "Will you skate with me, Mum?"

"Yikes! I haven't skated since I was about seventeen. I don't expect my skates are still around."

"I'm sure they are," her mother said.

Vanessa made a face. "I wish you hadn't said that."

"I think they're in that cupboard in the basement. You know the one, where we kept all the old games. Let's go look."

She was right. Behind the battered boxes of Monopoly and Clue, covered by the badminton racquets and net, was Vanessa's last pair of skates, the pale blue ones. "You're like a pack rat, Mom," Vanessa told her. "You don't throw anything out."

"You never know when things could be needed." Her mother's eyes glistened as they gazed down at the skates in her hand. "I remember taking you for your first lesson."

"That was a long time before these skates." Vanessa was too uptight at present to want to indulge in nostalgic memories. She held the skates, looking at them doubtfully. "I hope my feet haven't got bigger."

"Try them on, Mum," Roddy suggested.

"No, I'm sure they'll be fine. Anyway, we probably won't be skating for long. It's too cold."

En route to the Forks, they stopped at the Bay downtown store, where boys' skates were on sale. "An extra Christmas present," Roddy's grandfather told him, as Roddy beamed down at the black hockey skates on his feet. "Your grandma's right. A Canadian boy has to have skates."

Vanessa watched Roddy proudly swinging the skates by the laces as he walked to the cashier with his grandfather, and exchanged tremulous smiles with her mother. Both of them were intensely aware that the future was cloudy and uncertain, but for today, at least, everyone was determined to have a good time, for Roddy's sake.

Chapter 14

It was a memorable day. That was what Vanessa had intended, to create good memories for Roddy. Whatever happened in the future, she was sure that he would always remember the day he spent skating and sleigh riding with his grandparents in Winnipeg. She certainly would.

When they got home Vanessa declined her mother's offer of tea. "I'm going to call Jill."

"Good idea. I'll have a word with her when you're finished."

"Isn't it a little early?" Her father called out to Vanessa from the den, as she went upstairs to make the call. "Cheap rate's not until after six o'clock."

"I'll pay." She rolled her eyes as she went into the bedroom. Here she was, worried sick about losing her child, and her father was going on about a few extra cents for the call.

As she looked up the number of Jill's new condo in her address book, she thought of the last time she and Jill had been together, a few months ago in London. Fortunately, Colin hadn't come with her. He and Jill had never gotten along. He found her far too blunt. "It's the fact that she looks so much like you, but when she opens her mouth she's totally different," he'd told Vanessa after he'd met Jill for the first time.

At that time, early in their marriage, it had been important to Vanessa that Colin and her closest friend like each other. "She had a very difficult childhood," she told him, trying to explain Jill to him. "Her father left when she was a baby. Her mother drank too much. Jill and her brother, Steve, used to come to school hungry."

Colin didn't want to know that such problems existed, shrugging them off as if they never happened in his world. "I still don't understand how you two could have become friends."

"My mother sort of adopted her. Mom was always one for stray kittens and puppies or people in trouble. She tried befriending Mrs. Nelson, but Jill's mother didn't want what she saw as charity. Then Mom told me to ask Jill home for lunch. I didn't want to. She wasn't even a friend of mine. I'd hardly spoken a word to her at school. But Mom insisted. That's how our friendship started."

Jill hadn't liked Colin, either. "I realize you're madly in love with him," she'd told Vanessa. "You've always been a sucker for men like him, tall, blond, suave. But to me he looks like trouble, and I'm not just saying that because he's not my sort of man. Want some advice?" Vanessa had known she'd get it, whether she wanted it or not. "Make sure you keep a separate bank account. And don't tell him about it."

Jill's criticism of Colin had hurt Vanessa, but after another couple of disastrous tries, she'd accepted that it was best to keep her husband and best friend in separate compartments.

Now, as she punched in her number, she was wishing she'd taken more notice of Jill's opinion of Colin. But she also thanked God that her friend's warning had prompted her to maintain a separate bank account where she'd regularly deposited part of the money she earned. At first, hiding anything from Colin had made her feel guilty, as if she were betraying him. But later, when things began to get rough, she was glad she'd done it.

"Hello." Jill's voice answered on the fourth ring, just as Vanessa was preparing to leave a message.

"So you did get home," Vanessa found herself smiling into the near darkness of the bedroom.

"Hi, Vanny," Jill said excitedly. "I landed in here

less than an hour ago. How are you doing? Are you calling from bonnie Scotland?"

"No, I'm at home."

"You mean home Edinburgh or home Winnipeg?"

"Winnipeg. I got in last night."

"Wow! That's weird. I called your parents at Christmas. They never said you were coming in."

"They didn't know then."

"Okay. Something's wrong, isn't it?"

" 'Fraid so."

"I knew it. I told your mom I had one of those weird feelings about you. You know what I mean? The kind we always got when we were at high school. What's the golden wonder done now?"

"I've left him."

"About time." A moment of silence passed. "Sorry, that was a rotten thing to say. I truly am sorry that you're having a rough time. But I can't pretend to be sorry you've left Colin. He was a prick. What happened this time to make you take the big step?" Jill's voice rose. "He didn't hurt you, did he?"

"Physically, no. I don't want to talk about me, Jill. It's Roddy I'm concerned about."

"What's Colin done to Roddy?" Her voice rose even louder.

"It's more a fear of what he's going to do. He seems to be falling apart, suddenly. All the bad things you already know about seem to be escalating, so that he's hardly ever in at his office anymore. When I question him, he goes into a rage and tells me that most of his work is done by networking with people socially. He has these awful fits of anger over the smallest thing."

"Sounds like a sick man."

"You're right." Vanessa's hand clenched on the receiver. "Maybe I should have insisted he got some help."

"Don't be crazy. You've tried to get him to see a counselor before and it didn't work. I take it everything blew up at Christmas, the festive blowup season. What happened?"

Vanessa told her.

Jill whistled. "You poor thing. Having to tackle the family all alone. Sounds as if you did okay, though." She chuckled. "I'd like to have been at the castle when they found out you'd fooled them and got away."

"I'm worried about poor Morag. I'm sure she'll suffer for it."

"Oh, who cares! They all got what they deserved. I remember thinking at the wedding that they were like a bunch of *Masterpiece Theater* rejects."

"Amanda's okay. And Fiona's a dear. Poor Fiona." Vanessa sighed. "I wonder what she thinks of me now."

"Forget Lady Fiona. Have you heard from Colin since you arrived in Canada?"

Vanessa told her about Colin's call.

"Doesn't sound good. You've got to get out of there," Jill told her, "now that's he's pretty certain you're there. You should have left already."

"I don't need you to tell me that. I'm scared enough already. I keep thinking Colin's about to ring the doorbell any moment. Dad thought I should go back to Scotland and work it out with Colin."

"He would. I love your dad, but he'll always play it by the book. Don't you dare go back. If you do, you run the risk of losing Roddy entirely. You can bet your boots that Sir Robert the Bad will use all his considerable influence over Colin and his very considerable wealth on good lawyers to get Roddy. You have to buy time. And the best way to do that is for you and Roddy to disappear."

"That's what I thought."

"You have something they desperately want. Roddy. If you disappear completely for a while, they'll be more prepared to negotiate with you when you contact them."

Her father knocked on the door and put his head around it. "Sorry to interrupt," he said.

"Hang on a minute," Vanessa told Jill. "Dad wants

to tell me something." She slid her hand over the mouthpiece.

"I just spoke to Charlie Pieper on my cell phone," her father said.

"The lawyer?" Vanessa flared up. "I hope you didn't tell him—"

"I didn't say anything about you. I just said I was asking for a friend."

"Oh Dad," Vanessa sighed. "Everyone says that. He'll know it's about me."

"Just hear me out. Charlie says that even if a parent gets a court order in Manitoba, if you move to another province they have to reapply. And, of course, that means Colin would have to know exactly where you are in Canada before he could apply to the courts again."

Vanessa jumped up and hugged him. "Dad, you're a genius."

Her father smiled. "Well, that's a better reception, I must say." His smile faded. "I still think you'd have been better to work it out in Scotland, but as you didn't, it looks as if you shouldn't stay here any longer. I don't want you and Roddy to have to leave us, but . . ."

"Jill says I must." Vanessa hugged him again. "Don't worry, Dad. This will soon be over."

"I hope so. Give our love to Jill."

As he left the room, Vanessa picked up the phone again.

"What's going on?" Jill asked.

Vanessa told her. "I'm going to feel like a fugitive," she added, "trying to stay one step ahead of the law . . . and Colin. I hate the thought of it."

"At the moment, you're not breaking any laws. You've brought your son to visit his grandparents in your own country."

"But if I disappear? What then?"

"If you have qualms, think about Roddy being brought up with the crafty Craigmores, without his mother."

"Don't even say it."

"Right. That's what I thought. Here's what to do. Hang on a minute, I'm going to pour myself a strong glass of Perrier with a shot of Rose's lime juice, the way you limeys like to drink it."

"I'm not a limey," Vanessa protested.

"Good as. Don't interrupt my train of thought. Here's my plan. I'm going to call my travel agent and make all sorts of nutty bookings in my name. That'll throw them off the scent a bit. You get all packed up, ready to leave sometime tomorrow afternoon."

"Why not the morning?"

"Because I'm going to send you my Visa card by overnight courier, so you can use it, if necessary. You can forge my signature if you need it. We practiced that often enough when we were kids, remember? Tomorrow you're going to be me when you travel. You'll have to do some dodging about, but it's worth it to throw them off the scent."

"What about Roddy?"

"I've always wanted a son." Jill sounded as if she were having a ball. "Stand by for further instructions."

"I will. You're the first one to make me feel I've done the right thing. Thanks a million, Jill."

"Forget it. I owe you and your family. 'Bye, Vanny. Can I speak to Mom Marston now?"

"I'll call her. 'Bye."

When her mother picked up the receiver downstairs, Vanessa sank onto the bedroom chair, feeling like she'd been hit by a tornado. But she also felt that she was no longer in this by herself.

Chapter 15

"I intend to go to Winnipeg. I'm quite sure she's there with Roddy." Colin angrily stubbed out his half-smoked cigarette, so that it disintegrated into a mess of paper and tobacco in the large crystal ashtray. "Knowing Vanessa, she was probably listening in on the other phone," he told Ewen. "That's the sort of thing she does."

The lawyer sat at the desk in Sir Robert's study, papers spread out before him. He raised his thin eyebrows, but only repeated what he had said before. "I think that going to Canada would be unwise at this time."

Colin sprang up from his chair. "I know *you* think so, but I happen not to agree with you."

"Ewen's explained why," Sir Robert said, his voice sharp with impatience. "For God's sake, Colin, stop acting like a maniac. Ewen is trying to help us."

Colin was regretting even more his decision to engage Ewen. A couple of times now he'd caught that look in Ewen's hooded eyes which could very well be contempt. He wished he could find another lawyer, but it was too late now. What a fool he'd been to choose him. No doubt he had private discussions with his father, talking about him behind his back.

Trouble was, his father was paying Ewen's bill.

"I am happy to explain our position once again," Ewen said, "if that is necessary."

"Apparently it is," Sir Robert said, frowning at Colin, who, unable to remain still, had moved to stand by the window.

Colin stared out the tall window, which was draped with heavy dark-green brocade curtains that smelled faintly of mildew. Outside, beyond the terrace at the rear of the castle, rain was falling in a constant gray stream, mixing with the residue of snow, which was no longer white. Everywhere he looked he could see nothing but shades of gray. The stone terrace, the grounds, the sky . . . all were gray, with not a speck of color to alleviate the dismal sameness of it all. Even the greeny blackness of the pine trees had been faded to gray by the light covering of snow on their branches.

He turned from the window to light another cigarette and then went to sit in a chair close to the door. "Go ahead. Explain away," he told Ewen in a bored voice.

"It is important that you establish yourself as a good father for Roddy. The parent to whom custody should be given."

"What's the point of that if he's somewhere in Canada? And don't expect her to stay with her parents. Now she knows I'm on to her, she'll probably run again."

"That was why I consider your telephone call to your wife to have been ill-advised. Had you not called, she might have been content to remain with her parents."

Colin was irked by the implied criticism of his actions. "What good's that?" he demanded. "Roddy would still be in Canada."

"Not for long, I don't think. I've contacted a firm of solicitors in Winnipeg and they have advised me on family law in Canada. You have two alternatives."

"What are they?" Colin asked, growing impatient with Ewen's slow and painstaking manner.

"I am about to tell you, if you will permit me to do so." Ewen's tone was that of a schoolmaster reprimanding an unruly pupil. Colin felt like punching his pompous face.

"You have two alternatives. You can apply to the

court of the Canadian province in which your son is residing for an order requiring your wife to return your son to Scotland, to comply with the interim custody order made by the Scottish court."

"Let's do that, then."

"There is one problem."

"There would be. What is it?"

"As soon as your wife and son move to another province the court order will be invalid. You would have to make another application. This time to the court in the new province where your son is residing."

Colin was thinking. "That means that if Vanessa keeps moving around Canada," he said eventually, "she could keep escaping from any court orders that might be made."

"Apparently so."

"But that's absolutely preposterous," Sir Robert said, his tone suggesting that Ewen didn't know what he was talking about.

"Preposterous or not, that's how it is. And that is why Colin's call to his wife was the worst thing he could have done. Had you not contacted her," he told Colin directly, "she would probably have stayed in Manitoba. Now, it is—"

Colin interrupted him. "You said there was another alternative."

"Yes, there is. You could apply for custody of your son to courts in whichever province Roddy is currently residing."

"You mean get a court order for custody right there in Canada? Why the hell didn't you say so before?" Colin sprang up again, his face flushed with excitement. "That's what we'll do."

Ewen rubbed his thumb across his chin. "I would not advise you to take that course."

"Why the hell not?"

"Because you would have to prove your ability to be a responsible father to your son."

Colin's eyes narrowed. He went to the desk and

leaned his hands on it, bringing his face closer to the solicitor's. "So?"

Ewen did not flinch. "Your wife will be able to bring evidence—if she has any—of reasons why you would not be a fit father for full custody of your child."

"Well, that just about rules that idea out," Sir Robert said caustically.

Colin turned on his father. "I'll make that decision."

Ewen intervened. "The other drawback to applying to a Canadian court for custody is that you will not have the advantage of the Scottish connection."

"What do you mean?"

"I'm not suggesting, you understand, that a court in Scotland would lean unfairly to the side of a Scotsman, but I do think that they might be more inclined to take into consideration the fact that Roddy will one day inherit a Scottish title and estate. For that reason, a Scottish court would be likely to show more understanding of the need for him to be raised in Scotland. Whereas that factor might be of little importance to a Canadian court."

"Very well put," Sir Robert said.

Colin sank into his chair again and sat gazing into space for a moment. "Damn her," he said at last beneath his breath. "Damn her to hell."

"My advice is that we apply immediately to the Manitoba courts for a ruling for the enforcement of the Scottish custody order, requiring your wife to return your son to Scotland. If we receive that order, I should imagine that your wife's parents would most likely feel compelled to advise her to obey it. After all, they have to live and work in the community." Ewen touched the tips of his fingers together. "Of course, if she leaves her parental home, A, she will be beyond their influence, and B, we will need to track her down." He sat back in the wooden swivel chair. "North America is a very large continent in which to search for a mother and child."

"If I fly over tomorrow, I'd be able to find her in a few days," Colin insisted.

"We should engage a *professional* investigative firm immediately. But we must also give your wife the chance to return to Scotland. After all, even if she is with her parents, she has only recently heard about the Scottish court's ruling regarding interim custody. As I said before, I have sent a copy of that ruling by courier to her parents' address, together with a formal letter advising her to return your son to you immediately. Unfortunately your phone call will have weakened the effect of receiving such an official document."

"You're a bloody fool," Sir Robert told Colin, not even trying to hide his contempt.

Colin wanted to rush over and take his father in his hands, lift him bodily from the chair, and crush the life from him. He could do it easily. He even imagined what it would be like to feel his father's ribs crack beneath the iron pressure of his arms, to hear him scream with pain as they did so.

"Colin?" Ewen was saying. "Did you hear what I said?"

Colin became aware that he had risen halfway from his chair. Now he sank back into it, feeling nauseated and sticky with sweat, despite the coldness of the room. "Sorry," he muttered. "Tell me again."

"I said that you have a far better chance of gaining full and permanent custody of Roddy in the Scottish court. What you must do now is set out to prove yourself capable of giving a stable home to your son. Your wife's action in taking her son from the country without telling you is going to be a decided mark against her. You say that she is volatile, impulsive, and that you have proof of that. You must show, therefore, that you are a calm and steady influence on your son."

Sir Robert laughed outright at this, but stopped abruptly when Ewen turned on him. "And you, Sir Robert, would be far more helpful to your son's cause if you were to avoid the derogatory remarks you continually make of and to him."

Sir Robert visibly stiffened. "I *beg* your pardon," he said in his most haughty voice.

Ewen was obviously not intimidated in any way. He shook his head. "That's the trouble with families. They get so much into the habit of doing things among themselves that they don't realize how it seems to outsiders. A social worker might very well feel there was too much antagonism between both of you to accept this as a suitable environment for a child."

"That's one reason why I should stay in Edinburgh," Colin said. "And that's the home Roddy is used to, as well."

"And would you be prepared to stay there with him, no extended trips to London, no overnight sojourns elsewhere?"

Colin flushed. Insolent bastard! he thought. "I'll get a housekeeper."

"That won't help unless you've established yourself as a caring parent."

"Since when were men expected to care for their kids twenty-four hours a day?"

"Since they started applying to the courts for sole custody of those kids," Ewen replied. He leaned forward, pointing with his pen. "You'd better take this seriously, or you'll lose custody entirely."

"That's right," Sir Robert echoed.

"You as well, Sir Robert," Ewen said. "If, as you say, you are willing to have Colin live here with you and—"

"And give him a managerial position at the distillery now that he has lost his job." Sir Robert looked pointedly at Colin, as if waiting for thanks.

He wasn't going to get any. Colin knew his father was doing this for Roddy, not for him. All of this was for Roddy. It was like himself and his younger brother Alastair all over again. Until Alastair had been born, Colin had been his father's pride and joy. His firstborn son and a new heir to the title and to the Strathferness estate. Then Alastair had come along, with his sunny disposition and easy manner, and become his father's favorite. His mother's, too.

Colin could hear his father pontificating to Ewen, but he had escaped into his own thoughts. He seemed to do that more and more recently. Even the worst memories of the past were better than facing reality nowadays. His mother had never really recovered from losing Alastair. She'd always had that air of fragility about her, even when Colin had been a boy, but there had also been a sense of gaiety, of laughter bubbling beneath the surface, ready at any moment to burst forth like a fountain. Now it was as if she were an ethereal shadow, drifting in and out of the room, her mind never fully on the conversation. She always seemed relieved when it was time for her to rest or to go to bed at night, so that she could retreat to her small suite of rooms upstairs, to think her own hidden thoughts.

When Alastair disappeared, Colin soon came to realize that he had lost his mother as well as his brother.

"And I'm willing to pay all your debts," his father was saying. "If I can trust you to give me a comprehensive list of every one of them, not just a selection."

The old man would have a stroke if I did that, Colin thought. And wouldn't that solve a lot of problems.

The thought came unbidden to his mind, shocking even him with its candor.

"Did you tell your wife that you'd lost your position with your investment firm?" Ewen asked.

"No."

"Wasn't that rather odd?"

"Not really. We hadn't been communicating much recently."

"I understand that, but didn't she ask why you weren't going to work every morning, that sort of thing?"

"Going to the office at nine o'clock every morning was hardly my style," Colin drawled. "Nor was leaving on the dot of five-thirty every night. I saw clients in their own homes or offices, or at my clubs in London or Edinburgh."

"I see," was all Ewen said, but Colin, seeing the spots of color on his pale cheeks, felt he had scored a point. Then he realized, rather too late, that it might be more politic to try to get Ewen on his side, rather than baiting him.

"When I said that I didn't go into the office on a regular schedule I didn't mean—"

Ewen smiled. "I knew exactly what you meant. Now then, let's get this finalized," he said briskly, gathering his papers together. "You have Lady Craigmore's agreement to Colin's moving in here with you?" he asked Sir Robert.

"Of course. She'll be delighted to have him here."

"And you will put your house in Edinburgh on the market," Ewen reminded Colin. "The sooner the house is sold and the debts paid, the better, you understand? You say that your wife has not yet sued for a divorce?"

"No. She said she'd been to see a lawyer about a separation, but I think that was as far as it had gone."

"Have you any idea of the lawyer's name?"

"No, but I could probably find out through bills. The phone bill, that sort of thing."

"See what you can do. Talking of bills. Your wife will have credit cards—"

"I've put a stop on all of them," Colin said. "Did that last night on the twenty-four-hour phone service they have."

Ewen blinked. "That is unfortunate. We might have been able to trace your wife more easily from any credit card transactions she made."

"Shit!" Colin said, trying to ignore a similar explosion from his father. "Anyway, Vanessa's not stupid. She's got her own credit card. She can use that."

Ewen brightened. "But I'm sure the bills will come to your home in Edinburgh."

"I intend to get Roddy back a long time before the next bloody Visa bill comes in."

"Let us hope so. Meanwhile, we should file your suit for divorce as soon as possible." Ewen smiled his wan smile. "It never hurts to be the first one to do so. Makes it look as if you're the innocent party, if you know what I mean."

"I am the innocent party," Colin said, indignant at the lawyer's tone.

"Quite so." Ewen put the neatly arranged papers into his black briefcase and snapped it closed. "Good. I shall put all these measures into motion, particularly the investigation process. We must find out first whether or not your wife and son did indeed leave Britain and where they went. That shouldn't be too difficult. We'll soon be able to trace them."

"What happens when you find them?" Colin asked.

"That depends."

"You set the police on her," Robert said.

"Mother doesn't want the police involved," Colin told his father.

"What does she know about such matters? You know your mother, she lives in a fantasy world."

Ewen intervened. "There is no question of involving the police at this point. If the Manitoba court issues an order and your wife refuses to respond, then she could be acting in contempt of court. That's a matter for the police. But let us hope, for the sake of the family's reputation, that it won't come to that."

Sometimes Ewen reminded Colin of a lawyer in an amateur production of a play adapted from an early Agatha Christie novel. His pompous pronouncements had that element of the stage about them. Then, when you were ready to laugh derisively at him, he'd say something that hit you with all the subtlety of a sledgehammer.

"Show Ewen out, would you, Colin?" his father said unexpectedly. He held out his hand to the lawyer. "Thank you, Ewen. You seem to have everything under control. But if I think of anything else I'll give you a ring."

"Good." Ewen briskly shook his client's hand.

"We must get the boy back. He belongs here. Strathferness is his home."

"I'll do my best, Sir Robert. The rest is up to you and your family."

Colin opened the door and he and Ewen McKay left the room.

As he was pulling on his tweed wool coat and leather gloves, Ewen turned to Colin. "Would you like to come to my office for further discussion?"

Colin hesitated. "Is that necessary?"

"Not necessary, no. I merely wondered if you'd prefer to speak to me in my office about this matter."

This time Colin did not hesitate. "No, we've had too much bloody discussion already. I want action. And if I don't get it pretty quickly, McKay, I'm warning you I'll take action myself."

Chapter 16

Vanessa was still eating breakfast when Jill's package arrived.

"Saturday delivery," her father said. "Jill must have special clout."

"Nothing would surprise me where that girl's concerned." Lynne smiled as she served up more pancakes and back bacon.

Vanessa smiled, too. To her mother, she and Jill would always be "the girls."

"May I have more maple syrup, please?" Roddy asked.

"Help yourself." Vanessa handed him the syrup and then opened the package. The credit card was wrapped in plastic wrap. She hastily stuffed it into her jeans pocket. Knowing her father, he would definitely not approve of her using someone else's card, even Jill's.

She read Jill's letter and laughed aloud.

"What's so funny?" her mother asked.

"You should see the flights she's booked us on. Halifax, Chicago . . . even Churchill."

"You mean Churchill, Manitoba? You don't want to go there," her mother said. "You'd freeze."

"It can't be any colder than Winnipeg is at the moment. But she doesn't mean me to go to all these places. They're just camouflage."

"What's that?" Roddy asked.

"A kind of disguise," Vanessa said vaguely.

"When do you have to leave?" her father asked.

"Our first *real* flight is to Regina. It leaves at two o'clock this afternoon." Vanessa avoided looking at her mother. "Then we go to Calgary, before ending up at Vancouver. It's going to be a very long day."

"Why do we have to go to all those places?" Roddy asked.

"Because it's fun to see lots of different places when we're in Canada, that's why."

"I'd rather stay here," he said bluntly.

Vanessa focused her eyes on the wooden spice rack hanging on the wall above Roddy's head. "So would I, sweetie, but Jill wants to see us and she's going to be flying off to Tokyo sometime soon, so we have to go now."

She was getting used to making up things as she went along.

The morning rushed by far too fast. They had home-made pea soup and Vanessa's favorite pumpkin-and-ginger pie for lunch, and then it was time to leave for the airport.

Roddy sat in the front seat with his grandfather and Vanessa in the back, her hand clasped tightly in her mother's throughout the journey.

"I don't want you to come in with us," she told them when they arrived at the airport.

"Of course we're coming in." Her mother was half-way out the car. "You'll need help with the bags."

"We can manage them ourselves. It's not only that I can't stand good-byes, but I don't want to be seen with you."

"What on earth do you mean?"

Vanessa put on her dark glasses and pulled her tuque down farther over her hair. "I don't want *any* of us to be recognized, okay?"

"For heaven's sake, Vanessa. This is going too far!"

Hugh stuck his head into the car. "Do as Vanessa says. She's right. You can't be too careful."

"Now you're being just as silly as she is."

"I may not agree with what she's doing, but I respect her wish to do it."

"Okay, okay." Lynne grabbed the hand he proffered to help her out of the car.

Quick hugs all around. "Look after yourself," whispered her mother.

"I will. And we'll be back very soon," Vanessa promised, and then she and Roddy made a run for the entrance. Roddy turned to give one last wave before they went into the bustling airport.

The knowledge that she and Roddy were alone now was frightening, but also strangely exhilarating.

"Now, what's your name if they ask?" Vanessa prompted Roddy as they waited in line at the check-in counter.

"Rick Nelson."

"Excellent." Vanessa couldn't help giggling.

"What's so funny?"

"You just don't look like a Rick to me," she whispered, "but that's what Jill chose, so we have to live with it."

"I *like* the name Rick. From now on I'm going to be Rick."

"Great."

"Wow! Grampa gave me twenty dollars," Roddy suddenly said, taking out the bill his grandfather had tucked into his pocket.

Grampa had given Vanessa a lot more than that last night. Five hundred dollars. "Get word to me somehow if you need more," he'd told her, knowing she shouldn't leave a credit card trail.

"Jill will bail me out. I can pay her back later. Thanks, Dad," she'd whispered. "I know you think this is overkill on my part, but at least it buys me time. I promise it will all work out okay in the end."

"Of course it will."

As Vanessa sat on their third and last flight she sincerely hoped so. She was exhausted already from all the flying and the tension, and the effort of keeping her spirits up for Roddy. He, on the other hand, seemed as fresh as he'd been when they'd started out from Winnipeg hours and hours before.

Even fresher. He was going on adrenaline now and

becoming hyper and silly, bouncing up and down in his seat and singing some stupid commercial jingle he'd heard on TV, to the annoyance of the man sitting next to him.

Normally Vanessa would have apologized to the man, but she didn't want to draw attention to herself. She took Roddy's arm, forcing him to stop jiggling. "Roddy," she said softly, bending close to his ear. "Remember what I said about trying hard not to make people notice us? We're flying incognito, don't forget that."

He'd liked that word when she'd first said it. "Incognito," he repeated until he drove her crazy with it. He started doing it again, but this time she put a stop to it by raising her eyebrows at him in a way that he knew meant business.

"How about a game of naughts and crosses?"

"Too easy. I always beat you."

He was right. "Okay. We'll play Travel Scrabble then."

By the time they landed in Vancouver she was heartily sick of Scrabble and Hangman and I Spy, and ready to scream.

When they reached the arrivals' hall, she scanned the vast crowd of people waiting there. Her heart leaped when she saw Jill standing there. She was wearing dark glasses and a black coat, as she'd said she would, and Vanessa recognized her immediately. But it took Jill a moment longer. She was scanning the crowd, for a moment passing over the woman in dark glasses and tuque with the child, and then she caught sight of them and smiled.

"There's Auntie Jill," Vanessa told Roddy. "No, don't wave," she said quickly, catching his hand as it was about to go up.

Jill quickly joined them. "Let's get the hell out of here." She glanced around. "We can talk once we're in the car."

Chapter 17

It was hard to see anything from the car with the rain pouring down. Vanessa caught the occasional glimpse of mountains wreathed in gray mist, and, as they approached the city, the highway became a wide road flanked by mansions with large front gardens, but everything she saw was drenched with rain.

"Sorry about the weather, but that's how Vancouver can be in January."

Vanessa was disappointed. "It was so beautiful the last time I was here, but then that was years ago, in the summer."

"The weather's supposed to improve tomorrow."

"I do hope so. This is pretty depressing."

"I'm not taking you home," Jill explained, when they reached the downtown area. "That's what Col— they might expect, if they found out you were in Vancouver."

"Who's 'they'?" Roddy asked from the back of the car. "Is it Daddy who's chasing us?"

"Old eagle ears, there," Jill said under her breath.

"No one's chasing us," Vanessa said hurriedly.

"When why are we running away all the time? We couldn't even stay at Gran and Grampa's."

"I'll explain why when we get to where we're going."

"Where's that?"

"You'll see," Jill said. "You'll really like it, I promise." She turned to Vanessa, lowering her voice. "I thought of setting you up somewhere remote—perhaps on Vancouver Island—but then I thought you'd be better off somewhere where there's lots of people, so you'll just melt in."

"We hope."

"Don't be so negative. You're going to be just fine. They'll never trace you here."

Jill had found them a penthouse apartment in a new complex overlooking English Bay. "There's shops and restaurants, so you don't even have to go outside."

The thought of not being able to go outside made Vanessa fell like a prisoner.

"Security entrance," Jill said as they went up in the glass elevator. "Apartment's in my name, so always answer the buzzer as Jill Nelson."

"And I'm Rick Nelson," Roddy said.

"Right on, Rick," Jill said, grinning at him. She turned to speak again to Vanessa. "This apartment costs a bomb, but it won't cost us anything. It's been on our books for several months because of its price."

"Cool!" Roddy said as they soared up to the top floor. "Wow!" was his response to the lights that circled the bay like a misty glittering necklace when he entered the apartment and ran out onto the balcony.

"Be careful!" Vanessa warned him, as he leaned over.

"I am. Don't fuss, Mum."

"There's a special lock on the sliding door," Jill told her, "so you don't have to worry about him going out there when you're not around. The kitchen's through that door and there are two bedrooms and a den down the hall. This going to be okay for you?" she asked abruptly.

"It's much more than okay. It's absolutely gorgeous." Vanessa gazed around the large living room, at the mushroom fitted carpet and the furnishings of pale green and coral. When she looked back at Jill there were tears in her eyes. "You're the best friend anyone could have."

Jill looked embarrassed. She never had been able to take compliments gracefully. Vanessa hugged her, surprised, as always, by the solidity of Jill's body. Although they looked so much alike, she had never felt that her body was as sturdy as Jill's. If they were trees, Jill would be a stalwart oak and she, Vanessa, would be a willow, fluid in the breeze, but flexible. "God, it was so good to see you at the airport. I can't tell you how happy I felt when I saw you standing there."

"I was jumping up and down and screaming inside, but I thought it better not to draw attention to myself."

Roddy came back into the room. "It's really cool out there. I could see all kinds of boats down in the bay. Can I unpack my stuff?"

"Of course. Let's go see which room is yours."

"There's one big one for your mom," Jill told him, "and another, smaller one for you."

"No balcony, I hope," Vanessa said under her breath, as Roddy scampered down the hall.

"No. Only off yours."

They left him in his room, happily unpacking his bag, and returned to the living room.

"I've got a bottle of Chardonnay chilling in the fridge to celebrate."

"Not much to celebrate," Vanessa said with a rueful smile.

"There sure is. It took your breakup from Colin to get you out here to visit me in Vancouver. So we'll drink to Colin."

"You can forget that," Vanessa said.

"Oh, come on, Van. Don't tell me you've lost your sense of humor."

"It went a long time ago."

"Garbage!" Jill went into the kitchen to uncork the wine and pushed open the louvered doors of the hatch between the two rooms. She hauled out a tray and put the wine, a bottle of Perrier, and two glasses onto it. "Put that on the coffee table. I'll bring in the cheese and crackers."

"You're getting quite domesticated," Vanessa said, setting the tray down on the glass-topped table.

"Don't you believe it. Wine and cheese. That's the

extent of my culinary repertoire." Jill came through
and set a wooden board of mixed cheeses and a basket
of crackers on the table. She poured Vanessa a glass
of wine and herself some Perrier. "Here's to being
together again."

"That's the good part of all this. Here's to us."
Vanessa clinked glasses with Jill and took a gulp of
the cool, crisp wine.

Roddy suddenly appeared in the doorway of the
living room. "He can smell food a mile away,"
Vanessa said.

"Hi, buddy." Jill kicked off her shoes and tucked
her feet beneath her. "There's milk in the fridge and
cookies in a packet on the counter. Help yourself.
Your mom and I want to talk a bit."

"Don't expect that to get rid of him for long,"
Vanessa said, as Roddy raced into the kitchen.

"I don't remember us having that energy at his age,
do you?"

"You did. I certainly didn't."

"Oh you. You were the prissiest kid on the block."
Vanessa slapped her arm. "I was not."

"Were so. You used to come to school in long
dresses."

"Oh God, I did, didn't I? I thought I was Laura
from *Little House on the Prairie,* and you used to
make fun of me, so I'd run home and tell my mother."

When they'd stopped laughing, Jill said, "How's
your mother taking all this? Is she okay?"

"Not really. You know Mom. She's very worried."

"And your dad? Does he still think you should go
back and deal with Colin?"

"I don't know. He doesn't believe that Colin is as
bad as I say he is. He thinks I'm being overmelodra-
matic about it all."

"And are you?"

"When I was with Mom I began to wonder. Everyone used to say how like her I was. If that's true,
then I suppose I could be overreacting, because she
certainly does. But the more I thought about it, the

more I was sure that running away with Roddy was the right thing to do."

"Then that's okay, isn't it?"

Being with Jill was a tonic. She saw everything in terms of black or white. No room for gray in Jill's life.

They could hear Roddy humming to himself out in the kitchen. "You're going to have to tell him," Jill said.

"Tell him what?"

"Why you're hiding from his dad. He's not stupid, you know."

"I don't want to turn him against Colin."

"Just tell him the truth."

"That his father's no good?" Vanessa said in an undertone. "That he plays around with women and gambles and drinks too much? Isn't that a bit heavy for a boy his age?"

"He probably knows it already. Kids aren't blind. They know what's going on. Better you tell him the facts, so he doesn't imagine things are even worse than they are."

"Is that what you used to do?" Vanessa touched her friend's hand.

"Probably. Kids have a vivid imagination. But when my dad used to smash up the place he didn't leave much to the imagination." Jill gave Vanessa a twisted smile. "You're doing the right thing, Van. You're getting out before it gets really scary. Before Roddy sees things that keep replaying on the old mind video twenty years later."

This seemed as good a time as any to bring up the question that Vanessa had put off asking. "I know Steve's doing fine. You told me about his new job in Saskatoon when we spoke just before Christmas, but you didn't say how your mother was."

To her surprise, Jill smiled. "I've been waiting to tell you, but didn't want to do it over the phone or E-mail. You never know who's checking on you, nowadays. Mom's found a new job, a good one this time, and she's been sober for almost seven months. I'm

scared to say it after all the other times, but this time
I think she might make it."

"Jill, that's great news. You've been so good to her.
Stood by her all these years."

"Yeah, well . . . she's my mother, what else would
I do?"

"A lot of people would have let her get on with it."

Jill was about to reply when Roddy came back into
the room, carefully carrying a glass of milk in one
hand and a plate of cookies in the other. "Hey, you
could have used the hatch," she told him.

"Need any help?" Vanessa asked.

"No, thank you." Roddy was concentrating on not
spilling anything on the pristine carpet. He set the
plate and glass down with a sigh of relief and sat on
the sofa beside his mother.

Jill got up. "I'm going to get us some Chinese
food."

"But you've got in stacks of food for us!"

"You don't want to cook your first night here. I
won't be long. There's a restaurant less than a block
from here." Jill was already striding to the door.

Vanessa followed her. "I'm not hungry," she protested. "We've got plenty of stuff here."

"I want to make sure that people see me going in
and out of this place," Jill explained. "Don't forget,
the apartment's in my name. And Rick is my
nephew." She pulled on her black full-length coat with
the warm lining and fur-edged hood. "See this coat?"

"How could I miss it? It's gorgeous." Vanessa
rubbed her hand over the fabric, which felt like a firm
silk beneath her fingers. "I take it that it's waterproof
as well as warm."

"Naturally! It has to be, in Vancouver. I've got another one exactly the same for you. I left it in the car.
I'll bring it up later."

"Thanks, but I don't really need another coat."

"You're not thinking, airhead. We need to look like
the same person when we go in and out of here."

Vanessa had to laugh. "God, you're getting into this better than I am. You've thought of everything."

"Someone has to." Jill opened the door. "Speak to Roddy while I'm gone."

"Yes, ma'am."

"I'll get the usual for you. What about Roddy?"

"He likes everything but shrimp. Oh, and don't forget fortune cookies."

"Lock the door," Jill said as she went out into the hall.

Vanessa laughed. "You're even more paranoid than I am." Jill gave her a look over her dark glasses. "Okay, okay, I'll lock it." She did so.

"Can I watch TV?" Roddy asked when she went back into the living room. "Is it okay to say TV?"

"Sure. Why shouldn't it be?"

"You won't let me call it telly at home."

"That's different." She gave him a conspiratorial smile. "Things are more relaxed here."

"And Daddy's not here, right?"

Vanessa held her breath and then released it. "Right." She sat down beside him. "I want to talk to you about that."

"Can I watch TV first?"

"No. We must talk first. You can watch TV afterwards. Maybe we can find something we can all watch together."

"I like *Blue Peter.*"

"That's not on in Canada."

"I saw reruns of *Sabrina* on that special kids channel yesterday."

"Okay, we'll check in the television guide later." A moment of hesitation . . . and then she plunged right in. "You asked me before if we were running away from Daddy."

"What I *said* was, is Daddy chasing us?"

"No, he's not chasing us." At least Vanessa hoped he wasn't. Not yet, anyway. "But we *are* sort of running away."

"Why?"

"Because, as I told you before when we were driving to Edinburgh, Daddy and I are going to live separately."

"You didn't say why."

"Didn't I? Well, there's more than one reason, but it's mainly because I don't like Daddy gambling and drinking so much."

"And getting angry at us."

"Especially that. But when I told Daddy we were going to live in separate houses, he said that he and his family want you to live all the time with them, and I don't want that."

Roddy's eyes were as round as saucers. "You mean I couldn't ever see you again."

Vanessa hugged him tightly against her. "No, of course not. I mean they want you to live with Daddy—"

"Daddy on his own?" Roddy's voice rose in pitch.

"No, no," Vanessa said soothingly. "Daddy would probably take you to Strathferness to live, with your nanna and grandfather." That was a less frightening scenario for Roddy, and also quite possible. She couldn't see Colin setting up house on his own with just a housekeeper. Of course, she thought grimly, that depended on who the "housekeeper" was.

Roddy pulled away from her embrace and began to spread a triangular wedge of flavored cream cheese on a bran cracker. "I won't stay at Strathferness without you," he said in a low, intense voice. "And I don't want to go away to Daddy's crummy boarding school, either."

"You won't have to, pumpkin. I promise you that."

"Will I get to go to school in Canada, then?"

"Oh, I don't think it will hurt for you to take an extra week's holiday off from school, do you?"

"Yay!" Roddy cheered. "Only a week?"

"You wouldn't have been going back to school in Edinburgh for another week, would you?"

"I suppose not." Roddy stuffed another piece of peanut butter cookie into his mouth.

"We're not staying in Canada forever, you know. The reason we're hiding here for a while is to cool everyone down, give them time to think."

"Cool Daddy down, you mean." He mashed the cheese into the cracker. "He gets rather hot at times, doesn't he?"

"He certainly does. So does your grandfather. The idea is that we hide out here for a week or two. Then we tell them we're ready to talk to them."

"To negotiate, right?"

"Exactly. But because Daddy won't know where we are, once we reappear he'll be very happy to listen to what *we* want, rather than just what he and Grandfather want."

"So you and me are in this together."

"Sure are, pal. And Auntie Jill. And Gran and Grampa. They know all about it, too. We've got lots of help."

Roddy mashed the cheese even further into the cracker, so that it crumbled into pieces. "What if Daddy finds us before he's cooled down?" There was a slight quiver in his voice.

Anger seared Vanessa like a hot bolt of lightning as she realized how scared Roddy was of his father's anger. "He won't. But even if he did, I will always be here to make sure everything's fine. *Always.* Okay?"

He nodded. "Let's see what's on TV now."

She watched his golden head as he bent over the newspaper, looking through the television listings, but his last question was haunting her. She said a silent prayer that Colin wouldn't find them until he'd had time to cool down.

A few hours later, several thousands of miles away from sleeping Vancouver, it was early in the morning in Scotland. But not too early for an international incoming call that lasted less than two minutes.

The hunt was on. They'd left Winnipeg Airport yesterday afternoon. At present their destination was unclear, but the caller was certain that he'd find out within the next twenty-four hours. Colin's cigarette lighter illuminated the grim smile of his face. He set the telephone back in its cradle.

Somewhere else in the awakened castle a receiver was carefully replaced.

Chapter 18

For five long, excruciatingly boring days Vanessa had been cooped up in the apartment. They'd even stayed in to celebrate the New Year. Although Jill had brought in balloons and noisemakers and a sumptuous meal she'd ordered from her favorite Italian restaurant, it just wasn't the same as being able to go out.

Always an active child, Roddy was growing fractious and irritable, like a puppy kept tied up for too long.

"I have to take him out. He's getting impossible," Vanessa told Jill on Saturday, as she was putting away the groceries Jill had brought in for them. "And the sun's shining at last. This is the first day it hasn't rained."

"I'm not taking any responsibility for Vancouver's weather in the winter." Jill handed Vanessa a bag of carrots. "I can take Roddy out. Not today, though. I'll take him to the zoo tomorrow."

"I promised him I'd take him to Stanley Park today to see the totem poles."

Jill stood, hands on her hips, shaking her head at Vanessa. "How are you going to last this out, if you can't stay inside for more than a few days? Where is Roddy, by the way?"

"In the den, watching cartoons."

"Ah, good old Saturday morning cartoons. That brings back memories." Jill frowned at her. "You look as white as Casper the Ghost. I can see that you're getting cabin fever. Tell you what, I'll take Roddy out this morning for an hour. If you're really dying to get out, what I'd like you to do is go see Mike Chang."

They'd argued about this before. "No, Jill, I keep telling you I don't want to see a lawyer. Not yet, anyway."

"You're crazy. You have to know what the legal situation is."

Vanessa turned on Jill. "I know exactly what the legal situation is. Colin has been given temporary custody by the Scottish court."

"Yes, but—"

"That's not all. Dad called yesterday evening—"

"I thought we'd agreed he'd not call you here."

"He had to call," Vanessa said, with mounting irritation. "And he can't call you, can he? Colin knows your number."

"For God's sake, Van, quit being so paranoid. Even Colin can't arrange a wiretap on my phone."

"I wouldn't be so sure about that," Vanessa muttered. "Besides, it was you who said that anyone could listen in to your calls or read your E-mail nowadays."

"True, but I'm talking about professional snoops, not people like Colin."

"Knowing Colin and his family, it's professional snoops they'll have engaged to track me down." Vanessa ran her hands through her hair. "Let me tell you what Dad said. He'd just heard from a lawyer in Winnipeg that Colin was trying to apply to the Manitoba courts to have the custody order enforced there."

"Well . . . all I can say is it's a good thing you're not in Manitoba anymore."

"Oh, come on! You know if it applies in one province they can get me anywhere in Canada."

"You said Colin was *trying* to apply to the Manitoba courts."

"They have to be able to prove that Roddy is in Manitoba."

"How can they do that when he's here, in British Columbia?"

"They can't. But that's what bothers me. If they know he's not in Manitoba, they'll be trying to track him down."

"That's why it's essential that you see Mike Chang."

"I don't need to see him. I know exactly what he'll tell me. Take Roddy back to Scotland, find myself a good lawyer, and fight for custody."

"You're right. He will," Jill said briskly. "That's what I would have done in the first place. Stand up to the bastards."

Vanessa felt as if Jill had punched her in the stomach. "I thought you were on my side. You were the one who said come to Vancouver."

"I am. I did. But that was after you'd run off with Roddy. You'd burned your bridges by then."

Vanessa confronted Jill, heat flushing her face. "I still think I did the right thing. I know that you and my parents and probably everyone else in the world think I was stupid to run, but I still believe in my heart that what I did was right. I'm convinced a Scottish court would rule that Roddy should be raised in Scotland."

"Okay, okay. I'm sorry. I'm on your side, you know that."

Vanessa sank onto the kitchen chair. "You have to live with the Craigmores to know what a poisonous atmosphere they create. I'll do anything, *anything* to avoid sending Roddy back there."

"Oh, Van, I know. Tell you what. I'll speak to Mike, give him the story without names or places. See what he says."

Vanessa shrugged. "Whatever."

Roddy ran into the kitchen. "*Superman*'s finished. Can we go to Stanley Park now, Mum, like you said we could?"

Vanessa looked at Jill.

She shrugged and picked up her black leather briefcase. "I've got to go. Work to do."

"On Saturday?"

"A telephone conference. In this electronic age, my dear old friend, all the days are equal. There's a back entrance to this block. Go out that way. Give me a little time to get away before you leave."

"Now who's being paranoid?"

"It's catching. And remember to wear *our* coat."

"You sound like a Maxwell Smart rerun."

"More like *Mission Impossible,*" was Jill's acid comment as she went out the door.

Vanessa allowed about forty minutes before she and Roddy left the apartment. As she stepped out the door into the parking lot, she glanced around, just to make sure that no one was there waiting for them. She was growing increasingly nervous, which really bothered her. She'd always loved to do things on the spur of the moment, to act first and consider later. Having to worry about everything ahead of time made her feel anxious and claustrophobic.

As they crossed the road to walk along the path by the seawall, Vanessa smiled down at Roddy, who was already looking more relaxed. "Breathe in that sea air," she told him.

He took in a great gasp of air and grinned up at her.

"Smells good, eh?" Vanessa was feeling better already. This was the way she remembered Vancouver, sunlight sparkling on the water on one side, a breathtaking view of the distant mountains on the other. They stopped to gaze out at English Bay and the boats and tankers anchored there.

"Can we go on a yacht?" Roddy asked.

"Not a yacht, but maybe a boat. Jill says Granville Island's really interesting. Maybe we can take a boat trip there later."

As Roddy ran ahead of her, Vanessa stopped and turned to see if anyone was following them. Just a little way back, a sandy-haired woman in a long black raincoat paused to take a photograph. A young Asian man in a tan jacket was gazing out over the water. There were people everywhere, jogging and in-line skating and walking their dogs in the intermittent sunshine. No one appeared particularly interested in her and Roddy, but then how would she recognize a professional detective if she saw one?

She shivered a little in the chill wind that blew in

from the ocean, ruffling the water. Then she ran to catch up with Roddy. "I think we should get a taxi to the park. It's quite a long way to walk."

The taxi dropped them near Painters' Corner, where artists displayed their work beneath large umbrellas in case it rained. They walked down the shady pathway, passing a sign pointing to the zoo.

"There's a zoo here," Roddy said excitedly. "Let's go!"

"We'll walk around a bit more first. It's great to be able to get out and stretch our legs, isn't it?"

They walked along a long trail of damp earth, fallen leaves clinging to the soles of their shoes, until they reached the seawall again. Outlines of office and apartment blocks and hotels across the waters of Coal Harbour were half hidden by a fluid winter mist.

Roddy turned away and suddenly caught sight of the totem poles beyond the green cricket pitch. "Wow, look at those!" He took off, running ahead of her across a parking lot and a stretch of damp grass. Vanessa hurried after him, trying to keep him in sight. He sped across the open paved square to get closer to the towering poles with their ornate designs and brilliant colors.

It happened so fast that Vanessa didn't even have time to shout a warning. One minute Roddy was pounding across the paved square where the totem poles stood, flanked by trees and bushes, the next he had collided with the youth on in-line skates who was speeding across the square.

Both went down with a sickening crash.

Yelling Roddy's name, Vanessa tore across the square, her heart hammering in her chest. She felt as if her legs were made of cement, as if she were running on the spot, not gaining an inch. As she ran, her breath rasped in her ears.

A small crowd had gathered around the accident. A Japanese tourist helped the white-faced skater to his feet. Roddy still lay on the ground.

"It's my son," Vanessa said, frantically pushing

through the group of people standing around Roddy. "Please, it's my son!" They parted to let her through.

A dark-haired man was kneeling beside Roddy. He had taken off his jacket and was pulling off his pale blue sweater to form a cushion for Roddy's head. Blood welled from a gash on the right side of Roddy's forehead.

Vanessa fell on her knees beside him, her shoulder bag falling onto the ground. "Roddy. Roddy darling," she cried, taking his limp hand in hers. "It's Mummy. I'm right here."

"He must have knocked himself out falling on the pavement," the man said quietly. "The cut looks as if it was made by the Rollerblade. Could someone send for an ambulance, please?" he asked, raising his voice.

"I'm just doing that." The voice came from the periphery of the crowd.

The man gently ran his hands over Roddy's body as if he knew what he was doing. "I don't think he's broken anything. Have you got a clean handkerchief?" he asked Vanessa. "Mine's already used up."

With a sickening lurch of her stomach Vanessa saw the blood-soaked handkerchief in his hand. She fumbled in her bag, but could come up with only a packet of tissues. "That's all I have."

"That's fine." He made a pad of the tissues, applying them to Roddy's forehead and keeping pressure on them. He looked up at her. "Keep talking to him. He needs to know you're here."

Vanessa nodded, glad to find something she could do. "I'm here, Roddy. Mummy's here. You're going to be fine, I promise." She jabbered on, intensely aware of the horrible limpness of Roddy's hand and the gray pallor of his face.

Above the murmur of the people nearby came the whine of an electric cart. A first-aid attendant jumped out carrying his bag. "The ambulance should be here any minute now." He, too, checked Roddy for broken bones and replaced the pad on Roddy's forehead with a dressing. "You the boy's parents?" he asked.

"I'm his mother," Vanessa said. "This man—"

"I just happened to be near when he fell. He collided with a Rollerblader."

The attendant frowned. "They're a menace when they go too fast. Did he stick around?" He raised his voice. "Anyone see the guy on Rollerblades who ran into the boy?"

A Japanese tour guide dressed in a scarlet blazer stepped forward. "He disappeared soon as he saw the boy was down," she said. "He was scared, I guess."

Vanessa's heart thumped. *Disappeared?* Her mind whirled with sudden fear. Maybe it hadn't been an accident. Maybe it had been a setup. Maybe someone had followed them from the apartment and arranged this accident. But why would someone connected with Colin want to hurt Roddy?

"The ambulance is here," said the man with the blue sweater.

Vanessa's eyes widened. "Ambulance?" She heard the throb of the engine. Her hand tightened on Roddy's. "I don't want him to go in the ambulance."

"He'll be fine, ma'am," the first-aid attendant said. "Just you let them look after him."

"You don't understand," she said wildly. "I don't want my son to—" She was sounding like a crazy woman. She *felt* like a crazy woman. She wanted to gather Roddy up in her arms and run as fast as she could. Was it possible that an ambulance could kidnap them here, in front of all these people?

"It's okay," Roddy's rescuer said in a low voice. "They'll take your son to the nearest hospital."

Two more men converged on her. She could see only their uniformed legs as they bent over Roddy. "We'll take over now," one of them said. "Would you let him go, please, ma'am? We have to check him out before we put him on the backboard."

The dark-haired man put out a hand to help her up. "He'll be fine," he said softly. He picked up his black leather jacket and then, as they lifted Roddy, took his sweater from beneath Roddy's head. He

pulled on his jacket, but not the sweater. Vanessa
shuddered when she saw how heavily it was stained
with Roddy's blood.

"I'm sorry," she murmured.

He frowned. "About what?"

"Your sweater." She tried to swallow the moist
lump in her throat. "It's all—"

"It's not important." He tucked the sweater away
from sight beneath his arm.

She stood beside him, watching as they loaded
Roddy on the stretcher, only dimly aware that the
man's hand was now supporting her by the elbow, as
if he were afraid she might keel over.

"He's got a nasty bump on the back of his head,"
one of the ambulance attendants told her. "That's
probably what knocked him out."

They lifted the stretcher and were about to carry
Roddy to the ambulance when he stirred, lifted his
head, and suddenly vomited. "Mummy!" he cried in
panic.

"I'm right here, darling." Giddy with relief, Vanessa
darted forward to grasp his hand. Everything suddenly
seemed to slip into focus again, as if the sound of his
voice had restored her sense of reality.

"What's happened? My head hurts." He made a
little whimpering noise in his throat as if he were trying hard not to cry.

"You fell down and bumped your head hard. You'll
be fine. We're just going to the hospital to have you
check over."

She helped the attendants clean Roddy off before
they lifted him into the ambulance.

"You're the boy's mother, right?" the attendant
confirmed as she stood at the door, one hand on the
handle.

"Yes."

"Okay. In you get."

Vanessa hesitated and then turned back to the man
who'd helped Roddy. "Will you come with us?"

"You his dad?" the ambulance attendant asked.

"Only family can come in the ambulance," he added in an officious tone.

"I'll meet you in the emergency room," the man told Vanessa. "What hospital will you be going to?" he asked the attendant.

"St. Paul's," was the answer. "Ten-eighty-one Burrard."

"I'll meet you there." He held out his hand to Vanessa. "My name's Grant Kendall, by the way."

She summoned up a smile. "I don't think you want to shake hands with me at the moment. I'm a bit sticky."

Grant Kendall smiled back, a flash of amusement in his eyes. "See you at the hospital." He didn't seem to notice that she hadn't told him her name.

As the ambulance raced along the road that ran all the way through the park, Vanessa suddenly realized that she'd made a big mistake. She shouldn't have asked this Grant Kendall to come with them to the hospital. You're an idiot! she told herself. Even if she could trust him—and she felt instinctively that she could because of his genuine kindness to Roddy—he could well be an added complication in her already complicated life.

He walked into the waiting room about fifteen minutes after the ambulance got there. Despite her misgivings, Vanessa couldn't help feeling glad to see him. He was a familiar face in a room filled with strangers.

Returning her smile, he made his way across the busy waiting room and sat down beside her. He moved with an unhurried ease, a certain fluid grace, as if comfortable in himself and in the world around him. Vanessa envied him. At this moment she felt very far from comfortable.

"How is he?" Grant asked.

"They're just examining him now. Then they'll take him to be X-rayed, the nurse said."

"Mrs. Nelson," the clerk at the desk called. When there was no response, she shouted the name a second time.

Vanessa suddenly realized that *she* was Mrs. Nelson. She jumped up and went to the desk.

"Your medical card, please?"

Oh God! She'd given them Jill's name, but she didn't have her medical card. Vanessa swallowed hard. "Sorry, I—I don't have it with me. I left my card at home."

The desk clerk looked at her as if she were crazy. "Address?" she barked. Vanessa gave her Jill's address and the clerk pressed some keys on the computer. "Got it."

Vanessa's heartbeat slowed a little.

"But there's no child on this listing. Just you. Jill Nelson."

Grant came to stand behind her. "Problems?"

"I don't understand," Vanessa said to the clerk. "My son should be there, too," she improvised.

"Well, he's not." The clerk was getting annoyed now. "You said his name was Rick, right? Is that short for Richard?"

"No, just Rick." Vanessa was acutely aware of Grant standing close by her, listening.

"No Rick Nelson here."

"Well, he should be there," Vanessa said desperately, not knowing what else to say.

The desk clerk sucked in her breath. "Mrs. Nelson, we're holding up all these people." She waved her pen at the waiting crowd.

"Mrs. Nelson will bring her medical card in later," Grant said. "She's pretty shaken up by her son's accident."

Any other time Vanessa would have been annoyed at the suggestion that she wasn't capable of dealing with things herself, but Grant's intervention at this point was a welcome one.

"Okay." The clerk released a heavy sigh. "That's fine. Just as long as her son's on the card. Must be a computer screwup. We'll get it worked out."

"Thanks," Vanessa said to Grant when they sat down again.

He looked at her. She hadn't noticed before how very blue his eyes were, as blue as the Pacific ocean a short distance away from them. "Rick?" Dark, winged eyebrows rose above those intensely blue eyes. "I thought your son's name was Roddy."

Chapter 19

Head bent, Vanessa put her wallet back in her bag. "Oh, you know boys this age," she said in reply to Grant's question about Roddy's name. "He doesn't like the name Roddy much, so he decided to change it to Rick."

She could sense his penetrating gaze on her. When she looked up, he was looking at her intently with those very blue eyes. "I see," he said.

Vanessa was waiting for him to ask why, if Roddy had changed his name to Rick recently, the name Rick was on his medical card, but to her relief he didn't pursue the matter. She drew a shaky hand across her forehead. "I'm sorry." She gave him a wan smile. "I'm all muddled at the moment."

"That's understandable. Have you had anything to drink or eat?"

She shuddered. "I couldn't eat a thing."

"A coffee, then? I passed a machine when I came in."

"That would be great."

"How do you take it?"

"Just creamer. No sugar."

"Coming up."

She watched him as he walked away. Despite her preoccupation with thoughts of Roddy, she had to admit that Grant Kendall was good to look at, from the back as well as the front. Although not a tall man, he was above medium height and his dark hair curled attractively into the nape of his neck.

"Mrs. Nelson!"

She started as the name was called again. This time she responded immediately, crossing the floor to the waiting nurse.

"You can see your son now." The nurse led the way down the corridor, her rubber-soled shoes squeaking on the polished vinyl floor.

"How is he?" Vanessa asked.

"Dr. Sumner's with him now. He'll answer any questions you may have."

When they went into the small examination room Roddy was sitting on the side of the bed, looking pale and shaky, but decidedly better. Vanessa went to hug him.

"Watch out," he protested, holding on to his head as if he were afraid it might fall off.

"Sorry. I'm just so glad to see you sitting up."

Roddy rolled his eyes. *Mothers!* his expression said.

"Is he all right?" Vanessa asked the doctor.

"We have to take X rays, but I doubt we'll find anything more than a hairline skull fracture, if that."

"A skull fracture. Isn't that serious?"

"No. Very common." Dr. Sumner grinned. "Especially with lively youngsters like this young man. I've put three stitches in the forehead cut."

"Will it leave a scar?"

"A very slight one, perhaps, but his hair will probably cover it"—he glanced at Roddy's short hair—"if longer hair becomes the fashion again."

"Will you need to keep him in?"

"That depends on the X ray. If it's okay, he can probably go home."

"Yeah!" Roddy said.

They were about to wheel him down to X ray when Vanessa remembered Grant. Should she just let him think they'd gone? That would be the best way to avoid any further complications, wouldn't it? But how could she do that to someone who'd been so kind? Besides, he'd be bound to ask about them at the desk.

"Hang on a moment," she told the orderly, "I just have to tell someone where we're going."

Grant was standing by the bank of telephones, holding a Styrofoam cup.

"I'm sorry," Vanessa told him. "They called me in just after you'd left to get the coffee."

"How's he doing?"

She told him. "They're taking him to X ray now," she added. "We could be quite a while." She hesitated and then said, "No need to stay." A little pang stabbed at her. "I haven't even thanked you properly for all your kindness." She held out her hand. "Thanks so much, Grant."

He didn't take her hand. "You'll need a ride home. Did you leave your car in Stanley Park?"

"No, we took a taxi there. We can get another taxi home."

"I'll drive you."

"That's very kind, but there's no need to wait around. Thank you, though."

"I'll come with you to X ray." Grant nodded at the cup in his hand. "You haven't had your coffee yet."

"We have to go, Mrs. Nelson," the orderly called to her.

"Let's go," Grant said. He walked ahead of her to Roddy and the orderly. "Hi, Rick, I'm Grant."

Roddy frowned up at him. "My name's Roddy," he said.

Vanessa caught the amused glance Grant threw back at her before they started down the corridor. "I guess he's changed his mind again about his name," he said.

As they waited to get the X rays done, Roddy was at first wary with Grant, but it wasn't long before they were chatting away like old friends. Grant had a way with children that made Vanessa wonder if he had any of his own. As she listened to him, her innate ability with accents detected another element in his voice behind the slight North American accent. It hinted of another background. South America, perhaps.

So far, she hadn't taken part in the conversation herself. Her mind was too preoccupied with ways of getting rid of Grant Kendall before they left the hospital. But she was listening closely to their conversation. Roddy was, as always, asking questions, and Grant was answering them without hesitation.

"I make wine. I have a small winery in California," Grant was telling him. "In the Napa Valley."

"What are you doing in British Columbia?" Vanessa couldn't help asking.

"There's a thriving wine industry here, as you probably know. You *are* Canadian, aren't you? You have a rather unusual accent."

Roddy jumped in. "I'm part Canadian and part—"

"Yes, we're Canadian," Vanessa said quickly. She gave Roddy one of her looks, to stop him from volunteering any more information.

At that moment they were called in for the X rays, but when they'd finished and come out, Grant was still sitting in the small waiting room.

How in the world was she going to be able to shake him? Vanessa wondered. He was as tenacious as a bulldog.

There was no fracture. Roddy was free to go home, with a warning to rest quietly for a couple of days and to return to the hospital to have the stitches removed in a week's time. There was a nasty moment when Dr. Sumner asked who her family doctor was, but she said she was in the throes of finding a new one, as hers had recently retired. The doctor was too busy to pursue it any further, just telling her to be sure to call them with a doctor's name for their records.

It was a good thing she'd done a lot of improvisation work at theater school, Vanessa thought. She'd certainly had to put her skills to work this past week.

She still had to get rid of Grant Kendall, but she no longer felt able to summon up the energy to do it. As she waited for the doctor to finish off Roddy's papers, she suddenly felt so drained she had to sit down, the waiting room spinning around her.

"Are you okay?" Grant asked, his voice coming at her from a long way off.

"Sorry. I'm a bit light-headed, that's all." Even her own voice sounded as if it were far, far away.

"Delayed shock," he said succinctly.

He must be right. All she knew was that she felt nauseated and very dizzy. Part of her felt furious at this lack of control, but the other part just couldn't respond to her inner voice telling her to get up and get out quickly.

"I'll bring the car around to the front," Grant was telling her. "You sit here until I come back for you and Roddy." Vanessa felt him move away. "She's feeling a bit light-headed," she heard him tell the desk clerk. "Would you keep an eye on her?"

"Of course. You want Dr. Sumner to take a look at you, Mrs. Nelson?"

"No, I'm fine, thank you." Vanessa was embarrassed to have eyes swiveling to look inquiringly at her.

"You sit there with your son," the clerk told her. "Don't move until your friend comes back."

She didn't feel capable of moving. Resignation set in.

"Are you okay, Mum?" Roddy asked, his voice anxious.

"I'm fine. I expect it's what Mr. Kendall said. Delayed shock."

"He's okay, isn't he? I like him."

"Mr. Kendall? He was very kind to you," Vanessa answered slowly, wanting to trust her instincts, but still anxious. "I'm very grateful to him."

"But you're sure he's okay."

Roddy had had enough worries for one day. "Of course he's okay," she told him, her voice filled with confidence. "I wouldn't let him drive us home if I couldn't trust him, would I?"

But when they arrived at the apartment block, she rejected Grant's offer to accompany them upstairs. "We're absolutely fine. Really."

"Can't Mr. Kendall come up with us?" Roddy asked. "I wanted to show him my—"

"No, darling. Mr. Kendall has given up enough of his time for us today." Ignoring Roddy's rebellious look, Vanessa held out her hand to Grant. "Thank you so much for all your kindness."

How formal and inadequate it sounded! Beside her, Roddy was looking thoroughly miserable, his face extremely pale, but his jaw jutted forward, signaling one of his obstinate moods.

"I'm glad I could help." Grant looked at her gravely before taking her hand. She glanced away from him, smiling down at the glowering Roddy. She felt her hand pressed and immediately released.

"Look after yourselves. 'Bye, Roddy. Hope the head's better soon." Grant Kendall's hand rested for a moment on Roddy's shoulder and then he walked away to his car, leaving Vanessa feeling suddenly very much alone.

Chapter 20

Although Amanda had returned to London after Christmas, she flew back to Scotland again for the New Year festivities. Her father always gave the staff of the Strathferness estate and the distillery a Hogmanay dinner on New Year's Eve in the hall of John Knox Church. This was followed by a private dinner party at the castle for family members and close friends, complete with the piper of Strathferness in the kilt and full regalia piping in the haggis.

The staff dinner had been as riotous as ever, with many of the employees having to be assisted on and off the bus Sir Robert had engaged, to ensure that they didn't drive their cars in a state of intoxication.

The private dinner, on the other hand, had been an unusually somber affair this year. Not only did the physical absence of both Vanessa and Roddy put a blight on their enjoyment of the occasion, but each member of the family had been personally affected by the shock of Vanessa's flight with Roddy. They had never been a particularly close family, but now they were drawn together by their mutual sorrow at the loss of what, they all realized now, had been the one bright star in their lives.

Yet none of them, Amanda had realized as soon as she'd returned to Strathferness, had the capacity to give solace to the other. They had opened their ranks and themselves to the child who had loved them unconditionally, but now that Roddy was gone, each one of them had closed up like a flower in the darkness, furling its petals.

Amanda, who had probably spent the least amount of time with Roddy, was surprised to find how sorely she missed him. But what hurt her even more than Roddy's loss was seeing how withdrawn her mother had become this past week.

Ever since she'd come home, Amanda had tried to talk to her mother about Roddy, to draw her out of her melancholy, but her mother had always found a way to change the subject, turning it to questions about Amanda's work in advertising at Saatchi's Agency or what was on in London's theaters. Frequently Fiona retired to her rooms upstairs without anyone seeing her leave. Or she would slip out of the castle without anyone knowing that she had gone. And if someone noticed her absence, she would tell them upon her return that she had "just been to Alice Coombs-Hamilton's for a little game of bridge." Or to "Jessie Livingstone's house for a church meeting."

Amanda was staring gloomily into the fire, the Sunday papers strewn around her, when the library door opened and Colin walked in. "So that's where the paper is," he said, glowering at her.

"You look particularly ghastly this morning," she told him.

He grabbed the sports section from the floor, cursing as it fell apart in his hands, and threw himself into his father's leather chair.

"Are you okay?" she asked in a kinder voice.

"I'm just great. Couldn't be better." She could see the ironic twist to his mouth as he spoke. "Where are they?"

"The parents? Church, of course. In case you've lost track of time, it's Sunday today."

"You're right. I do lose track." He lowered the newspaper to stare at her, but she felt that he wasn't really seeing her. Looking through her rather than at her, really. "I start work at the distillery tomorrow."

"Yes, I know. You showed me your office, remember?"

"Oh yes. Right." His eyes were bloodshot. But it

was his voice that bothered her most. She hated it
when Colin shouted or was being sarcastic, but in the
last few days she'd noticed that he rarely raised his
voice. He seemed to be wrapped up in his thoughts,
and when he did speak, it was in a kind of monotone,
as if he were talking in his sleep.

"I think Dad's secretly quite pleased to have you
working here," she told him, trying to think of something upbeat to say.

"Is he?"

"He's always wanted you to join him in the family
business." Amanda felt a twinge of envy. Must be nice
to be wanted, even if Colin didn't seem particularly
glad about it.

"Well, now he's got me, hasn't he?"

Amanda hesitated, then said, "Any more news,
Col? From Canada, I mean."

"I know what you mean," he said, his voice edgy.
"Nothing new. Just that they've traced them to Vancouver. But you knew that already."

"What next?"

"Once they can get near enough to take a photograph with a telescopic lens, so that we can prove
that it's definitely Roddy, I can apply to the British
Columbia courts for an order."

He smiled for the first time. A little shiver ran down
Amanda's spine. "What then?" she asked again.

"Then I'll go and get my son."

"Dad said you shouldn't go yourself."

"I know what he said. He's not my keeper."

"I think he's right, Col. If Vanessa sees you or even
knows you're somewhere in the area, she's likely to
run again. And it will be much harder to find her if
she goes across the border to the States."

"She won't see me. She won't even know I'm near
until I pounce."

Amanda swallowed. "You won't do anything stupid,
will you? I mean . . . hurt her or anything?"

"What do you think?"

She looked at him directly, her blue eyes locking

with his brown. "I think you'll be so glad to get Roddy back you won't care what happens to her," she said evenly.

He nodded his head and kept nodding as he smiled a small smile to himself, but he said nothing in reply.

"I'm worried about Colin," Amanda told her mother later, as they walked around the garden after lunch.

Fiona had driven home separately from the service at St. Andrew's Episcopal Church, arriving half an hour after Sir Robert, because of the short meeting of the Altar Committee she'd had to attend. Amanda had been shocked at how pale and drawn she looked when she came in. And she'd barely touched the hearty lunch of roast lamb with mint sauce and all the trimmings.

Fiona's hand tightened on Amanda's arm. "Are you, dear?" she said in response to Amanda's comment about Colin. She released a small shuddering sigh. "It is a very worrying time for us all."

"He wants to go to Canada himself to get Roddy."

"I expect he does." Fiona shivered and drew her coat more tightly about her. "I do so hate January, don't you? The wind seems to cut through everything. Oh no!" She suddenly exclaimed, turning from the path to go to the bed of rosebushes, which were covered with straw to shield them from the perishing winter frosts.

"What's wrong?" Amanda followed her.

"I do believe the cold has destroyed that lovely Christmas rose that's lasted through so many winters." Fiona drew off her glove and bent to touch the blackened leaves of the rosebush with gentle fingers.

"How on earth could you tell that from the path?" To Amanda, gardening was like a secret society to which she definitely did not belong. She certainly hadn't inherited any of her mother's gardening skills.

Fiona gave her a faint smile. "Intuition." With infinite tenderness, she replaced the straw around the rosebush, as if she were covering a sleeping child. "It was blooming on Christmas Eve. Remember, I showed you how its petals were all frosted?"

"I remember," Amanda said softly.

"We had a little sunshine that day and the frost was glistening on the crimson petals. It was so beautiful that I took a photograph of it. Now it's dead."

Amanda drew her mother's hand through her arm again. She seemed inordinately upset by the demise of one rosebush. "But the other rosebushes look all right, don't they?"

Her mother didn't seem to have heard her. Amanda could feel her shivering, her entire body vibrating involuntarily.

"Are you cold? Shall we go inside?"

"I hope it's not an omen," her mother said.

"The rosebush? Of course it's not an omen."

But again her mother didn't appear to be listening to her. "I must tell Morag about it. Ask her what she thinks."

"You do that." Amanda guided her away from the rose garden and through the arbor to the sheltering trees of the grotto. "Talking of Morag, I've been meaning to ask how on earth you managed to persuade Father to keep her on."

Her mother glanced sideways at her from beneath her eyelids, but said nothing.

"After that terrible fight over Vanessa, I never thought I'd see her at Strathferness again," Amanda said. "I couldn't believe it when I came home to find her still here."

"I told your father I couldn't do without her." Fiona's thin lips quirked into a small, almost impish smile. "I said that she was the only one who could nurse me through one of my bronchial attacks. And you know, I get those at least twice every winter."

"You shouldn't be living in this dreadful climate, especially in a damp, drafty castle. Can't you persuade Father to take you to somewhere warm in the winters?"

"My dear Amanda, can you imagine your father lying on a sandy beach in his three-piece Harris tweed suit?"

They both smiled at the thought.

"Then you should go away by yourself." Amanda halted and turned to her mother. "Tell you what, why don't you and Morag take a couple of weeks somewhere sunny and warm? Barbados or Bermuda? It would do you a world of good."

"It sounds lovely, but I don't like to think of your father being left on his own."

"But he wouldn't be on his own now, would he? He'd have Colin."

"I suppose he would." Fiona drew the fur collar of her coat closer about her neck. "The thought of sunshine on my face is bliss."

"Think about it. I'd be happy to make all the arrangements for you."

Her mother patted her on the arm. "Thank you, darling. You are a source of great consolation to me."

Her words swamped Amanda with guilt. She hated coming to Strathferness, yet it meant so much to her mother that she knew she should come home more frequently.

"I'm glad you still have Morag with you. That was very clever of you. I'm impressed."

"I merely told your father the truth, that was all. We came to a compromise. As long as your father didn't have to have any dealings with her, Morag could remain at Strathferness in her position as housekeeper. So I've taken on a great deal more of the running of the castle, the housekeeping side." Again that little smile. "I think Morag prefers it that way."

"I'm sure she does. I have the feeling that you do, too." Amanda glanced at her mother. "You're looking cold. Let's go in."

"Ah, we MacKinnons are good Highland stock. We're much hardier than we appear to be." Fiona touched Amanda's arm. "Before we go in, there is one thing I want to ask you. What happened to the young man you brought home with you last week?"

"Oliver? He was a disaster. I dumped him as soon as we got back to London." Amanda grimaced. "Actually I dumped him *before* we got back to London. You can imagine what a fun drive it was, with him sulking and me trapped in the car beside him for more than five hundred miles."

"I wish you could find someone special with whom to share your life."

"So do I, Mother darling, so do I," Amanda said lightly. "But I don't think I'm the kind who wants to settle down with one man. To be absolutely honest, I don't like men much at all."

"Do you prefer women? Sexually, I mean?"

The question astounded Amanda. It was so utterly unlike her mother to say such a thing. She collected her thoughts. "If you're asking me if I'm a lesbian, Mother, no, I'm not." She sighed. "Sometimes I wish I were, so that I could have a sense of belonging somewhere. It's just that I don't like men very much. At least, not the men I have known."

"You must be patient and, perhaps, not quite so particular. No one is perfect."

"I'm not looking for perfection," Amanda said in a dry tone. "But I'd rather be alone than desperately unhappy because of a man's rotten behavior."

"I think there's someone special in the world for everyone. It's just a matter of finding him—or her."

"What a ridiculously romantic notion!" Amanda's voice was raw. "How in God's name can you, of all people, say that?"

"Because I believe it."

"You really think that Father was the man you were destined to be with?"

Her mother's pale blue eyes blinked rapidly. "It appears so, doesn't it? After all, I have been with him for almost forty years."

"Yours was more like an arranged marriage," Amanda said scornfully.

"Not entirely. I agree that it was our parents' wish that we marry. But your father had such energy, such verve and self-confidence. I found that very attractive. I was painfully shy and lived in the world of books and gardens. He was exciting. He brought the outside world to me. I was overwhelmed."

Amanda held her breath for a moment. Her mother had never before spoken of her relationship with her husband to her. Encouraged by this rare intimacy between them, she was about to bring up a forbidden topic when she heard Colin's voice calling her name.

"Amanda!"

"Yes?"

"Is Mother with you?"

"Yes."

"I've just had a call from Canada."

Amanda felt her mother's hand tighten on her arm. "Hang on, we're just coming in," she shouted back to Colin.

As they retraced their steps back to the front entrance of the castle, Amanda noticed how silent her mother had become. "It could be good news," she told her. Whatever constituted good news in this sorry matter, she thought to herself.

When they went indoors, the warmth in the library was extremely welcome after the raw chill outside. Her father was standing in front of the fire, but he quickly drew his wife's chair closer to the fire when they entered the room.

"You look absolutely frozen," he said to Fiona. "Come and sit by the fire and get warm. You shouldn't have kept your mother out so long," he told Amanda. "You know how frail she is."

"Sorry," was all she said.

"We enjoyed our walk." Fiona sat in her chair and held out her thin hands to the fire. She cast a smile at her daughter. "We so seldom have time to speak together."

Sir Robert cleared his throat. "I must prepare you for bad news, my dear. Colin has had a telephone call from Vancouver."

Fiona's hand went to her heart. Amanda could feel her own heart thumping as she waited for what was to come.

Colin stood in the center of the room, behind the large couch. "Roddy was hurt in an accident," he said.

"Oh no," Amanda said. "What kind of accident?"

"He was knocked down by a skateboarder or skater, something like that, in a park, and was taken by ambulance to a hospital."

"Oh my God," Amanda said. "Is he badly hurt?"

"Apparently not," her father said. "He's been released. But he was unconscious for quite a while."

"Oh, poor little Roddy."

Colin's hands turned to fists on the back of the sofa. "If I had that woman here now, I'd—"

Amanda interrupted him. "It's not Vanessa's fault. You can't blame her."

A flame leaped in Colin's eyes. "I do bloody blame her. She let this happen. She *caused* this to happen by kidnapping my son."

"For heaven's sake, Colin. It could have happened anywhere. Whatever you think of her, Vanessa adores Roddy. You know that. How did they find all this out?"

"I told you they'd discovered where she's staying in Vancouver, through following that bitch of a friend of hers, Jill whatsit. That was an inspired idea of mine, to put a watch on her."

Even now, with Roddy injured, he was gloating, Amanda thought disgustedly. "But how did they find out about Roddy's accident?"

"Roddy and . . ." Colin couldn't bear to speak Vanessa's name. "Apparently they hadn't left the apartment for days, but then yesterday they went out for the first time." He shrugged. "The PI followed them, not just in the park, but all the way to the hospital. This chap in Vancouver is reporting back to me regularly now."

"It didn't take long to trace them from Winnipeg, did it?"

"It pays to engage the best people for a job," her

father said. "I must say I was relieved to hear that the little chap isn't badly hurt. I expect you are, too, my dear," he added, looking at Fiona. She'd been surprisingly quiet since Colin had started telling them about Roddy's accident.

"Yes. I'm very glad." Her voice reminded Amanda of an automated message on an answering machine.

"Are you okay, Mother?" Amanda asked, concerned.

Fiona's hands gripped the arms on her chair. "Yes, thank you, dear. I'm fine. Just a little tired. And shaken by the news about Roddy, of course. What will happen now?" she asked Colin.

"There's good news, as well, thank God. The investigator's associate managed to take a photograph of Roddy as he was being lifted into the ambulance. He's going to send it to me on a special photo-imaging fax. Once I give a positive identification, we shall have definite proof that Roddy is in Vancouver. Then I can apply to the courts in British Columbia to have the Scottish court's ruling applied there."

"Now," said his father, beaming as if he were personally responsible, "isn't that good news?"

"I'll be bringing Roddy back to Britain in a few days," Colin added, his voice rising on a triumphant note.

His father's smile disappeared. "What do you mean you'll be *bringing* him home? You're not going anywhere."

"Now that we know where Roddy is, what's to stop me flying over and getting him?" Colin said, his tone belligerent.

"For one thing, you have a meeting tomorrow morning with our stillman, Donald Ross, and the brewer."

"Do you really think that the bloody distillery is going to take precedence over my son?"

"If you want to establish yourself as a responsible provider for that son, yes, I do."

Amanda recognized the acid tone in her father's voice. Watch out, Colin, she thought.

"And you have a meeting with Ewen McKay and the social worker on Wednesday."

"They can wait until I bring Roddy back."

"You'd better do as you've been advised or you may lose Roddy completely. Wait until the court in Vancouver has issued the court order. Then you can go and fetch him."

"I'll do as I goddamn please," Colin shouted. He was shaking with rage. "I'm not a child you can browbeat anymore, Father."

Fiona rose to her feet. She held out her hand to her son. "Please, Colin."

"Keep out of this, Mother," Colin roared at her. "Why don't you mind your own bloody business, the lot of you?"

His father advanced upon him. "How dare you speak to your mother in that way! Go to your room until you have regained control of yourself."

Colin laughed outright at this. "Go to my room? Go to my *room*," he repeated, still laughing. "Christ in heaven, Father, I'm nearly thirty-eight and you're still telling me to go to my room." He kept laughing while his mother stood, her face ghastly pale, staring at him. He moved forward, rounding the end of the sofa, to tower over his father.

Amanda darted across the room. "Come on, Colin, cool it." She grabbed his arm. "We're all so upset we don't know what we're saying." She could feel how tense he was, the arm muscles taut as a pulled bowstring beneath her hand.

Colin shook her off. Planting one hand in the middle of his father's chest, he shoved him so hard that he fell backward into his chair. Amanda's breath caught in her throat as she watched the blood rush into her father's face, turning it purple. She waited for the explosion.

From behind her came a long release of breath like a drawn-out sigh. She turned quickly, in time to see her mother crumple to the floor.

Chapter 21

Colin sat beside Amanda in the upstairs waiting room of the small private hospital in Inverness, an unopened copy of *House and Garden* in his hands. He felt a weight like a large slab of granite crushing him, sapping his strength, draining his energy, pressing so hard that his breathing was coming shallow and fast from high in his chest.

"Relax." Amanda put her hand on his arm. "I'm sure Ma's going to be fine."

Colin ignored her. Through the open door, he could see his father pacing up and down the corridor, up and down, unable to sit still. He blamed Colin for what had happened, of course. He'd actually said so. "If your mother dies," he'd said in a low voice when they'd watched her being wheeled on the stretcher into the hospital, "you will have killed her."

Colin couldn't think about that. Thinking about it only made him sink even deeper into the black sludge that threatened at all times to envelop him. If his mother died, there'd be no one left in the world who truly loved him.

No one but Roddy.

Dr. Jamieson, the cardiologist, looked into the room and then came in, followed by Sir Robert. Amanda went to them, but Colin remained near the window, maintaining as much distance as possible between himself and his father.

"Lady Craigmore has had a mild cardiac attack," Dr. Jamieson informed them. "I anticipate a full recovery, but you must think of this as a warning sign."

He turned to Sir Robert. "Has your wife been under some stress recently?"

Colin saw his father glance in his direction, his eyes like hard black pebbles. "Yes, she has," he replied. "Considerable stress."

"Then I must ask you and your family to do your utmost to remove any source of stress from her life while she is recuperating. She appears extremely anxious. It might help if I knew what the problem is."

Colin was about to tell Dr. Jamieson, but his father intervened. "A personal family problem," he said. "Nothing that we cannot deal with ourselves. We shall shield my wife from it, I promise you." Again he looked directly at Colin.

The doctor lifted his shoulders in a gesture of resignation. "Very well. I've ordered a sedative for her. Although she is not in any danger, she should remain here for a few days. That way we can monitor her progress once she has started on the heart medication I've prescribed for her. She has asked to see her son first."

"Me?" Colin was surprised.

"Yes, but no more than five minutes, please. She is tired and very weak." He frowned at Colin. "No stressful topics, please."

Colin nodded. He avoided looking at his father as he left the waiting room. At the far end of the narrow corridor was the room where his mother had been taken after she had been examined and treated in the emergency department. He waited outside the slightly open door for a moment and then pushed it open.

For a hospital room, the decor was surprisingly tasteful. Curtains and bedspread of a pale green cotton material, modern Scandinavian-style furniture of light wood. There was even a painting on the wall, a rather bland watercolor scene of Scottish hills. The steady beat of the heart monitor was the only sound.

His mother was lying in the narrow bed, her eyes closed. She looked so still and white that sudden fear made his breath catch in his throat. Then she stirred and opened her eyes.

"Colin?" she said, an upward inflection in her voice, as if she were surprised to see him there.

"Yes, Ma, it's me." He went forward, bending to kiss her forehead, which was cool and dry. He stood there at her bedside, feeling as awkward and tongue-tied as a gawky schoolboy.

"Sit down, dear." She tried to lift her head from the raised pillows. "I think there's a chair somewhere."

"I've got it," he said hurriedly. He carried the chair to her bedside and sat down. "How are you feeling? Are they looking after you properly?" He didn't know what else to say. Why in hell had she asked for him to come on his own? He'd have been much more comfortable had Amanda been there with him.

Her eyes closed again. Colin ran his tongue over dry lips. "You wanted to see me," he prompted.

She opened her eyes, trying to focus on his face. "I'm sorry, dear. The medicine they've given me makes me very sleepy."

"That's good," he said heartily. "You need lots of rest."

"It stops me from thinking too much."

A rush of guilt swept over him, but then he rallied himself. It wasn't his fault, was it? It was *hers*. Even in his thoughts he couldn't bear to speak his wife's name.

"Everything's going well, so you don't need to worry anymore," he told his mother.

One thin, brown-speckled hand grew agitated, clutching at the bedspread. Colin hesitated and then leaned over to cover it with his. "I want to see Morag," she said. "Can you arrange for her to see me? They told me only family members could visit, but I must see Morag." She blinked several times, pale eyelids covering pale blue eyes. "She's the only one who knows where all my things are," she explained.

"I'll make sure she gets in to see you."

"Today. It must be today." The hand trembled beneath his.

"Don't worry. I'll bring her here this evening, all right?"

"Thank you." Her hand slackened and then drew away from beneath his.

He looked at her other hand, attached by narrow tubing to the IV stand. He'd never seen his mother in a hospital room before. Although she'd always been frail in health, she usually took to her bed at home and had the faithful Dr. Strachan visit her there. They'd even had a private nurse living in for several weeks when she'd had a bad bout of pneumonia two years ago.

The only other time he could recall her being in a hospital was many years ago when she'd refused to eat and had lost almost twenty pounds in weight. He hadn't visited her then. She'd refused to see anybody, even her family.

Especially her family.

A shiver ran down Colin's spine. Hospitals terrified him. He hated the smells, the silences, the muted voices. He particularly loathed the atmosphere of enforced calm, imagining how chaotic it would be if everyone—patient and nurse and visitor—gave voice to the repressed fears they were all experiencing. It would be like the cacophony of hell.

His mother had fallen asleep again. He stood up, careful not to scrape back his chair.

Her eyes flew open. "I'm just dozing. Did I tell you everything?"

He forced a smile. "I don't know. You told me about Morag. Was there anything else?" He wished he'd been able to slip out before she woke again.

"Yes, there was." The left hand grew restless again, as if it had a life of its own. "Don't go to Canada, Colin."

He froze. "No need to talk about that now."

"Yes, there is," she insisted, her voice rising. "We must talk about it." The monitor on the wall reflected her agitation. "I don't want you to hurt Vanessa."

"Don't be ridiculous, Mother," he said, his voice contemptuous.

"If you go to Canada, Vanessa might run from you, and we shall never see Roddy again."

"Stop worrying about things like that, Mother. We've got it all in hand. Trust me."

"Listen to your father and Ewen. Stay here. Please."

His face hardened. "I think I know best how to deal with matters concerning my son's welfare."

The monitor's beeps increased. The door opened.

"Now, now, what's going on in here?" said a broad Scots voice. The stout nurse advanced to the bed, her blue skirt rustling as if it were stiffly starched. "Are you upsetting your mother?" she demanded, reminding Colin of one particularly intimidating, red-cheeked nanny he'd had.

"Promise me you'll stay in Scotland," his mother said, as the nurse bent over her.

"Now, that's enough talking, Lady Craigmore," the nurse said sternly, taking her hand to check her pulse. "You'd best be going," she told Colin over her shoulder.

"Not until you've promised me." His mother's voice rose in volume and intensity. Colin had never seen her quite so perturbed.

"Whatever it is your mother is asking," the nurse said, "you'd best give her your promise or she'll have another heart attack, and you don't want that on your conscience, do you?"

Colin directed a look of loathing at the nurse, but she'd already turned back to see to his mother. "I promise I'll stay in Scotland for now," he told his mother in a soothing tone. "So there's no need to worry any more about it, is there?"

He went around to the other side of the bed. His mother's eyes stared up at him, as if she were hoping to read the promise there, emblazoned in his eyes. He did not kiss her this time, but pressed her hand. "Rest now. No more worrying about matters that needn't concern you."

He drew his hand away. Behind his back, his left hand remained in the instinctive position of childhood, index and second fingers crossed.

Chapter 22

On the day after Roddy's accident, a large arrangement of flowers was delivered to the apartment in the afternoon, accompanied by a box wrapped in Superman paper with a label addressed to Rick Nelson. It was Jill who opened the door to the doorman, whose face was almost hidden by the flowers.

"Delivery for you, Ms. Nelson," he said.

Jill took them from him. "Thanks, Bill. Hang on a moment." She gave him a two-dollar tip and shut the door.

Vanessa came out of Roddy's room. "Who was that?" she began to ask, and then saw the flowers that Jill had set down on the table. A shiver ran down her spine. "Where did they come from?"

"Relax! They're probably from your Sir Galahad. Who else knows you're here? Look at the card."

Vanessa found the small card and ripped it open. "You're right," she said, with a sigh of relief. She read the message on the card aloud. "For Rick's mother. Hope you both recover quickly. Grant."

"Very nice," Jill said dryly, "but I still think you shouldn't have let him bring you back here."

"I didn't have a choice. For heaven's sake, I have to be able to trust *someone*, don't I?"

"I told you before, it could have been a setup. First the accident, and then the gallant knight coming to your aid."

"Colin wouldn't arrange for someone to hurt Roddy deliberately," Vanessa protested.

"Oh yeah? The Colin you've been telling me about

would do anything to get his son back. Besides, it could have been a setup that didn't work out the way it was planned. The accident was supposed to be a minor collision, but the Rollerblade guy mistimed it."

"Grant Kendall wasn't responsible for Roddy's accident. He *couldn't* have been. He was far too kind to Roddy. If you met him you'd feel the same way."

"Maybe I should meet him." Jill took the card from her.

"Well, you can't, can you? I've no idea where he's staying."

"It just so happens he's written another message on the other side of the card." Jill handed it back to her.

I'd like to know how Rick's doing, the message read. *I'm staying at the Bayshore.* Grant had written down the number of the hotel and his room.

The message gave Vanessa a feeling of assurance. "See?" she said. "He must be okay. He wouldn't tell me where he was staying if he wasn't. And that must be his real name."

"Anyone can use a fictitious name. After all, that's what you're doing, isn't it?"

Vanessa bit her lip. She desperately wanted Grant Kendall to be above suspicion. The memory of his kindness to her and, in particular, to Roddy, had lingered all through the previous night, so that her first thought upon wakening had been of him.

"He must be pretty dishy, this Mr. Kendall," Jill teased.

"It's nothing to do with his looks," Vanessa retorted. "Do you really think I'd be concerned about how someone looked at a time like this?"

Jill grinned. "You're not dead, girl. You can still be attracted to someone."

"Oh for heaven's sake."

What was building into one of their arguments was saved by Roddy running into the room. "The movie's finished. Can we go out?"

"Not today."

"I'm tired of watching television," Roddy moaned.

"The doctor said you must rest for a couple of days."

Roddy threw himself on the couch. Then he caught sight of the box and sat up. "What's that?"

"It's for you."

"For me? Wow! Where did it come from?"

"Mr. Kendall sent it. He sent these flowers as well. Aren't they beautiful?"

Roddy wasn't interested in flowers. He was already ripping off the paper from the box. "Hey! It's a Game Boy game." He started pushing buttons and the hand-held game emitted a high-pitched sound.

"That'll drive you crazy," Jill said beneath her breath.

"Anything that will keep him happy is fine with me," Vanessa said. "Have you got the instructions?" she asked Roddy, sitting beside him to look at the game.

"Yes, they're here." He thrust the booklet at her. "But I don't need them. I know how to work it."

"That's good, because I wouldn't have a clue. Wasn't that kind of Mr. Kendall?"

"Yes, it was." Roddy's head was still bent over the game. "Shall I phone him to thank him?"

Vanessa hesitated. Her eyes met Jill's over Roddy's head. "Yes, I think you should," she said firmly. "And I want to thank him for the flowers. Let's do it now before we forget."

Jill gave a small shrug, which Vanessa countered by saying. "We'll invite him over. That way you can meet him."

"Good idea. Whoever he is, there's not much point in hiding from him now that he knows where you are, is there? Besides, I'd like to get a good look at this mysterious Mr. Kendall of yours."

Vanessa made a face at Jill as she picked up the receiver and pressed in the number of the Bayshore Hotel. When she asked for Grant's room, the telephone rang twice and then she heard his voice. In-

stinctively, she turned her face away from Jill as she
spoke to him.

"It's Mrs. Nelson," she told Grant. "We're calling
to thank you for the lovely flowers and . . . my son's
gift."

"My pleasure," Grant said. "How's he feeling
today?"

"Much better. Bored, in fact. A good sign. I'll put
him on."

Roddy thanked Grant and then became engaged in
a conversation with him, answering questions that
Vanessa couldn't hear, until she became impatient and
whispered at Roddy to give her back the phone.

"Sorry about that," she said to Grant. "He can be
quite a chatterbox when he gets going."

"It's good to know he's okay. How about you?"

"I'm fine." Vanessa paused for a moment and then
said, "Roddy has to stay in today. Doctor's orders.
How would you like to come over and see for yourself
how well he's doing? I mean . . . if you have the time."

"Sunday's always a dead day for doing business. I'd
be happy to come over."

"You know where we are. I'll tell the doorman to
let you in."

"Great. See you in about half an hour."

As Vanessa put the receiver down she felt a sudden
rush of anxiety wash over her. What if her intuition
about Grant was all wrong? What if he was working
for Colin? Once inside the apartment, he could take
Roddy from them by force, especially if he had a gun.

"Now what?" Jill asked, seeing something was
wrong.

Vanessa shook her head, glancing meaningfully at
Roddy.

"I'll go speak to Bill," Jill told her. "And I'll ask
him to come and check on us half an hour after Mr.
Kendall arrives, just in case."

"Thanks, Jill." Their old ESP was still working.

"Just in case of what?" Roddy asked, lifting his
head from the game.

Jill rolled her eyes. "Old radar ears. In case we need anything," she told Roddy. "Bill's good for sending out for bagels or Chinese food . . . things like that."

"Who's Bill?"

"The doorman, noodlehead."

Roddy giggled at this. He bent his head over the game again, but as soon as Jill went out, he turned to his mother. "When I heard a man at the door I thought it might be Daddy." His eyes looked huge in his pale face.

Vanessa suddenly felt very cold. Roddy hadn't mentioned his father for quite a while. "Did you?" she said, lightening her voice.

"I thought he'd found us. That's why I waited in my room, to see if he was angry or not."

Vanessa put out a hand to brush Roddy's hair back from his forehead, her heart turning over at the sight of the dressing and the shaved section at the back of his head. "Daddy doesn't know where we are," she assured him. "He's too far away in Scotland to be able to find out."

"But he could easily fly here, couldn't he?" Roddy insisted. "Just like we did."

"Yes, he could, but he still wouldn't know where we are."

"It's not that I don't ever want to see Daddy again," Roddy explained, turning back to the game. "I just want to know when he's coming, so that I can be ready."

"You don't want him arriving unexpectedly."

"That's right."

"No need to worry about that. He'll be sure to call us before he comes."

"How can he call when he doesn't know where we are?"

"I meant he'd call Gran and Grampa in Winnipeg first and then they'd call us to let us know he was wanting to speak to us." Vanessa was improvising, trying to reassure Roddy, to rid him of the fear that his father was about to jump out at him from some dark corner at any moment.

The fact that she was suffering from the same fear did not help.

Grant Kendall arrived at an opportune moment. Roddy had come to a halt with his game and couldn't find out how to go on with it. Jill and Vanessa were trying to read the instructions, but all three of them had come to an impasse when Bill called up to them.

"Mr. Kendall's here," he told Jill over the intercom.

"Send him up."

"I've got stuck with the game," was Roddy's greeting when Grant appeared at their door a few minutes later.

"Have you? We'll have to see what we can do. Hello again," Grant said to Vanessa.

She'd remembered the blue eyes, but had forgotten about the warmth of his smile and the way it warmed those eyes. She returned the smile and then ushered him into the living room. "This is my dearest friend, Jill Nelson . . ." She paused in sudden confusion. Dear God, they'd forgotten to work out the names.

"Another Jill Nelson?" Grant said, amusement lurking in his eyes.

Jill was no help. She threw back her head and laughed like a hyena.

"Thanks a lot," Vanessa told her. "Great friend you are." She turned back to Grant, her face flushed with embarrassment. "I'm sorry. I think I'm going to have to explain."

Grant held up both hands. "No need. I can always call you Jill One and Jill Two."

"We're running away from my father." Roddy's sudden announcement came out of the blue, effectively putting an end to the conversation for several seconds.

Grant's black eyelashes blinked rapidly for a moment and then he unzipped his jacket. "I should hang

this up before it drips water all over your floor," he
said.

"Give it to me." Jill took it from him. "I'll hang it
in the bathroom." She frowned at Vanessa and then
went into the hall.

"Would you like some coffee?" Vanessa asked
Grant, to fill the awkward silence.

"Love some. It's not only wet out there, it's also
extremely cold. I'd forgotten how miserable Vancouver can be at this time of year. Seattle's even worse.
Nonstop rain."

They were into that safest and most universal of
topics, the weather. "It's so changeable," Vanessa
said. "Look how lovely it was yesterday."

"It was. More like a day in northern California."

Vanessa smiled. "Of course. I'd forgotten that's
where you live. No wonder you're feeling the cold.
The weather was good yesterday, but the rest of it
was dreadful." She looked directly at Grant. "I can't
thank you enough for all you did for us. I should be
the one sending the presents, not you."

"Not at all." He made a gesture at the sofa. "May
I?"

"Of course."

Grant sat down next to Roddy, who was kneeling
at the table, trying to get his game going again. "Let's
take a look at this," he said.

Jill came back into the room. "How about that
coffee?"

"I was just about to make it," Vanessa said.

"I'll do it. Got anything to eat with it?"

"There's some of that apple pie left . . . and oat-
meal cookies."

The two male heads were bent over the game, one
golden and bandaged, the other dark, almost black.
"Got it!" Grant said suddenly, and Roddy cheered.
Vanessa felt a glow of warmth as Grant patiently explained to Roddy what he had done to get the game
working again. She also noticed how Roddy leaned
comfortably against Grant's arm.

Grant suddenly looked up and caught her watching them. Vanessa felt her face grow warm. "You're very patient," she told him. "My son asks a lot of questions."

"That's the best way to learn."

She couldn't help thinking about the contrast between this man's patience with Roddy and Colin's impatience. Impulsively, she held out her hand. "I'd like to introduce myself again. Properly, this time. My name's Vanessa Marston."

His eyes widened perceptibly before he took her hand in his. "So your friend must be Jill Nelson?"

"That's right." Realizing that he was still holding her hand, she drew it away. "There's really not much point in continuing with this subterfuge."

"Not when you can't think up a second name, there isn't." His mouth quirked into a smile.

"I can't believe I could have been so stupid."

"You're obviously not used to aliases."

"You can say that again," Jill said, coming back into the room. "She's bloody useless. Never could keep a secret. You could always tell by her face. It went bright crimson if she was telling the smallest little lie."

Grant looked from one to the other of them. "I get the feeling you two have been friends a long time. In fact, you look like sisters."

"We've known each other since Grade Three," Jill said.

"Lucky you. A good friend is a treasure beyond price." He held out his hand. "Hi, Mrs. Nelson."

"It's Ms. Nelson . . . and Jill will do fine." She stood before him in her brilliant lime-green sweater and tight black leather pants, hands on her narrow hips. "Van tells me you have a winery in California, Mr. Kendall. Exactly where is it?"

"In the Napa Valley. Near Yountville, to be precise."

"How long have you lived there?"

"About four years."

"That coffee should be ready now," Vanessa said,

trying to stop Jill from asking any more personal questions, but Jill wasn't so easily distracted.

"Do you run the winery by yourself?"

"I have a partner."

"And you just happened to be in Vancouver this week."

"I come up here a couple of times a year. Our wines sell well in Canada."

"We have our own wines here, too," Jill said, a challenge in her voice. Jill had always been aggressively supportive of all things Canadian.

"Yes, well . . . we won't go into that," he said with a grin. He quickly changed the subject, turning to Vanessa. "Do you live in Vancouver, Mrs. Marston?"

"No. I'm . . . visiting Jill."

"But Mummy's Canadian," Roddy told him. "So am I."

"So you told me before. I'd never have guessed it from your accent," Grant said.

"I'm half Canadian, half Scots," Roddy said proudly.

"Okay, Roddy." Vanessa gave him a little frown. She had the feeling that he'd be spilling out his whole history and the fact that he was Roderick Angus MacKinnon Craigmore, the next heir after his father to the baronetcy and estate of Strathferness. Grant seemed to have that effect on people.

"Sorry, Mr. Kendall, but I think, in the circumstances, that it's best if we don't talk too much about ourselves."

"Quite right. I didn't mean to pry."

"You didn't have to," Jill said. "Between the pair of them, Van and Roddy have given most of it away."

"Well, not that much." He grinned. "At least I do know that Rick Nelson is actually Roddy Marston."

"Oops!" Vanessa covered her hand with her mouth. Grant's eyes met hers. "No wonder they couldn't find your son in the medical record," he said, unable to contain his laughter.

"I'm not Roddy Marston!" Roddy shouted. "I'm—"

"That's enough, young Roddy." This time it was Jill who interrupted him, bodily picking him up. "If you don't shut up I'm going to toss you over the balcony." She walked toward the sliding glass doors.

"Jill!" Vanessa protested.

"Don't be such an idiot. Roddy knows I don't mean it, don't you?"

But the color had drained from Roddy's face. Sensing his tension, Jill set him down and put her arms around his suddenly shaking body. "I wouldn't hurt you for the world, honey." Her troubled eyes sought Vanessa's. *I'm sorry,* she mouthed apologetically over Roddy's head.

"Once, when I was being bad, Daddy told me he'd throw me from the top of the peel tower at Strathferness. He picked me up and held me over the rampart wall."

Roddy's barely audible words struck like a dagger of ice at Vanessa's heart.

It was Grant who spoke first. "Dads say the worst things, don't they?" he said lightly. "And they play stupid games that scare us."

Vanessa held her breath as she watched the color seep back into Roddy's face.

"Did your dad do things like that to you?" Roddy asked.

"Sometimes. But here I am all grown up, so you can see that nothing happened to me."

"And you're probably bigger than your dad now, too."

"That's right."

"So he couldn't scare you, could he?"

"I think I'd be more likely to scare him now."

Grant's smile was immensely reassuring. It even made Vanessa feel better, although this new revelation from Roddy about Colin had appalled her. What other dreadful things had he done that Roddy had bottled up and not told her about?

"Have you got any other games?" Grant was asking Roddy.

"Yes, want to see?"

"Sure. Let's have a look."

"I'll get them." Roddy ran from the room.

Grant didn't waste any time. As soon as Roddy had gone he turned to Vanessa, his expression deadly serious. "It sounds to me as if you could do with some help."

Chapter 23

Vanessa was totally taken aback by Grant's cool statement. She had time only to exchange glances with Jill when Roddy came back into the living room with the games she'd managed to stuff into the bag she'd packed for him in Edinburgh.

"I've only got three," Roddy told Grant, and set them out before him on the glass-topped coffee table.

Vanessa hesitated for a moment. "Where did you park your car?" she asked Grant.

"In the visitors' parking lot," he replied. "Why?"

"Jill, would you mind waiting with Roddy for me? I want to speak to Mr. Kendall for a few minutes." Jill opened her mouth to protest. "Alone," Vanessa added pointedly.

"Is that wise?" Jill asked bluntly.

Vanessa glanced at Grant. "I think so," she said in a low voice.

Grant stood up.

"You're not going yet, are you?" Roddy said, dismayed. "You only just got here."

"Your mother wants to speak to me for a few minutes. We'll just be in the parking lot. I'll be back," Grant assured him. "I still haven't had that coffee I keep getting promised."

"Oh, I am sorry," Vanessa said. She swept her hair back from her face with one hand. "I'm afraid I'm not quite with it at the moment."

"So I gathered. You'll need a raincoat. It's still pouring down out there. And I'll need my jacket."

"I'll get it." Roddy was already gone.

"He really likes you," Vanessa told Grant.

"The feeling's mutual. He's a great kid."

Despite his warm words, there was something strange about the way Grant spoke of Roddy and a new severity about his mouth that disturbed Vanessa.

Grant pulled on the jacket Roddy had fetched for him.

"You will be coming back, won't you?" Roddy asked.

"I promised you, I would, didn't I? I don't break promises."

"Okay."

Roddy returned to his games, but Vanessa could see that Jill was not so easily reassured. "Stop worrying. I'm doing the right thing, I know it," she whispered as Grant went out into the hall.

"I sure hope so," Jill muttered. "You haven't changed a bit, have you? You always were too bloody impulsive."

"Roddy's already spilled the beans about his father, so what's the point? I might as well see what he has to suggest."

Glancing at Roddy, Jill drew her into the kitchen. "And what happens if Mr. Kendall just takes off with you in the car?" she demanded in a low voice.

"Why should he?" Vanessa whispered back.

"If he's working for Colin he could offer you in exchange for Roddy, couldn't he?"

"You've been watching too many lurid action movies."

"Have I? You always were naive, my dear old friend. There are people here in Vancouver that I could hire to rub someone out, no questions asked. It's been done before. And Colin's family has a lot of money."

Vanessa stared at her. "Surely you're not suggesting Grant's a hired gun."

"I'm not suggesting anything. Just telling you not to be so trusting, that's all."

"Okay, I'll be careful, but I still want to talk to him."

"Then do it here," Jill said, "not in a stranger's car."

"I don't want Roddy to hear us talking about him."

Jill shrugged. "It's your life."

Vanessa felt annoyed and disturbed by Jill's attitude, but this wasn't the time for an argument. She went into the living room. "We'll be back in a few minutes," she told Roddy, trying to keep her tone light and positive.

Damn Jill and her warnings, she thought as she went out into the hall to join Grant. She felt really spooked as they walked down the corridor to the elevator. When his arm pressed against hers as he leaned across her to push the basement button, she almost jumped out of her skin.

"Basement? I thought your car was in the visitors' parking lot."

"There's an exit from the basement that brings us out near to where I'm parked. Saves us getting too wet."

His explanation didn't ease her tension. She stood close to the panel, poised to push the emergency button if he made a sudden move. Thanks a lot, Jill, old pal! she said to herself.

The underground parking lot was well lit, but Vanessa was so tense she imagined shadowy figures ready to jump out at her from behind every car. Heart racing, she walked on taut legs down the center of the lane, making for the exit as fast as she could.

Grant Kendall walked a little behind her, saying nothing. As they crossed the parking lot, their footsteps sounded abnormally loud and she could hear her own hurried breathing resonate in her ears.

When she reached the exit door, Grant caught up with her and pushed it open, leading the way up the dimly lit stone stairway. When he opened the outside door, a wave of relief washed over Vanessa. She drew in a deep breath and slowly released it, feeling like a diver who'd at last reached the surface.

There were two rows of cars parked in the visitors' section. As they stepped into the open, the rain spilling down on them, her eyes caught a movement in the front seat of a car parked close by. Through the car's rain-streaked window, she was able to catch a glimpse of a large beak nose and high forehead, before the man's head was hidden by the pages of a newspaper.

She clutched Grant's arm. "I recognize the man sitting in that car," she hissed.

"Which one?"

"The red one. It looks like a Honda."

Grant turned as if he were about to walk over to the car. Vanessa's hand tightened on his arm. "Be careful," she said. "I don't want you to get hurt."

Without any warning, the car suddenly swung out of its parking spot and, with a screech of tires, raced past them, so close that they both had to spring back to avoid being hit. Vanessa crashed against the concrete wall and felt herself falling, but Grant grabbed her and dragged her against him.

As they stood there, his arms tight around her, hearts thudding in unison, she was acutely aware of the pressure of his body against hers and the warmth of his hurried breathing against her neck. Grant wasn't a large man, like Colin, but he was undeniably strong. His quick responses and the muscular tension of his thighs and shoulders told her that this was a man who used his body in work and play, as well as his mind.

He relaxed his hold a little, but did not release her. She looked up into his face and found that it was so close to hers that everything, apart from the warm brilliance of his eyes, was blurred. For a long moment her body remained pressed against his. Then she felt the chill of the rain on her face and more coldness as he moved away from her.

He took her hand. "Let's get into the car before we both drown."

Once inside the car, Vanessa began to shiver convulsively and her elbow was aching from having been slammed against the wall. "I'm s-sorry," she said through chattering teeth. "This is so stupid."

"It's just shock. I don't think he intended to run us down. He was trying to get the hell out before you saw him. What maddens me is that I couldn't read his license plate in this rain."

"It was a British Columbia plate, I'm sure of that."

"That's not much help, I'm afraid."

"I know." Still shivering, Vanessa stared down at her hands clutched in her lap. She looked up when Grant leaned across to wipe her wet face with some tissues he'd taken from the box behind him. "I must look a mess," she said, trying to smile.

He handed her the box of tissues. "A very nice mess." His gaze fixed on hers. "Tell me where you'd seen that man before."

"He was in the crowd standing around Roddy in the park yesterday. He had a baseball cap pulled down over his forehead, but nothing could disguise that large nose. I can remember thinking that it looked like the beak of the carved eagles on one of the totem poles. Strange how the mind works, isn't it?"

"Have you seen him at any other time?"

"I don't think so. But then yesterday was the first time I'd been out since I arrived in Vancouver." Another involuntary shudder passed over her. "He could have been hanging around here ever since I first arrived."

Grant pushed his seat back and sat sideways, facing her, his arm along the back of her seat. "Would you like to tell me what's really going on? No need to give me any details, of course."

"There's not much to tell, really." She crumpled the tissues she was holding into a tight ball. "We live in Scotland. I decided to divorce my husband. Because I needed time to work things out I said I wanted to visit my parents in Canada. He—my husband—applied for temporary custody in Scotland. And he got it."

She lifted her eyes to his. "I don't want him to get Roddy."

"I gather—" Grant cleared his throat. "From what Roddy said, I take it that he's afraid of his father."

For a brief moment Vanessa closed her eyes. "He's not the only one," she murmured. "I'm afraid my husband has taken this all very badly."

"You think you're being watched?"

"I don't know what to think anymore. It's got so that I imagine everyone's my enemy or out to kidnap Roddy. I'm not usually paranoid, but I feel I can't really trust anyone."

"Even me."

"Even you," Vanessa admitted. "My instincts tell me I should, but Jill tells me I shouldn't trust anyone." She gave him a faint smile. "I tend to do things on impulse. It's got me into trouble in the past. But this is the worst ever."

"You left your husband on impulse?"

Vanessa thought about that. "I hadn't actually planned to do it over the Christmas holiday," she said eventually. "Things just . . . sort of came to a head. I knew that I must leave him, right away." Her fingers traced the bright Christmas flowers on the tissue box. "I tried very hard to make our marriage work, for Roddy's sake. But then I realized that things were getting worse and that Roddy could be in actual danger."

"From his father, you mean?"

Vanessa nodded, her gaze sliding past his. "And his father's family."

"Was there no one in the family who took your side against your husband?"

"Not really. Not even his mother. She's a dear and I know she really cares about me, but she's far too terrified of her husband to think of going against his wishes. And although my sister-in-law has a strong personality, she's intensely loyal to the family. When it comes to outsiders, the family closes ranks and stands as one against anybody who's a threat. That means me now, of course," Vanessa said with a bitter smile. "I know it sounds weird, almost Victorian, but they're all, in their own way, under my father-in-law's thumb. He's extremely powerful." Her shoulders moved in a little shrug. "It's a very patriarchal family."

Grant's dark eyebrows rose and he gave a harsh laugh. "It sounds like the family from hell."

Vanessa resented his laughter. His response was entirely unexpected. Until now, he'd seemed so understanding and sympathetic. She sat up straight, moving back, severing the close contact between them. "My father-in-law is immensely wealthy as well. Money would be no object in getting his grandson back." She spoke more quickly now, wanting to put an end to this discussion of her life with a complete stranger. "If the law doesn't do it for him, he wouldn't hesitate to use other means."

"But the law so far is on your husband's side, isn't it? I understood you to say that he'd been granted custody by the Scottish court."

"Yes, but I'm here in Canada, with Roddy," Vanessa said with spirit. "I had hoped to hide out with Jill in Vancouver, but Roddy's accident put an end to that." She turned to grasp the door handle. "Thank you for listening, Mr. Kendall. You've been very kind to Roddy. I'd better get back or Jill will be worrying about me."

"She trusts me even less than you do."

Vanessa turned back to him, but her hand remained on the handle, ready to open the door. "Jill's a savvy businesswoman. She's learned not to trust anyone until she's absolutely sure about them. It's time I did the same."

He was half in shadow, his face lacking expression as he observed her. "I thought you were beginning to trust me. What changed your mind so suddenly?"

"Nothing at all," Vanessa said with a wry smile. "I have a bad habit of—of doing things that are inappro-

priate, that's all, like trusting total strangers and telling
them too much about myself."

"Open the door."

"What?"

"I said, open the car door."

Vanessa bit her lip. "Why?"

"Because you're obviously afraid that I'm suddenly
going to drive off with you. Open the door."

She stared at him, loosening her hold on the door
handle. He lunged across her, the sudden movement
startling her, and opened her door, pushing it so that
it swung open several inches.

Heart pounding, she sat very still beside him, not
making a move. She could hear his hurried breathing
and in the enclosed space inhaled the faint spicy fragrance of cologne he used.

"That's very impressive," she said at last. "But I
don't think I'd get very far if I tried to get away. You
could easily run me down with the car or drag me
back into it."

"I think it's time you learned to trust those bloody
instincts of yours." He was getting angry, the pleasant
facade slipping a little.

"I've learned not to from bitter experience."

"You can't always be wrong." His hand grabbed
her shoulder. This time she didn't flinch, but stared
straight back at him. "All I ask is that you listen to
what I have to say. Then you can go. I give you my
word that I won't try to detain you in any way."

She gazed into his eyes, trying to read the truth
from his expression, but in the semidarkness the bright
eyes were dimmed and all she could see was the shadows of the windswept trees beyond the parking lot
passing across his face.

"Will you at least listen to what I have to say?" he
asked, releasing his hold on her shoulder.

The wind was blowing in through the open door,
chilling her back. She pulled the door closed again.
"All right, I'm listening."

"First tell me this. Why didn't you stay in Scotland

and ask the Scottish court to give you custody of your son?"

"I had strong reasons not to do so." Vanessa stirred impatiently. "I can't tell you them without identifying my husband's family. Also the fact that the Scottish court has already given him temporary custody is an indication of the way they'd go."

"That's probably because you ran off with Roddy. The court wouldn't approve of that."

Neither did Mr. Grant Kendall, from the tone of his voice. "My husband has also applied to the courts in Winnipeg, Manitoba, where my parents live."

"That's where you went when you arrived in Canada?"

"Yes. My father found that out from a friend who's a lawyer there. That's why I knew I had to hide with Jill."

"But you now suspect that you've been followed to Vancouver. Which means that, if he can obtain proof that Roddy is definitely here—like a photograph, for instance—your husband can apply to the courts in British Columbia to get his son back."

Vanessa clenched her hands together. "I'm afraid so. I'd originally intended to hide out for a while and then contact Col—my husband—to negotiate an agreement. But now I'm convinced that I can't risk him getting his hands on Roddy again."

"Do you think he would physically harm his son?" Grant asked.

"I used not to think so, but now I'm afraid of what he'll do. Lately, his control seems to have been slipping more and more. You heard what Roddy said his father had done to him."

"You mean that thing about holding him out over the castle ramparts?"

"Yes," Vanessa whispered. "Now I'm wondering how many more awful things he did that Roddy hasn't told me about. I'm terrified that he'll not only have us followed, but also that he'll come and get us himself. I know that Roddy's afraid of that, as well."

Grant sat motionless in the darkened car, the only sound his measured breathing. Then he spoke. "You must get away from here as soon as possible. I can help you, but you'll have to believe that I'm on your side."

Vanessa hesitated.

"Do you trust me?" Grant demanded. "Or do you think I'm one of your husband's hired investigators?"

"I'm not sure. There's something about you that bothers me. I can't put my finger on it." She looked directly into his face, disturbed by the strong pull of attraction she'd been trying to resist ever since they'd first met. "Yet I can't help thinking about how kind you were to Roddy, and me, in the park. I really do want to trust you."

"Hold on to that thought." Grant leaned forward, his entire body emanating an intensity, like a magnet she couldn't resist. "Let me take you and Roddy back to California with me. Even if your husband's investigators follow you there, you'll be safe. I won't allow any harm to come to you or to your son."

She so desperately wanted to trust him, and his words were spoken with such powerful sincerity and compassion that they left little room for disbelief.

Grant leaned closer, his arm stretched along the back of her seat. "I give you my solemn word that Roddy and you will be safe with me." His words were seductive, his breath warm on her cheek. "Will you trust me enough to come to California with me?"

His assurances were like a cozy, down-filled quilt. A blizzard could be raging outside, but with Grant Kendall she felt that she would, indeed, be safe.

"Yes," she said. "I will. Thank you for your kindness." With a little sigh, she turned her cheek against his hand. It was a spontaneous movement and felt so right.

She felt the palm of his hand move down her face. His fingertips brushed against her jawline, sliding to the nape of her neck to lift her hair, sending delicious little shivers down her spine. She wanted more, but abruptly he pulled his arm away from her and opened his door.

"Let's go and tell Roddy." Grant got out of the car and came around to the passenger side to wait for her, but he didn't touch her again.

"And Jill," Vanessa said with a grimace.

Chapter 24

When Vanessa had finished telling Jill about Grant's offer, Jill didn't even try to be civil to Grant. "I want to speak to Vanessa alone," she told him in an icy tone.

"Certainly." His lean face showed almost no reaction to Jill's rudeness, but Vanessa caught the sudden tension around his mouth. "I have to go back to the hotel to make some calls." He moved toward the hall. "Where's Roddy?"

"Why?" asked Jill.

"I'd like to say good-bye to him before I go."

"That's not necessary. He's busy watching TV in the den."

"I promised him I'd come back." Grant's face registered no emotion, but Vanessa now had the impression of smoldering anger beneath the surface.

"For heaven's sake, Jill, stop being such a pain." She went to the doorway to call out to Roddy. "Roddy! Mr. Kendall has to go. Come and say good-bye to him."

Roddy came running from the den. "But you said you'd come back and play more games," he complained.

"Sorry, Roddy. I have to get back to work. Another time." Grant squeezed his shoulder. "I promise, okay?"

"Okay."

"What were you watching?"

"A film. *Honey, We Shrunk Ourselves*. It's really funny."

"Have you come to the Hot Wheels bit yet?" Grant asked.

"No."

"Then you'd better go back and watch it or you might miss it. That's the best part."

"Okay." Roddy dashed back to the den.

Vanessa gave Grant a quizzical look. "How do you know so much about children's movies?" Then, realizing that she was being as nosy as Jill, she hurriedly added, "Sorry, I didn't mean to—"

"That's okay. My partner has a couple of kids." He changed the subject abruptly. "Call me later, would you? Let me know your decision."

"Do you want our number here?"

"No, he doesn't," Jill said, before Vanessa could give it to him.

"Your friend's right," Grant said with a rueful smile. "You shouldn't give that number out to anyone, not even me."

Vanessa shook her head. "No wonder I'm so paranoid, with all of you giving me these dire warnings."

"Fat lot of good it does," Jill said, "considering how you ignore them." A buzzing sound came from her briefcase. "Excuse me, that's my cell phone," she said, pointedly looking at Grant. "I must answer it. I'm expecting a call from Hong Kong."

Grant got the message. He walked out into the hall and Vanessa followed him. "Sorry about Jill. She's not the most tactful person in the world, I'm afraid."

"Don't apologize. She cares about you. That's what matters." Grant moved a little way down the hall passage. " 'Bye, Roddy," he shouted. "See you again soon."

Roddy ran out again. " 'Bye. See you. Thank you for the game."

"You're welcome."

"Wait till my friends at home see it! They'll be pea-green with envy. 'Bye." Roddy disappeared back into the den and turned the television sound up even louder.

"He's obviously enjoying the movie," Vanessa said, with a smile. "Thank you for the game . . . and for everything." She stood there, searching for the right words, wanting to say more, to keep Grant here for just a few more minutes.

"My pleasure." He, too, seemed unsure of what to say next. Which was unlike him. Vanessa had never before met a man who was so calmly self-assured, without being obnoxious with it.

He took one step toward her. For one breathless, suspended moment, Vanessa thought that he was going to bend his head and kiss her. She wasn't sure how she would respond if he did. But, of course, it was all in her imagination.

"About California," Grant said briskly as he moved to the door, "discuss it with your friend. Then call me early this evening so that I can make plans."

"What's the time now? I've lost all track of time this afternoon."

"It's ten after four."

"I'll call you around seven o'clock. Will that be okay? That will give me plenty of time to talk it over with Jill and my parents."

He frowned. "Seven o'clock's fine. But I'm not sure you should tell your parents. If your husband goes to Winnipeg looking for you, they might give something away."

"I can't disappear into thin air without telling them where I am."

"I know it's tough, but it might be safer if you did. For now, at least. That way, if he asks, they can truthfully say they have no idea where you are."

"I suppose you're right. I'll think about it."

"Good." Without saying any more, he opened the door and went out into the corridor, pulling the door closed behind him. "Make sure you lock it," his voice said through the thickness of the door.

"I will," she shouted back, locking the door and sliding the chain across. She put her eye to the viewer in the door and saw his distorted figure walk down the corridor in the direction of the elevators. Then he disappeared from view.

When she went back into the living room Jill had completed her call. She stood in the center of the room, hands on her hips, obviously in a combative mood. "So, has Mr. Perfect gone at last?"

Vanessa sank into a chair. "Yes," she said, sighing. "Oh Jill. I don't know what to think. I know they've tracked us down here. I have to go somewhere else or Colin will get Roddy one way or the other."

"So you think that going to God knows where—"

"California."

"So he says," Jill scoffed. "How do you know that this winery of his isn't a total lie? And who's this partner with the children he talks about? You'll notice he didn't say if the partner was male or female."

"What the hell does that matter?" Vanessa said wearily.

"If he lies about that, he'll lie about other things. Besides, he's not likely to take you to California if he has a wife and two kids there."

Vanessa's head was beginning to swim. "But surely the fact that he's offered to take me there proves that he doesn't have a wife . . . or two kids."

"Sorry, Van, but there's something that just doesn't ring true about Mr. Kendall. He's far too smooth for my liking."

Jill's suspicions deeply disturbed Vanessa. Although she could sometimes be overhasty, Jill was usually a good judge of character. "How can I find out more about him?"

"I've already set up a check on him. That's what that call was about."

"Thanks, Jill. God, what would I do without you?"

"It shouldn't take too long. But don't you go anywhere outside this apartment until we get the results."

"Grant wants me to let him know my decision about California this evening."

"Bet he does. I'll tell you, dear friend of mine, if that man isn't working for Colin, he's sniffed out a good deal and is working for himself. Did you tell him Colin's family is filthy rich?"

Vanessa swallowed hard.

"No need to answer that," Jill said. "I can see from your face that you did. If, as I suspect, your Mr. Kendall's a smooth operator, he'll take you somewhere, then contact Colin and sell you to him."

Vanessa gave a nervous laugh. "Honestly, Jill! I'm starting to think it's you that's totally paranoid about people, not me."

"You're an actress, sweetie. You don't live in the real world. What's more, you're a Jane Austen–type actress, gliding around in frills and lace, flapping fans. I can't quite see you in *Trainspotting* or *Crash,* can you?"

"I should hope not." Despite her annoyance, Vanessa couldn't help grinning at Jill's suggestion, but her smile swiftly faded. "But you're wrong about me not living in the real world. You forget that I've had to contend with Colin and his ghastly father all these years."

Jill reached down and hugged her tight. "I was just kidding. I know you've had it tough. It's just that you always look for the best in people."

"And you see the worst. That's why we're such good friends, I suppose. Two halves making a whole." Vanessa hugged Jill back, grateful to have such a good friend. Then she sank back onto the couch. "Seriously, though, what is it you don't like about Grant?"

"Let me get you a drink first and then we'll talk. White wine?"

"Please."

Jill went to the kitchen and came back with the glass of wine and a tall glass of mineral water for herself. "Help yourself." Her leather pants creaking, she sat cross-legged on the floor in front of Vanessa. "What don't I like about him? It's not that I don't like him, really. There's something off about him, that's all. Maybe it's my one-quarter of intuitive Cree blood that senses all is not what it seems with Mr. Grant Wonderful. He's definitely good to look at, kind to children, caring to damsels in distress—"

"You make me sound like a right ninny."

"You're not. Only . . . you are extremely vulnerable at the moment, desperate for a way out of this mess. I'm trying to keep you grounded, that's all."

"I realize that. I told Grant that I was going to talk over this California idea with you. But before I do, you should know what happened in the parking lot." Vanessa told her about the man with the beak nose.

Jill's eyes became sloe-dark when she heard how close the car had come to Vanessa. "I don't want you leaving this apartment again until this is all over."

Vanessa shook her head. "That's not the point. The more I think about it, the more I'm convinced that Grant isn't involved with Colin. He was about to tackle the man, but the car raced off before he could."

"I hate to be so negative, Van, but the whole thing could have been another setup, designed to make you think that Grant Kendall is on your side. Didn't you think it weird that he'd ask you to come down to the parking lot, when the rain was spilling down? Surely he could have spoken to you here?"

"You're forgetting that it was me who asked him if we could speak in his car, not the other way around."

Jill waved an impatient hand. "Whatever. He jumped at the suggestion to get you on your own. Away from me."

Vanessa leaned forward. "I trust him, Jill. I have to go with my instincts."

"Your instincts aren't always right. Look at Colin. You thought he was perfect, too."

Vanessa winced. "Thanks a lot."

"Sorry. That was a punk thing to say."

"You're right, of course," Vanessa conceded, "but it hurts to be reminded. Especially now, when I'm desperate to get Roddy away from him."

"Look on the bright side, though. Without Colin, you wouldn't have had Roddy."

Vanessa nodded, tears gathering in her eyes. "He's a great kid, isn't he?"

"He sure is." Jill touched Vanessa's hand and then sprang up. "What time did you say you'd call Grant?"

"Seven."

"Before you call him, I'll get in touch with the guy who's doing the computer check on him. See what he's come up with, okay?"

Vanessa nodded. She took another sip from the glass of wine. "One more thing. I told Grant I'd call my parents and tell them I was going to California, but he said it wasn't a good idea to let them know."

Jill's thick dark brows lowered. "Why?"

"He said that it was better they didn't know where I was, in case my husband came looking for me in Winnipeg." Vanessa shivered at the picture this suddenly conjured up. Colin confronting her mother and father, demanding that they tell him where she and Roddy were, perhaps threatening them.

"Maybe he's right. If he's not playing games, I mean," Jill hastily added. "And if he does take you to California, I will know where you are." Her eyes narrowed. "And I'll know how to deal with Colin if he comes here looking for you, I can tell you."

Jill was fierce, but when Colin got into one of his rages, Vanessa thought, no one could deal with him. Except, perhaps, his father.

While Jill worked at her laptop computer in the living room, Vanessa passed some of the time by watching an old Stratford, Ontario, production of *Twelfth Night* on the Bravo arts network. It brought back memories of those happy times when she'd worked at the Stratford Festival herself, before she'd gone to England.

But, far too frequently, the face of Grant Kendall seemed to be superimposed on the screen, those intense blue eyes demanding that she think about him, not the televised play. Eventually she turned it off and went into the kitchen to make spaghetti for supper.

She opened the hatch into the living room, but Jill was so busy at her computer that she didn't even lift her head.

When everything was ready, Vanessa called down the hall to Roddy and then went into the living room. "I've made some spaghetti. Can you take a break?"

Jill looked up. "That's what smells so good." She sat at the large table by the window, surrounded by paper, and the printer was printing out more. "What's the time? Wow, nearly six-fifteen. Time sure flies when you're having fun." She grinned at Vanessa.

Vanessa stood surveying her. "You really do love your work, don't you?"

"Not so much the paperwork. I love the cut and thrust of negotiations best. That's what gets my blood beating. But you love your work just as much, Van."

"Yes, I do." Vanessa gave Jill a ghost of a smile. "When I get the chance to do it." She swallowed the lump in her throat. "God, Jill, I miss it so much."

"Don't worry, old pal. Once this mess is over, you can go back to working full-time."

"I've had to turn down so much work lately, I doubt anyone in the business will remember who I am." Vanessa turned away and went back to the hall. "Roddy!" she shouted. "Please turn off the television now and wash your hands for dinner."

"Before I clear everything off the table," Jill said, "I'll call Don to see if he's got anything concrete to tell me about GK."

"G . . . oh, yes. Grant. Why not wait until after we've eaten?" Vanessa wasn't sure she really wanted to know anything concrete about GK. Ever.

"No, I'll call him now and ask him to E-mail all the stuff he has. Don't forget you have to make that call at seven."

How could she forget? She'd been glancing at her watch constantly, the minutes slowly but inexorably ticking away, like the timer on a bomb.

She went back into the kitchen while Jill made her call, not wanting to watch Jill's face while she spoke to

Dan or Don or whoever, the man who could hold the key to her future in his computer. She clattered the pot on the stove, making as much noise as possible to drown out the sound of Jill's voice.

She was taking the bowl of sauce from the microwave when Jill came to the kitchen door. "He's got some stuff on him," she announced.

Vanessa's stomach lurched. "What?"

"I didn't ask. He said he'd E-mail it right away. We'll eat first before we read it."

Vanessa met Jill's dark eyes and then turned away to strain the pasta.

She couldn't eat more than a few mouthfuls of the spaghetti. Roddy was hyper from watching so much television. While he twirled his pasta, jabbering away to Jill about the movie he'd watched, Vanessa went through the motions of eating and warning Roddy to be careful not to drop tomato sauce on the carpet—this apartment was definitely not designed for children—and then cutting up pound cake and serving it with ice cream and raspberry sauce. But all the time her mind was on the information about Grant that simmered inside the computer.

When Jill got up and announced, "I'll check my E-mail messages," Vanessa felt positively sick. Like an automaton, she cleared the table, put the dishes in the dishwasher with Roddy's help, and carefully spooned the leftover tomato sauce into a container.

"What's Auntie Jill doing on the computer?" Roddy asked.

"Just work," Vanessa replied. "Want some more ice cream before I put your dish away?"

"Yes, please. Do you think she's got any games on the computer?"

Knowing Jill, Vanessa doubted it. Jill wasn't one for games. "You can ask her later."

"Cool! Can I—"

"May I," Vanessa said automatically.

"May I watch more television?"

"Why don't you read for a while? You've watched

far too much television already." Roddy should be
back at school in a few days' time, using up all that
excess energy in learning or sports, not stuck away in
this apartment, which was fast becoming more like a
prison than a haven.

"But I wanted to watch *The Simpsons*. It comes on
in a few minutes."

"Oh, for heaven's sake, watch it, then," Vanessa
snapped, and immediately felt guilty. Poor Roddy, it
wasn't his fault. She gave him a quick hug. "Sorry.
I'm feeling a bit cooped up today, with all this rain."
She gazed out the window at the gray water and sky.
How colorless Vancouver was at this time of year, all
gray and watery, like her feelings at present. "You go
and watch your program. After all, the doctor did say
you should rest for a couple of days. Maybe we'll
watch it together when I've finished clearing up."

And when she'd made that phone call to Grant.

Roddy went away happy, bearing another dish of
ice cream and cake.

As soon as he'd settled down in the den again,
Vanessa went through to the living room. Jill handed
her a sheet of paper. "I've done a printout. Nothing
much, I'm afraid."

Vanessa scanned the single page, catching the words
winery and *Brazil* and *Argentina*. Then she read it all
over again, this time digesting it. "So he does own a
winery," she said, almost weak with relief. "And he's
been in California's Napa Valley for four years, just
as he said."

"So it appears. Quite the world traveler your Mr.
Kendall. But you'll notice that his résumé only goes
back eight years. All that went before is a blank.
Don's going to dig further."

"You can tell him not to bother." Vanessa threw
the sheet of paper on the table. "This convinces me
that I can trust him." She gave Jill a triumphant smile.

Jill sighed. "I was afraid you might say that." She
looked at her watch. "It's seven. You'd better make
that call if you're going to."

Vanessa resisted the urge to lift her arms above her head and dance around the room. "I'll call him from the bedroom phone."

She went into her room and shut the door. Then, heart racing, she punched in the number of the Bayshore and asked for Grant's room. The line was busy.

The hotel operator came on the line. "Would you like to leave a message?"

Vanessa felt a sharp pang of disappointment. "No, thank you. I'll try again in a few minutes." She waited three minutes and then tried the number again. The line was still busy.

She tried again several times, but each time was told the line was busy. After almost half an hour, she was growing extremely frustrated. Grant knew that she was going to call him at seven. Why was he busy talking to someone else all this time?

Jill came into the room. "Any luck?"

"No, the line's still busy."

Jill raised her eyebrows, but said nothing and went out again.

At last, when she was starting to think he'd left the receiver off, Vanessa got the ringing tone and then Grant answered it. "Grant Kendall," he said in a curt voice.

"This is Vanessa Marston," she began. "I was trying to get you, but—"

He cut her short. "Sorry. Something urgent came up. I'm waiting for a call. I don't want to tie up the line. Give me your number. I'll get back to you."

She was about to remind him that he'd agreed that she shouldn't give the number out, even to him, but the urgency of his tone told her that this wasn't the time to argue with him.

She gave him the number. Immediately he hung up, leaving her with the hollow dial tone in her ear.

Chapter 25

Vanessa slowly set the receiver back in place. She turned, to find Jill standing in the doorway. "He couldn't speak to me," she explained to her. "He was waiting for an important call." Her eyes avoided Jill's. "He said he'd get back to me, but I have the feeling he won't."

For once Jill had the good sense not to make a snide comment. She came to Vanessa and rubbed her hand up and down her back. "Come and have another glass of wine."

As they went into the living room, Vanessa saw Jill glance at her watch. "Should you be somewhere else?"

Jill's cheeks colored slightly. "No, of course not." She poured Vanessa a glass of wine and set the glass down before her. "Drink up."

"Come on, Jill. We know each other too well to be able to lie and get away with it. You've got a date tonight, haven't you?"

Jill shrugged. "Forget about it. It's nothing important."

"Do you realize that we've talked about nothing but me and my problems ever since I arrived in Vancouver? Not one thing about you." Vanessa slumped onto the couch. "Come on, give. Is there someone new in your life?"

Jill gave her a sheepish smile. "Too new to know if I'm really interested, but I'd like to find out."

"Why didn't you say so before?"

"Because a casual date isn't as important as your situation, that's why."

Vanessa dragged Jill down beside her. "You've always been there for me whenever I needed you."

"Not as a kid, I wasn't." Jill grinned. "You've got a short memory. You've forgotten what a horrible kid I was. I also know you gave your mother a bad time because she wanted you to bring me home."

"That was years and years ago. I was a stupid nine-year-old then."

"But you still brought me home, didn't you, even though you didn't want to? And you told me what to wear, what was in and what wasn't, without making me feel like a nerd. And later on, when we were thirteen, fourteen, you took me along with you to all the school dances. Remember Kyle whatsisname telling you to dump me so you could go off with him in his car? You told him you couldn't leave me alone at the dance."

"I was probably using you as an excuse. Kyle may have been great-looking, but he had clammy hands." Vanessa grinned and then shook her head. "Imagine you remembering all that stuff. I'd forgotten most of it."

"No wonder. You've had something else to think about recently."

"I want you to go out and have a good time. You've been hanging around here far too much. You want to tell me about this new man?"

"Not much to tell. He's from Seattle. Loves sailing, like I do. We met last summer at the yacht club."

"Does he live here in Vancouver?"

"No, he's in town for the weekend."

"And you've spent most of the time with me. Why didn't you tell me, you fruitcake?"

"Forget it, okay?"

"Please go. What time was your date?"

"I was to meet him at Bistro, Bistro at seven."

"Oh no! It's almost seven forty-five."

"Stop worrying. I called him on his cell phone."

"Thank God for modern technology." Vanessa jumped up and grabbed Jill's arm, trying to haul her off the couch. "Come on, Jilly. Please go. I'll be fine, honestly."

"I don't want to leave you alone. Especially not after what just happened with your precious Mr. Kendall."

"Forget him. I've got Roddy to keep my company. We'll watch schlocky television all evening." Vanessa rolled her eyes. "To think I told him he could watch *The Simpsons.* If they knew *that,* Colin's family would have even more reason to accuse me of being an unfit mother! Please go, Jill."

"Okay, okay, I'm going. I know when I'm not wanted." Jill scrambled to her feet. "I'll just go and fix my makeup." She halted in the doorway. "I'll call you around ten, okay? The usual signal. Two rings, then I'll call again."

"Don't bother. You may be doing more important things at ten o'clock."

"Get lost." Jill grabbed a cushion from one of the chairs and slung it across the room at her.

Vanessa began clearing away the glasses. She was pushing them through the hatch when Jill reappeared.

"I've said good-bye to Roddy. Sure you're okay?"

"I'm absolutely fine. *Go.*"

But when the door closed behind Jill, Vanessa knew she wasn't really fine. In a short time she'd swung from the jubilation of discovering that Grant hadn't been lying to her to the shock of his icy reception of her telephone call. She felt like going to bed and pulling the covers over her head. Instead, she went into the den and found Roddy playing his new game, while the television blared and flickered from the corner of the room.

"Enough TV," she said, clicking off the television. "Let's do that new puzzle Auntie Jill gave you. It looks like a tough one."

"It is. I started it, but it's got lots of blue sky. I could do with some help."

"Well, that's what I'm here for. Let's do it on the coffee table in the living room."

Lots of blue sky. That was what she needed, Vanessa thought, both actually and metaphorically speaking. As she started to do the puzzle with Roddy, the rain was pattering steadily against the balcony window. The weather only helped to emphasize her feelings of gloom and disappointment. As she sat down by the coffee table, she released a heavy sigh.

She wished Grant Kendall had stayed at his bloody vineyard in sunny California and never inveigled himself into their lives.

They had done all the outside pieces of the puzzle and had made a good start on that blue sky when the telephone rang. Vanessa glanced at her watch. Nine thirty-five. Jill was early. She grinned to herself, guessing why. She picked up the receiver on the second ring and only then remembered that she was supposed to wait for Jill to ring again.

"Hello?" said a man's voice.

"Is it Daddy?" Roddy asked, hearing the male voice from the receiver.

"I don't think so." She put the receiver to her ear. "Hello?"

"Vanessa? It's Grant Kendall."

"Oh, hello," she said, keeping her voice cool and dispassionate. She could control her voice, but not her heartbeat, which had started racing.

"I must apologize first for being so rude when you called me. There was a slight emergency at the winery earlier on, but it's all been worked out now. You must have wondered what the hell was going on."

"Not at all," she said briskly. "I realized you were caught up with something important."

"Thanks for being so understanding. Have you had a chance to talk to Ms. Nelson? About California, I mean."

"Yes, I have."

"And?"

"I . . . I think it's far too much of an imposition on

you. After all, we are complete strangers, aren't we?" Vanessa knew that she was sounding like the worst kind of pretentious, upper-class English twit, but she had no intention of appearing overeager.

"You're right," Grant agreed, "we are strangers, but strangers can become friends. If you're prepared to trust me, I think I can help you and Roddy."

He sounded like the old Grant, warm and caring . . . and persuasive. It was as if the last telephone call had never happened. Vanessa drew in a deep breath and then released it in a long, silent sigh of relief. "When were you thinking of leaving Vancouver?"

"As soon as possible would be best, I think. Tomorrow morning?"

Panic swept over her at the thought of having to make an instant commitment, of leaving with him so soon. "Could you give me a little more time? I have an appointment at the hospital tomorrow morning for the doctor to check Roddy, to make sure he's okay. Also, I have to speak to Jill and I might not be able to do that tonight."

"Isn't she there with you?"

Vanessa bit her lip. Perhaps she shouldn't tell him that she and Roddy were alone in the apartment. Don't be such an idiot, she told herself. After all, she was talking about going all the way to California with this man, wasn't she?

"No, she went out. She should be back soon."

God, there she went again, hedging her bets, just in case.

Time to make up her mind, make that commitment. Either she trusted him or she didn't. "If you really mean it, about taking us to California, we could be ready by, let's say, two o'clock tomorrow afternoon. Would that be okay?"

"No problem," Grant said. "That will also give me time to work out a good way of getting you and Roddy out of the apartment without being seen by Mr. Beak Nose or anyone else who might be watching."

"I'll pack tonight. I take it we'll be driving, not flying."

"If that's okay with you. I have my own car with me, so I'll need to get it back to California, anyway. And crossing the border is far less hassle when you drive across than when you go through an airport."

It sounded as if he wasn't new to this game of evasion. Vanessa felt a rush of exhilaration. Suddenly everything had changed. "This is so kind of you. I don't know how I can ever thank you."

"Glad to help."

She almost laughed aloud at this typically male response to what was, after all, a considerable commitment on his part.

"I'll be in touch again," he told her. "Probably sometime around noon tomorrow."

When they'd exchanged good-byes, Vanessa told Roddy that they were going to California with Grant. He greeted the news with enthusiasm. "Great," he said. "I like Grant. He told me he could teach me to play chess." He looked up from the puzzle. "Will it be raining in California?"

"I certainly hope not."

When Jill called twenty minutes later, at exactly ten o'clock, she was surprisingly sanguine about Vanessa's decision. Either she was tired of arguing with her about Grant or her mind was otherwise occupied. Probably the latter, Vanessa suspected, smiling to herself. Jill promised to be at the apartment first thing in the morning and reminded Vanessa that she could call her on her cell phone at *any* time.

"Right," Vanessa drawled.

"I mean it," Jill insisted.

As soon as Vanessa put down the phone, she chased Roddy off to bed with the reminder that he had a nine o'clock appointment at the hospital tomorrow. This elicited a groan. He was far more receptive when she also reminded him that he would probably be up very late traveling on the road to California tomorrow evening.

Once he was in bed, she set to, packing everything she'd hastily gathered in Edinburgh, plus the few things they had accumulated in the past week, mainly gifts for Roddy from Jill—and Grant. As she took her clothes from the closet, she wondered when she'd be able to settle in one spot again for any length of time. After all, she wouldn't be able to remain in the Napa Valley for very long with a complete stranger, would she?

Even a stranger who was becoming such a good friend.

Next morning, to her relief, Dr. Sumner told her that Roddy was mending very well and confirmed that he was able to travel.

Vanessa was also told, by a member of the accounting department, that she would be sent a bill for Roddy's treatment, as his name did not appear on her medical coverage. She would have to take the matter up with the BC Health Department.

"Don't worry," Jill told Vanessa, as she drove them back to the apartment. "I'll pay the bill when it comes in."

When they got back there was a complex message on the machine from Grant, saying that he'd be coming by with first another car and then a truck and could Jill be around for them to do another "Double Jill Nelson stunt."

"Whatever that means," Jill said, making one of her comical faces. "I think your Mr. Kendall's getting his kicks out of this espionage stuff."

"I'm glad someone is."

Once she'd clarified Grant's message in a long phone call, Vanessa finished the packing and made sandwiches for the journey. Although Grant had said they could stop for something to eat once they crossed the border, Vanessa knew that Roddy could be pretty edgy if he was hungry.

Coached by Grant's intricate instructions, they

staged an effective and, they hoped, credible little scene at the front entrance of the apartment complex. Jill—who was supposed to be Vanessa—stood at the entrance beside Roddy, both of them waving to the real Vanessa—playing Jill—in her black coat and dark sunglasses, as she and her luggage were borne away by Grant at the wheel of a white limo.

A switch from limo to truck a few blocks away and then Grant, his face half hidden by a baseball cap, drove the truck back to the complex and into the underground parking lot. There he picked up Roddy, who lay down on the floor, and Grant drove the truck out, making his way down Pacific Boulevard.

"What about the truck and that other car?" Roddy asked, once he and his mother had transferred to Grant's own car. "You can't just leave them parked on the street, can you?"

"Quite right, young Roddy, I can't. I borrowed them from a couple of colleagues in the wine trade and they're going to pick them up. It's all arranged, so don't you worry about it." Grant glanced at a bemused Vanessa and said in a western drawl from the corner of his mouth, "Well, pardner, that sure should have shaken them rattlesnakes off the trail."

Vanessa threw back her head and laughed outright. It felt so good to be able to laugh again. She settled back into her seat, relaxing for the first time in ages, and said a silent prayer of thanks for Grant Kendall.

Chapter 26

The distillery that made Strathferness single malt whiskey was extremely efficient, but still used many of the ancient methods. Sir Robert preferred to germinate his own barley for the malting process, for instance, rather than bringing it in already prepared. He explained why he did this to Colin at great length—and in infinite detail—as they took a tour around the distillery on Tuesday morning.

Standing in the warm, damp malting house, Colin had to swallow hard to avoid gagging. He'd always enjoyed the mellow aroma and taste of fine whiskey, especially Strathferness, but after only two days in the distillery he'd become sickened by the stench of the mash and the fermented yeast. It seeped from the distillery itself into all the offices. Even after a long shower last night, he was convinced that his hair and skin still sank of it.

"How the hell do you stand working with this smell every day?" he asked Donald Ross, the stillman, who, Colin had soon discovered, was the most important person in the long process of producing their single-malt whiskey.

His father answered for the taciturn Mr. Ross. "It's the smell of money," he said bluntly. "Right, Donald?"

"Aye, that's right, sir," Donald Ross replied with a wry grin.

To Colin's fury, his father continued to harangue him in front of Ross and the brewer. "You've never balked at taking the money the distillery brings in . . . nor at drinking its whiskey . . . but you've taken hardly any interest in the family business. In fact, your sister has shown far more interest in it than you ever have. It's high time you got your hands dirty, became involved with how we Craigmores make our money, and not just enjoy the end products."

Colin felt an overwhelming urge to punch his father's heat-flushed face as he bent over the bubbling mash tun. It would feel even better to shove him into it and watch him boil to death in whiskey mash. A most fitting death.

Until now, he'd never realized quite how much the distillery meant to his father. He seemed to come into his own here, stalking around, barking out orders, even—on the odd occasion—praising someone for a job well done. He reminded Colin of a general reviewing his troops.

When Colin's tour ended, his father followed him into the cramped office that he'd been given. He pulled off his white coat and tossed it onto the chair behind Colin's desk, effectively staking his proprietorial claim. "I drove into Inverness last night to visit your mother at the hospital. Where were you? She said she hadn't seen you since Sunday."

"For God's sake, Father. This is only Tuesday. I was there twice on Sunday. I thought the doctor said she needed lots of rest. I intend to visit her this evening."

"You'd better do so. Your mother kept pestering me last night, asking me where you were. She was so concerned about you that her heart rate went up again. Exactly where were you, by the way? Off whoring, I suppose. You certainly weren't at home when I got back."

Colin gritted his teeth. It was galling at his age to have every move checked by his father. "As a matter of fact I was visiting a friend of mine who's an advocate. I wanted to get some more information about Canadian law."

"Why would you do that? Don't you trust Ewen to do the job properly?" His father's tone was belligerent.

"I want to make sure we have all the angles covered. Ian confirmed that Ewen is making all the right moves. Now that I have confirmation from the photograph that Roddy is definitely in Vancouver, I should be able to get some action."

"Yes, we should. Did you remember to fax Ewen back, to ask him to get those papers about the application for a court order in British Columbia couriered to you?"

Colin ignored his father's question. This was *his* business, not his father's. He swallowed hard, anger bubbling up inside him, like the whiskey mash in the vat. Forget him, he told himself. Focus on *her* and what she's done. That was far safer and more productive.

"Even though the photograph's blurred," he said, "you can see quite clearly that Roddy has a dressing of some sort on his forehead. What sort of frigging mother is she, to let such a thing happen to her son? A negligent one. Maybe worse." Colin's hands shook as he poured himself a cup of coffee from the vacuum jug on his desk, so that the liquid slopped over onto some papers. Cursing, he reached for a box of tissues to mop it up. "You never know, she could be knocking him around as well."

"Colin." His father's tone demanded his attention.

"What?"

His father's eyes narrowed to slits. "Have you any actual evidence that Vanessa ever abused him physically?"

"No. But she could be very volatile, as you know. These bloody actors are all the same, wrapped up in their own hysterical emotions, exaggerating everything. She was always swanning around with a script in her hands, not giving a damn about reality, that she should be caring for her child or cooking us a meal."

"From what I've heard," his father said, his voice dry as sandpaper, "you were rarely home, so why should she be cooking you a meal?"

Colin stared out the window at the snow-flecked pine trees and the slow-moving waters of the little burn that ran through the valley. "You know what I mean."

His father dragged out Colin's swivel chair from behind the desk and sat down. "Ewen called after you'd left this morning."

Colin turned. "Anything new?"

"No changes since he reported back yesterday."

"Good. It looks as if we've got that under control."

"So it appears. Ewen seems to think that this Canadian investigation firm is first-class." Sir Robert frowned. "Although I am concerned about that one part of the report we discussed."

"You mean the bit about another man being involved?"

"That's right. But apparently he's disappeared and hasn't been seen since the incident outside the apartment."

"I take it Ewen confirmed that our man didn't get the chance to photograph him?"

"No, apparently it all happened too fast."

Colin shrugged. He was tired of receiving secondhand reports, filtered through his father. He was biding his time. As soon as his mother was in the clear and able to come home to Strathferness, he'd be out of this place like a shot. It was time to take control of his own life. And as far as he was concerned, everyone was playing far too nice with that bitch Vanessa. Once he took over the hunt himself she'd soon find out what happened to people who thought they could get the better of him.

"Anything else you want to talk to me about?" he asked his father. "I have to get to those reports you wanted me to do."

Sir Robert pushed back the chair and stood up. "Right. I need them for that meeting this afternoon."

Colin looked down at his father's bald head with its fringe of gray hair. "They'll be on your desk by noon." He hid his clenched hands behind his back. If he didn't get out of this place soon, he wasn't sure he'd be able to keep his hands to himself. Ever since he'd moved into the castle his father had been riding him, never missing an opportunity to criticize his abilities or to emphasize his shortcomings. And, because of Roddy, Colin had to take it all meekly and not retaliate.

He sat down in the chair his father had vacated. I'm biding my time, he thought. He liked that expression. *Biding my time.* The three words held all the feelings of pent-up frustration, of vengeance deferred, that he was experiencing. They also held a satisfying sense of menace, speaking to him in a positive way of waiting for the right time to strike.

He poured himself more coffee and started humming the tune and then sang the words, "I'm biding my ti—ime; that's the kind of guy I—I am."

"What the hell have you got to sing about?"

Colin jumped, startled by the sound of his father's voice. He hadn't realized that he was still there, standing just inside the door. "I'm feeling optimistic." He pulled the computer keyboard toward him and began working on it.

"Humph!" said his father, and left the room.

When Colin visited his mother in the hospital that evening, she was up, sitting in a wheelchair, with Amanda beside her.

"Well, what a lovely surprise," he said, happy for more than one reason to see his mother out of bed.

She gave him a gentle smile. "Hello, dear." She held out one fragile hand to him. "It's equally lovely to see you." She looked as delicate as one of those figures made of spun glass, as if merely touching her would break her into tiny pieces. But she was obviously much better than she'd been on Sunday. Her face had lost that ghastly pallor and her cheeks were tinged with pink.

He bent to kiss her. "When did they allow you to get out of bed?"

"This morning. I slept for a while this afternoon."
She smiled at Amanda. "In fact, I was fast asleep
when your sister arrived. That's the best sleep I've
had in a long, long time."

He laid the expensive bouquet of early spring flowers on the bed. "For you."

"How beautiful. And how kind of you to bring
them, dear." One finger traced the delicate petal of a
half-opened daffodil. "A breath of spring in the midst
of winter."

"I'll get a vase for them," Amanda said. She picked
up the flowers and went out.

Colin took her place in the chair beside her mother's wheelchair. "It's wonderful to see you looking so
much better. Any news of when you'll be able to come
home?" He was glad Amanda had left the room.
Something told him she wouldn't have approved of
him asking that question.

"Nothing definite yet, but they do seem to be quite
pleased with me."

"That's excellent."

"Now, don't tell me you're all actually missing me
at Strathferness," she said, surprising him with the almost playful tone of her voice.

"I certainly am. I didn't come home just to live with
Father," he said, half joking.

His mother gave what sounded suspiciously—and
astoundingly—like a giggle. "No, I don't suppose you
did, my dear boy."

Colin stared at her, frowning.

"What's wrong?" she asked, startled by his expression.

"It's you, Mother. You—you seem different." He
wasn't sure he liked her this way. She seemed . . .
almost frivolous. Then he suddenly realized. "Oh, of
course."

"Of course what?"

"It's the pills you're on, right? Dr. Jamieson said
he was giving you a sedative as well as the heart
medication."

"Did he?"

"That's why you're in such a strange mood."

She stiffened and drew the edges of her rose-pink silk peignoir together across her knees, her back very straight. "I wasn't aware that I was in any kind of mood, strange or otherwise." The tone of her voice reminded Colin that his mother was an aristocrat through and through.

"Strange for you, I meant," he said hurriedly, not wanting to upset her.

"What's strange for Mother?" Amanda asked, coming back into the room bearing a tall vase filled with Colin's flowers.

"I was saying that she was in an unusually . . . lighthearted mood, considering all . . ." Colin almost floundered to a halt as Amanda's gaze fixed on him, issuing a warning, "all she has been through recently."

"She's being well looked after here and able to rest." Amanda put the vase on the chest of drawers and then went behind her mother's chair, bending to kiss her cheek. "And we're going to make sure she does more of the same," she added firmly.

"I should really prefer to go home," Fiona protested. It sounded to Colin as if this had been a subject of discussion before he came in. "Your father said he will engage a private nurse to take care of me. And I have Morag. I'd rather be at home, with my own things around me."

"You're better off here," Amanda said. "You know you won't be able to rest once you're at home."

"Why won't she?" Colin demanded. "If she has a nurse and Morag, she should be able to get plenty of rest."

"With Father roaring around the place? Don't be daft, Col."

"He'll have to be told to keep away from her. Surely he's got enough sense to—"

"Please stop it, both of you." Their mother's voice broke in, cutting Colin short. "I won't have you arguing across me." Her mouth quivered as if she were fighting back tears.

"I'm sorry," Colin said.

"Would you please help me back into bed," she whispered to Amanda. "I'm feeling rather tired all of a sudden."

Amanda glared at Colin. *You idiot!* she mouthed at him, before putting an arm around her mother's waist to help her back into the high bed.

"I'd better go," he muttered, glancing away from the sight of his mother's thin legs beneath the night-gown. "Just wanted to make sure you were being well looked after."

His mother sighed as she settled herself in the bed. "That feels so much better." She turned her head toward Colin as he hovered between the bed and the doorway. "Don't leave yet, dear. I want to hear how you're getting along at the distillery."

"I'll go and get a cup of coffee." Amanda gathered up her leather handbag and camel coat.

"You can leave your coat here," her mother said.

"I'll take it. I might fancy a walk before I come up again."

And a cigarette, thought Colin, grinning at his sister. She made a face at him and went out.

"I want a quick word with Amanda," Colin told his mother, determined not to be left alone with her again. He moved to the door of her room. "I'll be back in a few minutes." He strode down the corridor, catching up with his sister as she was about to step into the elevator.

"Traitor," he said, as he followed her in. "You bloody well knew that I didn't want to be alone with her."

"Oh, really? I thought it was time for a little mother-son bonding."

"I had enough of that on Sunday, thanks very much."

"You really are a shit, you know that?"

The elevator stopped and the door opened before he had time to respond. As they stepped out, Colin grasped Amanda's arm, but she shook herself free. "I'm your sister, remember, not your wife."

He stared at her. There was no mistaking the hostility in her eyes, the belligerent jutting of her chin. He felt betrayed. When had his own sister stepped over the border and allied herself with his enemies?

He held out a hand. "Come on, Mandy. Don't be like this with me."

"I'm not like anything. I'm just sick and tired of this situation. I need to get back to work and get my own life in order. I don't ever want to see Strathferness again. As soon as Ma is out of danger I'm getting the hell out of it." She stalked down the corridor ahead of him.

He caught up with her at the door to the small café. "Have you spoken to Dr. Jamieson?"

"No, but Father has. He's very pleased with her. Talking of sending her home in a couple of days."

"That's great news." He summoned up a grin, trying to lighten the situation, to coax Amanda back to his side. "They should keep her on those pills all the time. They've certainly brightened her up."

"I don't think it's just the pills. I think she's enjoying the peace and quiet of the hospital. Everything's too volatile at home at present. Whatever happens, she's far safer here, even when hooked up to monitors and IVs, then she would be at home."

Colin suddenly realized that Amanda was right. He knew it would be a shock to his mother when she heard he'd left Scotland and flown to Canada, especially after he'd given her his word that he would stay. But here, at least, she would be in the best place to receive instant treatment. Whereas, at home, she could . . .

"You're right. She should stay here."

Amanda looked surprised. "That's a sudden switch, I must say."

"I agree with you. There's far too much stress at home for her."

And there's going to be a bloody sight more stress

before I'm finished, he thought. As he picked up the tray at the counter in the tiny self-service café, his lips twitched with excitement at the thought of taking control. He covered his mouth with his hand to hide his jubilant smile from his sister.

Chapter 27

Vanessa was watching Grant's profile as they drove south along the Interstate to Seattle. After almost two hours she'd grown used to sitting here, close beside him.

He turned to glance at her and smiled. "Everything okay?"

She gave a satisfied sigh. "I should say it is." She circled her shoulders, feeling the tension easing from them.

"You seem more relaxed now."

"I was really tense going through customs. I felt sure they'd have been sent some sort of notice about me and Roddy, and they'd grab us and arrest us."

"Obviously your husband hasn't involved the police in this yet. Now that you've crossed the border into the States, it'll probably be even more difficult for him to get at you. So you can relax."

"I am. I haven't felt this relaxed for a long time."

Grant glanced in the rearview mirror. "How's it going back there?" he asked Roddy. "Hope you're not too squashed." They'd had to put Roddy's bag in the back with him, so that Grant's wine samples could be safely stowed in the trunk.

"I'm okay." Roddy sounded disgruntled, already tired of the driving. "When will it be my turn to sit in the front?"

"Sorry, pal," Grant answered for her. "You can't sit in the front. Air bags," he reminded Vanessa.

"Of course." She thought again of Jill's suggestion that Grant's "partner" with the children could be his wife. "That's very thoughtful. Not many single men would even think about children and air bags."

"That's a rather unfair comment, isn't it? There's been so much stuff about air bags in the media in the last couple of years I shouldn't think anyone would have missed it." His lips quirked into a smile. "Not even a single guy like me."

"Sorry. That was a stupid thing for me to say."

"That's okay." He glanced in the mirror again. "Maybe we should take a break before we reach Seattle. I'd prefer to keep going, but I think Roddy might like to get out of the car and stretch his legs. Am I right?"

"Yes, please!" Roddy shouted.

"So would I," Vanessa said, relieved that he'd suggested it.

"Sorry. You should have said so before. I have a tendency to keep driving unless someone speaks up. Take a look at the map, Vanessa, and see if there's a likely place we can stop."

It was the first time he'd called her directly by her name. She liked the way it sounded when he said it. *Vanessa.* As if he'd known her for a long time.

"We should be somewhere near Bellingham," he said.

"We passed it about half an hour ago."

"I thought you were asleep then."

"Of course not. I'm enjoying the feeling of freedom too much to be able to sleep."

"I'm really glad," Grant said softly. "You deserve it." For the briefest of moments, his right hand reached out to clasp her hand, which rested on the map of the Pacific Northwest. Vanessa felt warmth rising from her neck to her face.

"There's a small town coming up," she said, rustling the map to emphasize that her mind was on the journey, not him. "About another ten miles."

"I'm really hungry, too," Roddy said. "We didn't have much to eat for lunch."

That was true. "We've got the sandwiches I made," Vanessa said.

"Yuck! I hate sandwiches."

"I wouldn't mind some coffee, anyway," Grant said. "Why don't we stop, have something to eat, and then we can keep going for a few more hours before we stop for the night?"

"That sounds fine," Vanessa said. "Then if we get hungry later on, we've still got the sandwiches."

As Roddy groaned, she exchanged smiles with Grant.

"I'll count off the miles," Grant told Roddy, "so you'll know when we get close."

They found a Denny's within half a mile of the turn-off from the highway. Inside the restaurant, the aroma of coffee and cinnamon and bacon smelled better than the finest perfume to Vanessa. "Mmm! I didn't realize I was so hungry."

"That smells great," Roddy agreed.

"It's a special spray. Eau de Denny's," Grant said. "You can buy it at the desk."

"You can't," Roddy said, gazing up at him. But he wasn't quite sure about it.

"You certainly can," Grant teased. "That way you can make your home smell like a Denny's Restaurant. Mm-mm."

Vanessa laughed aloud, tilting her head back, so that people turned to look at her, smiling.

Grant was looking at her, too, a strange expression in his eyes. "That's the second time today I've heard you laugh properly."

"That's the effect you have on me," she said. Then her laughter died as she realized how intimate her remark might sound to him. She blinked. "I meant—"

"I'm glad I can make you laugh," he said, immediately putting her at her ease.

She was grateful to him. Her emotions seemed to be all haywire at present. She knew she wasn't in complete control of them and was even more likely than usual to blurt out the first thing that came into her head.

As they waited for a table, Vanessa watched Grant. Back straight beneath his black leather jacket, he stood behind Roddy, both hands on her son's shoulders. She loved the way Grant and Roddy had bonded. It was an immense relief to be able to put her trust in someone other than her parents and Jill.

Ever since she had first met Grant in Stanley Park, she'd had a sense of knowing him from somewhere else. Now it suddenly came to her. He reminded her of one of her favorite paintings, the wonderful Rembrandt portrait in Glasgow's civic art gallery that was called, very simply, *Man in Armour.* Grant had the same strong chin and sensitive mouth, the same sense of a man who was totally trustworthy. In the portrait, the man's eyes were hidden in the shadow of his gilded helmet, but she now knew instinctively that if they were visible they would be the same vivid blue as Grant's.

If you're not careful, she told herself, you'll be starting to think of this man as your guardian angel.

Grant turned to look at her and she found herself blushing. She sincerely hoped that he couldn't read thoughts.

"Your mother's very quiet," he said to Roddy.

"She isn't usually," Roddy said, and they all laughed, breaking the spell.

When they were shown to a booth, Roddy insisted on sitting next to Grant, opposite Vanessa. She sat next to their jackets, which they'd piled on the empty seat beside her.

Grant ordered the hamburger plate and Vanessa had blueberry pancakes. Roddy had a hamburger and fries, "A small hamburger, please, because I want waffles as well."

"I hadn't realized I was so hungry," Grant said when he'd finished, sitting back with a satisfied sigh.

"I've had enough," Roddy said, pushing his plate back.

"I should think you have." Vanessa handed him a clean napkin. "You've got syrup around your mouth."

"It's on my hands, too. It ran down my knife."

"Maple syrup's slippery stuff," Grant said. "Why don't we go to the rest room and get washed up?"

"Good idea." Roddy slid out after him.

"I'll ask for the bill," Vanessa said.

"That's fine, as long as you don't pay it."

"You're not paying for our food," Vanessa told him. "Especially when you're driving us all the way to California. Paying this bill is the least I can do."

"You can't use your credit card. That's too dangerous."

"I know that. I'm not completely stupid, you know."

"Sorry. Just being careful. Let me pay. I don't expect you have American money."

"Oh yes, I do. Jill gave me some."

Grant shrugged. "Okay, if you must."

"I must."

Vanessa watched Grant and Roddy as they crossed the room, and then took her compact from her bag to check her face in the mirror. What a fright she looked! Her face was shiny and her lipstick eaten off. As she pushed the compact back into her bag, her fingers encountered the soft leather of Grant's jacket.

Her hand clutched at the coat and then slackened as she became appalled at the thought that had rushed into her mind. Had Grant by any chance left his wallet in the jacket pocket?

She glanced around to make sure that no one was watching. Then she looked in the direction of the rest rooms. They were near the entrance, well past the long line of people waiting for tables. When Grant and Roddy came back they would have to make their way through the line. As long as she was careful, there was no way she could miss seeing them.

Without looking down, she slid her hand into the outside pockets of the jacket. Nothing in the left-hand one. Just a small packet, which she realized were tissues, in the right-hand pocket.

The waitress approached and Vanessa hurriedly withdrew her hand, feeling as guilty as a thief.

"More coffee?"

"No, thank you. Just the bill, please."

"Okay."

The waitress retreated.

Vanessa found she was trembling. She felt furious at herself. What she was doing was despicable. But all she wanted, the other half of her mind argued, was to verify that Grant was as trustworthy as she thought him to be. Surely there was nothing wrong with that. It's for Roddy, she told herself. He's more important than anything else.

Her gaze glued to the area beyond the line, she slid her hand inside the jacket, feeling for the pockets there.

A man and a boy appeared by the door. Heart racing, she pulled her hand out . . . and then relaxed. No, it wasn't them.

Again she slipped her hand inside the jacket. This time her fingers encountered what was unmistakably a wallet.

"There's your check," the waitress said, startling Vanessa. She put the bill on the table.

"Thank you," Vanessa said, but this time she kept her hand hidden inside the jacket, still gripping the wallet, until the waitress was safely across the room again.

Taking a deep breath, Vanessa drew the wallet out. She glanced in the direction of the entrance once again and then laid the wallet on top of Grant's jacket. She opened it with trembling fingers.

Dollar bills, both Canadian and American. Driver's license. The words blurred before her eyes and then cleared. Right name. Right address. Thank God for that. She began to breath properly again. Medical insurance card. Right name, again. Right address.

Her fingers felt behind the dollar bills and encountered the edge of what appeared to be a photograph. Yet again, she looked up to scan the entrance and the waiting crowd, and then slid the photograph out, setting it on the open wallet.

She looked, not quite able to take in what she was seeing. She bent her head to peer even closer, unable to believe her eyes. As she gazed down at the photograph, her heart pounded in her chest.

She had never seen the photograph before, but she recognized the picture all too well. It showed her dressed in her green velvet robe opening her Christmas gift from Roddy, with Roddy himself standing beside her in his new Superman pajamas.

As if it had all clicked into focus again, everything suddenly became extremely, horribly clear. The photograph had been taken on Christmas Day, just two weeks ago, by Colin. That meant that Colin had sent the photo to Grant.

Which meant that Grant Kendall was working for Colin and was her enemy. And Roddy's.

Her head snapped up. She had been staring down at the photograph for so long, trying hard to make sense of it, that she suddenly realized that she hadn't checked to see if Grant and Roddy were on their way back. But there was still no sign of them.

She looked at her watch. They'd been gone at least ten minutes. Ten minutes? She rose in her seat. Dear God in heaven, she thought, he's taken my son. Grant's taken my son.

Chapter 28

Vanessa scrambled from the booth and stood up, panic-stricken. She was about to yell, "Get the police!" when she saw Grant and Roddy, pushing through the crowd by the desk. Relief made her weak. She felt the chill dampness of sweat between her shoulder blades. Then she rallied, adrenaline pumping, as her mind registered what she was up against.

Hurriedly sitting down again, she slipped the photograph back behind the dollar bills. As Grant and Roddy came toward her, she smiled, raising one hand in a wave, while the other hand was engaged in sliding the wallet back into the inside pocket. For one heart-stopping moment it slid into nothing but silk lining, but then she found the edge of the pocket and the wallet glided safely inside it.

"Hi," she said brightly when they reached her. "You were a long time."

"Sorry," Grant said. As he sat down, he leaned forward to peer at her. "You okay?"

"Of course."

"We bought a bag of muffins." Roddy held up the paper bag. "In case we get hungry on the way."

Grant was frowning. "I should have come back first. Sorry to have worried you."

"I wasn't worried at all," Vanessa protested.

"You look as white as a ghost."

She summoned up a rueful smile. "I've eaten far too much, that's all."

He picked up the bill. "Good. You didn't pay yet." He leaned across to get his wallet from his jacket.

Vanessa held her breath as he opened it, praying that she'd put everything back in its proper place. He drew out a credit card. "Okay, everyone ready?"

Vanessa hesitated. She needed to go to the rest room, but couldn't risk Grant taking off with Roddy while she was in there. She nodded in response to Grant's question and picked up her jacket and bag.

"May I borrow your car keys?" she asked, when Grant reached the cashier.

He looked surprised.

"I can't find my lipstick," she explained. "I must have dropped it in the car. It probably rolled under the seat."

"Do you need it now?" He seemed reluctant to let her have the keys, which helped even more to confirm her suspicions. Not that she needed any confirmation. That photograph had been enough.

"I'm afraid so. I've eaten all my lipstick off."

He handed her the keys. "Want to come out and help me look, Roddy?" she asked, willing him to say *yes*.

"No, thanks. I'll stay with Grant. He said I could ask the lady for a special mug."

Vanessa felt like screaming. This was her one chance to get away. But if she insisted on Roddy coming out to the car, Grant would immediately know that something was up.

"Okay." She jingled the keys. "Thanks, Grant. I have to come in again, but I'll be quick."

"No hurry."

She went out to the car and opened the door. In case he was watching from the window, she bent over as if she were looking for something on the floor, and then held up the lipstick she had already slipped into her pocket.

When she came back they were waiting at the door for her. "Found it. Back in a minute," she said, before Grant could ask her for the keys. She went down the corridor to the rest room.

When she closed the door of the cubicle, she leaned

her back against it for a moment, feeling sick and lightheaded. Please help me, God, she prayed.

She'd lost this opportunity to get away in the car. If she told Roddy that Grant was an enemy he'd be bound to give them away either by arguing with her or not being able to hide his fear of the man he'd thought was his friend. It was likely to be the former. Grant seemed to have become Roddy's idol and it would be very hard to persuade him that he was actually his enemy.

Grant had said it would be best to make an overnight stop at a motel near Portland. She would have to change that plan, find some pressing reason for stopping at another restaurant or a motel somewhere near here. She must return to Canada as soon as possible. The farther away they were from the border, the more cut off from help she'd feel. But for now she must not allow Grant to see any change in her attitude to him.

Good thing she was an actress. This would have to be her finest performance . . . and no set lines, either. All improvisation as she went along.

She smiled as she rejoined them. "Sorry to keep you." She handed Grant the keys.

"See, I got a mug." Roddy held it up.

"So you did. That's great."

They went out to the car, the chill, damp air sending a shiver down her spine. Grant put a hand lightly on her back. "Cold?"

"It's a bit raw, isn't it?"

"I've got a blanket in the car. And a pillow for Roddy, in case he needs to get some sleep later on."

Vanessa stood by the car, wishing she could think of some way to avoid having to leave the bright lights and the friendly faces in the restaurant. "You think of everything," she told Grant. He opened her door and she got into the front passenger seat.

When he'd settled Roddy in the back, he handed her the blanket. "Here, wrap that around you." He got into the car and started up the engine. "Let's get some heat going."

"That's nice," Vanessa said when the warm air started flowing around her legs.

"How about some music?"

"Have you got any U2?" Roddy asked.

"U2! Where on earth did you hear U2?" Vanessa said, the pitch of her voice sounding unnatural in her ears. "Not at home, I know."

"John Culliton-Fraser has some U2 CDs."

"Sorry, I don't have any with me," Grant told Roddy. "Even if I did, I wouldn't be playing rock when your mother's tired and you're supposed to be getting some sleep. We've got a few more hours of driving ahead of us."

"I don't feel like sleeping," Roddy protested.

"We'll try a little night music." Grant turned out of the parking lot onto the highway and then slid in a CD. The music of Rachmaninoff flowed through the warm interior of the car. It was the second piano concerto. "How's that?"

"Fine," Vanessa said. She swallowed hard. Why did he have to choose this, of all things? The music was as sweet as maple syrup, the very essence of romantic melancholy. Exactly what she did not need at a time when she wanted to keep her mind alert, her emotions totally controlled.

"Quiet enough for you?"

"Perfect."

As the music ebbed and flowed around her, she turned her head away from Grant, pretending to doze off. But her mind was in overdrive. Not only must she get him to stop very soon, but she must also try to get the keys to the car from him, without him knowing. How could she possibly manage that?

One way came to mind, but she rejected it—for now. If she had to sleep with him it would definitely be her last resort. But if it was the only way to get the keys, she'd do it.

To ensure Roddy's safety, she'd do anything.

She let her mind dwell on the thought for a very brief moment and then hastily moved on. She'd tell

Grant she was feeling ill. He'd said at the restaurant that she didn't look well. Could you get food poisoning from pancakes?

"I don't like this music much," said a voice from the back of the car, breaking into her thoughts. "Have you got the *Jurassic Park* music? I like that."

"Sshh. Your mother's asleep," Grant said in a low voice. "Let's not wake her. I'll put something else on when this CD is finished."

"All right."

No one spoke for quite a long time, then Roddy said in a loud whisper, "Grant."

"Yes?"

"Are we going to stay with you for a long time, at the winery?"

"That depends."

"I mean, will I have to go to school in California?"

"Would you like to?"

"Yes, that would be neat." Another pause. "It wouldn't be boarding school, would it?"

"That depends on what your mother wants. And you, too, of course."

"My father wants me to go to boarding school. So does Grandfather."

"I see."

Vanessa's muscles tensed, but she kept her head averted and her eyes shut.

"I don't want to have to go to a school that's a long way from home."

"It might not be as bad as you think, you know. You'd probably make a lot of new friends."

Trust Colin's cohort to advocate boarding schools, Vanessa thought, gritting her teeth.

"Did you go to boarding school?" Roddy asked Grant.

"Me? Oh, I went to schools all over the place."

"But did you have to leave your mother and your friends?"

Vanessa decided it was time to break up this cozy conversation. She yawned and stretched her arms above her head. "Hey, you two woke me up with all your chattering."

"Sorry." Grant glanced at her. "Have a good sleep?"

"Not really." Vanessa wrapped her arms around her stomach and groaned. "I feel awful."

He frowned. "What's wrong?"

"I'm feeling really sick." Groaning again, she leaned forward, rocking back and forth in her seat as if she were in pain.

Grant slowed down and glanced in his rearview mirror to check for traffic. "Do you want me to stop?"

She nodded. "Would you mind? I feel as if I'm going to be sick."

"I seem to remember passing a sign saying there was a motel with a restaurant a few miles from here."

"Please don't mention restaurants."

"Sorry. Can you last for a few more minutes?" Grant asked, giving her another anxious glance.

"I think so."

"Okay. Hang on."

"You're not going to be sick in the car, are you?" Roddy asked, a hint of panic in his voice. Ever since he'd thrown up in his father's Jaguar and Colin had created a terrible fuss, Roddy had developed a horror of himself or someone else throwing up.

"No, darling. If I need to, I'll be sure to tell Grant in time."

"I can easily stop," Grant assured him.

For God's sake, stop being so understanding! Vanessa wanted to shout at him. It only made the situation worse. How much easier it would be to hate the man if he were a callous swine to Roddy and a sexist bastard to her.

Unfortunately, he was neither. Or, at least, she suddenly realized, he didn't appear to be. Grant Kendall was obviously a consummate actor. After all, until she'd seen that photograph he'd had her completely fooled, hadn't he? God alone knew what the man was really like.

Chapter 29

When they reached the next exit off the Interstate, Grant slowed down and turned off. The road approaching the small town soon became its main street, which was lined with a few single-story buildings on either side. Ahead of them were the mountains, their summits and slopes frosted with snow.

At the first intersection was a sign advertising a motel. "That might be a likely spot." Grant made a turn, drove a little way down the street, and drew up in front of the long, one-story building with a sign of a large sun converted to a happy face. "Sunshine?" he said doubtfully. "Well, it might shine here in the summer, I suppose."

Vanessa didn't respond. All she knew was that this was where she intended to part company with Mr. Grant Kendall.

He jumped out and came around to her side to help her out. She felt an impulse to kick him on the shins, grab Roddy, and run for cover. Instead she took the hand he proffered and slowly stepped from the car. She stood on the sidewalk, eyes shut, and, putting one hand to her forehead, moaned pitifully.

"Mum's really sick, isn't she?" she heard Roddy say in an anxious tone. How she hated having to upset him like this.

"Don't you worry. We'll soon have your mother feeling fighting fit again."

"That's alliteration, isn't it?" Roddy said.

"Whatever you say," Grant replied. With one hand

on Vanessa's elbow he guided her up the wooden steps and into the small foyer of the motel.

In less than ten minutes he'd arranged for two rooms for them and also asked about the availability of a doctor.

"I don't need a doctor," Vanessa said in a harsh whisper.

"Your wife pregnant?" asked the large woman in a gaudy floral sweater at the desk.

Seeing the twitch at the corner of Grant's mouth, Vanessa wished she could see the funny side of this, too. But there was nothing remotely amusing about the prospect of having to get herself and Roddy away from here, without Grant realizing that they'd gone until it was too late to catch up with them.

Grant drove the car around to the back and he and Roddy unpacked it. When he opened the door to one of the rooms and gestured to her to go in, Vanessa recoiled. The room was painted in a particularly gruesome shade of mustard yellow with olive-green paintwork. To add a little more color, the drapes and bedspread were a virulent mixture of orange and green.

There was also a predominant musty smell and, in the bathroom, when she inspected it, a patch of damp on the wall where several tiles had fallen out.

"If I didn't feel sick before, I certainly would now," she told Grant, who stood gazing about him with a look of revulsion.

"Want to try somewhere else?"

"No," she said quickly. "At least I can lie down. I couldn't have taken one more mile in the car. I'll be fine as long as I close my eyes."

Grant set down their bags. "Our hostess said there's a drugstore on the main street that's still open. Can I get you something to help the pain?"

"I have some Pepto-Bismol. That will be enough." Vanessa stretched out on one of the two single beds.

To her consternation, Grant came to her and lightly pressed the palm of his hand to her forehead. It felt soothingly cool against her skin. "No fever," he pronounced. "Thank God for that. I was concerned it might be appendicitis."

"I'll be fine once I get some rest," she told him.

"Roddy and I will let you sleep. We'll go and case this joint, okay?" Grant told Roddy from the corner of his mouth.

Vanessa had to think fast. She sat up again, holding her stomach, groaning horribly. "On second thoughts I think you'd better get me some Gravol, if you can." She held out her hand to Roddy. "Would you stay with Mummy, darling?" she begged, giving a particularly nauseating impression of a sick and clinging mother. "I don't want to be left alone."

Grant looked from her to Roddy, frowning. For a moment she didn't think he was going to buy it. Then he turned and went to the door. "I'll be as quick as possible."

She opened her eyes again. "Don't rush. I'll take the Pepto first, see if it works. Will you take the car or walk?"

"Why?"

"No reason. I wanted to make sure we had everything before you left, that was all."

The frown deepened. "I'll take the car. We brought in all the bags and Roddy checked to make sure he had all his stuff as well."

Vanessa closed her eyes, feeling the tide of disappointment wash over her. He was going to hang on to those bloody car keys all night.

"Anything else you need while I'm out?" Grant asked.

"No, thanks," Vanessa said, folding her arm across her eyes.

"I'll get some mineral water." He turned to Roddy. "And I'll bring back some Coke and chips, okay?"

"Thanks." Roddy sat on the edge of the rattan chair, swinging his legs. His face was pale. Vanessa knew that he was afraid of being left with someone who might throw up at any minute, but she couldn't risk letting him out of her sight.

"Right. As soon as your mother feels better, you can come and explore this place with me. Maybe there's a pinball machine somewhere."

Vanessa opened her eyes and saw how Roddy had visibly brightened. She felt a pain around her heart. Poor Roddy. It was bad enough having to run away from an abusive father, but then to have his new hero turned to ashes . . . Life was so unfair.

Grant put his hand on the doorknob, ready to open the door. "Look after your mother," he told Roddy. He went outside, pulling the door shut behind him.

"Has he gone yet?" Vanessa whispered to Roddy.

"I don't know."

"Check at the window. He left the car right outside this door."

Roddy gave her a questioning look, but did as he was told. He pulled the curtain back a little and looked out. "He's in the car. Now he's started it up."

"Good." Vanessa sat up and swung her legs to the floor.

"The car's moving away now. He's turning it. . . . Now he's gone."

"Great." Heart hammering, Vanessa dragged on her shoes. Roddy looked at her wide-eyed. "Stay here, all right?" she ordered him. "I'm just going to ask the lady again about that doctor."

"But you said you didn't—"

"I know what I said, but I have to speak to the lady again. If Grant comes back, please tell him that I had to find out about the doctor. He'll understand." Grabbing her bag and the room key, she ran to the interior door that led out to the hall. Then she ran back to the bewildered boy and grabbed hold of him, gazing into his eyes. "Whatever you do, Roddy, you must promise me that you will stay right here. Whatever Grant says, you must not leave this room until I say it's all right to do so, understand?"

He nodded, his large eyes like saucers. It was painfully obvious that he did not understand.

"You can turn on the television," Vanessa told him, and then rushed from the room.

She was glad to see that the woman was still at the desk, with no sign of anyone else being around. "Excuse me."

"Hi, there. Feeling any better?"

Vanessa took in a deep breath. She bent over the desk. "Can you keep a secret?"

The woman's eyes widened. "Well, I hope so."

"I'm not really sick," Vanessa said in a loud stage whisper, glancing around to make sure no one was listening in. "When I first saw you I thought you'd be the kind of person I could trust."

The woman nodded vehemently. "Sure you can, honey. Sure you can."

"What's your name?"

"Beth."

"Well, Beth, I'm in desperate need of your help. I have to get away from my husband. He's abusive to me and our boy."

Beth put her hands to her plump cheeks. "Oh my God, no. That poor little kid."

"And now he's kidnapped us."

"Kidnapped! Oh Lord, that's terrible. What can I do?"

"I need to rent a car. Do you have a rental place nearby?"

"Sam Riley runs a Budget Rental out of his service station."

"Would you do something for me?"

"Sure thing, honey."

"Would you call Sam for me and tell him I need a car later tonight?" Vanessa thought for a moment. "Eleven o'clock would be best. I'd call him myself, but my husband's due back any minute now and I don't want him to catch me on the phone." She gave a very visible shiver. "Heaven knows what he'd do if he knew I was talking to you!"

"I understand. Don't you worry. I'll call Sam and arrange it for you."

"I'll be driving the car to Vancouver, tell him."

"I thought you were Canadian, with that accent."

Vanessa gave her a faint smile. "Right. Here's my driver's license."

"Vanessa Marston Craigmore," Beth read from the license. "This here's not an American license. Not Canadian, either, is it?" There was suspicion in her voice.

"No. My son and I are living in Britain now."

"Your husband gave his address as Yountville, California."

"Well, we're separated, you see. He lives in California, but although I'm a Canadian I now live and work in Britain." She leaned even closer across the desk. "My son was over here visiting his father. I came to fetch him back. We were on our way to Vancouver Airport, but before I knew what was happening my husband took off with us."

"Sounds like a double kidnap to me. I should be getting the police in on this." Beth's hand was already on the phone receiver.

"Please, don't." Vanessa grasped her hand. Her look of alarm was all too real. "It's terribly complicated because of the international cross-border thing. Once my son and I get back into Canada we'll be completely safe."

"You sure about that?"

"Absolutely. Besides, you don't want to have the police coming to your motel, do you? It doesn't give a good image to the place, does it?"

"You're right about that. I recall the time when we had a bunch of kids here and—"

"I must get back to my room or my husband will guess something's going on." Vanessa picked up her driver's license and pressed it into the woman's hands. "If you see my husband, don't say a word to him, okay?"

Beth put her finger on her lips. "I won't breathe a word of this to anyone."

"Except Sam."

"Except Sam, of course."

"When he brings the car, give me two rings on the phone and then hang up. I'll know that's the signal that the car's here for me."

"Two rings and hang up," Beth repeated.

"No. Forget that." Vanessa clapped her hand to her mouth. "My husband's room is next to ours. He'd hear the phone." She thought for a moment. "I'll just come here at eleven, okay?"

"Here?"

"Here, to the front desk. At eleven."

"I'm not to call you. You'll be here at eleven," Beth repeated, by now looking a little flustered.

"And would you ask Sam to have all the paperwork ready, so that all I have to do is sign it?"

"Paperwork all done. I'll do that, honey. Now, don't you worry about a thing. I'll look after it for you." Beth's eyes glowed.

She's thoroughly enjoying this, Vanessa thought. It was probably the most exciting thing that had happened to her in years. "Thanks, Beth. I'll never be able to thank you enough for this," Vanessa said, and meant it.

When she went back to the room, Roddy was watching the television.

"Shall I turn it off?" he asked, looking at her with anxious eyes.

"No, sweetie. No need. Just keep the sound down. I'm going to lie down again for a while."

"Are you feeling okay?"

"I'm feeling much better," she said in a strong voice. "So you can stop worrying about me. To be honest, I was pretending I was feeling worse than I really was."

Roddy looked hurt. "Why did you do that?"

"Because I didn't want to be driving too long. We both need our sleep."

"Why didn't you tell Grant you wanted to stop? He'd have understood."

"Do you really think so? I'm not so sure. He said he doesn't like making stops on a journey."

"If you'd asked—"

"I didn't like to ask. Enough questions. You get back to your television. I'll rest."

She lay down on the bed, but a couple of minutes later the telephone rang and she sat up, guessing that it must be Beth. "Hello?"

"Is it okay to speak?" Beth asked in a loud whisper.

"Yes. It's fine. He's not back yet."

"I spoke to Sam. He says you can't drive one of his cars over the border to Canada, else how can he get it back?"

Vanessa's heart plummeted. "Oh no. I never thought of that."

"He said how 'bout he drive you to Seattle Airport, so's you can get a flight to Vancouver. It'll cost a fair bit, but it'll still be cheaper than if you rent and drive there yourself."

Vanessa felt hollow inside. She desperately wanted to get to Canada tonight. But what option did she have? She must get Roddy away from Grant as soon as possible. "Okay. If I can't take a car over the border, then this will have to do."

"Same time, okay?"

"Yes, I'll be at the desk at eleven. Thanks a million, Beth." She put down the receiver.

"Who was that?" asked Roddy.

"Just the lady at the front desk. Roddy," she said, "please turn off the television. There's something I have to tell you."

"What?" His eyes were still fixed on the flickering screen.

"Turn the TV off first," she said impatiently.

He did so, then turned to face her with a grumpy expression.

"You're not going to like this," Vanessa told him, "but I don't want you leaving me alone tonight."

"What do you mean?"

"I mean, I don't want you going off with Grant and leaving me."

"Oh, Mu-um, that's not fair! He said there might be a pinball machine."

"I know he did." Vanessa came to him and wrapped her arms about him. His body was stiff with resistance. "But I prefer that you stay with me at all times. So please don't argue with me later when I ask you to stay here, all right?"

He pulled away from her embrace and stared at her, eyes widening. "You think Daddy's coming here for us, don't you?"

Oh, God, she thought. What can I tell him?

"No, darling. I just think that you and I must stick together until this is over."

"But we can trust Grant. You said we could. Grant wouldn't let anything bad happen to us."

"*I* won't let anything bad happen, I promise you. Do you believe that?" She sat on the end of the bed, her hands on his shoulders, compelling him to look at her. "Do you?"

His mouth opened and shut. "Yes," he said at last.

"All right. Then you must do what I ask, okay? There has to be a leader on every mission and I'm it, so no questioning my decisions. Right?"

"Right," he said, with obvious reluctance.

"We're moving out of this place tonight, you and me, okay?"

"You don't need to speak in that stupid voice," he said. "I understand."

She grimaced. "Sorry. I thought it might be more fun if we pretended—"

"It's real, not pretend. I'm not a baby, you know."

"I know. I'm sorry. I do know how tough this is for you, but it's coming to an end now."

"Are we going to be running away from Grant as well as Daddy?"

Her heart constricted. "No more running away," she said firmly. "We're going to catch a plane to Winnipeg. We'll stay with your grandparents and work everything out."

"We should've stayed there in the first place."

"I think you're right. Anyway, that's what we're going to do."

"What about Grant?"

"What about him?"

"Will we ever see him again?"

Vanessa's pulse quickened. "We should be seeing him any minute now."

"You know what I mean," Roddy said with all the world-weariness a seven-year-old can summon up against an obtuse adult.

"Yes, I know. I'm sorry. To be perfectly honest, I don't think so. Once we go, I think he'll just . . . leave us alone and go back to his winery." Vanessa swallowed the choking lump that had developed in her throat.

"I wanted to see his winery." There was a very slight tremor in Roddy's voice.

"So did I."

"He does have one, doesn't he?"

Vanessa put one arm around his shoulders. Despite his courage, she knew that Roddy must feel that his world was constantly crumbling around him. She must leave him something tangible to hold on to. "Yes, Roddy, he does have a winery."

Again he drew away from her. He switched on the television again and sat, shoulders hunched, watching it. But Vanessa knew that, although his eyes followed the moving picture, his mind was engaged elsewhere.

"We mustn't let Grant think we've changed in any way, all right? When he comes back here, be his friend just like before."

"That won't be easy."

"No, I know it won't."

Roddy thought for a moment. "If he knew we were running away from him, would he hurt us?"

Vanessa took his head in her hands and turned it toward her, forcing him to look at her. "No, Roddy.

Whatever we did, Grant would never ever hurt either of us."

Later that night, lying on his bed in the silent darkness, straining his ears for every sound, Grant heard the interior door of the room next to his slowly open. He got to his feet and crossed the room.

Standing close to his own door, he imagined he could hear her painful intake of breath at the creak of her door's unoiled hinges. He cursed beneath his breath, knowing that somehow he'd screwed the whole thing up. As he heard them tread softly past his room and down the corridor, his muscles ached with the desire to rush out and confront them.

What was the point? He knew exactly where to find them.

Chapter 30

As it was far too late to catch a flight that night, Vanessa decided to stay at the Hilton at Seattle Airport, knowing that a major hotel would have better security and someone at the desk throughout the night if she needed help.

"Sure you'll be okay?" the friendly—and talkative—Sam Riley asked when he dropped her off outside the hotel.

"We'll be fine, thank you." Her head was pounding from the constant drone of his voice, but she was also immensely grateful to this man who'd brought her here safely. She showed her gratitude by giving him a twenty-dollar bill as a tip.

Once she and Roddy were settled into the room, she ordered chicken sandwiches from room service. Roddy had announced again that he was hungry.

He was also angry. Despite her explanation about Grant, he'd slumped, sullen and rude, in a far corner of the car, refusing to speak in anything but monosyllables. Now he went straight to the television and turned it on, without asking if he could. Vanessa decided to let him be. Better that than having a confrontation at this late hour, especially when she couldn't give him any credible explanation for their escape from the motel—and Grant.

What next? she thought, as she stood looking at the telephone. Should she stop at Vancouver tomorrow morning, see Jill before she went on to Winnipeg? By now she was finding it difficult to make decisions. Her mind was weary from stress and lack of sleep . . . and too much thinking.

She called Jill at her own apartment, but got the answering machine. "Damn," she said softly to herself. She hesitated when Jill's no-nonsense voice told her to leave her number. What was the point? If Jill was away, by the time she got home again Vanessa would have left Seattle. On the other hand, Jill might be picking up her messages from wherever she was.

Vanessa was about to leave a brief message with the Hilton's number when she suddenly realized that if someone was monitoring Jill's calls she'd be giving them what they needed: their present location.

The dial tone in her ear told her that she'd been cut off from Jill's machine. It was one of the lowest points in this entire debacle. Almost two weeks had gone by since she had left Strathferness and she was no further ahead. In fact, everything seemed far worse and infinitely bleaker than it had been on that first day, when she'd fled from Strathferness to Edinburgh and then Amsterdam.

"Is Auntie Jill at home?" asked Roddy through a wide yawn.

"She may be, but she's probably asleep. I'll call again and leave a message." She pressed in the numbers and this time, when prompted, said, "It's me. I'll call again in another hour."

When Roddy had fallen into a deep sleep on one of the double beds, Vanessa tried Jill's number again, but there was still no reply. She thought again of leaving the hotel number, but decided against it. She was quite sure that Grant was not working alone. This was a sophisticated operation. The man with the beak nose must be his partner, despite their little performance in the apartment parking lot in Vancouver.

Since she'd arrived in Seattle, she'd had a little time to think, and had already decided that the episode in the apartment parking lot had been staged to consolidate her trust in Grant. It was possible that Grant's beak-nosed partner had followed Grant to that grungy motel and then been left on the lookout. He would have seen them leave with Sam and reported it to Grant. It was highly likely, therefore, that Grant had followed them all the way to Seattle.

He could even be in the hotel at this very moment.

Vanessa checked the door again, making sure that she'd turned both locks and put on the safety chain. Then she bent to kiss Roddy good night and stretched out on the other double bed.

At first sleep just wouldn't come. Her mind was filled with swirling images, all tossed around, like debris being spun about by a tornado. Then came those ceaseless questions of what to do next. But, she told herself firmly, she'd decided that already. She was going home to Winnipeg. There, come hell or high water, she would make a stand and face Colin in whatever battle might ensue. She should have done that in the first place, and would have, but for the dread that crept over her each time she thought of losing custody of Roddy to Colin.

She was tempted to call her parents now, tell them she was coming, but decided that no one, not even her parents, should know her plans ahead of time. She wasn't about to trust any technology, least of all telephones. Only last year her mother had sent her a clipping from the *Globe and Mail* about a family whose house had been invaded by some technology wizard who'd taken over their electricity and telephones and pestered them day and night. Although it had turned out to be their own son, for several weeks he'd confounded even the experts.

No, she'd turn up at home unannounced and then she'd remain there, secure with the people she could really trust, and put herself and Roddy in the hands of a good lawyer.

"She and the boy have just boarded a flight to Winnipeg," the voice at the other end of the line told Colin on Wednesday evening. He'd been informed earlier that she'd stayed in Seattle the previous night. Now he felt a tremendous sense of elation. "Gotcha!" he said in a half whisper. "Trapped."

"What's that?"

"Nothing," Colin said. "Good work."

"I couldn't get on the plane. She took us by surprise. Left the Seattle hotel suddenly. They only just made the flight."

"It doesn't matter. She'll be going to her parents' place."

"I'll be on the next flight."

"I'm coming over to Canada myself. I can't get away tomorrow, but I hope to be able to leave here Friday."

"You want us to stay on the job?"

"Absolutely. You never can tell what devious tricks she's going to play. I can't afford to take any chances. My son's life and future happiness is at stake here."

"I understand."

"You go to Winnipeg. Keep reporting to me until I tell you not to. Once I leave Scotland, you can report to Mr. McKay until I arrive in Winnipeg."

"Not to Sir Robert."

"No," Colin roared down the phone. "I told you before, reports are to come directly to me. And if you can't get me, then to McKay. Understand?"

"Right, sir."

When Colin put away the portable telephone he found that he was trembling with excitement. She'd gone home. Like a trapped vixen, she'd gone home. Well, he'd soon have the dogs baying at her heels, damn her to eternal hellfire.

And he himself would be in at the kill.

Chapter 31

Lady Craigmore was coming home to Strathferness Castle. The doctor's decision to allow her to leave the hospital hadn't been made until late on Wednesday afternoon, so that all Thursday morning a retinue of people from the village had been busily scouring and polishing the castle under Morag Lindsay's direction.

Almost immediately after Fiona's heart attack, Sir Robert had come to realize the importance of Mrs. Lindsay to both his wife and the well-being of the household—and, therefore, to himself—and had effected a truce between himself and his erstwhile housekeeper. She was to be fully reinstated in her former position, but would not receive the benefit of his own commands or counsel.

"This will be our last discussion," he'd informed her at their one and only meeting since Fiona's collapse. "When Lady Craigmore returns you will apply to her for any decisions or orders regarding the running of Strathferness." The damned woman had merely said a quiet "Thank you" and left the room, her face impassive, as if she felt she'd received only what she deserved. Never again, he'd vowed at the time, would he deal with the woman himself or even acknowledge her if he passed her on the stairs. In his eyes, she was still a traitor to the family.

As he waited for the ambulance that was transporting his wife and the private nurse he'd hired from the hospital in Inverness, Sir Robert allowed his mind to dwell for a very brief time, a mere moment, on

what it would have meant to him if Fiona had never
returned to Strethferness.

His legs suddenly crumpled beneath him as if they
were made of corrugated paper. He sank onto the
footstool in his study, his forehead in his hand. He
hadn't allowed himself to consider it until now, when
it was no longer an immediate possibility. Strange how
he'd missed his wife these past few days. After all, she
did precious little around the place, other than sitting
at her tapestry or pottering in the garden, or cleaning
their extensive collection of eighteenth century silver-
gilt goblets and plates every week. Yet he had sorely
missed the quiet presence, the soft voice, even the
regular movement of the delicate hand holding a needle, pulling silks through the canvas before her.

That, in particular, surprised him, as he was forever
complaining to her about how much her needlework
annoyed him, particularly when she did it while he
was reading or watching television in the library. He
made a solemn vow that the next time she pulled her
tapestry frame toward her, he would not complain
about how it distracted him. Not the first time,
anyway.

Amanda was walking in the garden, along paved
paths slippery with frost. She thought of that last time
she and her mother had walked here together, their
discussion about marriage and love, and of the dead
rosebush. Her mother had said it was an ill omen.
Even in this modern age, Highlanders were very su-
perstitious. She hadn't exactly said what it meant, but
Amanda had suspected it presaged a death in the
family.

She shivered and pulled her thick mohair scarf up
around her ears.

Her mother's illness had terrified her. It had caught
her unawares. She'd taken it for granted that whenever she came home to Strathferness her mother
would always be there, a permanent part of the an-

cient home, like the faded tapestries on the walls of the hall.

Amanda now knew that to be a fallacy. Now she realized that things did not last forever, that life was short . . . and yes, although it was a hoary old cliché, sweet. And it was time she lived it, instead of frigging around on the periphery, as she was doing now.

As soon as she was sure that her mother was settled in comfortably at Strathferness, she was going to get back to London and give in her resignation. A high-powered, frantically busy position in advertising wasn't what she really wanted to do. She had several contacts in Edinburgh. She didn't belong in London; she belonged here, in Scotland. Alas, while her father was here, she couldn't think of living at Strathferness itself, but still she knew that, like the sleeping plants hibernating around her, this was where her roots were.

Morag Lindsay was checking Lady Craigmore's suite to make sure that everything was just right. She had allowed no one but herself to clean the bedroom and the small sitting room with the bay window that overlooked the garden. That way she could be sure that everything was done properly.

There were small vases of flowers or little pots of African violets on every surface. Lady Craigmore loved flowers. The rosewood dressing table gleamed, as did all the other furniture, and the silver-backed brushes and mirror shone in the soft light.

The electric fire burned low in the hearth. Several years ago, Lady Craigmore had insisted on their installation in all the bedrooms, saying that she didn't want to see anyone having to clean out ashes from log or peat fires upstairs.

How typical that was of her, Morag thought. As always Lady Craigmore was concerned with the welfare of others. She gazed around the bedroom, making sure that everything was in its proper place, glowing with the feeling of satisfaction that preparing these rooms for Fiona had given her. She could call her

Fiona now. Only in private, of course. To do so in public would not be correct. But during these past few weeks they'd moved from the relationship of respected employer and employee to that of close friends.

Morag knew a moment of quiet triumph as she thought of that conversation she'd had with Sir Robert. It was the last one he'd have with her, he had informed her in a pompous tone. Well, that suited her just fine, she thought with a smile. Just so long as she and Fiona were left in peace, to run the household the way they wanted, she would be content.

A shadow passed over her mind, like a gray cloud drifting across the sun. Well, maybe not quite content, she thought, remembering Vanessa and wee Roddy. Until this sorry mess was settled, none of them could be truly content.

Colin was in his room, making a call. He'd left the distillery at three, to be able to welcome his mother home to Strathferness with the rest of the family. "I'm checking in now," he said into the phone. "You won't be able to reach me for the remainder of the afternoon."

"She and the boy are in Winnipeg with her parents," he was told.

Colin breathed a sigh of relief. "Good. Make sure she doesn't catch either of you watching her. Ease off, so that she thinks she's okay there. That way she won't make any more moves. I want her to feel safe, really safe where she is."

"Don't you worry. She'll think we've all gone home, too."

He was expecting a laugh, but Colin didn't give him one. "I'll be in touch before I leave Scotland," Colin told him, and hung up. He put away the phone and went to the window, which overlooked the front drive. No sign of the ambulance yet.

The news that his mother was going to be released from the hospital had come as a shock at first. He'd

felt qualms for the space of a few minutes, but that
was all. He'd already made up his mind that, whatever
happened, he was definitely going to Canada. His
quest to rescue his son from that viper was vitally
important, more important than anything else in the
world, even his mother's life.

Anyway, what was her life? She was growing old.
In the winter, she sat around sewing aimlessly or she
played bridge with the church ladies. In the summer,
she deadheaded the roses. That was it. What sort of
life was that? And she was a slave to his father, had
always been so, subjugated, as they all had been, to
his will.

That was her choice, but it wasn't his. Not bloody
likely. He was going to show them all what he could
do . . . and without his father's help, too.

So, even if his mother did have another attack, a
far more serious—even fatal—one this time, because
she was upset by his leaving for Canada, wouldn't he
actually be releasing her from what was in essence a
miserable and pointless existence?

Of course he would. She had nothing to live for.
Oh, of course, she adored Roddy, but that was all. In
fact, he was convinced that she loved Roddy far more
than she'd ever loved him. Yet he, Colin, was her
firstborn son. Weren't mothers supposed to love their
firstborn sons best? His hands shook as he poured
himself a whiskey from the bottle he kept locked in
his bedside cabinet. That certainly hadn't been the
case with his mother. His mother had thought that the
sun rose and set on her bloody *second* son, damn him,
even though he'd abandoned her.

He drained the shot of whiskey down and poured
himself another. His mother hadn't cared much about
her firstborn son, so why the hell should he care about
her? To hell with her and all of them! All that mattered now was rescuing and punishing Vanessa. Before
the week was out, he'd have his son back and they'd
all congratulate him, but they wouldn't get their hands
on Roddy. No, once he got him back he'd make sure

that his son never came under this family's influence again. Roddy would belong to him alone.

It was growing dark by the time the ambulance drew up in the front of the castle. As Fiona was lifted into the wheelchair and carefully maneuvered up the six wide steps, she wondered if she'd done the right thing, after all, in begging the doctor to let her go home. The castle looked forbidding in the gray gloom of the early evening, a silvery mist shadowing the outside coach lamps that lit the entrance.

She would have preferred to go straight to her own suite, but knew that the family would want to gather around her, to welcome her home. And she definitely didn't want them crowding about her in her little sitting room upstairs. That was reserved for meeting the members of her family one by one, at her invitation. Or for pleasant conversations with Morag, while they had tea and chocolate digestive biscuits and watched *Coronation Street* or *ER* together.

Yes, that was what she was really looking forward to, the time when she could say good night and close her door on her family.

But here they all were, gathering around her: Robert, his face almost purple with pent-up emotion . . . and Amanda, suddenly looking older, a worried expression on her heart-shaped face . . . and Colin.

Fiona's heart cramped, making her clutch the arms of her wheelchair. Then she saw Morag coming down the main staircase and she felt a slight lessening of tension. Calmly, deliberately, she drew in several deep breaths and, with grace and composure, accepted their greetings.

But the image of Colin's eyes glittering feverishly in his ashen face stayed imprinted on her mind, like footprints in frozen snow, so that every time she woke up in her familiar bed in her familiar bedroom that night, it would be the first thing she saw.

Chapter 32

Returning to Winnipeg had been the right thing to do, Vanessa decided on her first night at home. After only a few hours of being there with his grandparents, Roddy seemed less tense and, for the first time, she found herself thinking about what she would do with her life once this was all over.

Since they had boarded the plane for Winnipeg, as if by tacit consent, neither she nor Roddy had mentioned the one gaping emptiness in their lives. She knew that this silence wasn't good for Roddy, but she couldn't bear to discuss it. It was like a raw, open wound. One day, when this was over, she would talk to Roddy about it, but not now.

Once she had given her parents a capsule version of all that had happened since she'd left Winnipeg, she tried very hard not to permit thoughts of Grant to enter her mind. That was easy enough while she was talking to her mother or watching the CBC news in the den with her father, but when she went to bed it was far more difficult. She lay there in her old bedroom, with the constant hum of the gas furnace blowing warm air through the register in the floor, staring at the poster of Evelyn Hart in *Swan Lake,* but it was Grant's image she saw.

Once during that long night the sense of abject betrayal engulfed her and she turned her face into her pillow. Other times, she ground her teeth and pounded the same pillow with fury at how gullible she'd been.

In the morning, she woke up suddenly, thinking of

him, and found herself gasping for air. Impossible to open the window, of course. It was frozen shut—and would be for another couple of months. She knelt on the bed and peered out the double panes of glass, but could see little more than the yellow glow of the streetlight, as the inside window was etched with ice patterns. How strange it was, she thought, that you could be so toasty warm in the house when it was minus thirty degrees Celsius outside.

Maybe that was the charm of being here, that sense of being holed up in a safe and warm place, hibernating like the bears and the other wild animals, until spring came and thawed them out.

That sense of safety was shattered, however, when she heard from Jill after breakfast. "What the hell is going on?" was Jill's greeting when Vanessa took the telephone from her father. "I stay away from my apartment for a couple of nights and I come home to your frantic messages on the machine. I've been worried sick. Why didn't you tell me where you were, so I could call you back?"

Vanessa explained why, wincing inwardly at every mention of Grant's name.

"Shit!" Jill said. "I knew you shouldn't have trusted that guy. He was too damned good to be true. I told you that, didn't I, several times?"

"Yes, you did," Vanessa said wearily. "I should have listened. Anyway, I'm here with my parents now and—"

"He called me."

"Who did?"

"Grant," Jill yelled down the phone. "He called and left a message, begging me to get back to him at some hotel."

Vanessa's heart started racing. "Where?"

"It's okay. Relax. He was in Vancouver."

"Yes, but that means he's followed me back to Canada. Oh God."

"Now, don't start panicking."

"I'm not. It's just that . . . that I hoped he'd go on

home to California and we'd never hear from him
again. What did he say when he called?"

"He said you'd gone off with Roddy and that you
were in danger."

Heat flared in Vanessa's face. "I certainly was.
From *him*! I can't believe he'd have the nerve to call
you. Did you call him back?"

"Yes, but he'd checked out."

"God, Jill, he could be on his way here."

"Did you tell him where your parents live?"

"Not the actual address, but he knows their name
and that my father's an accountant."

"Bigmouth! You had to tell him all that stuff,
didn't you?"

"I trusted him, Jill."

"I know you did, sweetie, I know. Sorry, I'm just
mad as hell that the guy I put onto it didn't find out
more about Grant. I feel kind of responsible."

"That's ridiculous. No one's responsible. It was
just fate."

"Fate? You've got to be kidding. You mean the
dreamy Grant Kendall just happened to be around
when Roddy got hurt? Hello-*o*, Vanessa, anyone in
there?"

"That would mean Grant orchestrated the whole
thing, arranged for Roddy to be hurt."

"Got it in one. So you can stop thinking of the man
as your caped crusader."

"I'm not exactly stupid," Vanessa said, her voice
pinched. "I just didn't think he was capable of hurting
a child."

"Depends how much he was paid, I suppose. Any-
ways, that's in the past. You'd better go to the police
and see if you can get some sort of protection."

"How can I, when I've got a court order against me
in Scotland? Possibly here as well, for all I know. If I
go to the police they'll probably order me to take
Roddy back to Scotland right away. Then I'll be back
where I started."

"Well, you're not any better off holed up there, are you?"

"I've made arrangements to see a lawyer later this morning."

"Good. Maybe she can make some sense of all this."

"It's a he, actually."

"Women are better for custody cases."

"Don't be so sexist." Vanessa hesitated. "Jill . . ."

"What?"

"Did Grant say anything else? I mean . . . I need to know exactly what he said."

"I told you. He said you'd gone off with Roddy and that you were in grave danger."

Vanessa thought for a moment. "It doesn't make any sense. Why would he warn me of danger from himself? It's almost as if he's regretting having worked for Colin and wants to let me know that I'm in danger from him."

"From who?"

"Colin, of course."

Jill heaved an exaggerated sigh down the line. "Dream on, buddy. No wonder you're in the theater. Fantasyland is the only place for you. You're determined to whitewash this guy."

Vanessa gritted her teeth. "You make me really, really angry, Jill Nelson. I'm not whitewashing him. I can't tell you how mad I was when I found that photograph in his wallet. But he could be having second thoughts."

"About what?"

"I agree he was working for Colin, but perhaps he was horrified by what happened to Roddy and wants out."

"Whatever you say. Look, I have to fly to New York this afternoon for a meeting tomorrow. Do you want me to cancel it and come to Winnipeg instead?"

"No, thanks. I can manage fine. Give me a call tomorrow evening and I'll let you know what happened with the lawyer."

"I'll do that." A pause, then Jill said, "Van . . ."

"What?"

"Please be careful. I love you, you know."

"I know that. Love you, too. Before you go . . . it wasn't like you to be away and not check on your messages. What happened?"

A stretch of silence and then Jill said, half laughing, "I had an unexpected invitation from my yachting friend."

"Aha! I guessed as much. Where?"

"Florida."

"Get much of a tan?"

"Nope."

Vanessa chuckled and, after a moment, Jill joined in. "Good for you," Vanessa told her. "But next time choose your timing a little more carefully, would you?"

"I'll check with you first, okay?"

Vanessa found herself still smiling as she put down the phone, but the smile faded as she began thinking again about Grant's message on Jill's machine. Why had he talked about her being in "grave danger" as if this were some new threat?

And why, when she knew that he was working against her, that her son was in danger from him, did she still feel this burning desire to have him here beside her?

Chapter 33

When Colin didn't appear at the breakfast table the morning after their mother's return to Strathferness, Amanda suggested that he might have left early to go to the distillery.

"That'll be the day," her father said, slathering thick-cut marmalade on his toast with the back of the spoon. He bit into the toast, marmalade sticking to his mustache, chewing while he talked. "Don't often catch our Colin going in to work early."

Amanda looked down at her copy of the *Daily Telegraph*. Watching her father eat turned her stomach. He was like a starving man who'd had his first meal in weeks set before him.

"Where's your mother?" he asked.

"In her room. Where else would she be?"

"Never mind." He shook the creases out of the *Times*.

"Surely you didn't expect her to come down for breakfast." Amanda was genuinely amazed.

"Thought she might," he muttered. "Usually does, when she's at home."

Amanda was tempted to let it go, as she usually did, to avoid a row, but this was too much. "Father, would you put your paper down for a minute, please?"

He lowered it a couple of inches, peering over the top. "Why?"

"Because I want to speak to you."

Frowning, he slammed the paper down on the table, rattling the china and silverware. "Well?" He glanced at his watch. "Make it short. I have a meeting at nine."

"I'm leaving tomorrow morning."

"You can't leave. Your mother needs you."

"No, she doesn't. What she needs is lots of rest and to be left in peace, something this family has never seemed quite capable of."

"She'll get her rest."

"She needs to have peace of mind as well. Living here is like being in a battle zone and I refuse to be the peacemaker all the time."

"You're havering, girl." He snorted. "Some peacemaker. You're hardly ever here."

"No, and that's why I'm not." Amanda leaned forward. "Ma's very ill and you're still expecting her to come down to breakfast, because you don't like changes in your life. Well, that's too bloody bad."

"Watch your mouth, young lady."

"Oh for God's sake, Father, stop being so ridiculous. I'm thirty-three. I live in the real world where women swear, okay? You're not going to have everything your own way anymore. Ma will need to be looked after until she's strong enough to do things herself again, which means you have to stop this stupid vendetta with Morag, unless you want this place to fall down about your ears."

He drew himself up, his spine stiff against the high-backed chair. "I refuse to speak to the woman."

"Then send notes to her, but you can't bother Ma with questions about what's for dinner tonight and who's going to show the school group around the castle on visiting day."

"I will have no dealings whatsoever with that woman," he said through clenched teeth.

"Then engage someone else as a go-between. Get a part-time house secretary . . . or something. It's not as if you can't afford it, for God's sake. And while we're about it, we need more help in the kitchen. Morag shouldn't have to be helping with the cleaning and washing up in there."

"Why not? She does precious little else in the place."

Amanda sighed and slowly shook her head at him. "Honestly, you just don't have a clue what goes on here, do you? Ma and Morag have kept everything running so smoothly all these years that you thought it was a breeze to look after. Well, you're soon going to find out it isn't."

He muttered something to himself, but this time he didn't bark back at her. "What is it that needs doing?"

"Morag will tell you. She was talking to me last night, after Ma fell asleep."

"If she talked to you, you can tell me."

"No, Father. I'm going back to London tomorrow. You'll have to deal with Morag yourself."

He set his mouth in a stubborn line. "If you won't tell me, I'll ask your mother. She'll know what to do."

Amanda recognized blackmail when she heard it. That was one of her father's favorite methods of getting his own way. "Start worrying her about what's going on here and you'll soon have her back in hospital again. Is that what you want?"

"Of course not."

"Then leave Ma alone."

He glared at her from beneath bushy eyebrows, but for the first time in her life Amanda saw fear in the dark depths of his eyes and she suddenly realized that he wasn't entirely invulnerable. He cleared his throat. "Tell you what, why don't you stay here at Strathferness, take over the running of the place?"

"You must be joking!"

"No, I'm deadly serious. We could make this place as popular as Cawdor or Crathes."

"You mean have hordes of people piling through it every day, high heels puncturing the putting green, lunch with the Laird of Strathferness . . . that sort of thing?"

He seemed to recoil at the thought. "I was thinking of something rather more . . . upscale."

"Why? It isn't as if you need the money, is it? Not with the distillery doing so well."

He looked around him, his gaze taking in the new crack in the plastered ceiling above them. "This place eats money. You've no idea how much it costs to keep it up. Damp courses, constantly repairing the stonework, gardeners, groundsmen . . ."

Amanda pushed back her chair. "To be perfectly honest, I'm not particularly interested in Strathferness. In fact, I don't give a damn about it." Her heart pinched even as she said it, but she wanted to hurt her father and she knew that this was the way to do it.

He looked utterly shocked. "You don't mean that."

"Sorry, but I do."

"But . . . Strathferness is the ancient home of your ancestors."

"That's great, but I'm more interested in the future than the past." Amanda came to the middle of the table. "I know how much you love the place, but for me it has too many negative memories. I care about the people, but not the place. So if you're talking about gathering all your children about you in your old age, please count me out." She gave him a bitter smile. "Isn't having Colin here enough for you?"

As if on cue, the door opened and Morag entered. "Forgive me for disturbing your breakfast, Sir Robert," she said, adopting the special plummy accent she used only with him. "But when Betty went to make Mr. Colin's bed she found this note on his pillow. It's addressed to you."

She advanced into the room, but handed the note to Amanda, not her father. He stood, shoving back the heavy chair, and took the letter from Amanda.

"Thanks, Morag," she said. Morag retreated to the doorway, where she hovered half in and half out of the room.

Sir Robert glanced at the sheet of paper in his hand. "He's gone."

"Colin?" Amanda said. "Gone where?"

"To Canada, the bloody fool." He handed Amanda

the letter. "If that woman finds out Colin's coming after her, she'll start running again and we might never find her and Roddy." He went to the fireplace and stood glaring into the fire, one hand on the cluttered mantelshelf above him.

The note was brief. Amanda read it aloud. " 'Gone hunting in Canada. Tell Ewen I'll let him know when he can call off the hounds.' " She looked up. "What does it mean?"

Her father turned around. "You know as much as I do. The Canadian investigator's last report was that Colin's wife and Roddy were flying to Winnipeg. When I discussed it with Colin he told me he would now be able to pursue the matter in the Manitoba court, as we'd originally intended. We had Ewen dealing with it."

"Has Mr. Colin gone to Winnipeg?" Morag asked from the doorway.

Amanda had forgotten she was still there. "Looks like it, I'm afraid." She saw her own fear reflected in Morag's eyes. "I wish he hadn't. He should have left it to the lawyers to deal with." She hesitated for a moment and then turned back to her father. "I'm afraid of what might happen. Colin's not . . . not very stable at present."

Her father swung around. "Colin's never been stable. He's got his mother's genes. That branch of the MacKinnons was always too highly strung." His gaze sought Amanda's. "Your mother's going to take this badly. What are we going to do?" It was the first time he'd ever asked her for advice on a serious matter.

"Phone Ewen."

"It's only five past eight."

"Then call him at home. This is urgent." Amanda turned to Morag. "What time did Betty—"

But Morag was no longer there.

Chapter 34

The light was flashing on the answering machine when Vanessa, Roddy, and her parents arrived home from the appointment with the lawyer. There were three messages.

Her father pressed the button to play them back, just as Vanessa was about to fill the kettle with water for tea. She stopped, frozen, as Amanda's voice issued from the tape.

"Vanessa. It's Amanda. I really need to get hold of you. Call me at Strathferness." Vanessa went to the machine and hurriedly clicked off the tape.

"Who was that?" asked her mother, taking the kettle from her and filling it at the sink.

"Amanda, Colin's sister."

"Colin's sister?" her mother repeated. "Why would she be calling you?"

"We'll never know," Vanessa said.

"Aren't you going to call her back?"

Hugh Marston stared at his wife. "Of course she's not. The last thing she wants to do now is let that family know where she is."

"Don't be silly, Hugh," Lynne Marston said. "Colin's sister called her here, didn't she? So of course they know that Vanessa's here."

"They don't know for certain," Vanessa said. "They're just guessing." But of course the Craigmores knew where she was. She was merely trying to calm her mother. "Anyway, I'm not about to speak to any of them. They might fight each other, but when it comes to the crunch they work as one, that family." She clicked on the tape again.

Amanda's voice again. "Vanessa, this is Amanda again. It's—let's see—it's just before five British time Friday afternoon. I phoned you about an hour ago. You probably don't want to call here. I can understand that. I want to let you know that we found out this morning that Colin intended to fly to Canada. He probably left here really early this morning, so I imagine he was going for the flight that leaves Glasgow around noon."

During the pause that followed, Vanessa heard her mother's sharp intake of breath and "Oh dear God" from behind her. Then Amanda's voice said, "This is a warning, really. If you're at your parents' house I think it would be best if you weren't around when Colin gets there." Another little pause, then, "I'm sorry I didn't call before, but . . . I knew you'd be asleep. Good luck. Give my love to Roddy."

Again Vanessa clicked off the tape, heart beating painfully fast.

"Oh my God," her mother said again. "He's coming here. Colin's coming here. We'll have to call the police."

Vanessa stood staring at the machine and then turned slowly to face her parents. "There's no point, Mom. They wouldn't come just because we thought Colin might be violent. You heard what Charlie Pieper said at our meeting. We have no actual proof of any of Colin's threats. In the eyes of the law, he had every right to hire investigators to track me and Roddy down. From a legal viewpoint all we can do is put this in the hands of the lawyers here in Winnipeg and let them deal with it."

"But what are you going to do about Colin coming here?" her mother asked, her voice rising. "We must call in the police."

"I'll call Charlie," Hugh said, "but I know what he'll say. That Colin has this court order from Scotland, so he has a right to come and get Roddy." He patted Vanessa's shoulder. "I'm sorry, sweetie, but that's the way it is. Why don't I ask Charlie to come over? That way, if Colin does come here, Charlie might be able to sweet-talk him into sitting down and discussing this sensibly."

Vanessa's mouth trembled, but her voice was quite steady when she spoke again. "It won't work, Dad. If we don't get out of here before Colin arrives I could be endangering Roddy. I can't do that. I don't want to leave, but it's not worth the risk if I stay. If Colin comes here, all of us could be in danger."

"Come on, now, it's not as bad as all that. Colin's never actually threatened to harm you, has he?"

Vanessa was tempted to tell her father that Colin had done so on many occasions, but what was the point of worrying her parents even more?

She turned to the answering machine and was about to put it back to the recording mode when she remembered there was a third message. She switched it on.

It was Grant. To hear his voice there, in the familiar surroundings of the family kitchen, sent such a flood of longing throughout her body that she had to turn her face away from her parents.

"Who is it?" hissed her mother, but Vanessa shook her head, tears stinging her eyes.

"This message is for Vanessa. Please make sure she gets it as soon as possible. Vanessa, I know something happened on our journey to stop you trusting me. God knows what it was, but you must listen to me and trust me now. *Please.* You and Roddy could be in danger. I'm staying at the Holiday Inn on Portage Avenue." He pronounced *Portage* in the French way, which made her mouth flicker into a fleeting smile. He gave her the number of the hotel. "Please call me back as soon as possible. I have no intention of harming you or Roddy. I just want to help you."

The message was over. She swallowed the moistness in her throat. She wanted so much to believe him, but how could she? She rewound the tape.

"So that's Grant Kendall. He sounds very credible,"

said her father. "Are you certain he's working for Colin?"

She turned on her father. "I told you. I found the photograph in his wallet."

Her father put up his hands in a defensive gesture. "Okay, okay. No need to attack me."

Vanessa sighed. "Sorry, Dad. I didn't mean to." She pushed her hand through her hair. "This is all getting a bit too much, isn't it?" Her mind was spinning. Now Grant was after them again, as well as Colin. She knew she must take action right away, but what?

"The Holiday Inn," her mother said, glancing nervously at the doorway into the hall, as if Grant might appear there suddenly at any moment. "That's not that far from here, is it?"

Miraculously, her mother's fear calmed Vanessa. "No, it's not," she said. "That's why I must get the hell out of here. If he and Colin come here together we haven't a chance." The adrenaline was pumping now. She turned to her father. "Dad, do they still plow the road to the cottage in the winter?"

Her father frowned. "The cottage? Sure they do. Several people have winterized their places, like I did, so they can go down there occasionally in the winter, for Christmas or cross-country skiing."

"Good," she said. "Then that's where Roddy and I will go to hide out. Once Colin's cooled down, I can come back and negotiate with him. As long as I have a lawyer there," she added, "in case Colin makes any threats."

Her father shook his head. "I don't know that driving to the cottage is such a good idea. That wind's pretty strong and the temperature's rising. That's a bad sign. Could be a storm blowing up. We'll need to check on the forecast." He went to the door.

"Forecast or not, I'm going to the cottage."

"But you're not used to winter driving," her mother protested.

"For heaven's sake, Mom, you don't forget how to drive—"

"I'm talking about *winter* driving," her mother insisted. "You know what that's like."

"That's right. I *do* know. Scotland can get bad weather, too, you know. Stop worrying, Mom. I'll be fine. I just want to get out of here before Colin comes."

"Relax," her father said. "He can't possibly be here until this evening at the earliest."

"That's what I thought."

"I'll drive you."

Vanessa smiled at him, glad that she had him on her side now. "Thanks, Dad, but I can manage. I want you to hold the fort here. You'll know best how to deal with Colin. If Roddy's not here—and he can even search the place to make sure—Colin will go away and not bother you."

"He was at the cottage, remember?" Her father frowned. "Maybe—"

"He was there one weekend. And hated every moment of it, too. What an idiot he was! He wouldn't have a clue where the cottage is. Just pretend I never came here."

"This guy Kendall obviously followed you here. He'll have told Colin that."

"And what if this Grant comes looking for you?" her mother asked.

"Just tell him I'm not here." Vanessa gave her a faint smile. "You can do it, Mom. You're a great actress. Besides, by that time it'll be true."

"It's not one bit funny."

"I know it's not, but we have to find the humor in this somewhere, don't we?" Vanessa hugged her tight and then gently pushed her away again. "Be a darling and pack some food in a couple of coolers for me, would you? I take it there's canned stuff in the cottage?"

"Stacks of it. So you'll want eggs and milk and bread, that kind of thing, right?"

"Perfect. You'll know what we need. Some peanut

butter for Roddy. And some of your homemade straw-
berry jam, if you've got any left."

"Of course I have. You'll need bottled water, too."

As Lynne went downstairs to the basement,
Vanessa exchanged glances with her father.

"I'm tired of running away, but I think this is the
best thing."

"I'm not so sure," her father said. "But I get the
feeling that you know more about Colin than we do.
And his sister does, too, and she said you should
leave. She sounded pretty sensible."

"Amanda? Yes, she is. She and I could have been
good friends had it not been for her understandable
loyalty to the Craigmore family. I must say, I was
extremely surprised that she called me. Normally, for
the sake of peace, she takes the family's side—or ignores what's going on. That's what makes me feel that
I must get out of here. She's obviously genuinely worried about Colin coming here."

"So is that man."

"Grant?" Vanessa shook her head. "I don't know
what his motive for calling me is. I'd like to think it
was genuine concern, but I just can't trust him."

"He sounds Australian. Is he?"

"I believe he said he worked in South Africa for a
while—and he was in South America. Anyway, who
cares?" She turned abruptly and went past her father
into the hall. "I'll get Roddy ready."

"I'll go fill my car with gas and check the oil."

"Mom's car's fine."

"You're not taking her old car out on the highway.
Anything you need at the supermarket?"

"Mom will know. Ask her."

He was about to go down to the basement, but then
stopped and turned. "Someone could follow you when
you leave here, you know."

Vanessa was halfway upstairs. "You're right." She
thought for a moment. "You said last night that Uncle
Jerry had taken early retirement since he'd got sick.

He and Aunt Doris haven't gone to Florida, have they?"

"No, he's no longer well enough to travel."

"Do you think he would lend me his car?"

"What good would that do?"

"He still lives in that apartment block on Pembina Highway, doesn't he? You could drive Roddy and me there. We could lie on the backseat, with a cover over us. Uncle Jerry could let us into the underground parking lot and we could switch cars. Even if anyone follows us, once we're in the parking lot they won't be able to see us switch cars, will they?"

Her father looked doubtful. "I don't want to worry Jerry. He's too sick. Anyway, he's really fond of that car and—"

"He's also really fond of his niece and great-nephew, isn't he? Give him a call. Oh . . . and make sure he fills up his car with gas."

Her father looked at her, admiration in his eyes. "You're getting quite an expert at this stuff, aren't you?"

"It's not out of choice, I can tell you. Okay, Dad, you call Uncle Jerry. I'll get Roddy and all our things ready. We're moving out of here," she shouted as she ran upstairs.

Only to herself did she add, Let's just hope that this time I'm making the right decision.

Later that afternoon, Vanessa drove her uncle's car out of the underground parking lot. She was wearing her uncle's parka and a decrepit old tuque, into which she'd tucked her hair. Roddy was lying on the back-seat, covered by a blanket.

As she swung into Pembina Highway she caught sight of a brown minivan parked on the roadside. It looked very like the one that her father had said was following them when they left their house.

She moved into the outside lane and was delighted to see when she checked her right mirror that the minivan was still sitting there.

"Foiled you again," she said in a cartoon voice.

"Can I come out?" Roddy asked. "It's hot under here."

"Wait just a few more minutes." She checked her mirror again. The minivan was not following her.

She didn't see the beige sedan that had pulled away from the curb when she drove out.

Chapter 35

Roddy gazed out the window at the leaden clouds and the vast stretch of fenceless fields covered in snow. He listened to the wipers' steady rhythm of rubber against glass, sweeping the snow from the windshield. He could see nothing up ahead except swirling snow. It was like they were driving into a big, white nothingness.

"Roddy?"

He turned his head.

"Everything okay?" his mother asked.

"There aren't any houses. There's nothing at all."

"Around here, you mean? Well, there are probably some farms, but we can't see them because of the snow."

A big truck that had been following them for a while pulled out and drove beside them for a moment, its tires humming. Then with a whoosh it passed them, pulling ahead of their car. Roddy hoped it would stay there, within sight.

"Damn," his mother said. "I hate being behind these things."

"Overtake it, then."

"No, this fresh snow makes it a bit icy. I'm going fast enough." Roddy could see how her hands were gripping the steering wheel, so that her knuckle bones stuck out. She didn't usually hold on that tightly. She glanced at him. "Warm enough?"

"Yes, thanks." He looked down at the map on his knees. "How far do we have to go?"

"We stay on this road, Highway 15, for a while and

then take Highway 44 to Rennie. Can you see Rennie on the map? That's where we take the road that leads to the cottage."

"Yes, but how *far* is that?" She wasn't answering his question.

"You mean how long will it take to get there? Probably another hour. This snow is really holding us back. So just sit back and enjoy the ride."

He didn't like to tell her that he wasn't enjoying it one bit. He had never been anywhere that felt quite so . . . so empty before. Even the Scottish Highlands weren't as bleak as this in the winter, and there were a lot more cars and trucks on the A9.

He wished Grant were here with them. It seemed such a long time since he'd seen Grant, yet it was really only three days since they'd been driving with him to California.

The big truck had disappeared into the whiteness. There was no telling how far away it was now. He strained his neck to be able to see out the front window, but still could see nothing but snow. It was coming at them sideways now, and there was a lot more of it. As soon as the wipers made one pass, more snow came down and obscured their view. "I can't see that truck anymore."

"I know. They go very fast, don't they? And the snow's blowing now, so it's hard to see up ahead. Let's turn on the radio."

"That's what you said before."

"Before when?"

"When we were driving to Edinburgh. When we were running away from Daddy."

"Actually, we were driving away, not running."

"Ha, ha, very funny," he said sarcastically. He didn't appreciate his mother's humor at the moment. "Now we're driving away from Grant. Maybe Daddy as well."

"I keep telling you, Roddy, neither of them knows where we are."

"I wish Grampa was with us."

"I do, too, but he had to stay behind with Grandma."

"To deal with Daddy, right?"

"What?" His mother looked surprised and rather cross.

"That's what you said."

"You listen to other people's conversations far too much, young man."

"Well, it does all revolve around me, doesn't it?"

His mother glanced down at him, with that sort of little smile that crinkled just the corners of her mouth. "I suppose it does, really."

His mother hadn't smiled much since they'd left Vancouver. No, that wasn't quite right. She hadn't smiled much since that time in the Denny's Restaurant when he and Grant had come back from buying muffins and she'd looked so strange because she wasn't feeling well. At least, that's what she'd said.

"It's all going to work out, pumpkin. I'll make sure of that."

He knew she would. At least, he hoped she would. He didn't even want to think about the chance that she wouldn't. What if this time they couldn't escape from whatever they were running away from? It made his stomach feel all gloppy.

"Turn on the radio," she told him. "Let's see if we can get some good music to drive through snow by." She was changing the subject. She *always* did that when she thought he was worrying too much about something. She'd talk about it with him and then, after a while, she'd switch to something unimportant.

They drove for a while without speaking, an easy-listening station on the radio playing what his mother called Golden Oldies, some of which she sang along with. She was doing it for his benefit, he knew. He wished she wouldn't. He hated it when she pretended everything was fine, when it wasn't. It made him feel even more scared. But he played along with her, pretending to hum tunes he didn't know, just to make her happy.

"Isn't this great?" she said. "I used to love going to the cottage in the winter. It was always a big treat."

He smiled back at her and then turned his head away, to avoid more stupid conversation, and gazed out the side window. What was so great about being hurled into white darkness, he thought, with no end in sight? At least the scenery was more interesting now, with masses of dark pine trees lining both sides of the road, but it was hard even to see them. In all his life he had never realized there could be this much snow. It was far more than he'd ever seen in Scotland.

"I've forgotten the name of the place where we take the 44," his mother said after they'd been driving through the forest part for ages. "Can you see on the map?"

"It's getting too dark to see."

"Then use the little flashlight Uncle Jerry said he had."

"Flashlight?"

"Torch. Uncle Jerry said he had one in the car."

"Where is it?"

"Oh, for heaven's sake, Roddy. You're supposed to be the navigator, aren't you? Try the glove compartment."

He glared at her, but she wasn't looking. She was too busy concentrating on the road, peering past those wipers and the blinding snow. Maybe he was being mean not helping when she had to do all the driving. He opened the glove compartment and fished out the little flashlight from a bundle of old maps and a pair of pliers tangled in bits of rolled-up string.

"Why do they call them glove compartments when nobody keeps gloves in them?"

"Don't ask me."

"I just did." At least *that* made her laugh.

He switched on the little flashlight and opened the map to the section his grandfather had shown him earlier. The beam of light illuminated the map. He followed the red roads with his index finger.

"Can you find the intersection?"

"Yes. You turn left on Highway 11 at Elma."

"Elma. That's right. I couldn't think of the name. That should be coming up soon."

"After that you turn right on 44 to go to Rennie."

"Great. Keep the map open and you can talk me through. I couldn't do this without you. You're a great navigator." She patted him on the knee. "We're into the last stretch now. Won't be long before we're lighting that log fire and drinking hot chocolate."

They were not far from their last change of roads when a new noise started. It sounded like hundreds of tiny pebbles hitting the car. He could see them bouncing off the road as well, in the light from their beams.

"That's all we need," his mother said, slowing a little.

"What is it?"

"The snow's turning to ice. Those are ice pellets you can hear hitting the car."

"Is it dangerous?"

"Not really. Thank heavens it didn't start earlier, though, or we might have had to turn back."

Roddy shivered. He didn't like that constant patter of ice on the car. Somehow, it made it seem colder and more scary. "What do they do?"

"Ice pellets? Not much, really."

He could tell from her voice that she was lying. She was scared.

She slowed down. He could see in the headlights' beam that the road ahead was now all shiny. He gripped the flashlight, liking the warm feeling of the rubber against his fingers.

After a few more minutes his mother glanced down at him. "Relax, Roddy."

"I am."

"It's fine. Honestly it is. Driving on ice just takes a little adjusting, that's all. Don't forget I lived here for more than twenty years before I went to Britain. Snow and ice—even floods and blizzards—mean nothing to us sturdy Manitobans."

This time she sounded okay. Lulled by her assurance and the steady sweep of the wipers, Roddy closed his eyes, his grip on the flashlight loosening.

"Wakey, wakey. We're here."

His mother's voice seemed to be right in his ear. When Roddy opened his eyes, he saw that he was right. She was bending right over him. And the car had stopped. He was glad of that. He sat up, rubbing his eyes.

There were trees everywhere, surrounding them on all sides. Big pine trees and smaller white-trunked trees with no leaves, and some even smaller bushes. The car was parked in a clearing by the log cabin.

"Come on, lazy bones, bestir yourself. I need some help carrying this stuff inside. Put your parka on, though. This ice stuff is cold."

He pulled on his parka, putting up the hood, and jumped from the car. The ice pellets hit his face. "Ouch! That hurts."

"Pull your hood right down." His mother ran into the cottage, carrying a thermal cooler. Roddy went to the trunk and dragged out a couple of plastic bags filled with stuff. Although they were heavy, it was so cold he began to run, and then he slipped on the stone path and almost fell. It was like walking on a skating rink.

His mother appeared in the doorway of the log cabin. "Be careful. The path's really icy."

"I know. I almost fell." He grinned at her and went inside.

He put the two bags on the big round table in the center of the living room and gazed around at the rustic maplewood furniture and the huge picture window overlooking the lake. The back door led to a wide veranda the length of the cabin and beyond that was the old swing hanging from the tree near the barbecue pit.

Apart from the snow and ice, the place hadn't changed a bit from the last time he was here. He was glad. But he still felt as if he and his mother were the only two people for hundreds of miles in this wintry ice world.

It took several more treks in and out before they'd completely unloaded the car. Then he helped his mother get logs from the covered woodpile at the side of the cottage and soon they had a fire going.

"Before we unpack anything, we're going to have that hot chocolate I promised you."

"With marshmallows?" Roddy asked.

"With marshmallows." His mother knelt down and hugged him tightly against her. He smelled her familiar perfume and felt how softly warm she was. Then she set him at arm's length, her eyes glowing with the reflected light of the fire. "We're safe here. No one but Grampa and Grandma knows we're here. And we're not cut off. Grampa gave me his cell phone, so we can call them and tell them we're okay."

"Let's do that now." Roddy was eager to hear other voices, to know that they weren't totally alone.

"Good idea. They'll be anxious to hear that we arrived safely, especially with all this snow." She pressed in the number. "Answering machine," she whispered to him. "They're monitoring calls."

"Maybe they're at Uncle Jerry's."

"No—they—" She broke off. "Hi, Mom and Dad," she said, in that loud voice people used when they were talking to an answering machine. "We arrived about half an hour ago. You must have been a bit worried, but it took us much longer to get here because of the snow. We had ice pellets falling as well." She paused.

"It's a terrible line, lots of crackling," she said in an aside to Roddy. "I'm waiting for them to pick up." Then, when they obviously didn't pick up, she continued with her message.

"It's great here. I'd forgotten how cozy the cottage can be in the winter. We feel beautifully safe and warm here. We've got a fire going and we're just about to have some hot chocolate. Oh, I nearly forgot . . .

if Jill calls from New York tell her I'm fine. I'll be in touch with her later. Please be sure to call me back, just to let me know everything's all right. We love you both."

She switched off the phone and stared down at it, frowning. "Strange they didn't answer when they heard it was me."

"They could be out," Roddy said again.

"You're right. They could be. Maybe they did go back to Uncle Jerry's place. Anyway, at least now they'll know we've arrived safely. They'll probably call us back later. Let's go make that hot chocolate. We deserve it after hauling in all that stuff."

Chapter 36

As Vanessa's message ended, Colin smiled to himself. "So that's where she is, the cottage," he said, switching the machine back to the answer mode.

He went downstairs to the family room in the basement. "That was your daughter on the phone. She left a message, bless her little heart. She's at your lakeside cottage. But of course you knew that already, didn't you? I hadn't realized it was possible to get there in the winter."

"*You* certainly wouldn't be able to," Hugh Marston said through stiff lips. Beside him, hands bound tightly behind her back like his, Lynne was sobbing quietly.

"Oh, you must never underestimate me, dear Father-in-Law." Colin swayed a little on his feet, but the hand holding the small, black handgun did not waver. "That's the trouble with all of you, my family included: You underestimated me."

Ever since they'd answered the doorbell a short while ago, to have Colin burst into the house flourishing that gun, Hugh had been racking his brains to find some way of getting it away from him, but though Colin had obviously been drinking, he'd never let down his guard for a moment.

When the telephone rang, Colin had been binding them with a length of heavy twine that Hugh kept in his workshop. Lynne had begged him to let her answer it, but Colin had merely laughed and continued binding her hands, wrenching them even tighter so that she gasped with pain.

When he'd finished tying them up, he'd gone upstairs and switched the machine on full volume, so that they could hear every word, despite the heavy static. It had been agony to hear Vanessa's voice, so happy and confident, telling them that she had arrived safely at the cottage. *Safe and warm,* she'd said, her voice buoyant with relief.

"The police are watching this house," Hugh said, wishing to God they really were. "They'll be here any minute."

"All the more reason for me to get the hell out of here."

"Our friends the Merciers are coming over this evening," Lynne said, her breath coming in gasps. "They'll soon know something's wrong when we don't answer—"

"Shut your mouth." Colin's eyes glittered with hatred as he glared down at her. "No, I'll shut it for you." He turned away and went into Hugh's workroom. "Tape, tape. Where's some tape?" they could hear him mutter to himself. "Aha!" He came back with a roll of duct tape.

Lynne's terrified gaze sought Hugh's.

"Colin," he said, "please don't use that tape on us. We promise not to say anything more. Lynne has heart trouble. You know that. Please."

Colin seemed to hesitate. Then he started to cut a length of tape. "You'd be on the telephone as soon as I leave."

"How could we be? We can't even move."

Colin surveyed them and laughed. "You look like a couple of trussed capons lying there. If only I had a camera handy. What a perfect picture you'd make for the Marston family album."

"Please don't, Colin," Lynne begged him. *"Please!"* Her voice rose to a scream. It was cut off with sickening suddenness as the piece of gray tape was placed over her mouth.

She gasped for breath, her chest heaving, eyes staring with panic.

"Don't breath through your mouth, Lynne," Hugh

shouted. "Breath through your nose. Keep calm for Vanessa's sake, darling. You're going to be just fine. Keep breathing through—"

His words were cut short as Colin clamped another piece of tape over his mouth, pressing it down hard with the heel of his hand. Now Hugh felt the horrible panic that had engulfed his wife, and he forced himself to breathe through his nose, slowly, calmly.

"Damn you. Damn you to hell," he said. But the words came out as grunts.

"Now I don't have to cut the telephone wire," Colin said. "That way, if Vanessa calls again, she won't suspect there's anything wrong. And neither of you will be able to answer it," he added, chuckling to himself.

He dragged Hugh across the carpeted floor, away from Lynne. Then he grinned down at him. His look of blatant self-satisfaction made Hugh want to throttle him.

Lynne was making small whimpering sounds and breathing heavily and rapidly—far too rapidly— through her nose. *God in heaven, please help her to calm down,* Hugh prayed. Why the hell hadn't he made some special arrangement with Jerry, just in case this happened?

But he knew why. He'd always thought that Vanessa was exaggerating about Colin. Exaggerating, just like Lynne did about every small thing. He hadn't really believed that the man who was married to his daughter was capable of actually harming people. Oh, he was a jerk, that had been obvious from the way he'd been behaving. The gambling and drinking . . . *that* he believed. But all the rest, Colin's violent temper and the danger to Roddy . . . all the stuff that Vanessa had worried about, he'd put down to a woman's hysteria.

Now he knew that he'd made a huge mistake, a potentially fatal mistake, in not taking his daughter's concerns seriously.

"Good-bye, dear parents-in-law," said Colin's voice from the foot of the stairs. Hugh twisted his head around and saw Colin turn as if he were about to leave. Then he turned back again. "Oh, by the way, you might be interested to know that I have an old address book of Vanessa's that I happened to find at home in Edinburgh. In it is not only the address of your palatial summer home, but also details of how to get there."

He went up the stairs—two at a time, from the sound of it. Hugh could hear him turning the locks, putting the chain on the back door. Then he went out the front door, slamming it behind him.

All Hugh could hear then, above the sound of his wife's painfully labored breathing and her ceaseless whimpering, was the moaning of the wind and the patter of ice on the windows.

Chapter 37

Grant had spent a frustrating couple of hours that evening at, first, a local police station, and then the main downtown station, trying to persuade the police to check on the situation at Vanessa's parents' house.

As soon as he'd arrived in Winnipeg, he had rented a car and then checked into a hotel on Portage Avenue, which was fairly near the airport. From what he could see on the map, it seemed a good strategic point.

Once he was in his room, he called Vanessa's parents. No one had responded to the message he'd left. Yet he was almost certain that Vanessa and Roddy were there. He was tempted to go to their house and batter on their door, demand that Vanessa see him, but they'd probably call the police and he'd be locked up. What help would he be to them then? No, he had to be patient and wait. Patience didn't come easily to him. Especially not when it involved Vanessa and Roddy.

He'd decided to go to the house, anyway, and keep watch there. The house was on a street lined with large old elm trees. It was detached, well kept, modestly sized, but with a large front yard, which was presently piled high with snow. This was the house in which Vanessa had grown up. His heart turned within him as he thought that she and Roddy could be in there at this very moment.

At first he sat outside in his car, parked a little way down, on the opposite side of the road, so they couldn't see him from a front window. The snow had started falling quite heavily after a while, restricting his view of the house. He could see nothing but a few chinks of light filtering through spaces in the closed curtains. No one came in or out.

He drove around to the back to check it out. The garage was at the rear, with a back lane entrance. Risking the chance of being seen by someone, he pulled into an empty car port a little way down the lane. After a while, an older man, whom he took to be Mr. Marston, drove out of the garage and down the lane. He appeared to be alone, but it was hard to see through the blowing snow. Knowing Vanessa's resourcefulness, Grant decided to follow the car, a gray Honda, in case she and Roddy were hidden inside it.

After driving for about ten minutes, the Honda took a right turn off the main road and drove around to the rear of an apartment block. A few minutes later, it disappeared into the underground parking lot, where Grant was unable to follow.

He waited in a nearby parking spot on the main road. Keeping the car heater on and having to use the wipers periodically to clear the snow from the windshield, he kept his gaze glued to the apartment block exit, fervently hoping that there wasn't another exit at the rear. He began to wonder if Vanessa and Roddy had been in this apartment block all the time and that Vanessa's father was picking them up from here.

More than an hour had passed. A couple of cars had come out, neither of them a gray Honda. Then Mr. Marston—if that was who the driver was—suddenly drove out the exit and made a U-turn, apparently making for home again.

Grant swiftly followed him and made his own U-turn. Only then did he notice the brown minivan that had been parked on the opposite side of the main road. As soon as the Marston car passed the minivan, it swung out and followed at a discreet distance, driving in another lane.

Grant revved up and moved into the lane next to

the minivan. He glanced across at the driver. It was the man with the beak nose.

Grant quickly dropped back, before the man could see him. If he goes all the way to the house, he thought grimly, I've got him.

But, to Grant's surprise, when Mr. Marston's car turned down his own road, the minivan continued on down the main road. Making yet another split-second decision, Grant decided to follow Mr. Marston back to the house. If Colin turned up, at least Grant would be there, too.

He hovered at the end of the lane until he saw the Honda turn into the Marstons' garage. When he drove slowly up the lane, the garage door was descending.

He was right back where he'd started. Vanessa and Roddy were still in danger and he had no way of knowing how to get to them in time. If they were elsewhere, it was likely that Colin's investigators knew where they were. If they were still in this house, Colin could arrive at any time and grab Roddy. It was obvious that he couldn't watch both entrances to the house at the same time. He needed backup.

It was then that he'd decided to go to the police. He'd expected to get help immediately. Now, after almost two hours of being sent from the local station to the downtown station, and from one department to another, he was growing increasingly frustrated—and frantic.

"Don't you understand?" he shouted at the sergeant in the downtown station, who'd started asking the same questions all over again. "A kidnapping could be taking place at this very minute and you're doing bloody all about it."

"It's hardly a kidnapping, sir, when the father is retrieving his son from a mother who took him without permission. From what we've been able to find out, the father was granted custody in Scotland. He's been given the right to take his son."

"Not if he uses violence to do so."

"Have you any evidence to prove that he might be violent?"

"You'd be able to get that evidence from the child's mother."

"But you don't know where they are, you say? Have you tried calling them?"

"Yes, several times," Grant said wearily. "And your constable also tried. We keep getting the machine."

"Then why don't I send a patrol car along to take a look at the Marstons' house, to make sure everything's okay there?"

Grand couldn't believe what he was hearing. After all this time, he was getting what he wanted. He quickly recovered. "That would be a great help. Thank you."

"Then if my officers report back to me and say everything's fine, we can wrap this thing up and forget all about it."

Grant didn't think that was likely, but he nodded. "Thanks, Sergeant Miller. I'd like to go along with whoever you're sending to the Marstons' house. That way I'll be sure that the family's safe."

"You can follow the patrol car. They'll be driving without the siren. This is not an emergency situation," he added, in case Grant protested.

Grant took a deep breath and kept his mouth shut. If this wasn't an emergency situation, he didn't know what was.

"Thanks again."

"You're welcome. I don't suppose we'll see you again, sir. Unless we're ordered by the court to get the boy back to the boy's father. You say you're a close family friend. Try to get her to return the boy to Scotland. It can get messy if we have to take over."

Again Grant nodded, not able to trust himself to say anything.

He tailed the police car to the front of the Marstons' house and then got out and followed the police constable up the path to the front door. Neither ringing the bell nor knocking repeatedly brought any response.

Yet the lights were on and they could hear music playing inside the house.

"Probably watching TV," the young officer said. He went around to the back door and rang the bell there. Still no response.

"Try knocking," Grant said, now desperate.

"I could hear the bell ring inside, sir." *Get off my back,* his tone said. "They're either out or don't want to answer the door. That's their choice."

"It might not be." Grant leaned across the policeman and hammered with his fist on the door.

"Now, that's enough." Grant found himself being shouldered away from the door. "If you're a family friend, as you claim to be, I'm starting to wonder why they won't answer your calls. There's no sign of any trouble here."

"That doesn't mean there isn't any." Grant could feel anger, fueled by frustration, building inside him. Cool it, he told himself.

"You leave these people alone," he was told. Having swept the backyard with the powerful beam of his flashlight, the policeman led the way back to the waiting car.

"Anything?" asked his partner, who had waited in the car for them.

"Not a thing. Everything looks fine. Right, sir?" the officer said pointedly to Grant.

"It *looks* fine."

The officer stood with his hand on the car door handle. "You heading back to your hotel now, sir?"

"I think I'll watch the house a little longer, just in case."

"We don't want to get called in with a complaint from these people that some guy's stalking them," the officer said. His meaning was absolutely clear.

"You won't. Unless Colin Craigmore turns up. Then you might."

The officer opened his notebook. "Where is it you're staying?"

Grant told him.

"Room number?"

He gave it to them. No doubt he'd be getting a call from the police shortly. Too bad. He wouldn't be there.

"Right, sir." The policeman slicked back his dark hair, replaced his peaked cap, and got into the car beside his partner.

The constable leaned out the open window. "Don't worry, sir. We'll be checking back later, just to make sure everything's fine."

And that I'm no longer here, Grant thought. "Thanks for all your help, officer. Good night."

"Night, sir." The patrol car drove off slowly, stopped beside his car, no doubt to make a note of the license number, and then sped off.

As soon as they were out of sight, Grant raced around to the back of the house. He rang the bell and knocked repeatedly. He wanted to yell Vanessa's name, but was afraid the neighbors might hear and come to check on what was happening.

He opened the outer screen door, adjusting the top catch so that it remained wide open. Then he examined the inner door. It was made of solid wood and had a lock in the handle. That would be easy enough to open. Unfortunately, there was also a deadbolt lock.

Hands numb with the bitter cold, head and face pelted by barbs of ice, he tried to get the lock open with a credit card. One lock responded, but when he tried turning the handle the door wouldn't budge. It was obvious that the deadbolt was engaged.

Making sure that the outer door was fully open, he balanced himself, concentrating all his energy in his legs, and gave the door an almighty kick. The door shuddered, but held.

Grant stepped back, then slid and almost fell on the ice-covered concrete. Cursing, he steadied himself by catching hold of the storm door. This bloody ice made it hard to get a firm footing.

He gave the door another massive kick. A bolt of

pain shot up his thigh. This time he heard the welcome sound of splintering wood. He paused, ear to the door, straining for the sound of voices. He heard nothing.

Drawing in a couple of deep breaths, he summoned up the focus and concentration he'd learned at the martial arts classes he'd taken in his youth. The next kick shattered the door frame, sending the chain flying. He stumbled into the back entrance of the house.

"Vanessa!" he shouted, slamming the door shut behind him. The music was loud, drowning out any other sound. "Mr. Marston!"

Then, his ears attuning themselves, he heard something else. It sounded like some sort of animal, but it could be someone moaning. The sound was coming from below. He dashed down the flight of stairs that led to the basement.

When he saw the two trussed bodies he thought for one sickening moment that they might be dead, but then he saw that both pairs of eyes were fixed on him. The woman's eyes pleaded with him to help her. The man began to struggle against his bonds.

"Hold on," Grant shouted. "Keep still. If you struggle, it'll make the knots tighter. I'll get a knife."

The woman, whom he guessed must be Vanessa's mother, was moaning piteously. He found a knife in the workroom and sawed at her bonds, wincing when they fell away to reveal bleeding wounds where they had chafed her wrists.

She made urgent sounds, her numb fingers touching the tape that covered her mouth. He was afraid that he'd tear skin away if he took off the tape too fast.

"Can you try to ease it off yourself?" he asked her. "I don't want to do any more damage."

She nodded, understanding. Her face was gray. Warm tears poured from her eyes, dropping onto his hands as he worked. Grant cursed silently, using every word he'd ever learned in that land of vivid cursing. *Colin, I swear I'll make you pay for this,* he vowed.

His hands shook as he knifed the bonds away from Mrs. Marston's feet. He rarely prayed, but now he was doing so nonstop. *God, don't let him get to Vanessa and Roddy.*

Having to know what happened, he turned to Vanessa's father, who was lying still; only his eyes, wild and bloodshot, were painfully alive. He tried to speak to Grant, but couldn't, and became extremely agitated.

Grant put a hand on his shoulder. "Relax. It won't take me a moment to get these off. Then you can tell me what happened."

He sawed away at the thick twine. "Okay, Mrs. Marston?" he called across the room. He glanced up, to see that she was dragging herself across the carpet toward them, propelling herself with her left arm, while the right hand was engaged in peeling the evil-looking tape from her mouth.

Dropping the knife, Grant went to her and lifted her up, depositing her at her husband's side. She leaned over him, stroking his face with her left hand, while the other kept working at the tape on her mouth.

Now Grant cut away the last of the rope from Mr. Marston's ankles and he sat up, his back against a cupboard. He was more ruthless than his wife with the tape, dragging it from his mouth.

"He's gone after them. That devil's gone after Vanessa and Roddy." His speech was slurred, thick, but Grant, anticipating what he would say, could understand.

"Oh Hugh." Weeping, Mrs. Marston buried her head on her husband's chest.

His arm went around her. "It's all right, sweetheart. You'll be okay now."

"It's not me," she said through swollen lips. "It's them. Vanessa and Roddy."

As neither of them could walk without aid, Grant helped them both to the sofa, seating them side by side. Hugh Marston drew his wife close against him again. He looked at Grant. "I take it you're the Grant Kendall that Vanessa was telling us about."

"Warning you about, you mean."

"I can't understand your connection with this at all. Neither could she."

"I'll explain later. I'm sorry, but before I do anything else to make you comfortable, I must know where Vanessa and Roddy are."

Mr. Marston hesitated, but Mrs. Marston did not. "They're at our cottage in the Whiteshell Park," she told Grant. "Vanessa drove down there with Roddy."

"In this snowstorm?" Grant was appalled.

"It wasn't this bad when she left," Hugh Marston said defensively. "And she's done it many times before." His voice broke. "It was the one place Vanessa thought she might be safe with Roddy."

"Did you tell Colin where they are?"

"We didn't have to. He picked up Vanessa's message on the machine when she called us from the cottage."

Grant cursed aloud. "But how did he find out how to get there?" he asked.

"He had Vanessa's old address book. The directions of how to get there were in it."

And he's used to winter driving with snow and ice, thought Grant. "We have to get the police in right away. Is there a phone down here?"

"On the desk over there. The number's in the black book beside it."

"I have the number already," Grant said. "They were here just a few minutes ago to check on you."

"The police were?" Mrs. Marston said. "Is that who was ringing and knocking? We tried to shout, but we couldn't." Her eyes filled with tears again. "I was so relieved. Then they went away. We could hear the car drive off again."

Her expression showed that she was reliving the anguish she'd felt at the time.

Grant's mouth twisted into a wry grin. "Then I broke down your door. Sorry about that, but it was the only way."

"Don't be sorry. We thank God you came."

Let's hope it's not too late. Grant did not speak his thought aloud. He started to punch in the number of the police station.

"I've just had a thought," Hugh Marston said. "It'll be the RCMP you'll need."

"Why?"

"The Winnipeg police are for the city only."

"I still think I'll call my friends at the station. It will give me some satisfaction at least," he added with a grim smile.

It didn't take long to persuade Sergeant Miller to get the RCMP involved, once Grant told them he'd found the Marstons bound and gagged. The sergeant promised he would come to the house himself right away, and he'd bring an RCMP colleague.

"I'll be going with the police to the cottage," Grant told the Marstons after he'd completed the call, "but first I must get someone in to look after you."

"I'm fine," Hugh Marston said. "But I'd like to have a doctor check Lynne over."

She was sitting beside him, tightly holding on to his hand as if she would never ever let it go. "I'm fine, too. All I can think of is what's going to happen to Vanessa and Roddy if Colin gets to them before the police do."

Grant didn't even want to think about it. "Don't worry," he said, assuming a cheerful, optimistic tone that he was far from feeling, "the police will get there and they'll be fine. Now would you please give me the name and number of a neighbor or friend I can call?"

"There's my brother Jerry, but I don't want him to worry about us. He's very sick."

"He'll have to know sooner or later," Lynne Marston said.

"Yes, but I'd rather tell him myself once it's all over." Grant's gaze met Hugh Marston's and saw the despair in their depths. "Call the Williamsons next door. I hate to bother them, but they're good friends. They can drive us to the hospital to have Lynne checked." Hugh glanced down at his shaking hands. "I don't think I'm able to drive."

Grant could see how difficult it was for him to admit such a thing.

"I'm not going to any hospital," Lynne said. "I'm fine."

Grant picked up the telephone again.

Hugh Marston was looking at him, a frown creasing his forehead. "Before you call the Williamsons, I want you to tell me something. And I want the truth."

Grant replaced the telephone. "What do you want to know?"

"You're not a private investigator, are you?"

"No, I'm not."

"It's obvious you've got some emotional involvement with my daughter and grandson. What's your connection to Colin?"

Grant told him.

Chapter 38

Vanessa had been trying to call her parents all evening, but all she could get was a loud crackling on the line. The storm was obviously affecting it.

"Can't you get them?" Roddy asked, his voice tight with anxiety.

"The line keeps breaking up. Must be all that ice." She sat down on the large cushion in front of the fire. "No need to worry. They've probably gone back to Uncle Jerry's place. They'll get our message when they go home."

Outside, the wind gusted and whistled, battering the cottage, but its strong log walls withstood the onslaught.

A sudden thump on the roof made Roddy jump to his feet, his eyes round with fear. "What was that?"

"Probably a branch falling onto the roof. I expect it broke from the weight of the ice." Vanessa smiled, determined not to let him see that she, too, had been startled. "It's easy to see you're a city boy."

"I am not," he said indignantly. "Strathferness isn't the city, is it? And I spend lots of time there."

Vanessa tried to hide the involuntary shiver that ran across her shoulders. "You certainly do."

"And whenever I'm there, Grandfather takes me around to inspect the pine forest and the grouse moor and the distillery. And in the shooting season I get to meet all the tenants and workers and shake their hands."

The young laird speaking, thought Vanessa with a rueful smile. "Of course you do. I was forgetting about that." Roddy would one day become the Laird of Strathferness. Whatever else happened, that was one inevitability she must accept.

"I'm just not used to being out in blizzards," Roddy reminded her.

Vanessa bent forward to poke at the fire, sending bright sparks flying up the chimney. "Well, this is definitely not a blizzard, just a heavy snowfall with some wind. And I wouldn't exactly call this being out, would you? We're as cozy as we can be. We have this fireplace and the woodstove in the kitchen, and piles and piles of logs. And we have enough food to last us for a couple of weeks, at least."

"And no one knows we're here." Once again, Roddy was seeking reassurance.

"No one except Grandma and Grampa knows we're here."

"And Uncle Jerry and Auntie Doris."

"Of course. But that's all. Shall we get on with our game?" She looked down at the checker board on the floor in front of them. "Maybe not. You've got me cornered, I believe."

Roddy chuckled. "You shouldn't have made that last move." He sat down again.

"Hey, don't rub it in." She tried to concentrate on the board, but now the eerie sounds of the storm were making her nervous, although she knew that the cracks and thumps were only the trees bending and creaking in the wind.

"Make your move," Roddy demanded.

"Okay." She moved her black checker and he promptly wiped her out, as she knew he would.

"Yeah! I won," he shouted, leaping around and pumping his fist.

A loud thumping on the door cut through the noise he was making. He froze in the center of the room, staring at his mother. "That's not a branch."

Vanessa scrambled to her feet. "No, it's not." She felt as if she were solid ice, unable to move.

The thumping continued and now there was a man's

voice shouting, but they couldn't hear what he said above the whooping of the wind.

"Who is it?" Roddy whispered.

Vanessa slid her tongue over dry lips. "It's probably Ted Sinclair."

"Who's that?"

"Have you forgotten Ted? He looks after the cottage for us in the winter and does odd jobs in the summer. You met him the last time you were here."

Roddy's hurried breathing slackened a little. "I don't remember him."

"He probably saw the lights and the smoke. I should have let him know I was coming." But still she didn't open the door.

"Let him in, then. He'll get cold outside in the storm."

"Yes, you're right." The hammering and shouting continued. Vanessa moved toward the door. "You stay there by the fire, Roddy. I don't want you to get cold. The snow will probably come in when I open the door."

Heart pounding like the blows on the door, Vanessa crossed the living room. If only she could see who it was out there . . . but the door was built of solid pine, with no peephole. Who would need a peephole here in the countryside?

She wished she had some sort of weapon. Maybe she should go into the kitchen and get the sharp knife her father used to cut slabs of raw steak. But Roddy was watching her closely and she didn't want to scare him.

It was bound to be Ted.

Or perhaps it was Grant. Her heart leaped spontaneously at the thought . . . and then plummeted. Grant Kendall's your enemy, not your friend, she reminded herself.

"Maybe it's Grampa, come to see if we're all right," Roddy said.

"Maybe it is." It was a possibility. Her father hadn't been happy at her driving in the storm. Armed with this hope, she went to the door. The knocking had stopped for a moment; now it started up again with renewed vigor, but this time there was no shouting.

She undid the latch and then turned the handle slowly, her shoulder braced against the door, ready to shut it quickly if she didn't know who the person was. She was about to open the door a little farther when it burst inward with a rush of wind and snow, sending her flying. She managed to save herself from falling by grabbing the doorknob of the coat closet.

The door slammed shut again. A tall snowy figure stood there, breath puffing in white clouds, frosted face hidden by the fur-lined hood of his parka. But Vanessa knew even before he pushed the hood back that it was Colin.

"Daddy?" Roddy's faltering voice came from behind her.

Vanessa spun around, but before she could go to Roddy, Colin had shoved her aside and gone to his son.

"Hi, Roddy. How's my boy?" As he spoke, Colin was shivering uncontrollably. "I am so cold, son. Your mother kept me waiting out there in the blizzard. Do I smell a fire?"

Roddy nodded, but made no move. Vanessa quickly stepped to his side. "How did you get here?" she asked Colin. He'd been drinking. She could smell the alcohol on his breath.

Colin ignored her. He held his hand out to Roddy. "Would you take me to the fire, Roddy? I'm terribly cold."

Roddy looked with round eyes from Colin to his mother. "It's just through here in the living room," he told his father.

Colin took off his gloves and unzipped his parka, dropping them on the floor. "Thanks, son." He followed Roddy into the living room, turning once to give Vanessa a smile.

The smile negated any doubts Vanessa might have

had about Colin. It was a malignant smile filled with triumph and malice.

She knew now that she—and perhaps even Roddy—were in deadly danger. She must remain calm, keep all her wits about her.

"God, that looks marvelous," Colin said, squatting down before the fire, holding his hands out to it. "I don't think I've ever been so cold. This is a bloody awful country, isn't it, Roddy?"

Roddy stood at a distance from him, looking uncertain, his nervous glance going from Vanessa to his father and back again.

"Come and give me a hug," Colin said in that unnaturally hearty voice he kept using with Roddy. "That'll soon warm me up."

Roddy looked at his mother.

"Did you hear me?" Colin roared suddenly, startling both of them.

Roddy chewed on his lip, trying hard not to cry.

"Give Daddy a hug, Roddy," Vanessa said. "He must be very cold."

Roddy went to his father and put his arms around his neck, but all his movements were jerky, tense, like a wooden marionette.

"That feels so good."

Colin clutched him hard against his chest, so hard that Roddy protested. "You're hurting me, Daddy."

The grip relaxed. "Sorry, son. You know I would never hurt *you,* don't you?"

The emphasis on the *you* chilled Vanessa.

"Don't you?" Colin's voice rose. "Goddammit, Roderick, answer me when I speak to you."

Roddy blanched. "Yes, Daddy, I know," he said hurriedly. "But . . . but you mustn't hurt Mummy, either."

Vanessa tensed, loving Roddy for his courage, but wishing he hadn't said it.

Colin shook his head solemnly. "Mummy's been bad. She's done a very bad thing."

"What's she done?" demanded Roddy, eyes flashing.

"She kidnapped you. Kidnapping's a crime. Your mother's probably going to go to prison for a long time."

"No," Roddy yelled. "That's not true. You won't go to prison, will you?" He swung around, about to take a step toward Vanessa, but Colin grabbed his arm, gripping it tightly.

Vanessa took a shuddering breath. "No, darling, I won't." She gave Roddy a reassuring smile. "There's no need to upset him," she told Colin, striving to keep her voice calm and low, when inside she was screaming.

"He needs to know the truth. You've filled his mind with filthy lies about me. It's time he knew the truth about his bitch of a mother." Colin maintained his hold on Roddy's arm.

"Don't call her that." Roddy struggled to get away.

"A bitch? But that's what she is. I want you to say it, too. Repeat after me: *My mother is a bitch.*"

"No, I won't." Roddy glared at his father, struggling even harder to free himself. "You can't make me say it."

Colin smiled. "Oh, can't I?"

"You look so cold, Colin," Vanessa said, her heartbeat ragged. "Why don't I make you some nice hot coffee?"

"You know what you can do with your frigging coffee." Colin shook Roddy. "Stop defying me. Say what I told you to say. My mother is—"

"I won't say it. I *won't.*" Roddy cried out when Colin gave his arm a vicious twist. "You're hurting me."

Waves of nausea and fury swept over Vanessa. "Please let him go, Colin. It's me you want to hurt, not Roddy. You love your son."

"That's right. I do love him. And that's why you're going to rot in hell for taking him from me."

"Roddy, go and see if Grampa left some whiskey

in the kitchen." Vanessa tried to keep her voice as normal as possible. "He used to keep it in the cupboard near the door, the lower one." Colin had already been drinking heavily. If she could get him to drink some more, he might just pass out. Or at least be sufficiently befuddled for her to be able to get Roddy away from him.

"I don't need anything to drink," Colin said, but there was a spark of interest in his voice.

"You must be so terribly cold." Vanessa spoke in a soothing voice, soft as velvet. "A drink will make you feel all warm inside."

His eyes narrowed. "What are you up to, bitch? You're up to something."

She shook her head. "I'm only trying to make you feel more comfortable."

His glare wavered. "Right, then. We'll all go into the kitchen and see what your stupid old fart of a father has got there."

Vanessa caught Roddy's eye just as he was about to protest again. She gave him an urgent shake of the head. *No,* she mouthed.

Colin leaped at her so fast she didn't have time to move. The stinging blow across her face snapped her head back, sending a bolt of pain through her neck. "Don't utter one more word to my son, understand? Not one frigging word, or it'll be the last one you'll ever speak."

Vanessa stood before him, shaking, feelings of raw hatred welling up inside her. What distressed her most was to hear her son crying and not to be able to go to him and comfort him.

"Please, Colin, I'm begging you." Although her head was pounding and the room was swinging about her, she spoke calmly in a low, earnest voice. "Please don't hurt Roddy. You love Roddy. He's your son. Don't hurt him."

He drew his arm back, ready to strike again. "Shut your mouth or I'll shut it for you."

Roddy dashed to him, grabbing at him. "Don't hurt my mother. Please don't, Daddy. *Please.*"

His father stood, arm still raised, frozen in mid-action. Then he turned away and the arm was laid around Roddy's shoulders. "Okay, let's all go into the kitchen and find something to eat." He turned around and smiled at Vanessa, an extraordinarily charming smile. "Maybe if we're nice to her your mother would make us some of her super sandwiches."

Vanessa saw for one fleeting, heart-stopping moment the man she had fallen in love with years ago. She smiled back. "Of course I will."

His volatility terrified her.

"Good." Colin led the way into the kitchen and started opening and then slamming shut the doors of the maplewood cupboards Vanessa's father had installed with such care.

"We've got a tin of ham," Vanessa ventured.

"Excellent. Won't that be great, Roddy? Ham and lettuce and English mustard. Must be good hot English. None of that tasteless Canadian crap."

Vanessa nodded. If the man wanted English mustard, that's what it would be, whatever it said on the label.

Colin opened another door. "Where's this whiskey your mother was talking about?"

Roddy looked bewildered. "I don't know."

"Try that cupboard in the corner," Vanessa said, praying fervently that her father had left a bottle. Too late she recalled that he usually cleared liquor out of the cottage in the fall in case someone broke in.

Colin reached into the cupboard, rattling cans of soft drinks. Then he said, "Aha!" and brought out from the depths of the cupboard a half bottle of Canadian rye. "I can't believe your father would drink this crap," he said in disgust, "but I suppose it's better than nothing."

He poured himself a large measure of rye and looked up . . . to catch Vanessa watching him. "Monitoring me, as usual?"

She shook her head and went to get the can opener from the drawer.

He was there like a shot, slamming the drawer shut, missing her fingers by an inch. "Nice try. Thought you'd get a knife out, didn't you?"

It had certainly been in her mind to try. "I was looking for the can opener."

"There's one on the wall." He stared at her with loathing in his eyes. "You must think I'm really stupid."

"I'd forgotten. It's been a while since I was last here," she murmured apologetically. God, how she hated him for turning her into an abject little mouse. But she knew that she must do everything possible to keep Colin from losing it altogether.

He went to the drawer and took out the large knife her father used to carve roasts and hams for family feasts in the summer. She saw Roddy blanch and her own stomach squeezed with fear.

A slow smile crossed Colin's face. He came close to her, so close that she could smell the rye on his breath and see the shadow of a beard on his skin. He held up the carving knife and brought the sharp point close to her throat. She held her breath. Just the mere act of swallowing would bring the tip of the knife in contact with her throat.

Colin laughed aloud and moved the knife down. "Bring me that tin of ham, Roddy. I'll slice it up so Mummy doesn't have to soil her delicate little hands." His eyes glittered at Vanessa. "That was just as good as one of your shitty little telly melodramas, wasn't it?"

She said nothing, but stood watching the hands with the long aristocratic fingers that had once caressed her body, brought her to ecstasy, dexterously slicing the ham.

As she made the sandwiches, her mind raced and her eyes sought for something that could be used as a weapon, but she could see nothing small enough to hide without Colin seeing it. And he wouldn't let her near the drawer where the knives were. Besides, she knew very well that with his superior size he could turn a weapon back on her.

Roddy was watching her from the corner of the kitchen, his eyes dark pools in his colorless face. When Colin went to turn off a dripping tap, she gave Roddy a smile and a small reassuring nod behind Colin's back. But she didn't dare speak to him.

She piled the sandwiches on a plate. "There we are," she said brightly. "Would you like to eat them in the living room by the fire?"

"You really are stupid, aren't you? Wrap them up. We're taking them with us."

Vanessa swallowed. "Taking them? Are we going somewhere?"

"Very clever deduction," he sneered. "We're going home. Home to Strathferness." He smiled at Roddy. "Won't that be great, Roddy?"

Roddy nodded, but his terror was clearly visible.

"Well, you could show a bit more enthusiasm when your dad's come thousands of miles to rescue you. How about a thank-you?"

"Thank you, Daddy," the boy whispered.

Vanessa's heart turned in her breast. Roddy was learning fast not to upset his father. Two abject mice. "When are we leaving?" she dared to ask.

"You can't keep your mouth shut, can you?" He loomed over her, his height and size that had once been part of his attraction now a source of menace. "*We* are not leaving. Roddy and I are driving back to Winnipeg. *You* are expendable."

Oh God, he was going to kill her first and then take Roddy.

"Take me with you. I promise not to get in the way," she gabbled. "Roddy won't be happy if you leave me behind."

Roddy's face was so white she was afraid he might faint. He made a sudden dash across the kitchen and grabbed her around the waist. "You're not going to hurt Mummy," he yelled. "She's coming with us."

Colin advanced on them. "Get away from her." Roddy shook his head, clinging desperately to Vanessa. "I said, get away."

"I'll move if you promise you won't leave her behind. She could get buried by the snow. Wolves could eat her up." Roddy was inventing madly as he went along. "There's bears that don't have enough to eat in the winter and they break down doors and tear people apart and eat them."

Colin began to laugh and kept laughing. Vanessa felt Roddy's body shaking against hers. She slipped an arm about him and hugged him close, then released him before Colin could see what she was doing.

"Oh Roddy, my Roddy, what a lad you are!" Colin said, his laughter dying. "I can't think of a more worthy fate than to have your mother eaten by wolves and torn apart by bears."

"I don't want that to happen to her!" Roddy cried.

"What do you care? She's a bad person. That's what happens to bad people. Remember all those witches in our Hans Christian Andersen book of fairy tales? They get eaten—or burned. There's an idea, we could tie her up and set fire to this crummy little cabin."

Roddy lifted his chin. "I know you wouldn't do that," he said. "You're too nice to do that."

A shadow passed across Colin's face, subtly shifting his expression. "Quite right. I wouldn't do that. Very well, my son. At your request your mother will accompany us to Winnipeg and then we'll turn her over to the police."

Vanessa willed Roddy not to protest. She fixed her gaze on him, trying to make him look at her. *We've achieved this much,* she told him silently. *Don't spoil it by asking for more.*

"I'll go and pack again," Roddy said.

"No time for packing," Colin said. "Just get your coat and whatever else you need in this godforsaken weather."

Weather! Vanessa thought. How could she have forgotten the storm raging outside? "I don't think it's safe to drive in this storm," she said. "Maybe we should wait until the morning? At least it will be light by then."

"Who asked you for your opinion?"

"I just thought—"

"Stop thinking. Just do as I tell you. Wrap up the sandwiches and let's go."

He took up the bottle, which had only a couple of inches of liquid left in the bottom.

"Roddy may need something to drink."

"Roddy, get some cans of Coke or whatever it is you like. Let's get going."

He marched them into the living room.

"I should dampen down the fire," Vanessa said automatically . . . and immediately regretted it.

"Leave the bloody fire. Who the hell cares if this dump burns to the ground?"

He had been glad enough to get inside "this dump" for shelter and warmth, she thought bitterly. As soon as they had scrambled into their coats and boots, he forced them out, not even allowing Vanessa to lock the door behind her.

Colin's car was covered with snow and ice. "I'll get another snow brush and scraper from the other car," Vanessa shouted to Colin as he started the engine.

"I'll get it," Colin shouted back. He got out of his car and held out his hand for her keys. Not trusting her, he took Roddy with him. When he returned, she'd cleared much of the snow from the front windshield and was scraping the ice from the rear window.

"Well done," Colin said. "You Canucks have some talents, I see."

As fast as they swept snow from the car, more covered it. The wind had died a little, but the snow was falling even more heavily. It was madness to try to drive in this. But then, thought Vanessa, everything about this night was madness.

At least, thanks to Roddy, she was there with them. Not left back at the cottage, worrying herself sick.

Or perhaps not able to worry at all. Ever.

If only they could get as far as the highway they might be okay. If they broke down there, the RCMP patrol might find them. But if they got stuck here, on the local road, they could freeze to death before anyone discovered them. Few people came to their cottages in the winter and certainly no one in their right mind would do so in this weather.

Once they'd cleared the car as well as they could, Colin ordered them to get in. "You go in the back," he told Vanessa. "Roddy sits by me."

When Colin shoved her into the backseat, Vanessa made no protest. There was a chance she could lean over and try to throttle him from behind. But not while he was driving.

That idea was dashed when Colin produced a length of rope. "What's that for?" Roddy asked.

"To tie your mother's hands behind her back. I don't trust her when she's sitting behind me."

"Then let her sit in the front," Roddy said. "I can sit in the back."

"Keep quiet," Colin told him, his tone sufficiently menacing to stop Roddy from arguing with him.

Vanessa said nothing as Colin came close to her. He leaned over her, his body in the bulky parka pressing against hers. He chuckled. "Now if Roddy weren't here I just might—" He leaned closer to whisper in her ear.

She tried not to show any response, but her body tensed with revulsion.

"This is just for old time's sake," he added, and leaning his full weight on her, he savagely kissed her, his tongue probing against her clenched teeth, forcing her mouth open. She felt as if she were going to be sick. She sent her mind somewhere else, anywhere, to escape, and it alighted on Grant and their shared laughter at the restaurant, before she found the incriminating photograph. Oh Grant, if only you were here now, she thought.

If he were, her other self reminded her, he'd be helping Colin tie you up.

"What's the matter, sweetheart? Lost your zest for kissing me?" Colin forced her to turn around and wrenched her arms behind her back, tying them tightly with the length of rope. "Good. Now I don't have to worry about you." He turned her about again and fastened the rear seat belt around her. "Mustn't forget to put your mother's seat belt on, must we?" he said to Roddy. "Can't have anything happen to her." He gave a mocking laugh.

When he first tried to drive the car out of the driveway, the car's wheels spun, but after another couple of tries, he managed to reverse out into the narrow road.

The car bumped and skidded along the twisting, tree-lined road beside the frozen lake. Colin had always been a skillful but daring driver. Vanessa had found his thrilling style of driving exciting when she was younger, but recently it had raised fear, not excitement.

Sensing the treacherous surface, Colin kept to a moderate speed on the lakeside road, but once he was out on the highway he put his foot down. The driving snow slanted across the highway, blowing from the north, at intervals piling up in drifts on the highway itself, so that frequently he had to swerve to avoid them.

They'd been traveling for more than three quarters of an hour when they almost plowed into a drift in the center of the highway. Vanessa's breath caught in her throat, but Colin managed to avoid the pile of snow. As he braked to make the sudden detour, the car slid sideways.

"It's very icy," Vanessa said, when he'd recovered control of the car. "If you go too fast you could go into a major skid."

"Thank you for that helpful information. I think I know how to drive." He gave her a menacing glance in the rearview mirror. "Either you shut your mouth back there or I'll just toss you out onto the road and let Roddy's wolves eat you all up."

As time passed he became more and more reckless,

not even slowing down when he came to a snowdrift on the highway, merely turning the wheel and skidding from side to side, as if enjoying the challenge Mother Nature was throwing at him. Knowing how treacherous this kind of ice could be, Vanessa was terrified that he wouldn't be able to recover from the next wild spin.

Her shoulders ached from being wrenched back in an unnatural position, her wrists raw where she'd been trying to loosen the rope. She'd given that up after a while, knowing that it was useless. She'd thought of even trying to kick Colin in the head, but he checked her constantly in the mirror and doing anything to take his concentration away could cause a fatal crash. Their survival had become her primary concern.

She could only sit there, raging at her inability to do anything, and hope to God that someone somewhere knew that she and Roddy were in grave danger.

For a very long time Roddy had been silent. She was desperately worried about him. He'd been in a state of shock in the cottage. Several times she'd opened her mouth to speak to him, but was afraid to draw Colin's wrath again, in case he carried out his threat to throw her out of the car.

Eventually, she couldn't stand it. "Are you asleep, Roddy?"

"Shit!" Colin roared. But it wasn't her he was yelling at. A deer loomed in the beam of their headlights. It froze, its antlered head turned to watch the car bearing down on it. Colin slammed on the brakes and spun the steering wheel.

It all seemed to happen so slowly. The sickening feeling of the car going out of control, sliding on the ice beneath them. Colin cursing. Roddy's high-pitch screaming. And her own voice crying out for her son. The side of the road suddenly appeared in front of them, then the bank of the pine trees. Metal screeching, glass tinkling . . . She felt a blow on the side of her head, blinding light, whirling darkness, and then . . . nothing.

Chapter 39

It was Grant who saw the car. He was sitting in the rear of the RCMP four-by-four, on the left-hand side, and caught a glimpse of a dark object on the other side of the highway. It was partially covered by snow and rested at a bizarre angle at the edge of the pine forest.

"Looks like a crash over there," he shouted, his heart pounding.

"Where?" shouted Wayne, one of the Mounties. The other Mountie, Dave, slowed down, the antilock brakes creaking as the tires started to skid on the ice and then steadied.

"Back there on the other side of the highway," Grant said. "Looked like a car had crashed into the trees."

"We'll go take a look." Dave drove on a little, then did a U-turn from a turning lane and went back the way they'd come, this time driving very slowly. All three men peered out into the snow-swept darkness.

Grant dredged up a brief silent prayer. *God, if it is them, let them be okay.*

"There is it," Wayne shouted. "Looks like a crash, all right. They must've skidded off the highway."

They pulled into the verge at an angle, so that the full beam of their headlights picked out the car. It had hit the trees head-on. "Doesn't look too good," the driver said. He reported in on his radio, stating his position.

Grant opened his door and started wading through the snow. Wayne, who was already out of the car, stopped him. "You stay here, Mr. Kendall. You never know what the situation might be."

"I'm coming with you."

Wayne shrugged. "Okay. But make sure you stay behind us."

They left the car running and the radio on. As Grant followed the Mounties through the snow, he saw that both officers had drawn their guns.

The hood of the car was crumpled like a concertina, steam—or smoke—coming from beneath it. The windshield had shattered, spewing glass over the driver. Although Grant couldn't see Colin's face, he recognized the golden hair on the head that rested against the steering wheel.

"He's still alive," pronounced Wayne.

Grant didn't have time to decide whether he was glad or sorry.

"Roddy, Vanessa!" he yelled.

Blinded by the snow, he could only see vague figures, a small one in the front passenger seat and a larger one in the rear. He yanked at the rear door, but it wouldn't budge. "The door's stuck!" he yelled through the wailing wind. He went around to the other side and tried it. "So's this one."

"Wait," Wayne shouted back. "The boy's in the front."

"Is he okay?" Grant yelled. "Roddy, are you okay?"

Then he heard a small sound that turned his heart over. "Grant?" He plowed through the snow to the open door at the front of the car.

"Watch out," Wayne said. "We have to fix that neck wound."

Grant didn't need the warning. He could see the blood pouring from the gash on the side of Roddy's neck.

"Keep him as warm as possible." Wayne ran to get his medical kit.

Grant knelt down in the snow and put his arms around the shivering boy. "Hi there, Roddy, old pal.

Everything's going to be fine now. The Mounties rode in to rescue you."

"On . . . their . . . horses?" Roddy whispered.

Grant grinned, blinking frozen moisture from his eyes. "With their horsepower."

"My neck . . . hurts."

"Wayne's going to fix it for you."

"Where's Mummy?" Roddy tried to turn his head.

"Don't move. Once Wayne gets back, I'll see how she's doing, okay?"

"She's in the backseat. Daddy tied her up. She was screaming when we crashed. I was, too."

Grant swallowed the hard lump in his throat. "I bet you were. It must have been pretty scary."

"Is Daddy dead?"

Wayne had returned and was leaning over him now, seeing to the cut. "Your dad's not dead, but he's still unconscious. We'll deal with him in a minute. You just hold still now while I check you out. Does it hurt anywhere else?"

Knowing Roddy was in good hands, Grant straightened up. Again he tried first one and then the other of the rear doors, using his full force to wrench at the handles. They wouldn't budge. He plowed back to the front of the car, where Dave was checking the engine, having spewed foam on it from the extinguisher. "What about Vanessa?" Grant yelled at him. "Are you just going to leave her there?"

"Before I do anything else, I have to make sure this isn't going to blow," Dave said patiently. "If it caught fire before we got them out, we could all go sky high."

"Sorry. It's just that I can't get either of the rear doors open and she hasn't made a sound."

"Soon as I've got this tamped down, we'll get her, okay?"

"What can I do?"

"We've called for an ambulance, but it could take a while. If the boy's okay we can carry him into our car and keep him warm. You can stay there with him."

"I will, but not until we get Vanessa out. Have you got some sort of crowbar I could use?"

"Sure." Dave bent down and rummaged in his tool kit, then handed Grant a crowbar. "You keep shouting at her, see if you can get a response. Soon as I've finished up here I'll come and help."

Grant went to Colin's side. He bent his head and peered into the darkness, trying to ignore the warm metallic smell of blood. "Vanessa!" he shouted urgently into the shadowy darkness. "Vanessa! It's all over. You're safe now. It's all over. Vanessa!" Then he went to the rear door and started prying it open with the crowbar, all the time shouting her name.

From somewhere a long way away a voice was calling her, urging her to wake up, but she wasn't sure she wanted to. She was cocooned now, floating in darkness, safe. Waking meant fear and action—and pain. Yet that voice kept at her, urging her, telling her she was safe now, that there was no need to worry anymore.

There were terrible noises happening around her, banging and screeching sounds. She shrank from them. Then came a rush of cold air gusting around her and a bright beam of light blinding her.

"Vanessa! Thank God you're alive." She felt hands gentle on her and that voice she thought she'd never hear again talking to her all the time. "Hang on. I'm just getting the seat belt off."

"Don't move her till we're sure nothing's broken," warned another, unfamiliar voice. That voice, too, seemed to come from a long way off, and it echoed in her head. *Broken, broken, broken* . . . as if she were in a vast cave.

Now they were turning her. She flinched as the bonds tightened momentarily on her chafed wrists and then felt them loosen. "I can't . . . move any arms," she whispered.

A face came close to hers. She was sure it was Grant, although he was wearing a hood and his dark eyebrows were frost-tipped. "No wonder. You've had them tied behind your back for a while. Here, let me help." Slowly, gently he eased her arms forward. Pain shot through her. She clenched her teeth to hold back a cry. She began to shiver uncontrollably. "I'm so cold," she whispered through chattering teeth.

"As soon as Dave has checked you over we'll get you into the other car where it's warm."

"Roddy?" she asked, suddenly remembering. Her voice rose in panic. "He's got Roddy."

"Roddy's right here."

"Mummy!" cried his voice from the front seat.

"Oh Roddy." Tears coursed down Vanessa's cheeks. "Are you okay?"

"I'm okay."

"Oh thank God—" Vanessa's voice caught.

"Don't cry, Mum. We're safe now. Grant and the Mounties saved us."

"Mounties?"

"That's right. Grant said they rode to our rescue."

She laughed and sobbed at the same time. "That sounds like Grant." She turned and grasped hold of his sleeve. "Don't leave me."

"Never." Grant bent to kiss her forehead, a gentle kiss with no pressure. Then he kissed her again, this time a more lingering, reassuring kiss on the cheek, that told her far more than words might have done that she was safe—and that she was safe with him. "Soon as we know you're okay, no broken bones, we'll get you to the car."

As Dave ran his hands expertly along her legs and spine and arms, she tried to answer his quiet questions, but she was so cold it was hard to get the words out.

"Nothing broken," he told her. "You and your son are going to be fine."

She hesitated. "Colin?" she asked.

"Still unconscious. We've wrapped him in blankets to keep him warm. Looks like he hit his head on the windshield. Wasn't wearing his seat belt. Could be in-

ternal injuries. Can't be sure until the medics come.
You're lucky people."

"Lucky?"

"The bank of snow must've slowed you down when
you went off the road."

"It was a deer. It suddenly appeared right in front
of us."

"That happens. Pretty scary, eh?"

She had to smile. The trite phrase summed up everything that had happened to her recently.

"Okay, ma'am. We've got a very willing guy here
ready to carry you to the car."

A blanket was wrapped about her and she felt herself being lifted out of the car. As she laid her head
against Grant's chest and felt his arms tighten about
her, a weight seemed to lift from her heart. She'd been
right about him all along, except for . . .

"The photograph. Why did you have that photograph in your wallet?"

"What photo— Oh!" Grant said with a long sigh of
realization. "So *that's* what happened. It's a long story.
I'll explain later. Now I'm going to put you in here,
next to your son, Roddy the Intrepid."

She felt herself being lifted into the rear seat of the
car and the blanket tucked around her. "Roddy's a
hero," she whispered. She gathered her son in her
arms, relishing the warmth of his body against hers.

Grant shut the door on them to keep the heat in
and, opening the driver's door, slipped into the seat
there. He looked back. "Are you okay here, the two
of you?"

Vanessa nodded, too weary to speak. She welcomed
the painful tingling in her hands and feet. It told her
that warmth was seeping into her body, bringing her
back to life.

"I have to go and help the others." Grant leaned
into the back of the car and touched his fingers to first
Roddy's face and then Vanessa's.

"Ouch, your hand's cold," Roddy complained.

Vanessa managed to lift her hand to trap Grant's

against her cheek. She turned her face and pressed her lips against his palm. "Stay," she whispered. "You're so cold."

He leaned even farther into the warm cocoon in the rear of the car. Taking her face between both hands, he kissed her lips, his mouth warm and infinitely gentle against hers. "I'll be back soon," he whispered, and then he was gone.

Vanessa had no sense of time passing. The constant static and sound of voices on the two-way radio in the front of the car filtered through her state of semiconsciousness, but she understood nothing that was said. She was aware of the hum of the engine, the slight chill of the air that blew in the slightly open window, the constant whir of the heater fan blowing warm air into the car, but all of these were merely a background to the quiet, easy breathing of her sleeping son, whose head rested in her lap.

She must have dozed a little, for she awoke with a slight start when she heard the door open and then Grant's voice. "Are they okay?"

"Sleeping soundly," said the voice of the Mountie called Wayne.

"Good." A little moment of silence, then Grant said, "I hate to leave them."

"I'll look after them, sir. Don't you worry."

"In the circumstances, I think it best that I stay with Colin."

Vanessa wanted to cry, *No!* but for some reason she couldn't get the word out.

"You don't have to worry," Wayne told Grant. "Not with Dave in the ambulance with you."

"I wasn't worried." Another pause. "Thanks, Wayne," Grant said. "See you at the hospital."

"That's right, sir. We'll get them both checked over and then you'll be sure they're okay."

Vanessa sensed rather than heard Grant walk away from the car. She wanted to dash after him, beg him to stay with her and Roddy, not to go with Colin, but it was too late. Grant was gone.

The car moved off. As it settled into a steady pace, she alternated between dozing and waking. When she slept, she dreamed strange unsettling dreams of being chased down long tunnels or windowless corridors. When she was awake, her brain was in overdrive, pondering why on earth Grant would choose to travel in the ambulance with Colin rather than in the car with her and Roddy.

Chapter 40

The following few hours passed in a blur for Vanessa, as if they were happening in one of those half-waking, half-sleeping dreams she'd been having. The journey, the arrival at the hospital, and the subsequent medical examinations and police questions all seemed to be happening to someone else.

When her parents were allowed to see them both, while they were waiting for Roddy to have his head X-rayed, Vanessa began to feel some semblance of normalcy returning. She answered all their questions as best as she could. It wasn't until they were absolutely sure that she and Roddy were going to be all right that they told her how Colin had attacked them.

Vanessa was horrified. "Oh my God!" she whispered. "I can't believe it." Tears rushed to her eyes. "Colin really has lost it completely. I am so sorry he put you through all that."

"Why are you sorry, honey?" her father said. "It's not your fault."

"It *is* my fault," she said vehemently. "I was the one who married him."

"Well, that's all in the past," her mother said, with a little warning glance in Roddy's direction. "I can only thank God that Colin's brother found us when he did."

"Colin's who?"

"His brother, darling. Grant. Such a nice man. Of course, you didn't know about that, did you? He said you didn't know. He's been with his brother most of the time since they brought Colin in."

Vanessa shook her head impatiently. "You've got it all wrong, Mum." Her mother really was getting more and more addle-headed every day.

"No, I'm absolutely certain. After all," Lynne said indignantly, "it was Grant who knocked down the door and discovered us. We might have been dead otherwise."

"I'm not disputing the fact that Grant rescued you, Mum. But he's not Colin's brother."

"I'm sorry to have to tell you this, but I am."

They all turned with a start to find Grant standing in the doorway of the little room.

"Hi, Grant," said Roddy. "I had to have stitches in my neck."

Grant came forward and rested his hand on Roddy's shoulder. "Did you? Hope it didn't hurt."

"Not much."

"That poor old head of yours. That's the second time you've bashed it. It must wonder what it's done to deserve all this."

Roddy chuckled.

Vanessa had been staring at Grant ever since he'd first spoken. "Will someone please explain what's going on here? I don't understand. This is like just one more crazy dream. How can you be Colin's brother?"

As if no one else were in the room, Grant pulled up one of the plastic chairs, placed in front of Vanessa, and sat down in it. He took her right hand in his and kissed it. "I wanted to tell you this later, explain it all when you'd had some rest and were feeling stronger."

"But I had to go and blurt it out," Lynne said, her face scarlet. "I am so sorry. I just didn't think."

Vanessa heard her father's heavy sigh, but all he said was, "Come on, Lynne, let's go for a coffee. Back in a few minutes, honey," he told Vanessa, giving her a bear hug that hurt her shoulders, but was balm to her spirit.

Roddy sat beside Vanessa, staring at Grant. "If you're Daddy's brother, then you're my uncle. I didn't even know I had an uncle."

"Well, you have one now."

"Hold on a minute," Vanessa said, her mind now aching as much as her physical body. "I thought Colin had only one brother: Alastair."

A slow smile spread across Grant's face. His mouth pulled down at the corners in a wry grimace. "That's me."

"You mean . . . you're the notorious Alastair Craigmore who ran away from home at sixteen?"

"Seventeen. Yes, that's me."

"The one who's rotting in jail in Australia?"

Grant's smile became a little grim. "That sounds like something my beloved father might have said."

"Actually, it was Colin who said it. I'm sorry, but I'm finding this all so incredible. How on earth did you know about me and Roddy? It surely couldn't be coincidence; that would be too creepy."

"No, it wasn't coincidence at all. I had a major mole at Strathferness."

"Of course you did. But who was it?" She stared at him. "Of course. It must have been Amanda."

"No, not Amanda."

"Then who?" Vanessa was totally baffled. Who else was there who would work against Colin and his father?

"Maybe it was Morag," suggested Roddy.

"No, not Morag, either, although she was an invaluable accomplice." Grant grinned at Vanessa's consternation. "Do you give up?"

"Of course I do. There's no one left. Not inside Strathferness itself."

"Oh, but there is." He waited a moment, for dramatic effect. "It was my mother."

"Your mother?" Vanessa was absolutely stunned.

"Nanna?" Roddy said, sounding just as stunned.

"I can't believe it," Vanessa said. "Fiona would never ever cross Sir Robert in any way."

"In her quiet way my mother is far stronger than you think."

My mother. How strange to hear Grant talking of

Fiona as his mother. That, more than anything, convinced Vanessa that she was hearing the truth. "I still find it almost impossible to believe. How on earth did she know where to find you?"

"She knew exactly where to find me. She always has. My mother and I have been in constant touch since the first few weeks after I left Strathferness."

Before Vanessa could say any more, Roddy was called in for his X ray. He insisted on going in on his own.

After he'd left the waiting room, Vanessa turned back to Grant, still utterly bewildered. "But . . . but how did you and your mother communicate? Colin's father—I mean *your* father—collects and opens all the mail."

"I wrote to her care of her church and bridge friends. A small select group was in on the secret. If one friend was away or sick, another would offer her services. Morag worked as a sort of liaison officer, picking up or mailing letters when my mother wasn't able to get away from Strathferness."

"My God, that must have been quite an organization those women had going! I just can't believe that Fiona would do such a thing. Just think what would have happened had your father ever found out . . . I don't think he'd ever have forgiven her. I know he never allowed your name to be mentioned in the house."

"So I heard." Grant's mouth twisted.

Vanessa put a hand on his sleeve. "I'm sorry," she said softly.

"Don't be. I knew what would happen when I left Strathferness. It was worth it."

"Your mother took a big risk getting you involved in our predicament. Why did she do it?"

"She'd lost one son because of my father's dictatorship. She couldn't bear to see her grandson go the same way, or worse still have his spirit broken by another father in the traditional Craigmore mold. She called me and begged me to help you, to find you and Roddy before Colin—or his investigators—did.''

"How did you find us? After all, you weren't expecting Roddy to have an accident, were you? I take it that wasn't planned.''

"Not to my knowledge it wasn't. I can't believe that even Colin would go that far. Every bit of information that came into Strathferness was being fed back to me by my mother. Colin had anticipated that you would seek out your friend Jill in Vancouver. I drove up there so that I could be hot on the trail. Once they'd tracked you down to the apartment block where Jill had installed you, I was there as well, watching you.''

"My God, no wonder I had that creepy feeling of being watched all the time.''

"There must have been at least three of us. Two of Colin's people, plus me. I just happened to have been tailing you and Roddy that day you went to Stanley Park—''

"Roddy's all finished,'' the nurse said. "Just wait here for the X rays, so you can take them back to the doctor.''

"What have I missed?'' Roddy asked, sitting down beside Vanessa again.

"I was just explaining to your mother how I happened to be in Stanley Park when you had your accident. When that Rollerblader skater crashed into you, it gave me the perfect opening to become friends with both of you.''

"Why didn't you just tell us right away you were my Uncle Grant?'' Roddy asked.

"Good question. There were two reasons. One, your grandmother didn't want anyone to know what she was up to.'' Grant fixed Roddy with a serious look. "And you have to swear that you won't ever mention it to anyone at Strathferness, Roddy. Okay? Because we don't want her getting into any trouble, do we?''

Roddy nodded earnestly. "I swear.''

"My second reason for not telling you about my

connection with the family was that I was sure that
your mother wouldn't trust me if she knew I was your
daddy's brother. More than once she told me that,
however bad their squabbles might be, the Craigmore
family always stuck together against all outsiders. I
wasn't going to take the risk of her turning against
me because I was a member of the family, just when
I had won her confidence."

It wasn't just my confidence you'd won, Vanessa
thought. "Then I found the photograph."

"Yes, then she went through my wallet when my
back was turned and found that picture." Grant raised
his eyebrows at Roddy. "See what happens when
you snoop?"

"I thought Colin must have given you the photograph," Vanessa said, "and, therefore, you must be
working for him."

"I can understand why you thought that. But, in
fact, my mother had couriered the photo to me, so
that I'd be able to recognize you both. She told me it
was the most up-to-date picture she had."

"It certainly was! Taken the day before we left
Strathferness. You can see why I thought Colin had
sent it."

A sudden pall fell over them all. Vanessa swallowed. "How—how is Colin, by the way?"

"He's conscious. No broken bones. Just concussion."

"Have you spoken to him?"

"No, I left just before he came around. Wayne
the Mountie's sitting beside his bed, so you're
quite safe."

This was directed as much to Roddy, Vanessa knew,
as to her. Her gaze met Grant's. *But for how long?*
was her silent question.

"I won't let anything happen to you or Roddy," he
answered her softly. "I'm not going anywhere."

Roddy looked from her to Grant. "I'm glad you're
here, Uncle Grant," he said suddenly. "We make a
good family, don't we?"

Vanessa felt her cheeks redden. She looked down at her hand tightly locked in Grant's.

"We sure do," Grant said.

But they both knew that the nightmare was not now—and might never be—truly over.

Chapter 41

Colin was lying in the narrow hospital bed, staring at the picture of ducks flying across a flat golden prairie, which hung at a crooked angle on the wall. His head was throbbing like a generator and he felt as sick as a dog. They'd hooked him up to an IV as he couldn't keep any food down.

"Concussion plus a hangover," the kid masquerading as a doctor had told him with a sneer. "That's a potent combination, Mr. Craigmore."

The doctor, Vanessa, her parents . . . they could all go to hell, for all Colin cared. But Roddy . . . Tears oozed from beneath his closed lids. He'd lost his son. Because of that one stupid, infantile act of tying those idiot parents of Vanessa's up, he'd lost the one good thing in his life.

And with his son he'd lost all his will to fight. Nothing else mattered to him now.

The worst part would be returning to his father without Roddy, admitting that he'd screwed up, that because of his lack of control they could have lost Roddy forever.

No judge in any country, not even Scotland, would give him custody now.

He heard footsteps. A nurse came into the room and bent to whisper in Wayne Plod's ear. The policeman had told him his correct name, but Colin liked to call him Mr. Plod. The name suited him perfectly. Wayne, the earnest, plodding Mountie who always got his man. He'd sat there, hour after hour, waiting for Colin to give him a statement, but Colin had refused to speak to him. They'd offered him a lawyer. Still he'd refused to talk. Now something new was happening.

"You've got visitors, Mr. Craigmore," said Mr. Plod in a hearty voice.

"I told you before, I don't want to see anyone."

"Your son has come to see you."

His heart gave a little leap, but then fell back into the black pit again. He turned his head away. "Hi, Daddy," said a slightly wobbly voice from the door. Colin couldn't resist looking. Roddy was clutching his green dinosaur. He was well flanked. Vanessa to his right, another cop to his left. The group advanced a little way into the room, moving in unison, as if they were joined together at the hip.

Another man followed them into the room and went to stand beside Vanessa. Colin stirred uneasily. There was something vaguely familiar about him. As he watched them from beneath his eyelids, he saw Vanessa glance sideways at the man, her lips sliding into a secret little smile when their eyes made contact.

Colin's heart clenched like a fist when he saw her expression. A long time ago, she'd looked at *him* that way. No one, particularly himself, could mistake the radiance that mantled her face. Whoever this man was, Vanessa was strongly attracted to him.

"Are you feeling better, Daddy?"

Better? Colin felt like laughing. It wasn't possible to feel worse than he did now. "My head's less sore," he said. "How about you?" Roddy had a large taped dressing on his neck. I did that to him, Colin told himself, nausea rising at the sight of it.

"I'm okay."

"I'm sorry I crashed the car."

"It was the deer. Mummy told me that."

Colin's eyes flicked to Vanessa and away again. "Yes, it was the deer. I couldn't stop on the ice." He held out his hand to his son. "Come a bit closer."

Roddy flushed. "I—I can't."

Colin's hand dropped onto the bed. "No, of course

you can't. Sorry." His gaze raked the others. They were like a bloody gallery of onlookers, watching the sport, gloating at his demise. He felt like a mortally wounded stag and they were the huntsmen crowding in for the kill. "I didn't mean to hurt you," he told Roddy, his face flushing with embarrassment at having to speak this personal stuff in front of them all.

Roddy didn't say anything.

"He knows that." It was the stranger who spoke, his voice like a long-forgotten echo in Colin's mind.

"How the hell would you know anything about my son?" Colin demanded.

"Must be in the blood." The man smiled a strange half-smile . . . and suddenly Colin was seeing that picture of his mother that hung in the gallery, the one that his father had commissioned the first year of their marriage. Not the same hair, of course. This chap had dark, wavy hair. Colin's mother had the golden hair that Colin had inherited from her, but this man bore the same fine, aristocratic features, the same dark eyebrows arching over vivid blue eyes. His mother's eyes had faded over the years. This man's eyes were brilliant and alive.

"Who the devil are you?" Colin asked in a harsh whisper. But he didn't even wait for a reply. "Alastair?"

His brother came forward to the bed. "It's been a long time, Colin."

"What the hell are you doing here?"

"Protecting my nephew."

"From me?" Colin snorted. "Little Alice protecting my son from me."

Alastair had always hated it when he called him Alice, as Colin had often done in their youth. When he was very young he'd gone crying about it to his mother. Now he merely raised those winged eyebrows and looked down at Colin with that bloody pitying look in his eyes.

"Come to gloat with the rest of them, I suppose," Colin said.

"Hardly."

"A man of few words, I see."

His brother shrugged. "What is there to say?"

"Where have you been all these years?"

"Many places. Australia. South America. I'm in California now."

"Doing what?"

"I run a small winery in the Napa Valley."

Colin grinned. "That figures. Whiskey would be too tough for you."

"I prefer the climate." There was a wealth of meaning in the words.

Brown eyes met blue. "I wish I'd had the guts to run from Strathferness like you did," Colin said in a low voice. "If I had, things might have turned out very differently." He turned away . . . and encountered the steady gaze of the Mountie at his bedside. "Writing all this down, are you, Constable Plod?"

"I think this visit's lasted long enough, Mr. Kendall."

"Who the hell's Mr. Kendall?" Colin demanded.

"I am," his brother said. "I changed my name legally to Grant Kendall." He met his brother's gaze again, but this time there was no hint of pity in his expression. "I never did like the name Alastair."

"When did—"

"That's enough, Mr. Craigmore," the Mountie said. "If you're well enough to ask your brother questions, you're well enough to answer mine."

"Give us two more minutes, Constable," Grant said, "and then he's all yours."

"Okay, sir. But just two minutes."

"Thanks." Grant turned back to Colin. "You're going to need a lawyer. You've got quite a few charges against you: criminal assault, carrying an unregistered firearm—"

"When did you meet my wife?"

"When I was asked to keep an eye on her and Roddy."

"By whom? No, you don't have to tell me. It was Amanda, of course. She'd be the traitor in the family, damn her."

Grant did not respond.

"Is there something going on between you and Vanessa?" Colin asked in a low voice.

"I think you should ask your wife that question, not me."

"My wife?" Colin's voice rose. "She's not my bloody wife anymore."

The constable stood up. "Right. This visit's over now."

Colin grasped his brother's arm, drawing him down. "Can you get me a bottle of whiskey?" he whispered in his ear. "Anything will do. This has all been such a shock. . . . I'll go crazy if I don't get a drink."

Grant pulled away from him. "I'll get you a lawyer, that's all."

Colin swore at him. Grant went back to the group by the door, but then hesitated. Turning, he took Roddy by the shoulder and brought him to Colin's bedside. "Say good-bye to your father," he told him.

Roddy stood there, hands twisting together, face very pale. " 'Bye, Daddy. See you soon."

Colin held out his hand. The constable instantly loomed farther over the bed. "Good-bye, son," Colin said.

A long spell of silence ensued. Then Roddy took his father's hand, squeezed it, and stepped back, pressing his spine against Grant. Grant's arm went around the boy's chest in a protective gesture. "Good boy," he said softly. Still holding him close, he met Colin's gaze. "Don't worry," he told his brother. "I'll look after him."

Colin saw how Roddy looked up at his brother, his eyes full of hero worship, and the knife of jealousy turned in his heart.

His son would never again look at his father in that way. Whatever happened, however hard he tried to redeem himself, the only expression he'd see in his child's eyes would be fear.

As he watched his family walk from the room without a backward glance, Colin felt despair fall on him like a cloak of suffocating black velvet.

He answered all the Mountie's searching questions with indifference, responding in monosyllables in a flat expressionless voice. Then he was given more sedatives, this time in a small paper cup, the nurse watching him to make sure he put the two pills in his mouth.

She didn't see him take them out again a few minutes later. Nor did the new constable who had replaced the weary Wayne. He was a younger man, less experienced, but unfortunately less inclined to doze than Wayne had been.

Colin bided his time. He sang the tune in his mind. It had become his theme song. *I'm biding my ti-me . . .* He was growing desperate for a drink. The earlier sedatives had helped a little to alleviate the desire. Without them, he was starting to get the shakes. If he didn't make a move soon he'd be a zombie.

His clothes were hanging on a wire hanger in a small metal cupboard by his bed. He'd seen them when the nurse had opened the door to look for his reading glasses. If he was going to get out of this place, he had to get his clothes and put them on without the Mountie seeing him. It seemed impossible.

Then the cop showed him the way. The next time the nurse came in to check on him, Colin feigned sleep. "Out like a light," the Mountie told her.

"The doctor ordered a good strong dose of sedatives."

"That makes my job easier," the constable said. "Could you do me a favor?"

"Sure. What do you want?"

"I can't leave him and I'm dying for a Coke. Could you get me one?"

"Sure thing. Back in a minute."

She was, too. Colin, lying there with his eyes closed, heard the cop thank the nurse and the squeak of her rubber-soled shoes as she left the room. Then came the pop of the tab being opened and the fizz of the drink. He even heard, in the quietness of the room, the *glug-glug* as it went down the mountie's throat.

Colin suddenly gave a loud moan and threw his arms wildly in the air, knocking the small oval pan they'd given him to throw up in onto the floor with a loud clatter.

"Shit!" The Mountie set down the can of Coke on the cabinet beside him and came round to the other side of the bed. He checked Colin first and, assured that he was fast asleep, bent to pick up the pan. In a flash Colin had grabbed the two pills from beneath his pillow and slipped them into the aperture in the can of Coke.

It was done in a few seconds. By the time the Mountie went back to the other side of the bed, Colin was lying on his back, emitting loud snores.

The ensuing half hour was the longest in Colin's life. As he lay very still, pretending to be asleep, nerves were jumping all over his body and he had to fight the urge to yell the place down. If he didn't get a drink very soon, he'd need a straitjacket to keep him from rampaging through the hospital.

After a while, the Mountie's breathing became deeper, heavier. Colin turned very slowly, to find that the man's chin had sunk onto his chest and his arms were hanging by his sides.

Colin lay there for at least another ten minutes, his eyes fixed on the man, steeling himself not to make a move in case it would awaken him. Then slowly, stealthily he tore the plaster from the IV needle and drew it out of his hand, wincing at the pain. He stuck the piece of plaster onto his hand, hoping it would stem any bleeding.

Then he lay back on the bed for another few minutes, in case his movements might awaken the cop, but he was far away by now, his mouth hanging open, gasping snores coming from it.

Colin eased himself across to the other side of the bed, trying not to gag as the movements made his head throb sickeningly again. He set his feet on the

floor and stood up, but had to grab hold of the side
of the bed as the room swung wildly around him. God,
he was in a bad state. Was it possible to get out of
this place when he couldn't even stand straight?

You have to, he told himself. The alternative was
prison and disgrace. His father would never forgive
him for that. All the time, as he opened the metal
door to the clothes closet with a scrape of the lock
that he was sure would awaken everyone on that floor,
never mind one sleeping policeman, and then got
dressed, he told himself that he must restore Roddy
to Strathferness. That was all that mattered now. If
Vanessa got custody of Roddy, she would make sure
his son never returned to Strathferness, at least not
while he, Colin, was there. That would mean the end
of the family line.

It was remarkably easy to get out of the hospital.
He just walked down the silent corridor to the stairway exit. His room was on the second floor. He stag-
gered down the flight of stairs and then made his way
out, following the red exit signs. Not one person even
glanced at him. He was just another doctor or late-
night visitor in the busy hospital.

It wasn't until he reached the revolving door leading
outside that he remembered the storm.

"Better zip up your parka, pal," a man who was
coming in said to him. "The wind's died down, but
it's a bastard out there."

He was right. As Colin stepped outside, the cold
knifed through him, shocking him awake. He was so
light-headed now that his vision was blurred. Little
gusts of wind kept swirling the snow about so that the
world constantly moved about him, like a carnival
ride.

A taxi pulled in to deposit a very pregnant woman
who was bent over in pain, her anxious husband hov-
ering about her. As they went into the hospital, Colin
quickly grabbed the handle of the taxi, shouldering
aside another man who was about to take it.

He sank into the backseat with a great sigh of relief. "Take me to the nearest bar."

"Not many open this time of night," the driver told him.

"I'll make it worth your while."

The driver shrugged. "Okay. There's a place I know stays open pretty late, but I'm not sure in this storm if—"

"Give it a try."

"You were lucky to get me," the driver told him, as he drove through the deserted city streets, weaving between stalled cars, skidding in the rutted snow. "I've been on fourteen hours straight. I was about to sign off."

The bar was still open. It was a few miles from the downtown area, attached to a motel that was filled with stranded motorists. Now they were passing the time in the bar until the highways were cleared.

A surprisingly festive atmosphere prevailed. Colin could understand why. It was so bloody cold outside that to be warm and safe inside this place must be like heaven to most of the revelers. He did not join in the excited chatter and interchange of personal stories that the storm appeared to have inspired, but sat in a corner of the bar, drinking straight whiskey with a chaser of still mineral water.

By the time he'd had his third double, the shivering had stopped, the headache was less severe, and his mind seemed clearer. Yet the clarity only served to emphasize his dilemma.

Someone tried to start up a conversation with him and he brushed him off. He was growing increasingly weary of all these people around him, of voices yelling and laughing, the whir and clatter and canned music of the lottery machines, and the blare of rock. He was in an utterly alien world. Or perhaps it was he who was the alien in this world.

I don't belong here, he told himself. But then where did he belong? With his wife and son in their large Victorian house in Edinburgh? In his old financial firm dealing with asinine investors who bored him to tears and turned him to drink? In his cramped office in the distillery where—despite his affinity to the final product—the stench of whiskey mash that permeated everything made him feel violently ill? Or within the stone walls of Strathferness Castle, the ancient home of his ancestors—and, currently, of his father? And even when his father was dead and he, Colin, was laird he would have to know all about sheep and fermenting barley and peat and tourists taking the whiskey trail, and to dance at the annual Hogmanay ball with the tenants from the tied cottages. Was that to be his life?

No, not one of these things gave him any sense of belonging or of pleasure.

But, perversely, he wanted it all for his son, because Roddy, he knew intuitively, loved Strathferness. Roddy belonged there. Roddy was not yet blighted by the legacy passed from father to son by generations of Craigmores.

But what happens to Roddy if I get hold of him again? Colin asked himself. He thought of the scene in the kitchen at the cottage and of Roddy's look of terror as he saw his father hold the knife to his mother's throat. The memory of his son's expression made Colin break out in a cold sweat. How long would it be before fear sapped Roddy's spirit from him, so that love of home and the Highlands and the family inheritance no longer brought him joy? "It doesn't take long," Colin murmured aloud.

"What's that?" the man on the stool next to him asked.

"Nothing," Colin murmured. He swung himself off the stool and stood there, the room tilting slightly before his eyes.

The bartender came over. "Anything else, sir?"

"Yes." Colin leaned closer. "Can I buy a bottle? I'm staying in a room here." It was a lie, but who cared?

"Sorry, sir. Can't sell you a bottle. Tell you what,

though. I can give you a couple of doubles in a large glass, okay?"

"Make that four doubles in a very large glass."

The bartender gave him a wink. "Right." He poured the drinks and handed the glass filled with whiskey to Colin. "There you go, sir. You'll sleep like a baby after drinking that."

Colin jerked up his head, sending a pain shooting through his temples. "Will I?" he said absently. The thought of a long sleep was extremely inviting.

"Better set your alarm to wake you up if you've got anywhere to go in the morning."

Colin had nowhere to go. He didn't want to be woken up. He wanted to sleep. Besides, there was a snowstorm outside. Where could he go?

What did they say about sleeping in the snow? That you mustn't do it or you'd never wake up. If you were lost in a blizzard, you must keep walking or you could fall asleep in the snow and freeze to death.

There were worse ways of dying. Far worse, far slower ways of dying. Dying by torture. Dying by degrees. Dying while you lived a living hell.

He picked up the glass of whiskey, signed his credit card bill, and opened the door that led to the motel foyer. There was a map on the wall. An arrow pointed to the motel on the main road, stating, *You are here!* A short way down from the motel, on the same side of the road, was the entrance to a park.

"Is the park open?" he asked the tired-looking woman at the front desk.

She looked at him as if he were crazy. "The park?"

"Yes, the park," he said impatiently. "Can you get into it?"

"Sure you can. There aren't any gates." She glanced at the glass in his hand. "You sure you want the park? It's pretty cold out there tonight."

"That's my business."

The woman shrugged and went back to telling a man that she was sorry she didn't have any rooms left, but he could sleep in a chair in the lounge for the night, no charge.

Colin zipped up his parka and pulled up the hood. He took a long drink from the glass, the whiskey like liquid fire warming his blood.

He paused at the front door to drain the glass, then carefully set it down on the top shelf of the coat rack before he opened the door and stepped outside.

The night was still, sounds muffled by the snow, blissfully quiet after the raucous commotion inside the bar. He set off down the road, plowing through the snow that had piled into drifts in places. Hardly any cars drove by. The city was sleeping beneath its mantle of heavy snow.

He saw ahead of him, through the snow that was falling lightly now, the end of the row of buildings on his side of the wide road and then the trunks and bare branches of trees marking the beginning of the park.

He could no longer feel the cold. In fact he felt so warm that he unzipped his jacket and put back the hood, relishing the cooling caress of snow on his face.

When he reached the park entrance, he felt as if it were inviting him in, the curved pathway saying, "Welcome." There were no barriers here, no fences, only the sloping banks that led down to the frozen river. Although its waters were turned to thick ice and it was covered in snow, he could see, in the glow from the streetlights behind him, the river's path outlined by the leafless trees that lined both banks, winding and curving away as far as the eye could see.

He started down the sloping ground, slipping and falling where the snow was deep and the incline steep, and came to the riverbank. Everywhere he looked the snow lay white and pure, untouched, like drifts of cotton wool, soft, inviting.

Nothing moved, nothing except his own body weaving and swaying beside the silent river. In that silence he could hear his heart pounding and the hum of the whiskey in his ears, in his veins. He sat down on a wooden bench covered in snow. It felt cold at first, but he soon grew used to that.

There was something he knew he must do before he slept, but he couldn't remember what it was. Then in a moment of lucid consciousness it came to him. His numb fingers fumbled in the pocket of his jacket, searching for his small black notebook and pen. It was hard to hold the pen with no feeling in his fingers, and the letters kept blurring before his eyes, but he managed to write the four short lines on the ruled page.

Then he put the notebook and pen back in his pocket and, knowing he had done all he could, moved along the riverbank. In a deep snowdrift beside a clump of trees, he sank down, burrowing into the cool softness like an animal hibernating in the winter, drawing it over his head like a quilt of the softest down.

For a moment, when his breath wouldn't come, he struggled, but soon, very soon, sleep came to him, gathering him up in her icy arms, and peace was his at last.

Chapter 42

The media made little of the report. A man had wandered away from the hospital after suffering concussion in a car accident and had died of hypothermia in a city park. Such things happened in winter storms in Manitoba.

At the inquest, mention was made of four cryptic lines in the deceased's small notebook, but as neither the man's wife—who was a local woman, born in Winnipeg—nor his brother, who happened to have been visiting at the time of the accident, could see any particular significance in them, they were soon forgotten.

The verdict was accidental death and the grieving family was allowed to take the body back to Scotland, where the deceased had lived.

Although two black funeral cars had been sent, no member of the family was at Glasgow Airport to meet the little entourage when they disembarked from the Air Canada plane.

Vanessa was glad of that. Since the news of Colin's death had hit them, she and Grant had been so caught up with the inquest and making arrangements for their return to Scotland and taking care of Roddy, they'd had precious little chance to think about themselves or the future. The journey to Strathferness would at least give the three of them some time alone.

As they started out from the airport, Vanessa sat in the rear of the second car—which was following the car containing Colin's coffin. One hand clasped Grant's, the other was on Roddy's knee. It wasn't

going to be at all easy, but she knew she could face
what was to come with Grant at her side.

She also knew that this was going to be even harder
for him than for her. He had vowed never to return
to Strathferness. Now, after eighteen years, his sense
of duty, his love for his mother, and his wish to support Vanessa were forcing him back. But, most of all,
it was his desire to see his dead brother's wishes carried out that was driving him home to his roots again.

They had plenty of time to discuss the future on
that long drive northward, but they were discussions
of a practical nature, not really touching upon the
deeper emotions they felt. There would be opportunity for that later . . . much, much later.

The shock of Colin's sudden death was still upper-
most in the minds of all three of them.

By the time they were moving at a suitably slow
pace down the driveway leading to Strathferness Castle, they had resolved to stand steadfast together
against the coming onslaught. And Vanessa knew that
she had Grant's absolute support. He, too, believed
that Roddy's safety and happiness were paramount.

As the ancient gray walls came into sight, Vanessa
could feel Grant's muscles gather into a knot in the
arm pressed against her side, see his tension in the
grim taut line of his jaw. She squeezed his hand.
"We're in this together, remember?"

Frowning, he glanced down at her as if, for a moment, he'd forgotten she was there. Then he smiled,
squeezing her hand very tightly. "Thank God for
that."

They were standing on the steps, the three Craigmores, all dressed in black. What shocked her was
how very small Sir Robert looked as he stood near,
but aloof from, the two taller women.

"My God, he's shrunk," Grant said in a low voice.

His father hadn't shrunk, but his shoulders were
hunched and his spine less erect than it had been
before.

Grant stood back to allow her and Roddy to go

before him. Vanessa went first to Fiona, whose face was haggard and drained of color, but her eyes were dry and alert.

"My dear Vanessa, welcome home." Fiona's cheek pressed against hers and then she bent to kiss her grandson, offering him the same welcome, but adding, "We have missed you so very much, Roddy dear," and a little embrace.

Only then did Fiona allow her gaze to dwell with ill-concealed hunger on the face of her younger son. Grant had stayed apart from the welcoming group, but now he came forward and, with a strangely old-fashioned gesture of love and respect, kissed both of her thin hands before being taken into her arms.

Neither of them spoke. Vanessa could hear Amanda quietly sniffing behind her and Roddy was staring at them, not quite understanding what was happening.

Then Fiona patted her son's shoulder and put him from her. "Go to Amanda and your father," she told him, her face composed again.

Vanessa stepped back as Grant came to his sister. "Mandy, you haven't changed one bit," he said, as her arms were flung about his neck.

"Welcome home, Alastair," she said, kissing him. He pulled her close, hugging her tightly against him.

There was an awkward silence and then, like his mother, his sister gently pushed him away and both of them turned to the man who waited nearby.

"Father?" Grant said with an upward inflection in his voice. He went to him with outstretched hand.

For one horrible moment Vanessa thought that Sir Robert was going to ignore the hand that was being held out to him, that he would turn and walk away from his only remaining son. But then he took it in his, releasing it after a brief moment. "Welcome home to Strathferness, Alastair," he said. The words came slowly, dredged up from some deep well within him.

"Thank you, Father." Grant's tone was crisp, unemotional.

Vanessa released her breath in a silent sigh of relief.

Grant signaled to Roddy to come to them. "And here's your grandson, safe and sound." The clichéd words were like balm salving Vanessa's heart.

"Welcome to your ancestral home, my boy." No hugs, of course, from Roddy's grandfather, just a firm handshake. "You are now the Master of Strathferness, heir to the title and estate that has been in the Craigmore line for—"

"Well, I think all that can wait for a while," Grant said, cutting in on his father.

Sir Robert looked shocked. His eyes, beneath heavy eyebrows, glowered at his son.

"We're all very tired, especially Roddy," Grant explained in a quiet voice. "We've had a very long journey after an extremely stressful week."

Sir Robert seemed to gather himself together. "Of course," he muttered.

"You'll have plenty of time to talk to Roddy after he's had some sleep."

"Good. There's much to be discussed," Sir Robert said in a gruff voice. His gaze kept going to his son's face as if he sought to reconcile the youth who had fled from this place and the self-assured man who seemed to be taking charge. "The rector is inside, waiting for . . ."

His mouth trembled and, for the first time in her life, Vanessa felt pity for him, but she also noticed how studiously he avoided looking at her.

Grant took his father's arm. "Why don't we go and wait inside, then? It's too cold to stand out here. We can wait in the hall."

"I had intended a short ceremony of prayer to . . ."

"A good idea. Let's all go inside," Grant said again. "Perhaps we can have a quick drink together first to warm us up. And something to eat. Then, once everything's prepared, we can gather in the chapel."

Vanessa felt weak with relief. She flashed Grant a gateful smile. She was desperately tired after the overnight journey across the Atlantic and it would be so much better not to have to watch the melancholy sliding out of the coffin and the silent solemn carrying of it into the chapel.

The gathering in the library was an awkward one. There were so many questions hanging in the air, waiting to be asked and answered. At least the long journey had given them time to prepare for them.

They'd expected the questions to come thick and fast tomorrow, after the funeral at St. Andrew's was over, perhaps, but to their surprise and dismay, as they were taking their first drink, the rector, Mr. Ogilvie, asked Alastair the first significant question.

"Are you planning to come to Strathferness to live, Mr. Craigmore?" he asked quite casually, not at all realizing what a bombshell he was dropping.

When everyone turned to him, Grant realized that the rector had addressed the question to him. He looked rather shaken for a moment and then quickly recovered. "No, Mr. Ogilvie. My home and my livelihood are in California. I intend to stay there." He smiled to lighten the answer. "I've lived in too many warm climates to be able to take the cold winters here."

He avoided looking at his father, but Vanessa could see that Sir Robert's eyes were clouded with something that could well be disappointment.

"I'm going to have to rely on wee Roddy to help me, then," he said, his hand resting on his grandson's shoulder.

Grant gave Vanessa a warning frown, but she didn't need it. She knew well enough not to open that can of worms today.

"Perhaps Amanda can help with the distillery," Fiona said, quietly dropping her own bombshell.

Obviously, no one was more surprised than Amanda herself at her mother's suggestion. "Me? You must be joking, Mother."

"Not at all. I think you'd make an excellent partner for your father."

Amanda's laughter was scornful, but there was a look of surprised speculation on her face that made

Vanessa think this might not be the last time that the subject would come up.

Morag rolled in the food trolley, bearing several plates of sandwiches and little cakes. "Thank you, Morag." Vanessa smiled at her. "I believe I have a lot more than food to thank you for," she added softly.

Morag smiled. "We'll have time later to speak together," she told Vanessa, casting a warning glance at Sir Robert.

This is how matters had always been resolved at Strathferness. Later. In small, private conversations. Not together as a family around a large, round table where everyone could contribute openly to the discussion.

Vanessa turned . . . to meet Grant's eyes gazing at her. They exchanged secret smiles and she knew that he was probably reading her mind.

When they gathered in the tiny, dimly lit chapel a short while later, Grant breathed in the familiar musty smell of ancient dampness sealed in ancient stones. He knelt beside Vanessa, his arm pressed against hers, and felt a surge of quiet exhilaration at the thought of getting to know Vanessa the real woman, not the haunted, suspicious wife of his tormented brother.

They had so much to talk about, so much to plan. Their primary task must be to tackle the thorny problem of Roddy's place of residence and the fact that he would be allowed to make only well-supervised visits to Strathferness in the coming years.

But they had Roddy's own father's guidelines for that. Grant took the little black notebook from his pocket, turning it to the creased, water-smeared page, and again read the brief message his brother had left for him.

Alice, the words read. *The boy belongs to Strathferness, but make sure he follows your example, not mine, until it is his turn to be laird.*

The cryptic message was for Vanessa as well, of course. She had wept when she first read it. Weeping for times gone by and the qualities she had found and loved in Colin. But, most particularly, these lines were for Roddy. His last, caring message from his father.

As the family bowed their heads to pray that Colin might rest in everlasting peace, Grant met Vanessa's little inquiring look. He slipped the notebook into her hand. "Keep it somewhere safe for Roddy," he told her.

Tears came to her eyes. Blinking them away, she took the notebook from Grant, managing to give his hand a little squeeze as she did so. She slipped the notebook into her handbag. Seeing that Roddy was watching her, she gave him a reassuring smile and a brief hug.

Then, thinking of both Colin and Roddy as well as herself, she said a brief, fervent prayer of thanks that, at long last, they were all safe from harm.